Finton Moon

A NOVEL

© 2012, Gerard Collins

We gratefully acknowledge the financial support of the Canada Council for the Arts, the Government of Canada through the Canada Book Fund (CBF), and the Government of Newfoundland and Labrador through the Department of Tourism, Culture and Recreation for our publishing program.

Cover Design by Todd Manning
Layout by Joanne Snook-Hann
Printed on acid-free paper

Published by
KILLICK PRESS
an imprint of CREATIVE BOOK PUBLISHING
a Transcontinental Inc. associated company
P.O. Box 8660, Stn. A
St. John's, Newfoundland and Labrador A1B 3T7

Printed in Canada by:
TRANSCONTINENTAL INC.

Library and Archives Canada Cataloguing in Publication

Collins, Gerard, 1963-
    Finton Moon / Gerard Collins.

ISBN 978-1-897174-90-6

I. Title.

PS8605.O465F55 2012   C813'.6   C2012-901096-0

Finton Moon
A NOVEL

GERARD COLLINS

*For Monique —
a kindred, beautiful soul with a
vagabond heart.
Hope you find your heart's
home*

Gerard Collins

killick press
an imprint of Creative Publishers

St. John's, Newfoundland and Labrador
2012

For Norma,
Healer, Inspiration, and Goddess of Weekends

The moon is my mother. She is not sweet like Mary.
Her blue garments unloose small bats and owls.

Sylvia Plath

It is believed by experienced doctors that the heat which oozes out of the hand, on being applied to the sick, is highly salutary. It has often appeared, while I have been soothing my patients, as if there was a singular property in my hands to pull and draw away from the affected parts aches and diverse impurities, by laying my hand upon the place, and extending my fingers toward it. Thus it is known to some of the learned that health may be implanted in the sick by certain gestures, and by contact, as some diseases may be communicated from one to another.

Hippocrates

That is part of the beauty of all literature. You discover that your longings are universal longings, that you're not lonely and isolated from anyone. You belong.

F. Scott Fitzgerald

Foreword

The savvy reader understands that this is a work of fiction and, as such, the people and places represented in this novel are products of my imagination. Darwin isn't a place I've lived, but it has characteristics, foibles, and a certain *je ne sais quoi* that are common to all small towns.

Likewise, Finton Moon`s family is not my family, but, rather, like all families has its share of good fortune and misery, arseholeishness and kindness. A family of any other kind, as Frank McCourt writes, is "not worth your while" in literature.

And, while I'm at it, the school represented is not a school I've ever attended, the teachers not like any I've ever had, and the clergy far removed from any I've known personally.

However, the burgeoning disillusionment with certain institutions, the endless search for answers in a confusing world, and the unmitigated sense of wonder and love of life are all mine. Those, I own and did not make up.

GC

Prologue

A few days after his eighth birthday, Finton Moon scaled the large, burly spruce at the edge of his parents' property and nestled into the sturdiest branch. High above the earth, as the morning sun arose, he felt safe from the clamour and concerns of daily life and the need to adapt to his ill-fitted surroundings. The branch yielded to his body and bent to the wind as the climber surrendered to the comforting bough.

In the distance, his mother yelled: "Finton Moon, where the hell are ya?" Her shrill voice stung his ears. "Get your arse home!" she called. "It's time for mass!"

He closed his eyes and went invisible, became but a breath upon the wind. Now and then, he opened one eye and watched various family members scouring the property—his mother usually enlisted one of his brothers, either Clancy or Homer, to find him. At last, he lay back and smiled, drew a deep, calming breath and shut his eyes. The tree spoke to him in creaks and groans, telling the tale of supple saplings in another time.

"Finton!" Elsie Moon shouted from fifty yards away, coming closer to his tree. His eyes came open in a state of alarm, and his body jerked upright, the involuntary maneuver causing him to slip. As he grasped for something firm to ease his fall, a painful explosion seared his left elbow. The ground was hard and unforgiving. At the base of the tree he sat, dazed and relieved, gripping his arm and hoping it wasn't broken.

He whimpered only once, then swallowed the pain. The last thing he wanted was for them to discover his place. There were other trees, sure, but not like this one. So he sat, with eyes closed, rubbed his arm and whispered a prayer. As the world went dark, he grew lighter of mind and body, and he drifted skyward—far above the burly spruce, beyond the clouds, and into another dimension.

He reached a great height, far above the earth, then slowly descended towards a lush, grassy surface and, from every direction, a celestial object mesmerized him. High above, shooting stars. Across the horizon, a blazing comet. Suspended in the air and all around him, dazzling orbs of every hue. Far below and gently approaching was his Planet of Solitude—a prominent, white apple tree kept him transfixed with its soft, green leaves and fruit-bearing branches bent low. When he'd finally landed, he found a spot beneath the tree and leaned back to gaze in wonder at the indigo sky. He'd been there before, in dreams and visions. But never before had he felt so alone. Never had it looked so stunningly real. As he scanned the vast plane, a prayer came to mind.

When he awoke, he was bent over near the spruce at the edge of his parents' property, holding his arm. But the pain had subsided and, upon examination of his elbow, the only sign of injury was a small, dark bruise.

"There you are," his mother said as she stepped through the high grass and crossed the boundary between meadow and woods. She was wearing her Sunday clothes, including the white, silk scarf he'd given her last Christmas. "Where did you go?"

"I've been here all along," Finton said. "I didn't hear you."

She narrowed her eyes. "Did you hurt yourself?"

"Just bruised."

"Well," she said skeptically, "it's time to go to mass."

He nodded and patted the tree trunk, then followed his mother home.

Nativity
1960 (Darwin, Newfoundland)

Finton Moon was a spring baby with a natural propensity for falling.

In his younger years, Finton loved to hear the story of when he was born, but the constant revision of details worried him—his parents, Elsie and Tom, sometimes forgot the doctor's name, the number of nurses, or the time of delivery. There weren't any pictures either—not of his mother's pregnancy nor of Finton's infancy. Sure, his parents didn't own a camera, but he wondered if some relative might have taken a photograph or two. Still, he wouldn't inquire too deeply. He was terrified of discovering an awful truth: that it didn't happen the way they said it did, or that he'd actually never been born at all.

According to Elsie, when Finton was born, the nurse dropped him on the bed and said, "Oops!" But he didn't cry. "You just lay there," his mother told him. "Deep, blue eyes, just lookin' at us all like you had a hundred questions." She shook her head and put a hand over her mouth to stifle a laugh. "You were quiet as dirt." The nurse scooped him up and examined him, but there wasn't even a mark on his tiny body.

According to Elsie Moon, the delivery was easy—a mere forty-five minutes from first contraction to famous first fall. "Time enough for a good shit," her husband Tom added as he sat at the kitchen table smoking a Camel and projecting a wispy grey "O" of smoke into the air. Nanny Moon peered up from her Bible, silver-rimmed glasses perched on her nose, and mused that her newest grandchild was merely doing penance for the fall of man. "'Twas just as well he get used to the cruelty," she liked to say, then returned her gaze to the consoling lines of the Good Book.

In the rest of the story, he didn't cry until two days after he was born. "The moment I set foot on that doorstep," Elsie said, "you started yowling to beat the devil—and we thought you'd never stop." For the next twenty-four hours, nothing—not his mother's coddling, his father's swearing, his grandmother's prayers, nor his brothers' funny faces—could halt the howling.

She deposited him in the hall closet with the door closed, but an hour later she took him out and set him in the back room that was undergoing construction. "Tom's a wonder for startin', but he never finishes," his wife often said. When Elsie went to fetch him, she noticed that the crib had attracted several spiders. "Nasty buggars," she clucked as she brushed them away and sent the ugly creatures scurrying back to the shadows.

Five-year-old Clancy suggested they sing, but Elsie frowned as she jostled Finton in her tired arms. "I don't know any songs," she said.

"Elvis!" Clancy began hopping around and swiveling his hips, singing, "Since my baby left me!" into his fisted right hand. Elsie shook her head and cleared her throat before trying "Love Me Tender," which only heightened his bawling. "Amazing Grace" caused the child to gag until his face turned a light shade of blue, which nearly sent his mother into a panic. Resisting the urge to shake him to a more natural hue, she forced out an "Irish Lullaby," which only made him cough and spit as he clenched his upraised fists in mounting frustration.

It was Tom who snatched him up by the armpits and crooned, "You're Nobody Till Somebody Loves You," while both boys, the mother, and even Nanny Moon hummed along on the chorus. Finton stopped coughing from the middle of "somebody," ceased choking on "loves" and slowly abated his whimpering by the end of the first verse. Before the song was done, the vexed baby committed to slumber, the sign of which was the steady rise and fall of his tiny chest with every life-affirming breath. "A bloody miracle," the grandmother whispered as she blessed herself.

"Thanks be to Jesus," Elsie Moon declared. He slept through the night and, from that day on, Tom's version of the Dean Martin ballad became Finton's lullaby even though no one knew why that song, and seemingly no other, would serve.

And that, more or less, was the story of Finton's birth.

Confirmation

Morgan Battenhatch, the eleven-year-old babysitter, kissed Finton's forehead and buried her nose in his little neck, inhaling the dueling smells of sweet talcum powder and Sunlight soap from his fresh-scrubbed skin. "He's adorable, Mrs. Elsie." She cooed and cradled him in her confident arms as she crossed the threshold to take him to church on the first Sunday morning in April—Finton's first mass. The child gazed up at the underside of Morgan's chin, occasionally waving a chubby hand at the split ends of her straight, blonde hair and warbling a pleasant, private language.

"Poor Morgan," Elsie Moon would say whenever she recounted the event. "She was always a bit... *strange*."

"Finton was the sacrifice," Nanny Moon would become fond of saying, glancing under her glasses from her knitting or the Bible.

Morgan was being confirmed that day at the Sacred Heart of Mary church, and Finton's presence would render the occasion more auspicious. "Poor Morgan," as she was often called, looked quite refined for a girl whose mother was a witch and whose father had died when she was a child. Given the squalor of the Battenhatch house, no one questioned Morgan's preference for eating the occasional meal with the Moons, and now that they had Finton, it gave the girl something to keep her occupied. The Moons, simply put, were her anchor in the world. "It's like bringing the savage to God," said Nanny Moon. At a young age, Morgan spent a lot of time with the Moon women, learning about religion, men, and the evils of the world. She didn't get along with her own mother and, almost imperceptibly, she had gained the status of unofficial adoptee and babysitter.

With Finton nestled in her arms, she proudly stepped over the threshold in a perilously long, white dress. Because of the heat, Elsie had shortened the sleeves of the second-hand garment, but she had neglected to hem it for ease of gait. The two siblings—Clancy and Homer—were already stuffed into the sweltering Valiant, where they squabbled over the back seat. While Clancy repeatedly punched him in the shoulder and ordered him to sit up, three-year-old Homer lay stretched across the seat, determined to have it all to himself. Their father leaned indifferently against the side of the car, stealing a last cigarette before committing to the drive. Their mother, meanwhile, was rummaging through her black handbag, preparing to leave the house and asking, "Now have ya got everything, girl?"

Morgan's occupied arms were trying to nudge Elsie through the door. "Yes, ma'am."

"Prayer book?"

"In my purse."

"Got yer purse?"

"Yup." She hoisted her right shoulder as evidence.

"Envelope?" The envelope contained money for the church collection. Elsie had laid it on the fridge, and Morgan had forgotten to slip it into her bag.

"Shit!" She wheeled around, an abrupt about-face motion that instigated an unfortunate chain of events. Morgan's weak knees, shaky hands, and silky white gloves combined with the forward momentum of tripping in her hem to generate a thrust and lift that launched the child into the bright April air, a flight that was aborted by the kiss of his tender cheek on the jagged corner of the concrete doorstep. His blanket picked up some pebbles as his tiny body rolled over three times, falling away from the step.

He did not cry, but lay peeping up at them from the ground, dazed and confused. "He's bleeding!" Morgan squealed as she rushed forward.

"Oh, bloody Jesus, he's gonna lose an eye!" Elsie nudged the girl aside and snatched up the child. "You'll be a state, girl, if ya handles him."

Mistrustful of her daughter-in-law's maternal abilities, and equally suspicious of any physician as young as Abel Adams, the grandmother insisted on accompanying them to the hospital. Since Morgan still had to be confirmed, Tom dropped child, mother, and grandmother off at Emergency. "Church would do him more good," Nanny Moon clucked to no one as she sat in the waiting room, smoothing her starch-stiff, blue dress with her white-gloved hands and needlessly straightening the brim of her straw hat. "Nothing heals proper without God's help." Tired of being ignored, she took out her Bible and read.

"Nothing for me to do," Adams shrugged. He had arrived in his lime-green softball uniform, complete with catcher's knee and chest pads. Finton's bleeding had subsided before they reached the hospital, and the cut had closed over by the time Adams could be reached. Upon carefully checking the baby, the doctor declared, "He's healing fine on his own. Take him home and..." Adams glanced at the grandmother, leaned in closer to Elsie, and lowered his voice. "I'd be more careful with him if I were you."

"The nerve of that quack," Nanny Moon muttered on the way home in the taxi. She was just as perturbed by Adams' whispering as by his warning, which Elsie relayed as they waited for the cab. The mortified mother sat fuming in the back seat with Finton staring up at her with his guiltless blue eyes. When Elsie finally could stand his gaze no longer, she averted her eyes to the passing scenery. As they passed the Battenhatch house, she glanced worriedly at Nanny Moon, who pretended not to notice.

"Adams says Finton healed him*self*."

Tom Moon sat at the kitchen table where he practised blowing Camel rings. He watched disinterestedly as Elsie placed Finton in the crib and stood staring at him, hands on hips, shaking her head. Now and then, she'd back away slightly, then circumspectly approach the crib, arms folded across her chest, and peer anxiously at the child.

"That's just foolish," Tom said and squished out a cigarette when his mother darkened the doorway.

In the dim light, Nanny Moon squinted and said, "I wouldn't be surprised if he's a bit odd, that one."

Taking notice of his wife's dismay, Tom sat blowing zeroes over his son's head. "He's branded now," Nanny Moon said with a toss of her silvery head. "He might be took for a Moon with a mark like that." She made the sign of the cross over his head, then ambled away, still mumbling to herself.

To Tom, the gesture appeared more like an exorcism than a blessing. "Not to worry," he said. "There's nothing wrong with him that can't be fixed."

Two weeks later, Finton's scar was barely visible, but his mother sometimes traced her finger across its shadowy arc and wondered how much the child had been damaged.

Sawyer

Welcome to Darwin: God's Country, Pop. 2500

"Lies," his father would say each time they rumbled past the large green sign on the side of the highway. "The works of it is nudding but dirty-arsed lies."

One of Finton's favourite pastimes was sitting in the front seat of the powder blue Valiant, cruising from one end of Darwin to the other, while his father drove. They'd roll across the umbilical steel bridge connecting Darwin to the rest of the world, then a few more miles to the highway before turning around and heading back towards town. His father's guiding hand was centred at the top of the wooly steering wheel, his left arm dangling out the open window, a smoke protruding like an extra digit between his yellowed fingers. "Population's goin' down, Finton. More likely to see Satan than God—so it's not God's country no more, if it ever was. And no one here likes strangers."

Legs dangling above the muddy floor mats, Finton would crane his neck to look up at his father when he spoke. He loved those rants about what was wrong with the world today. Tom Moon rarely alluded to days gone by. No one did, which left Finton to assume that the past was irrelevant. The bare historical fact was that Darwin was an insignificant trench created by a gargantuan glacier that scraped slowly across the face of Newfoundland a thousand centuries ago on its way to the ocean. As if in recompense for its accidental and violent birth, thousands of years later Darwin found itself cradled by ocean and hugged by forest. While farming such hard, salty land was a formidable vocation, Irish and English fishermen in the 1700s pegged the low-lying flatbed as an ideal refuge from which to instigate a cottage fishery. Their descendants in the late-twentieth century would regret the choice when the cod fell away, and Darwin became a town that could sustain existences but not livelihoods. But Finton knew nothing of this history and, furthermore, was unconcerned.

The tranquil life was tedious to some, but to a curious, young boy every tree boasted a fairy and every rock concealed a monster. Fields of tall grass were oceans to swim and the Laughing Woods teemed with bears, wolves, and Indian braves. In a secret alcove in the woods beyond the perimeter of the red schoolhouse, Finton rode a tree that was supple and strong, his getaway horse from marauding Apaches. From high above the ground, he could hear the clanging call of the teacher's handbell, though he sometimes pretended otherwise. "Hiyo, Silver, away!" he'd cry, and he rode like the wind. In a dark thicket only minutes from home, wounded by an arrow and hiding from the Indians, he retreated to the foxhole, a bowl-shaped hollow in the forest floor, stockpiled with spruce cones and other crude weapons. The Laughing Woods concealed many enemies but gave refuge to those who knew its secrets, and Finton was one of the chosen few.

Another favourite hiding spot was the front seat of his parents' sky-blue Valiant. On summer days, he would scrunch into the front seat, with the vehicle parked at the top of the lane a few yards from the house and no one around to disturb him. One day when he was eight, as he inhabited a hardcover of *Man O' War*, a frantic thump on the driver's window jolted him upright. His mother had placed both hands to the glass, cupped her thin lips and mouthed, "SAWYER MOON!" Before the blue-tinged half moon of her breath had faded from the window, Finton had scrambled to unlock the door.

"Winnie called and said Sawyer Moon is on the go!"

Finton slammed his book shut, clutched it to his chest, and scurried behind his mother. He glanced back only once to catch a glimpse of the familiar figure on the road, slouching towards the lane.

"Oh God! He's gonna see us!" his mother hissed. "Come on, Finton!"

Perpetually on the move, going nowhere and everywhere simultaneously, Sawyer Moon always kept his hands plunged deep into the pockets of his baggy, brown trousers, head bent forward as if fighting a cruel wind, legs reaching forward, grabbing ground in the manner of a soldier attempting to take a hill that will not be won. Sawyer didn't have friends, though he often talked to Finton's father. Most people skittered away, locked their doors and pulled the shades upon his approach. Tom Moon was the only one who never avoided

Sawyer—a fact which made Finton question his father's sanity, but also filled him with admiration for his remarkable kindness.

Sawyer was hunched over like a Grimm brothers' troll in his khaki-green Army jacket with its lamb's wool lining that was yellowed and stained brown with tobacco, grease, and turpentine. A sprawling, dark splotch across his chest looked like Jesus on the cross, while another one on his arm resembled a map of Africa. He wore a red hunting hat, and from under his coat protruded a plaid polyester jacket over a white shirt with two buttons undone, revealing the round neck of a white t-shirt. Sawyer's rumpled outfit had deteriorated from having served as pajamas on numerous occasions in various sketchy locales.

Ever since Finton could remember, people had warned him about Sawyer. "He's outta the mental for the weekend," someone would report, and the word would spread like a virus.

The most popular theory was that Sawyer had lost his mind in the war, had come home at nineteen with an arm injury, a red dragon tattoo on his left shoulder, and a small pension to reward him for being one of the few survivors of a bloody battle in Korea. Since then, and before, he had always lived with his mother Minnie. He couldn't dress himself. He had sent away to Sears for the girl in the pink bra and panties on page forty-eight. When he was a boy, he had thrown his mother down the stairs while she was pregnant, which is why she was so stunned and he was an only child. He ate only raw meat that he killed with his bare hands, and on nights when Sawyer couldn't sleep, he trolled the woods in search of dubious sport.

Finton had no reason to doubt any of this. His teachers would sometimes cancel recess because Sawyer Moon was "on the go." Once, Finton's whole gang was caught by surprise when Sawyer leaped out from behind a boulder, arms outstretched like the Mummy, his terrible pink tongue hanging to one side of his mouth and dripping saliva, his eyes blazing red. The children bolted, and Finton ran too, though he often wondered what would happen if he let Sawyer catch him.

Now ushered inside, his heart pounded like a bodhran beating the rhythm of a Celtic reel. "Don't look out the window!" His mother peeked through the curtains. These moments, like thunderstorms or fights between his parents, terrified him. Finton didn't speak, but he rarely did anyway. "There's times," his mother would tell people, "Finton can be as quiet as death."

Elsie slightly lifted the kitchen curtains and quickly let them fall. "He's comin' up the lane." She crouched beside the cupboard, in front of the humming refrigerator; her hand lay absently upon the silver handle as if she were thinking of climbing inside. Gently, but firmly, she pushed her son away, indicating that he was to hide on his own. Finton panicked and dropped to the floor. He crawled under the table a few feet from the door, whose window was devoid of a drape and potentially exposed him to the enemy.

"Don't make a sound," Elsie whispered, plucking the black rosary beads from around her neck and running them through her callused fingers. "Not a single word." He wondered what would happen if one of his brothers were to make a sudden appearance, but he figured they were down at Bilch's, playing pool and drinking Pepsi.

Laying *Man O' War* spine-up on the canvas, Finton grasped the table leg before him, fist over fist, and closed his eyes. Like the arrival of a storybook giant, footsteps stomped the concrete steps: *tap-tap-stop*, followed by knocking—*Pound! Pound! Pound!*

Finton opened his eyes and saw a wizened face peering through the window, the vacant eyes searching for human life. The voice slurred like a wounded bear: "I knows yer in there… hidin' from me, ya bash-turds!"

Finton tucked his head between his knees and hugged them close, assuming this posture would make him invisible. He shuddered and hugged them closer when Sawyer struck the door again.

"Let me in!" he roared.

As Finton looked up and caught Sawyer's gaze, they were both transfixed. With his big-fisted paw, the intruder alternately hammered the door and rapped on the glass. Finton felt like crying. "Gotta go to the bathroom," he whispered.

"Don't you dare move! If he sees you we'll have to let him in."

Wrapped in a tight bundle, Finton quivered beneath the table and silently prayed to Jesus to make Sawyer go away. Just like counting the time between crashes of thunder, Finton breathlessly tallied the seconds separating Sawyer's barrages. Longer spaces between poundings meant that Sawyer was getting tired and soon would leave. At first the blows rained continually, but then grew lighter, with time in between. After a while—maybe half a minute—Sawyer seemed to take breathers. The first break was eight seconds; the next was fourteen; then it was forty, and Finton could hear talking—a shout of greeting. Finally, when the knocking had stopped for several moments, he peeked out the window and saw no Sawyer. He thanked Jesus and made the sign of the cross. The storm had passed. He still dared not move, but waited for a word from his mother. She knelt on the floor, her brown, permed head bowed against the hard, white fridge and her hands clasped as she whispered a rosary.

"He's gone," Finton said, feeling the wonder and relief of certainty. She shot him a sharp look and finished a Hail Mary before blessing herself and going to the window to peek through the curtain.

"What in the name of Jesus—"

"What?"

"Your father—what's he doin' out there?"

"What?"

"He's talking to Sawyer Moon. There's more sense in a cow than there is—don't tell me he's bringin' 'im in. Sweet Jesus—" She jerked away from the door and folded her arms across her chest defensively.

The door handle rattled, but Finton's mother had locked it. His father kicked the door three times, making the windowpane jostle in its frame. "Else! Open the door!"

Elsie obeyed and stepped aside to let Tom and his guest enter.

"Else, have we got five dollars to lend Sawyer?" With his right index finger, Tom repeatedly jabbed his left palm, for he rarely rested his hands in his pockets; he was always gesturing, smoking, clutching or clouting. "Till Thursday?" When he laid one brotherly hand on Sawyer's shoulder, Finton's gaze fixed on his father's grease-blackened knuckles, which meant he had been labouring on someone's car. He was proud that other kids' fathers had to come to his for such important repairs. While Tom was known to be a bit of a hard ticket who always had trouble finding steady work, he was well regarded for his talent in saving cars from the junkyard.

"I have twenty," Elsie said, a slight quiver in her voice, placing her hands on her hips in mock defiance. "But we need groceries, and I wouldn't mind a night o' bingo to get outta this friggin' house."

Finton watched as Sawyer stood in the doorway, rubbing his grizzled chin with his left hand, a sly expression on his face as he looked around. To the boy, who couldn't help but rankle his nose and rub his eyes from the stench of sweat and turpentine, he appeared to be appraising the meagre contents of the kitchen. Finton had never known any visitor but the parish priest to exceed the boundaries of the kitchen; very few saw the inside of the slightly more comfortable living room that was just beyond it. He would often hear stories about parties and good times in the tiny living room "in olden times," which was what Nanny Moon called the days when people laughed and danced so roughly that the McNulty Family record would skip from beginning to end on the suitcase turntable that had come in the mail from relatives in Boston. There would be beer and cake, chips and Cheezies, and sometimes even a pot of homemade turkey soup. Someone always brought a guitar for Tom to play and sing "My Lovely Irish Rose." But those were the good old days, which seemed to have ended just before Finton's coming.

Sawyer's presence emphasized that people rarely came to the Moon house anymore. To Finton's admiration, he did not seem to be the slightest bit discomfited to be standing in someone else's kitchen asking for money. He had removed his cap, however, and tucked it under one armpit in what Finton took as a show of respect. It was the first time he had seen Sawyer's bare head, and it surprised him to learn that his hair, though shorn close to his scalp, was still brown and thriving.

Tom, meanwhile, had joined his hands in supplication, not for the money, but for his wife to stop talking in that whining voice. "Do we have it or not?"

Elsie sighed and stared at the closed curtains through which the light begged for entry. Finton knew she had noticed the clasped, tense hands. "I'll get me bloody purse," she said and stomped to the bedroom. Upon returning, she gave a crisp, blue bill to Tom, who thrust it towards Sawyer's ready hand.

Finton scrutinized the soft manner in which Sawyer took the bill with his thick fingers. "Thanks, Tom, b'y." His raspy voice had taken on a pathetic, conciliatory tone that made Finton's stomach queasy. "Ye were always good to ol' Saw."

Tom again laid a hand on Sawyer's shoulder as if to offer absolution. "Is that enough, now?"

"Oh yish, yish. Go' blesh ya, ol' buddy." He winked at Tom, who looked away out the kitchen window, and assessed Elsie as if he didn't quite trust her not to smack him. "You too, Elsie Moon. Yer a good soul to poor ol' Shawyer."

"Yer welcome," she said, and Finton thought her face would crack from the strain. He wondered, *Is this really the woman in the stories from* "*olden days*"? He doubted his mother had ever been happy, let alone jumping to the McNulty Family record and making it skip.

When Sawyer had shuffled out the door, the arguing began. Voices bellowed and arms waved angrily. Finton sat on the floor, his back to the wood stove, wringing the spindles of a chair in his hands, wishing he could conjure a genie to whisk him away on a magic carpet to some foreign land.

"I wouldn't mind if you were gettin' work from the garage, but that money—"

Tom raised his hands to his ears. "I don't wanna hear it."

Elsie suddenly turned her back to her husband and snapped the faucet on full force. Dishes clanked with a distressing din over which she was forced to shout, "My father used to say, a fool and his money are soon parted!"

With an angry slap at the back of a kitchen chair, Tom stomped into the living room and forced himself to sit in front of the floor-model television, which was switched on with the sound turned down. *The Friendly Giant* was on in the usual black and white, with the two musical cats blowing noiselessly on their French horn and saxophone; Rusty the Rooster strummed on a tiny acoustic guitar specially sized to fit under a chicken's wings, and Jerome the giraffe swayed his long, spotted neck, while the white-haired giant in his tunic, arms folded, surveying all, smiled benevolently and pretended to enjoy the racket.

Finton heard the angry shuffle of matchsticks in a box, the flare of the flame, the first puff, the release of breath. A billow of white smoke floated from the corner of the room towards the television set. He heard his mother's nagging voice, still chasing her husband to his resting place: "Don't know what we're gonna do for groceries now. There's nudding there for supper, and Clancy registerin' for softball tomorrow." She paused for a response, and Finton held his breath until she continued. "Just like the rest o' yer family. That's why none of the Moons never had nudding, never will have nudding. Either drinkin' it, smokin' it, or givin' it away."

"Stop!" Finton shouted, clutching the spindles, his small face peering at her from behind the bars. "Yer only makin' 'im mad again."

"Go read a book, Finton. Get outside on a nice day like this."

"But you told me to come in 'cause of—"

"Yer mother told you to get out!" a voice roared from the living room.

Finton flinched and bumped the back of his head on the iron handle of the oven door. "I wish ye'd make up your bloody minds." With one hand, he rubbed his head and inspected his fingers for blood. He squeezed back the tears that blurred his vision, not wanting them to assume it was because he was sensitive.

"Lord thunderin' Jesus—" Then the pattern unfolded: the matchbox struck Rusty's beak; his father's feet pounded the canvas as he whipped out his brown leather belt, rushed towards Finton, grabbed his shoulder and whacked him on the arse.

"Don't you ever talk back to your mother again! What'n hell do you think?"

"I just wants ye to stop fightin'. Yer always at it!" His own tears blinded him, and he rubbed his eyes, growing angrier at nearly letting them see the extent of his pain. *Don't you cry*, he told himself. *Don't you cry.*

"Get out, ya goddamn sissy!" his father said and whacked his behind again as Finton skittered past him, bending down to snatch up his book. With *Man O' War* clutched to his chest, Finton stumbled into the daylight and didn't stop running until he'd gotten far away from that house. Deep in the woods, he collapsed into the foxhole.

"What'n hell do you think?" His father always said that when he was hitting someone, though he never expected an answer, just wanted to point out the confused nature of the antagonist.

Finton lay back, his head against a rock, *Man O' War* open flat on his chest, its spine raised upward as if in readiness. With black flies buzzing around him, the occasional one pitching on his face, his only thoughts were of hatred and revenge. He was capable of killing his father when he cursed and hit him, asking, "What'n hell do you think?" He despised his mother for stirring him up. Why couldn't she just give in to him? She always had to struggle and make it worse for them all.

The longer he lay there, gazing up at the tree tops and savouring the singing of hot, boiling sap, the more his anger subsided into helplessness. He'd never felt like a part of this family, with their rough ways. It wasn't just the constant swearing or the loud voices, but the way those voices talked to, and about, one another in a casually callous way. It was the insensitive manner in which they treated most living things, whether slapping a child's face, drowning unwanted kittens, or eating a good meal without seeing the need for gratitude. It was the way his mother, like a good Darwin wife, complained in a high, shrill voice about her husband's drinking, while he, in her absence, like a good Darwin husband, would call his wife by indelicate names. But more than their voices, it was their silence that bothered him: their unwillingness to speak words that could easily build bridges, settling for careless actions that, instead, built fences or moats.

None of them were readers, except for an occasional *Word Jumble* or his father's Mickey Spillanes. But Finton lived his life in books. They all complained he was too reclusive. "Too much to yourself all the time," they mocked him. His father would call him "the lone wolf." Novels were his means of escape, and he was keenly aware that they sharpened and defined the separation between him and them. The nature of that separation was something he couldn't quite name, and yet he was sure it was symbolized by the fact that both of his brothers were given bicycles on their respective eighth birthdays, and yet Finton remained bikeless, walking everywhere. It wasn't a big deal and yet, it was, for the small neglects contained larger meaning. His difference was further emphasized each time he was called out of bed to entertain some stranger with his ability to read. Sleepy-eyed and dressed only in his pajamas, Finton would stand in the kitchen in front of a visitor, and his father would hand him a book. "He's some hand to read—just watch," Tom would say. "Finton, read for the man. Show him what you can do." The reward for meeting their expectations was usually a quarter, though sometimes as much as a dollar. But the effect on Finton was a burgeoning sense of difference, as they made a show, for strangers, of his ability to do something they themselves found mysterious and useless. The more he thought about it all, the more he wanted to get away.

Somewhere in the thicket behind him, a twig snapped and suddenly the woods seemed to split wide open. Flipping onto his stomach and supporting his rigid body with his elbows, Finton scanned the trees. Ceased breathing. Listened for another noise. His heart hammered. The hungry eyes of a girl he knew peered back at him from the shadows. A flash of red. For a half-minute, he didn't breathe. Gazing and gazing, but finally, seeing nothing more, he gasped for air. The hungry eyes of Alicia Dredge had vanished, and the twig-snapping became increasingly distant. Although she never spoke to him, sometimes Alicia seemed to be constantly waiting for him and scouting him from a distance. To Finton, her behaviour was annoying.

He wanted nothing to do with her. As he was thinking that fact, a mosquito buzzed near his ear, and he flicked it away.

Tucked away in the bottom bunk bed that night, staring at the picture of the tortured Jesus that hung on his wall, he wondered if there was anywhere in the world where he could ever feel secure and normal.

Battenhatches
(Autumn 1969)

By the time he'd turned nine, Finton had scurried hundreds of times past the Battenhatch house's grim exterior. Arms flailing and heels kicking himself in the backside, he wouldn't slow down until he had turned into Moon's Lane a few yards down the road. He would peek out of one eye as he passed the mangle of birch and spruce that festooned the front yard. The interior layer of trees formed a ruddy wall of impenetrable red pine that cradled the house as the arms of a frail woman would embrace an unattractive baby. Their intent wasn't to nurture, but to hide and suppress.

There had never been a husband as far as he knew—questions to his parents initiated a change in subject—and Miss Bridie Battenhatch's daughter Morgan was rarely home. Lately, rumour had it, Morgan split her time between Moon's Lane, her mother's house, and the psychiatric ward at St. Clare's in St. John's. Sometimes, though, her dead father's relatives would send for her to come stay with them in Halifax. "For her own protection," Tom would say, as if twenty-year-old Morgan was harmless to anyone else.

For most of his life, Finton saw her only as his golden-haired babysitter, but there were often whispers that Morgan wasn't normal. She was always swearing and talking back to her mother. Although most of what happened behind Battenhatch doors was unknown to the rest of Darwin, a passerby could hear bloodcurdling screams and the shattering of glass against walls, furniture being upended—all adding to the legend of Miss Bridie and, increasingly, that of her untamable daughter. While he didn't witness any of those wilder moments, Finton could distinctly recall a specific summer afternoon when Morgan had demonstrated to Finton and Homer how to fry ants in their backyard with a magnifying glass, the sun's rays, and a little patience. They'd accidentally set fire to the grass and Homer had dashed inside to tell. After Clancy and Elsie put out the blaze with buckets of water, both disciples were grounded and Morgan was sent home with a whack on the arse.

"The girl is not right," Elsie said. "I don't want her babysitting anymore." Finton complained bitterly, since he was in love with how Morgan sometimes made fudge for the boys, swore violently when she lost at poker, and let them stay up late when their parents were gone to the Saturday night dances and political rallies. Nanny Moon agreed with Elsie, however, remarking how the Battenhatch girl sometimes stared off into space and talked to herself. "With a mother like that? It just goes to show," Elsie said.

"All they've got comin' in is Morgan's babysitting and Miss Bridie's welfare cheques," Tom argued, but to no avail. Ultimately, he gave in to the nagging and banned Morgan from babysitting at the Moon house. Still, there were plenty of other places in Darwin for her to find work. Gradually, however, word had spread of Morgan's exploits, and there was a rumour going around that she'd been caught in bed with one of the boys she was supposed to be looking after.

The other rumour was that, when she was eighteen, Morgan had thrown a rope over an exposed beam in her bedroom, stood on a chair and put a noose around her neck. Even bending her legs, of course, the ceiling was too low, and her mother had caught her before she could kill herself, throwing her arms around Morgan's legs and thereby saving her from "an eternity in purgatory." Instead, Morgan was sent to the psychiatric ward at St. Clare's in the hopes that she could be cured of the darkness tormenting her soul.

One cold night in early September of '69, there came a thunderous pounding upon the front door. Finton was parked on the floor, hugging a pillow and watching *Gilligan's Island*, thinking he would never want to leave any island that had both an exotic Ginger and a pretty Mary Ann. He heard mumbling from the porch: "Morgan home from the mental—Miss Bridie—fire, Tom."

As if on cue, a mournful siren's wail pierced the night. Finton dashed to the kitchen and climbed onto the kitchen counter to peer out the window. He was just in time to watch the sleek, red truck, glistening in the moonlight between gathering dark clouds, its blood light flashing as it pulled in front of the ghostly residence.

Tom cursed under his breath, wondering aloud what that "bloodofabitch" was after doing now. He slipped his feet into his shoes and tied them rapidly. "I'll go have a look, Else."

Finton hopped off the counter in his bare feet. "I'm goin' too!"

"Nearly bedtime for you. I'll tell you about it in the morning." Tom popped a cigarette between his lips, a frightened look in his cobalt eyes that made Finton all the more eager. Both of his brothers were out—likely down at the fire. So Finton feigned sleepiness, went to bed, and waited for the telltale creaking of his mother opening and closing the front door. Careful not to make the floorboards squeak outside Nanny Moon's bedroom door, which was always barred tight when she was praying, he crept out into the night air.

Even from his own front step, he could see that the blaze had painted the sky a lurid orange-blue. It was like stepping inside the hell of his nightmares. Flames seeped like liquid from the eaves of Miss Bridie's house. Orange sparks spattered upward and twirled about like fireflies before settling mischievously among black branches. Suddenly, Finton was terrified: it had been a warm, dry Indian summer up until that day, and the fire would spread quickly to the trees and houses on Moon's Lane.

He galloped down the lane, feeling as if he were entering the screen of a colour television like he'd seen on display at Sam's Stereo. About a hundred Darwinians had congregated before the burning house while, all around them, treetops blazed and the velvet stream that flowed between Moon's Lane and the Battenhatch estate glowed silent orange and blue. Red parking lights winked on and off for half a mile, while the flashing lights of an RCMP patrol car bathed everything in hysterical crimson.

At first, Finton watched the show from the bottom of Moon's Lane. Nearly everyone he knew was standing there, driven out of their homes and drawn to the flames, curiosity and fear etched on their faces. Some, like his father, were lured by compassion for a woman whose daughter was trying to burn her home to the ground. Most were drawn by the desire to witness the unveiling of Bridie Battenhatch.

Strange visions too clear to be real presented themselves inside his head. Miss Bridie rocking back and forth, counting blue ceramic rosary beads with her spindly fingers, wheezing an old song from her blackened lungs. Beside her, a man genuflected on one knee, using one hand to protect his eyes from the overpowering smoke. He grabbed hold of the woman's arm just as a flaming beam crashed from above and hurled him backwards, smacking his head on a table and leaving him dazed on the floor.

Finton blinked—not exactly seeing, but imagining. He had these kinds of visions occasionally and they sometimes came true. *Didn't I dream this?* he wondered in a voice that seemed outside himself. Blinking again to reset his focus, he identified his mother at the fringes of the crowd, peering into the fire, double wrapping her orange-lined navy parka around her as the wind riffled through the grey fur trim of her hood. She always seemed to be cold and alone. Just off to her right his mother's sister-in-law, Aunt Lucy, leaned forward like a dying willow over her nine fatherless children who huddled like strewn petals at her feet. A quick scan of the crowd showed his best friend Skeet Stuckey smoking and sputtering a string of curse words; Winnie and Francis Minnow, arm in arm, chatting to each other in soft, calm voices; young Doctor Abel Adams; Davey Doyle, star pitcher of Clancy's softball team, the Esso Extras; his mother's Uncle Tim with the red cheeks and gleaming, bald head; and Albino Al Kelly with his older brother Lance, the bartender at Jack's Place. Also guest starring were various teachers, particularly Father Power, who stayed in his car with the windows rolled up, as well as Miss Fielding and Miss Woolfred, who stood talking to each other, their eyes shining with fear. He also noted a murder of Crowleys that included his mortal enemy, Bernard. Behind the Crowleys stood a flock of Dredges, including the pretty one, Alicia, with the hungry eyes. Beside her was a gaggle of girls Finton knew from school. Tall, strong Dolly Worchester looked as if she could lead an army of Amazons into battle. But Mary Connelly, with her needle-thin body, seemed in perpetual need of a hug; he wished he had the nerve to offer her one.

Standing atop the culvert where the river ran beneath the road, Finton observed the rolls of black smoke spewing out from the windows and eaves in an ominous cloud that extended as far as he could see, above all their heads and over his parents' house at the crest of Moon's Lane.

A dark figure bolted out of the house and fell face forward onto the ground. It was his father, he quickly realized, who stumbled as if drunk, then rolled onto his back to suck the dense air into his lungs, his sweaty visage reflecting orange and black. Two men with worried expressions hovered over him. They kept looking at the house where billows of smoke poured out the broken front window and the open door.

Sliding invisibly through the awestruck throngs, Finton sidled onto the ground beside his father.

"She won't come out," Tom Moon was saying. "Stubborn as they come, she is."

"What's wrong with 'er?" one of the men asked.

"She's just sittin' in her chair, rockin' back and forth with everything going right to hell around her. 'Let's go, Miss Bridie,' I says. 'You'll be burnt to death if you stays here.' She don't even look at me. Just rockin' and singin' 'The Wabash Cannonball'."

"Sounds like she's in shock," said the other one.

"Couldn't stay no longer, b'ys." Tom spit a black glob onto the ground in front of Finton. While the boy was still gazing at the shiny dark stuff that came from his father's insides, Tom stood up shakily.

"Yer not goin' back in!" the first man said, wiping the blackened sweat from his brow.

Tom stopped. Glared at the ground, absently rubbing a sore spot on his crown. "Are *you* goin' to?"

Silence. Tom spit again—not angrily, but as a sign of covenant. Without another word—although Finton thought of a few things *he* could have said to the cowardly men—Tom darted into the flaming building.

Time stood still as he watched the front door. Presently, he felt a well-meaning hand on his shoulder, which turned out to belong to one of the cowardly men. Finton shrugged it off and dashed to the front step. As he peered through the smoke, the heat threatened to melt the flesh from his face. Finton shielded his head and stepped back.

He observed no more, for one of the cowards stepped in front of him, inadvertently posing a barrier between the flames and the boy. The man, who was Mayor Munro, seemed to be considering his options. Lucky for His Worship, and for Finton, Tom Moon's backside broke the spell as, swearing like a madman and pulling with all his strength, he partially emerged from the curtain of smoke.

"Come on, Miss Bridie! There's nudding in here for you now."

"Morgan!" she was sobbing. "My Morgan's still in there!"

"Morgan's up at my place, Miss Bridie. She's best kind. Now come on." He jerked the rocking chair, in which the hysterical woman sat, onto the threshold. But they both came up solid in the door frame as she refused to be dragged any farther.

"S'me home, Tom! I can't leave me 'ome!" Clinging one-handed to her blue ceramic rosary beads, she grasped both sides of the door frame. The sight of those beads was paralyzing; except in his vision, Finton had never actually seen them before. Meanwhile, Tom Moon kept tugging at Miss Bridie's chair and swearing at her.

"I wants to go back home!" Bridie leaped from the chair and scampered inside the house, clutching her long, grey hair, rosary beads dangling from one hand.

"Jesus!" Tom spit on the porch once more. "You're askin' to get the two of us killed." He hauled the rocking chair outside on the porch and flung it aside.

Finton lurched forward and grabbed his father's belt above the left hip. "Don't go in again, Dad!"

Tom didn't hear him, though, and Finton got dragged a few feet before he fell aside. He wondered what sort of moral code reasoned that the life of a suicidal hag was worth a man leaving his family without a provider. Regardless of the reason, he left his youngest boy lying on the porch of a burning building. It was the closest to an apocalypse Finton assumed he would ever come: the flames, the heat, the smoke, the hordes, and the abandonment. This time his father returned in mere seconds, carrying Miss Bridie in his arms. He fell across the porch with her and pinned her to the ground as she flailed in her bare feet, crying out for her daughter.

The Girl in the Pink Coat

At the breakfast table, everyone talked about last night's fire, but Finton ate quickly. Upon finishing, he mumbled gratitude to his mother, grabbed his bookbag, burst out of the house, leaped over the steps, and ran down the lane. Right about now, she would be emerging through her own front door and on her way to the red schoolhouse at the top of the hill. Rubbing his invisible power ring, he called on Green Lantern to help him fly at the speed of light, and his feet seemed to lift from the ground.

Before he veered right at the bottom of Moon's Lane, he glanced to his left at the burnt remains of the Battenhatch house. It appeared more haunted than ever, especially now that he could see right through the dark, open space where the front door once concealed the secrets of those within. The stink of burnt wood and smoldering ash assaulted his nostrils as he flew past the awakening bungalows, towards Mary's house, where he could see her in the distance, strolling and chattering with Dolly Worchester.

He couldn't recall a time when he didn't know Mary Connelly, and yet he would always remember the first moment he saw her. It was Grade One, the beginning of the school year. He was five and she was six because the results of a test administered by the Darwin School Board Authority deemed Finton more advanced than most children his age, and so he was permitted to skip kindergarten. Thus, he would always be a year younger than nearly all of his classmates. That first day, there was a girl wearing a pink nylon jacket so bright that it hurt his eyes. She had just hugged her father after letting go of his hand, and she strutted away from him like she was ready to attack the world.

Despite her small frame and wide, brown eyes that gave her the air of a fairy princess, she had a warrior's spirit that was enhanced by the upward turn of her small nose, the quiet set of her determined chin, and the way her fine brown hair stranded across her face in the breeze. He'd been so entranced by that first sight of her that, as she approached him, he forgot to move. He just stared at her, admiring her luminous jacket and the confidence with which she tread the earth. She stopped in front of him, mere inches away, and only then did he realize he'd been standing in her path.

"What are you looking at?" she'd asked.

"Your coat."

"Why would you stare at my coat?"

"It's really pink."

"Haven't you ever seen a pink coat before?"

"Not like that one." The bright September sun had arisen behind her in the crisp, fall sky, illuminating her hair in golden red.

"What's your name?"

"Finton Moon." Squinting, he looked away to the trees surrounding the schoolyard. He felt slightly destabilized whenever he said his own name aloud, as if each time he did so, he was giving away something of himself. He could imagine a day when he wouldn't speak it at all, and when someone asked, he would offer a made-up one.

"Mine's Mary Connelly," she said, looking first at the ground and then into Finton's eyes. "Wanna be my friend?"

Finton nodded. "Okay." Then Mary began telling him what Grade One would be like and what the teacher would say. She seemed very wise for one so small and fragile. *Someone ought to be protecting her*, he thought. *Sir Finton Moon of the Laughing Woods—slayer of dragons, saviour of damsels in distress.* In a way, of course, she was also looking out for him. She was his queen, and for her he would lay down his life.

They sat beside each other in class, occasionally whispering a comment on the strange things the teacher said. But Mary had several such friends around her, all just wanting to be in her world, perhaps all thinking they would stand guard for her while she reigned over them and protected them. Finton shrank in his seat, defeated by the idea of competing for friendship.

As the school year went on, Mary slipped gradually away from him and into the exclusive realm of girls. Her best friend was Dolly Worchester, the Amazon queen. While Mary was small and delicate, Dolly was tall, strong, and more athletic than most boys. In the games at recess in the school grounds, Dolly would battle more fiercely than anyone and was always a member of the victorious team.

"Hey, Moon! Wait up!" Hearing the voice of Skeet Stuckey, Finton instinctively halted on the side of the road. Resignedly, he watched the girls disappear over the hill.

Every day at recess and when school let out, he would watch Mary go off with her girls while he fell into a stream of babbling boys that usually headed for the woods. He often wished he could go with her, but she was beyond his grasp. Even to be seen talking to Mary would mean being mocked by the other boys, especially Bernard Crowley and his minions. Eventually, he took to sitting with the boys on the far side of the classroom, opposite the girls. He often felt the pressure of such restraint as if he were bound in a straitjacket, each authentic emotion buckled, every dangerous thought shackled.

"Did you hear about Miss Bridie?" Skeet panted from running to catch up.

"I was there."

"Yes, b'y! I managed to sneak out for a few minutes, but Mudder caught me and dragged me home. What a bitch, man." Finton shrugged and kept walking, while Skeet scrambled to keep up. "I heard Morgan started it, and now's she in the mental."

"No one knows what really happened."

Skeet drew a huge gob of spit into his throat and hawked on the ground in front of Finton's feet. "One in and one out."

Finton shook his head disgustedly. "What're you talking about?"

"Morgan's gone in and Sawyer Moon's out."

Finton halted near the top of the hill. Skeet laughed heartily as he paused beside him, then glided past. "You scared o' Sawyer?"

"No... not really."

"That must be why you're running."

"Shut up."

"Oh—I get it." Skeet slowed and nodded towards the schoolyard. "Trying to catch up with your girlfriend." He motioned towards Mary, who by now was standing around with a circle of girls, no doubt gossiping about last night's fire.

"She's not my girlfriend."

"Well, let's catch up with her then."

"No!"

"If you won't talk to her, I will." Skeet took off running, straight for the girls at the edge of the small crowd while Finton muttered to himself and trudged behind.

Seeing the boys approach, Dolly pushed her glasses up the bridge of her nose and nudged Mary with her elbow. "Did you hear about Sawyer?" she asked.

"He's outta the mental," Skeet said testily. "We know."

"We just saw him." Mary pointed towards the thicket. "Over there."

Skeet spit on the ground. "Scared, are ya?"

Finton peered nervously into the woods, imagining the madman could be lurking behind any tree.

"Better to be scared than to let 'em catch ya," Mary said. "That's what Dad says."

"I'm not scared o' nuttin'."

"Yeah, we'll see about that when Sawyer gets ya. Then you'll run home cryin'." Dolly's prediction sent the three of them into peals of laughter. Skeet didn't laugh, though. He seemed embarrassed, which was always funny to see because Skeet was so much bigger than everyone else.

Skeet stuck his hands in his pockets and winked at her. "You know what you needs, Dolly?"

"What do I need, Skeet Stuckey?"

"A man."

"What would I do with a man? Everyone knows women are better."

"Someday you'll need a man to protect you—then we'll see who's better."

"Well, if you see one around, let me know."

"B'ys, shut up—women are just as good as men." As he spoke, Finton noticed Alicia Dredge sitting on the steps with her big-eared, older brother Willie. When she caught him looking, she shifted her gaze towards the road. Conversations went on all around them, but the two siblings sat in seclusion. They didn't even talk to each other.

To most people, Alicia was invisible. But Finton often noticed her, in spite of himself. She never spoke, preferred the shadowed periphery and eschewed attention. She often averted her eyes as if she'd been discovered—and discovery was certainly not on her agenda. For she was a Dredge and, as such, not just unworthy of attention but disdainful of it. The Dredges were like spiders in the corner of a shed, or a bottomless black hole at the far end of an overgrown yard—it was best to pretend they didn't exist. Alicia didn't call attention to herself, but Finton was sometimes aware of her watching him with those unnaturally large eyes. Despite being a Dredge, she was not unattractive. In fact, he sometimes wondered what it was like to be her, the only flower in a neglected lawn. Of course, he would never admit that she intrigued him, for she was a Dredge, and a Dredge never met with anyone's approval.

"Hey, I got an idea." Skeet nodded towards the school. "Fielding don't even know we're here yet. We should take the morning off."

"No!" said Mary, clutching her books to her chest. "Mom would kill me."

"Come on, girl." Dolly nudged her friend. "It'd be fun!"

"Moon?" Skeet's plan was obvious—since most of his previous attempts had failed, he was trying to embarrass Finton into skipping school.

Inside the schoolhouse, the first bell rang, creating a knot in Finton's stomach. "Not me."

"What if Mary went with us?"

"Not likely," she said.

"Come on, b'ys. It's only one morning. No one will know."

But Finton knew the teacher would call his mother, and there'd be a lot of explaining to do, and the next thing he knew, he'd be staying after school and being grounded at home, and everyone would be mad at him, so he'd have to tell the priest what he did, and then God would be mad at him, and he'd have to do penance, and even that wouldn't make up for the all the guilt he'd feel. It was better to stay innocent than to face all the punishment. Even if no one else knew, skipping school felt wrong.

When the second bell rang, Skeet began to panic. "Fine. I guess I'll just have to go in the woods by meself."

"Sawyer's in there," said Mary.

"Think I'm scared o' him?" Skeet laughed just as Miss Fielding was opening the doors to the school, and he ran off towards the thicket. "Chickens!"

"You can't let him go by himself," said Dolly. "Go after him, Finton."

"You go after him. He's big enough to handle Sawyer."

"But it's Sawyer," said Mary. "He might do anything."

Finton stared at the ground, then looked at Mary, who was clearly disappointed in him. He looked at Dolly, who stood with her arms folded and lips twisted skeptically, practically daring him to prove his masculinity in front of the girl he obviously loved. He glanced to the doors, where he could just see Miss Fielding herding the children inside. In fact, the Dredges were already entering, with Alicia casting him a backwards glance. She always seemed to be looking at him.

"Hurry up!" Dolly said. "Sawyer Moon's on the go!"

Mary looked to the woods. Finton's heart pounded furiously. "Fine," he said. "If Miss Fielding asks where I am, tell her I forgot something and went home to get it." He started to run, but stopped. "I'll be right back with Skeet."

Both girls nodded and exchanged worried glances. When Mary and Dolly turned the corner of the schoolhouse, Finton dashed for the woods. Only when he'd reached the first line of tall, skinny birch did he stop and catch his breath. "What the hell am I doing?" he grumbled to himself as he took up a brisk walk, the hard plastic handle of his bookbag making his palms sweat. The path in these woods was worn from many generations of school-skippers that likely included Finton's own father. So there was little doubt which route Skeet had taken.

"Skeet! Where the hell are ya?" He waited and listened. A few yards off, a crow called from a towering spruce, but the only other sound was the distant clanging of the final bell, signaling that he was officially late.

Finton walked into the thicket, where the birch and spruce bramble was densest, and pushed his way onto the path. Within moments, he entered a clearing and heard the fading footsteps of someone running.

But it was already too late for him to turn. On a stump in the clearing sat a man, with his head bowed and his hands covering his eyes. His head was bobbing up and down while he chanted something indecipherable in a low, guttural voice.

Despite serious misgivings, Finton stood his ground, his heart pounding furiously. A gasp must have escaped his lips because Sawyer looked up at him with the pus-filled, narrowed eyes of a rabid dog. His face was unshaven, his mouth drawn tight like a keyhole. He shook his head and started beating the air in front of him with open palms as if he were encased in a water-filled glass tank and was trying to escape. Finton's instinct was to turn and run. But he was frozen in place.

Sawyer wiped his nose on his sleeve. "Do you know me?" he asked.

"I do," said Finton. "I knows you." He steadied his breathing as best he could, trying not to show any signs of fear. "My father is Tom Moon. He's a friend of yours."

A dim light came on in Sawyer's eyes. "Good ol' Tom. Yish."

Finton glanced around. The path lay ahead, but he preferred not to cross near Sawyer. The only safe route was the way he had come. "I have to go to school," he said.

Sawyer stood up, taller than Finton remembered, wearing the same khaki Army jacket with the stains of Africa and the crucified Jesus. His hands kept fidgeting and swiping at his face as if to rid himself of an invisible web. As he shuffled forward, dead twigs snapped beneath his boots. "You knows me, sure." He kept coming closer, and Finton was prepared to bolt. "I'm a friend o' your father's." Every now and then, he blinked several times in rapid succession, and when he stopped, his eyes were redder.

"Tom." Finton took a step backwards. "Tom's my father."

"You're a good lad," said Sawyer. "Come here till I tells ya something."

"What is it?" asked Finton, too petrified to move. He'd always wondered what this moment might be like, and now that he knew, he wished he didn't.

"Come here till I tells ya!" Sawyer said, and with one hand that was quicker than Finton would have guessed possible, he grabbed Finton by the shoulder, shook the bookbag from his hand, and drew him in close. He could smell Sawyer's smelly breath. He gazed into his mongrel eyes. "You tell 'em I'm not goin' back."

"What? Tell who?"

"Not for no one."

"I don't know what you're—"

Before Finton could get the words out, Sawyer shoved him to the ground and lay on top of him, pinning him with one hand. Finton kicked and flailed, but his size was no match for a man who had once been a soldier.

He found himself staring into those deep-set red eyes, that engorged nose, and those yellowed teeth that had consumed raw flesh. The grey, stiff bristles and weather-chewed skin. Finton wanted to scream, but Sawyer had taken his voice.

Finton closed his eyes and focused on the whistle of the breeze, the beating of his own heart. The crow cawed and, somewhere farther off, children chattered. It took only an instant for the world to go black. Then he could no longer hear or feel. All around him was a blanket of darkness beset with a panoply of brilliant, spinning stars of burnt orange and lemon yellow. Here, there was no Sawyer, no danger—just tranquility.

An invisible force tugged at his pant legs. Finton clamped his hands on his belt, resisting the humiliation with all his strength. A voice commanded him to open his eyes, said it was going to be okay. But he couldn't open his mouth to respond; he was floating above the starry planet. Finally, when he felt a slap on his cheek, he opened his eyes. There, leaning over him and blocking out the sun was Skeet.

"You came back," Finton said.

"Good thing too. Rotten bugger wasn't long runnin' when he saw me comin' after 'im." He pulled a cigarette from behind his ear and lit up, panting and grinning, his forehead glistening. He pointed to the darkest part of the woods. "Went that way, the bastard. You okay, Moon?"

"I'm all right." Finton tried to stand up, but he felt woozy and had to sit on the stump.

"He was like an animal," Skeet said. "Worse than I ever seen him before."

"Yeah. Me too."

"Did he say anything?"

"Not much." Finton shook his head. "Something about not wanting to go back."

"To the mental, I suppose. I mean, who would, right?"

When Finton finally felt up to it, the boys decided they'd skip the rest of the morning. Their parents and the teacher would just have to understand.

"I'm not telling anybody about this," Finton said.

"Understood." Skeet blew a ring of smoke into the wind. "I wouldn't either."

Together, they ambled down the road, avoiding the path until they reached an opening in the brush, where they followed a secret path through the woods, all the way to the foxhole.

In the sunlit hollow, Skeet plucked a cigarette out of his pocket and coolly lit it with a match. "Sawyer almost had you, man. I thought you was a goner."

"He had me pinned," Finton said. "But he couldn't get to me."

Skeet looked at him curiously and held the cigarette towards him. Finton shook his head. "What do you mean?" Skeet asked.

"I was long gone." Finton thought about Sawyer. He could see that mean face and those tortured eyes, staring at his own death—fear and sorrow eclipsing each other. And then he saw Sawyer's body, face down on the ground, not moving.

"Earth to Finton." Skeet shook him by the arm, the cigarette stuck in one side of his mouth, a worried look in his eyes. "Jesus, b'y, you're like a fuckin' zombie."

"Sorry. I was just thinkin'."

"Sometimes you really weird me out," said Skeet.

"Sometimes I weird myself out."

A crow cawed as it flew overhead and perched in a tall spruce behind them. Skeet seemed lost in thought, reminding Finton of how little he actually knew of Skeet's motives. To his mind, Skeet was brighter and kinder than most people gave him credit for. He had a hard reputation—always cursing, smoking, and getting into trouble—but Finton saw a side of him that no one else did. Skeet was protective over Finton like a big brother would be, with a sense of justice that perpetually courted trouble. More than anything, it was his insistence on doing right by people that impressed Finton. In Darwin, nearly everyone struggled to get by, and most people did only what they needed to do. The town had more than its share of bullies—the Crowleys, who lived on the edge of town on their ramshackle property, were the best example of Darwinian ethics.

Bernard Crowley was perpetually trying to goad Finton. In Darwin, any child who read books, went to mass, and stayed out of trouble was simply trying not to stand out. It was the safest method of ensuring one's survival. Likewise, you didn't jump onto the ice pans in spring, you didn't go joyriding out on the highway at night, and you didn't hang around at Bilch's after dark. But Finton drew attention no matter what. It just seemed that the more invisible he tried to be, the more he attracted unwanted notice. If he went for a walk in the woods, wasps would sometimes buzz around his head. Mosquitoes would zip towards him and sometimes flit right into his eye as if he wasn't there. Butterflies would pitch on his head as if he were a tall plant, and rabbits would occasionally hop towards him on a path, eyeing him curiously. Likewise, people like Bernard Crowley inevitably took an interest in him. It was as if he were an alien species they were intent on studying.

It was common knowledge in Darwin that you didn't mess with the Crowleys. They were crouched at the edge of town in their rundown house full of youngsters and animals—mangy dogs, barnyard cats, a host of chickens and ducks, and a bedraggled horse. Even by Darwinian standards, the Crowleys were dirty, foulmouthed and poor. The parents lived on welfare, and none of the children went to school regularly. Bernard was probably better off than most; at least he came to school once in a while, even if his chances of passing were slim. In fact, his nickname was "Slim," not just because he was as scrawny as a junkyard dog, but because Miss Fielding had once asked him in front of everyone, on a day he'd been acting up worse than usual, what he thought his chances were of passing Grade Two. Bernard had already failed it once, mostly because of chronic absence combined with an inability to count or spell. When he shrugged nonchalantly, the teacher bent over, looked him right in the eye and said, "Slim." Then she said it again. "Slim, slim, and slim. Those are your chances of passing." Sure enough, he failed, and the name stuck. Some people forgot his given name and just called him Slim. Finton, however, preferred to call him "Bernard," which seemed more suitable.

He used to be in Homer's grade starting off and Homer still told the story now and then about when Slim Crowley pissed in his pants in front of the whole class. The teacher had made him stand in front of everyone until he apologized for stealing some money from Homer. He never apologized, but his bladder let go, staining his pants and making a big, yellow puddle at his feet. He ran out of the school and didn't come back that year, so he failed Grade One. The following year, Miss Fielding just put him ahead, which most people took as an act of surrender.

Now in the same grade as Finton, Bernard would go out of his way to antagonize him; on the school grounds, he occasionally gave Finton a shove with his shoulder to make sure the smaller boy knew who was boss. "Hey, faggot," he'd say. "Did your grandmother dress you this morning?" Finton would say, "I dressed myself." One day, he'd had enough and just told Bernard to go to hell. Bernard smirked and shoved him, but Finton stood his ground, fists curled, ready to fight. Bernard took him in a headlock and punched him in the nose. Eyes watering and nose bleeding, Finton squirmed to be free. Then, from out of nowhere, Skeet rushed at Bernard and knocked him back against the side of the school, forcing him to let go of his captive. He raised a fist to Bernard's face and told him, "Lay another hand on 'im, Slim, and I'll beat the livin' shit outta ya."

"Yeah?" said Bernard. He looked fearfully up at Skeet, who was a couple of inches taller. "You 'n what army?"

"Just watch yerself." Skeet spat on Bernard's shoes and released him.

Bernard skulked off with his gang, but not before turning with a scared, spiteful expression, shouting at Finton, "Yer boyfriend won't be always there to save ya, faggot!"

Skeet stuck his hands in his pockets and turned to Finton, who wiped the blood from his lip and licked it away. "If he gives you more trouble, just give us a shout."

"Thanks," said Finton, as he flicked away a ladybug that had landed on his sleeve. "But I can take care of myself."

"I'm sure you can. But people like Slim won't quit till you puts them in their place. I'm used to dealing with quiffs like him."

Finton nodded and wiped his nose again. The bleeding had already stopped.

"Jesus, I thought you were gonna bleed to death," said Skeet.

"Fast healer," said Finton.

Sitting in the foxhole with Skeet, nursing his psychological wounds from dealing with Sawyer, Finton was reminded of why he was friends with this odd boy, who smoked and swore and often did things Finton would never do. He supposed it was because he admired Skeet's moral code—he'd often seen him stick up for other "weak" members of the Darwinian tribe. But he didn't fool himself. Skeet Stuckey was also a part of Finton's own plan to survive Darwin's brutality. As long as Skeet was around, Finton had a guardian angel. Skeet, too, had failed a grade, but had quickly found a use for his new, smaller friend— someone to help him with the occasional piece of homework.

"Thanks for saving my arse," Finton said.

Skeet spit into the foxhole, near Finton's feet. "No problem—that's my job."

"Why?"

"I dunno." Skeet shrugged. "It just feels like it should be."

Finton didn't push it any further. After all, even a lone wolf could use a friend.

The Gathering Storm

Tom thought it would be a good idea to take Finton with him to Taylor's Garage, where he worked, although Finton wasn't sure why. He had no interest in cars except as places to read a book or listen to the radio. But he was the only one of the three boys who showed no aptitude for vehicle repair. Clancy was heir to Tom's wealth of automotive information, and even Homer, who preferred woodworking to car maintenance, could change the oil, fix a tire, or help out with a brake job. Finton was mystified by his father's mechanical world, with its language of carburetors, belts, lubricants, and manifolds—hard words that rebuffed emotion, neglected wonderment, and resisted interpretation beyond the mundane.

That morning, his mother had looked pale and complained of a headache. The older boys, because it was Saturday, would spend the day with friends, but Tom thought it would be good to show Finton his place of work. "Who knows? Maybe he'll take to it."

But, after only a few minutes, Finton desperately wanted to go home. Tom must have seen the discontentment in the boy's face because he told him, "You're here at least until I'm off for lunch, so you might as well get interested. What's wrong with you?"

He didn't answer, just wandered around the garage, poking at old tires or kicking loose screws around on the dirty concrete floor. When he finally got bored enough, he pulled a *Tintin* comic from his jacket pocket and sat reading in the corner on a gigantic grader tire. Now and then, some man came into the garage and Tom would nod towards Finton and say, "That's my boy over there." Finton would look up, give a two-finger salute, and return to the fantastic world of Tintin, Snowy, and Captain Haddock.

The bright-coloured pages, simple dialogue, and the captain's cursing kept him amused while his father lay under a jacked-up, black Volkswagen, making clanking noises with a wrench and occasionally muttering obscenities. Tom seemed happiest when he was working on cars, but that was also when he did the most swearing.

It was the scraping, metallic sound of something giving way that made the boy look up, just as his father screeched a bloodcurdling, "Fuck ya!" One of the cinder blocks had slid away, lowering the Volkswagen just enough to pin Tom underneath. It was only by a hair's breadth that he escaped being crushed. "Finton!" he yelled. "Come here!"

Within seconds, Finton was on his knees beside his father's blue-clad leg, looking underneath the car and asking if he was all right.

"See can ya pull me out, b'y—Jesus' sake! Hurry up!"

Finton positioned himself at his father's feet. A quick look around confirmed that no one else had come running, so he grabbed his father's ankles and pulled.

"Harder, b'y! Put some muscle into it!"

"I'm trying," he said, panic setting in. "I'll be right back." He scurried outside and yelled, "Somebody! Help! Dad's stuck under a car!" Within seconds, three men came running from the scrap yard, assessed the situation and, within a short time, two men—and Finton—lifted the small car while another man pulled Tom from beneath the VW. His father was dazed, even a little shocked, as he sat on the concrete floor, holding his grease-blackened, quivering hand in front of him. Blood dripped onto the concrete between his legs and pooled into a dark circle.

"We've gotta get you to the hospital, Tom," said the oldest of the three men, with grey sideburns and wearing a baseball cap with "Pat" on the front. Finton recognized him as Pat Taylor, who owned the garage.

"I'm coming," said Finton.

"No," said Tom. "Stay here with Pat. These men will take care o' me."

"No—I'm going."

"I'll get my car," said one of the men, and the other one followed him, while Pat stayed behind and bent down to assess Tom's hand.

"Looks pretty bad, b'y—I'll get ya a clean rag. Must be one somewhere. Look after yer old man, young fella." He gave Finton's hair a quick scrub and went off to look.

"Give it here," said Finton.

"Wha'?" Tom looked startled, as if the boy was speaking a foreign language.

"Let me see it—quick."

Appearing stunned, Tom held out his trembling hand for Finton to see. It was bruised so ugly that Finton couldn't look at it. The blood ran freely and was particularly dark around the wound in his father's palm, where the skin had been scraped and pulled. The bluish discolouration reminded him of a cut he'd had in his own palm once when he'd wrecked Homer's bike in the lane. That one had healed within seconds and had needed only to have the rocks picked out of it. This one was much worse.

Carefully, he cupped his hands and placed one on each side of his father's bloody palm. He drew a deep breath. The hand quivered violently, but Finton managed to steady it enough. Within seconds, his father's breathing began to stabilize. "Holy Mary Mother of God," Finton kept saying over and over. Eyes closed, he imagined a place far away—high above the garage, in a different dimension, beyond the earth and its planets—and, at last, his Planet of Solitude.

"We're here," he said and glanced down to see his father's head in his lap, peaceful and happy, no angry lines on his face. "Everything's okay, Dad. I'm here."

Tom didn't speak, just kept beaming up at his son.

"There," Finton said. At the sound of a voice, he opened his eyes. He was holding his father's hand, while Tom was sitting up, head laid back against the side of the Volkswagen, his face twisted in anguish and appearing ready to pass out.

"This should do the trick," said Pat, getting down on his knees beside the patient and snapping open a first-aid kit. He pulled out a gauze bandage and began to unroll it. "This might hurt a bit, Tom. Hold out your hand."

With glazed eyes, Tom scrutinized his boss and then his son, as if unable to recognize either one. He opened his hand.

"Hmm." Pat cautiously, awkwardly began winding the gauze around Tom's hand. "Put your finger there, Finton. That's the boy. Your dad's gonna be okay." He stopped what he was doing and peered at the injury. "Doesn't look too bad, though, Tom, b'y."

"Whattya mean?"

"Jesus, b'y, I thought you were gonna bleed to death. But it's startin' to heal already. Looks like the wound's closed up on its own. Still might need stitches, though."

After Pat had firmly wrapped the wound and asked Tom to hold it closed with his good hand, they stood him up. "I'm not crippled," Tom said. But they helped him to the other man's car. Finton accompanied them to the hospital and sat in the back seat with his father.

"What did you do?" Tom asked him in the waiting room.

Finton shrugged. "I did that thing."

"That thing?"

"That thing I can do."

"Oh. That thing."

Finton wasn't sure if his father didn't know what he was talking about or simply didn't believe him. Regardless, when the doctor saw Tom about twenty minutes later, he informed him that the wound was mostly healed, that he was a lucky man and should be more careful next time he was getting under a car.

When they were in the Valiant and on the way home, Finton finally exhaled. Tom lit a cigarette and said, "Don't tell your mother."

"Why not?"

"It would worry her."

"Which part—you getting hurt or me fixing your hand?"

Tom blew a smoke ring and said, "Don't tell her anything."

As soon as he got home, Finton washed the blood from his hands and went in to check on his mother. He knocked gently on the bedroom door and she told him to come in. Elsie lay on her back, covered in blankets and looking up at the ceiling. Her face was flushed. Finton crept over to the bedside and laid a hand on her forehead.

"Are you all right, Mom? You've got a fever."

"I'm all right." She didn't look at him. "Enjoy your morning at the garage?"

"Not really."

"Why not?"

He shrugged. "I'd rather be home."

Elsie smiled wanly. "I'm beginning to worry about you. You need to take more of an interest in things." He laid his hand on her forehead again. "I'm okay," she said and closed her eyes. "That feels kinda good, Finton. Your hand is cool."

He stood beside her for fifteen minutes, long enough for her to fall asleep. Before he left the bedroom, he kissed her forehead, noting how he felt kind of dizzy. Fifteen minutes on the Planet of Solitude will do that, he reminded himself, thinking it wasn't a place he could stay for very long.

"I'm not staying here if she comes." Elsie clanked the dishes so hard in the sink that Finton was amazed they didn't break. It had only been a day since her "spell," as she called it, but Elsie was already up and back to normal. Her fast recovery didn't surprise anyone, though, since no one but Finton knew how sick she'd been.

"She got nowhere else to go." Tom ran a hand through his mass of black hair, obviously exasperated. He winced from the pain in his bandaged hand. He'd told Elsie he'd slammed the car door on it, and it was nothing to worry about.

"Don't she have family in the States? And what about her good-for-nudding nephew?" Finton heard desperation in his mother's voice. She didn't like visitors because, as a general rule, people were just too much trouble.

He nibbled his dry toast. "She smells funny, Dad."

"Well, so do you, but we don't send you to the States." His father winked in a way that made the boy wonder if Tom might actually consider doing it. He wished they would. He'd probably like the States. It had to be more fun there where they had The Wonderful World of Disney.

"She looks at me funny."

"'Cause you are funny." His father munched on his toast and blueberry jam, sipping his milky tea every few seconds. He wiped a smear of butter from his chin, and the motion made a scraping sound.

Finton fell silent. He felt odd enough without having his elders point out his shortcomings. "Everybody in school says Miss Bridie is a witch." He laid down his toast and looked pleadingly at his father. "I can't sleep in the same house as her."

Having long made a study of his father's habits and moods, Finton knew he would seriously consider his fears. Tom had certainly heard the same rumours, but had dismissed them as gossip based on the rundown appearance of house and person, the secretive manner in which the door was always barred, and the fact that Miss Bridie lived without electricity or telephone. The house was always dark, lit at night by a candle on the kitchen table. If you wanted to talk to Miss Bridie—which no one except himself ever did—you had to knock really hard on her front door. Even then, no one would answer. The only time she came out of the house at all was to hang clothes on the line, run errands at Sellars' store or, once in a blue moon, go for a walk down at the landwash or in the woods. Finton had seen her down by the saltwater once, humming "Molly Malone" while she was bent over to pick up a piece of driftwood, which she then stacked atop the pile of wood in her arms. He ducked behind some large spruce trees and waited for her to wander down the shoreline. Everyone seemed to know that she wandered the beach and the woods by herself sometimes. Phonse Dredge had stopped by the house for a beer one night and mentioned casually that he'd seen her one evening, standing on the shore looking out to sea. Elsie had added that she'd seen Miss Bridie in the woods one time, sitting under a big spruce and saying some kind of prayer. "Although not like any kind of prayer I ever heard before," she'd said. But Tom had always concluded that none of those things made her a witch.

"People are just afraid of her because she's different. She's just lonely," he said.

"She's a witch," said Finton. "That's why people are afraid o' her."

"She's not so harmless as all that, and you bloody well know it." Elsie suddenly stopped scraping dishes and turned to face her husband, a frilly blue apron around her waist, a green cup towel attached to her right hand and a peanut butter glass pressed to her left. Her eyes shimmered with fear. "She might be lonely, but she made her own bed. She shoulda kicked Morgan outta the house the day she quit school. I know I wouldn't have the like in my house. And I wouldn't have her mother either. She's wicked, Tom. I don't like the way she looks at me." Her voice trembled, as she pounded the glass once against her thigh. "It's like she hates my guts or something."

Tom sighed, swallowed his tea. "You're imagining it, Elsie. She looks at everyone that way."

"The youngsters—especially Finton." Finton's head jerked towards his mother. But she would not meet his gaze, merely continued to focus on drying the glass in her hands until it surely verged on cracking. "The youngsters are all afraid of her."

"And I s'pose you're not." Tom set his tea cup gently in its saucer. Then he deposited the saucer onto the empty plate, eliciting a tiny clinking sound. He stood up, walked out the front door, and closed it softly behind him.

"To bring that woman under this roof," he heard his grandmother rasp unseen from the dark living room where the curtains were drawn shut, "is dancin' with the devil. And we all know how that works out." Her rocking chair creaked steadily. "Whole nudder tune then, by God." Finton hadn't a clue what she meant, but her words gave him chills. His mother draped her cup towel over the oven handle and crept to her bedroom where she stayed for the rest of the morning.

Miss Bridie's living situation wasn't mentioned again. She simply continued residence in her burnt-out home. The shell remained intact—the roof would hold, but would certainly leak when it rained. The outside was charred like burnt paper and smelled of smoke. But at least the Indian summer had returned, and the nights were usually not too cold.

Finton was impressed by how hard his father worked all month and well into October. Joined on the weekends and in the evenings by kindhearted Francis Minnow, Tom toiled every day at Miss Bridie's house, first installing a new plywood door, then systematically pulling out the burnt planks of siding and hammering in new ones before tackling the roof that needed to be rebuilt. Homer would help out occasionally by driving the nails where his father told him. The middle brother seemed to enjoy his apprenticeship role, demonstrating a talent for making and building, while Finton preferred an observational position. Clancy was more interested in mechanical repairs, but even he showed up at Miss Bridie's to help with painting and lifting. All autumn long, the pounding of nails echoed like gunshots from across the river. Sometimes Finton would perch on a large branch overhanging Moon's River and watch, pretending he was under siege and singing "Davey Crockett" to himself.

He saw Miss Bridie only once that whole autumn when she brought out glasses of water to the three amateur carpenters. In her twig-like hands, she held forth the sweaty tumblers as if they were gold goblets of Communion wine; she plodded in a way that reminded Finton of a prisoner of war—head down, taking small, unsteady steps. And yet in daylight she appeared surprisingly young. Perhaps she had even been nice-looking once. In fact, he could imagine her as a fine lady, twirling an umbrella in her white-gloved hands while the men bowed to her on bended knee, requesting her hand in marriage. But the sound of present-day voices brought him back to reality, and everyone returned to being who they really were.

Resting at the two-thirds rung of the rickety wooden ladder, Tom wiped his glistening forehead and took the proffered glass in the same hand. He nodded his thanks and hoisted the glass as if to toast the lady of the manor. "Got to get this sealant on before that big storm gets here. She's gonna come on pretty hard, I hears."

"I got trust in ya, Tom. I dare say I'll be better off than most." Miss Bridie didn't stay for long. "Ye got work to do, so I'll leave ye to it." She stayed for a few minutes and watched, then said something to Tom which made him stop his work and look down at her. Laying a hand on the toe of his boot, she spoke again in a low voice that Finton couldn't hear. His father nodded, appearing to be thinking about something, and then the woman ambled back to the house.

Finton had heard about the tropical storm on the news last night. After cutting a swath through the Carolinas and killing over a hundred in Pennsylvania and New York, she was destroying houses and stranding tourists in her sweep up the Eastern Seaboard. According to the radio reports, people in Maine were boarding up their houses and heading inland. That same brute was hurtling towards the coast of Newfoundland.

That night, with his eyes closed as he lay in the bottom bunk, he thought about Miss Bridie, probably also lying awake in a leaky old shell, exposed to the wind and rain, too frightened to get out of bed. He also wondered about Sawyer Moon, whether he was out in the woods tonight, huddled in a secret cave somewhere, having fallen over and injured himself, unable to get up.

Finton's eyes came open, confronted by the dark window at the foot of his bed. A low, angry rumble preceded a faint blue flash that lit the sky. As the noise died down, he heard murmuring from his parents' room. Finton's stomach knotted. He loved thunder and lightning, thrilled to booming winds and pelting rain. But he knew what would happen next. He had just pulled on his pants when the thunder growled, followed by a blink of yellow light. He sat upright in his bunk, holding his breath.

Footsteps flew. Knuckles tapped on the bedroom door. "Boys!" his mother called. "Get up. We're sayin' the rosary!"

Finton groaned. It wasn't the storm he feared, but the rosary.

Clancy had his own bed in the same room, and he wasn't keen on leaving it. "Why do we have to go through this every time? It'll pass without the rosary."

Heavy footsteps and no whispering from the father. "Get out in that living room, get down on your knees, or I'll brain ya!"

Homer had already clambered down from the top bunk, dressed, and exited to the kitchen. But Finton lingered in the doorway to witness this latest squall between his oldest brother and their mother. Surprisingly, Clancy flipped the covers away and tramped past Finton in his underwear, bare feet slapping the hallway canvas.

Elsie Moon was an acknowledged master of the ancient Catholic art of Speed Rosary, in which punctuation was forbidden. "Hail Mary full of grace the Lord is with thee blessed art thou amongst women and blessed is the fruit of thy womb Jesus holy Mary Mother of God pray for us sinners now and at the hour of our death, Amen." No one could plow her way through a Hail Mary as fast as her. Finton aspired to keep up, but he left out words, and his tongue felt like a pebble skipping across a lake. The haste only added to the mystery since Finton didn't have a clue what he was saying. "Blessed is the fruit of thy womb" was particularly mystifying, as was the exclamation "Jesus!" each time.

When rosary began, Finton felt as if he were a passenger on a runaway bus. When he was asked to lead a section, it was like being made to drive, without lessons, without brakes, and with no idea how to stop—and he dragged his whole family with him. It was supposed to be a sombre "Our Father" followed by ten Hail Marys, as counted on the beads that Nanny Moon had given him for his birthday— simple math. But Finton was always speeding up or forgetting where his fingers should be.

"That was only nine," his mother would say with a sigh. Or, "That's twelve, Finton." Sometimes she'd just bring it to an abrupt end, inserting an "Our Father" and crashing the rosary bus into a wall.

The worst times were when one of his brothers started to laugh. Mirth was even more sinful than hesitation, for his father knew that once it started, rosary laughter, like funeral laughter and school laughter, was impossible to contain. And it would always end badly, with someone getting hurt.

The night of the storm, Finton didn't feel like laughing; he was frightened by his mother's behaviour—the way she cringed with each crash of thunder, the way she gripped her beads as if God was a dog that was trying to get away from her. Between rounds, Finton asked if someone should check on Miss Bridie. But his suggestion was met with silent indifference. He realized it was wrong to speak nonrosary thoughts at such a time, but he thought God would not mind him voicing concern over one of his lost flock. He glanced out the window and thought he saw someone slip past.

In the middle of Finton's rosary, an anxious knock came on the outer door.

"Keep going," Nanny Moon urged. In a grey flannel nightgown that reached her ankles, she knelt on the rough carpet, leaning forward, hands clasped and elbows resting upon the mahogany coffee table, whose spindly legs buckled slightly.

"But—"

"Don't stop the rosary, Finton." Elsie Moon spoke in a rising, barely controlled voice. *What's wrong with her?* he wondered. Couldn't she hear the person at the door? A gust of wind slammed the house and made it groan. A burst of light fractured the darkness, and thunder rumbled a sermon. Finton sputtered, "The Lord is with thee," but the pounding on the door punctuated each syllable. "Blessed—art— thou—amongst—"

"Tom!" came the shout from outside, like a plea for refuge.

He looked at his father, who finally stood up in his white undershirt and underwear, trudged in his wool socks out to the kitchen, across the linoleum, and grabbed the doorknob. "Keep going," he commanded Finton, who forgot about "women" and started on the next "Hail Mary."

"Hey!" he was shouted down by Clancy. Nanny Moon and Elsie raised their voices: "Holy Mary Mother of God, pray for us sinners now—"

He heard rushed mumbling, his father swearing, and the door crunching shut. "And at the hour of our death, Amen."

"Elsie." Tom leaned against the doorway, one hand on the door frame as if to support his entire weight.

The praying paused. Elsie Moon glared at her husband. "Come finish the rosary."

"Morgan's here."

"Tell her to come in and say the rosary."

"You can say it yourself," said Tom. "I got to go."

"It's always something with that woman," said Elsie. "She can bloody well wait. Now, kneel down and finish the rosary."

Tom glared daggers at her, then rushed to the bedroom.

With a glance towards Morgan, Elsie resumed the rosary, the slowest one Finton had ever heard, the words ridiculous and yet terrifying. He shuddered when she recited, "Pray for us sinners, now and at the hour of our death, Amen," because he realized they were praying for souls already lost.

Meanwhile, Morgan stood in the kitchen, jean jacket drenched, blonde hair rain-dyed brown, head bowed and dripping onto the linoleum. With her face hidden, she appeared small and distant, yet somehow sturdy and rational. Not speaking, she simply just stood there waiting, a nightmarish vision.

Tom emerged fully dressed and paused only long enough to don his shoes and grab his coat. "Come on," he said and seized Morgan by the elbow to lead her out.

Minutes later, the rosary done, Finton blessed himself and leaped to his feet.

"Where are you goin'?" His mother's eyes narrowed and her lips clenched.

"Miss Bridie's. I wanna see."

"Get to bed, Finton."

But, if only for that moment, he was more his father's son than his mother's. He raced out the front door in his bare feet and brown corduroys. His mother unsuccessfully grabbed for his arm, but she managed to block Clancy and Homer from following.

The rain lashed his face and the wind pulled him forward, down the dark lane. When he reached the river, lightning torched the sky behind Miss Bridie's house.

He saw his father's black shadow on the Battenhatch front porch, timorously pushing open the brand new, glistening door.

Finton veered the corner of the lane. No pause, no punctuation—skipping steps. He leaped onto the front porch and, with a soft thud, landed inside.

In the blackness that swallowed him, a sour stench brought tears to his eyes. His head pounded in unison with the beating of his heart.

He could make out his father's silhouette—a black ghost kneeling beside the motionless body of a woman.

He wanted to ask if she was dead, but felt he shouldn't speak. Inwardly he prayed a Hail Mary, closed his eyes and listened to the sound of his father's voice, a half-whispered, hushed, and reverent tone that the boy found soothing. Tom spoke her name as a statement: "Miss Bridie." He expected a reply. "Open your eyes now. Yer bleedin' and we gotta go to the doctor."

He'd seen dead people on *Gunsmoke*, so Finton knew she was gone. But some native authority in his father's voice inspired an expectation that she would obey.

A whistle of wind through cracks in the eves pulled Finton's eyes open. Raindrops plopped from every corner of the ceiling. Puddles on the bare plank floor progressed into small ponds. One dark pool he knew did not leak from above, but from Miss Bridie herself. It seeped from her stomach and spilled over the sides of her thin frame—as if she had laid herself down in a pond of blood.

He had no idea how long he'd knelt there, watching the two shadows that seemed linked by the darkness between them. In the dark, not speaking, not staring at anyone, Miss Bridie seemed human. He could almost feel sad for her. Could almost love her because of her uncompromising monstrousness. He wished with every fibre of his body and soul that she would not be dead.

His father raised his voice, more demanding but without fear or questioning. "Miss Bridie."

Finton almost believed in her life, so much that he felt his fingers tingling and his hands vibrating. Within moments, his fingers, hands, arms, and chest throbbed so hard that he wondered if he might possibly die from the pain. Obeying some primal instinct, perhaps instilled by the rosary, he found himself squatting beside the body and barely knew how he had gotten there. "Holy Mary Mother of God, Holy Mary Mother of God," he kept whispering over and over, almost to himself, vaguely aware there was more to the prayer. His knees hovered inches above the black spot in her left side, his bare toes tucked beneath the edges of her dress, bathing in her blood. "Holy Mary Mother of God, Holy Mary Mother of God." On the kitchen table was the dark shape of a kitchen knife.

Balancing like a baseball catcher, he spread his hands over Miss Bridie's wound, her body taut and unyielding. "Holy Mary Mother of God." He closed his eyes and gently rocked, feeling dizzy and unsure of why he was acting this way, just knowing it was the thing he ought to be doing. He leaned forward and kissed her cheek.

"Finton," he heard his father gasp and clear his throat. "That's enough. Yer mother—she—"

But the boy discerned only a distant presence as if his father was yards away, calling to him through a funnel. The smell of her sweat filled his nostrils even as he rocked and trembled, hands throbbing, body overheating. He would have to let go soon, but if he could just believe, she might actually come back. Suddenly, the darkness was replaced by a galaxy of light, with a swirl of colourful stars and planets all around. In his mind, or so it seemed, he sat beneath an apple tree that appeared long dead and Miss Bridie lay in his arms. She stared up at him with a face as blank as an unpainted wall.

"Oh Tom!" He heard her crackling voice wheeze as if it were the last two words to be squeezed from her lungs. To Finton's amazement, she sighed and said, "You brought 'im." He heard her lick her parched lips, heard the sharp rise and fall of her chest. As he opened his eyes, her head turned to the side so that he couldn't see her face.

Finton felt his father's hand on his shoulder. Their eyes met for a flickering moment, and then quickly, self-consciously, disengaged. In his father's eyes, he had seen both relief and something else. Maybe that other emotion was fear—but of what?

Sirens filled the house as a wolf's howl fills a forest: as if it belonged. The banshee cry of sirens and soothing flash of blood-red lights were such common occurrences at the Battenhatch house that they were a part of it, forever associated with it, as much as ticks and lice, stormy nights, or Miss Bridie Battenhatch.

His father held her hand, even stroked her hair as they loaded her onto the stretcher and aboard the ambulance; he sat with her in the back. He looked briefly at Finton, who sat on the dilapidated front step, his bloody feet tacky on the damp wood, sticky hands tucked beneath his armpits. He struggled to catch his breath, muttering a grateful prayer as the ambulance rolled away, bathing him in blood-light and siren's wail. His lips still tasted the cold stink of her flesh, and his body was wracked with pain.

Although trembling with fear and the faint stirrings of a headache, he crept back into the kitchen, curious to see the knife that Morgan had used to slice open her mother. But it wasn't there. He massaged his temple, blinked and stared. But the tabletop contained only a wrinkled doily, a half-full bottle of Five Star rum, and an upset tumbler. The knife was gone.

By morning, his headache had disappeared. The dried bloodstain on his pillow was easy to ignore. Half asleep, he glanced at the dark spot, drew his finger across its crusty surface, scraping most of it away with a fingernail and flicking away the residue. In the bathroom mirror, he noticed a brown blemish on his face created by a trickle of blood that had dried overnight. Using a wet face cloth, he washed away the stain.

Gods and Devils

Finton told no one about what had happened that night at Bridie Battenhatch's house. For several days after the incident, whenever Finton entered the same room, Tom would grow visibly tense, with a longer drag on his cigarette or a nervous tapping of his index finger upon the Camel package in his left hand. If he was watching TV when Finton entered the living room, Tom would leave. Whenever Finton appeared as if he was going to speak to him, Tom would depart. The police had come around, but Finton overheard his father say that Miss Bridie's wound was self-inflicted. "She gets riled up sometimes when she talks about stuff—probably stabbed herself by accident," he said. In the end, there were no witnesses, since even her mother wouldn't say a word against Morgan, and Miss Bridie spent only a day or so in hospital.

Two days prior to Halloween, as the other children and the teacher were leaving for the day, Finton approached Father Power after religion class. The sun's golden rays illuminated the classroom as the priest sat on the edge of his desk and listened gravely, nodding wisely and furrowing his eyebrows. Finally, he clasped his hands on his lap and asked, "What exactly do you think you did?"

"Like Jesus did with Lazarus, Father." He looked down as he spoke, afraid to meet the priest's analytical stare. "Kind of."

Father Power cleared his throat and gazed out the window into the bright, golden sun. "Why do you think that?" He ambled toward the boy and smiled, though Finton found no comfort in this facial construction, which seemed intended to put him at ease and actually achieved the opposite effect. The priest, only in his thirties, had a thin, angular face and hawkish nose that complemented his raven-like hair and rendered him treacherous on sight alone. "I mean—she likely was never dead to begin with. Don't you think?" The priest planted a firm hand on Finton's shoulder that kept him locked in place and, in a confusing flash, ran his fingers through a shock of the boy's hair.

"She looked dead." Finton glanced at the floor, happening to see his own hands, which he had scrubbed consistently with scalding hot water and Sunlight soap for the past two weeks, but the stains of Miss Bridie's blood remained.

With one long finger, Father Power lifted Finton's chin. "But we both know there's a difference between looking dead and being dead—don't we?"

"I s'pose."

"Look." Father Power placed both hands on Finton's shoulders. "What you're talking about is a miracle, my son. And you—that is to say, your family—"

Finton glared into his dark eyes, daring the next words. That his father was just a hard luck fool who couldn't support his family. That the Moons were poor and couldn't possibly be expected to perform extraordinary deeds.

"You shouldn't misplace your faith." The priest suddenly relinquished his grip. "Or else you'll be lost. Do you know what I'm saying, Finton?"

"Yes, Father."

"Besides, what you're suggesting is sacrilege, my boy. And to commit sacrilege is a mortal sin. And you don't want to go to hell, do you?"

With barely a mumbling farewell, Finton took his books and ran home. The farther he got from the schoolyard, the more convinced he was that the priest was right—that Miss Bridie had not been dead. He could accept a great deal of punishment, but the thought of spending eternity doing the devil's dirty work in the dark was enough to pretty much assure him he'd been wrong about the whole thing. It was all just a bad dream, he had decided, just as he was passing by the Battenhatch estate.

For the first time ever, he didn't run past, but stood at the unlatched gate, and tried peering in through the window, piecing together that night in his mind. But the windows were dark. The bloodstain on the front door had been whitewashed away. He couldn't feel or see the resurrection, could barely even recall the particulars. Therefore, it didn't happen. And so there was no need for him to wind up in hell. But as he sauntered up Moon's Lane, he wished he could talk it over with Miss Bridie.

"It's the God's honest truth," Tom was saying as the boy walked in. "Phonse Dredge says he saw him, plain as day."

"Who, Dad?" Finton had entered the kitchen in time to see his father banging the table with his fist, making the glass sugar bowl spill some of its grainy, white contents onto the brown Formica. Clancy and Homer sat at the table while their mother stood at her usual spot by the kitchen sink, a wet dishrag in her hands, bubbles foaming and hissing in the dish-filled water behind her. Nanny Moon sat in the living room, tucked mostly out of sight, rocking back and forth, going "tut-tut-tut" whenever Tom swore, and knitting something on brown yarn the colour of a dirty dog.

The boy caught his father and mother exchanging glances. "Tell me," he said.

"Well," Tom said in between sips of beer. "Me buddy Phonse Dredge was on duty last night down at the watch shack for the department o' highways. Right at midnight, the lights went out. Black as pitch. But Phonse had his big flashlight. Figuring that someone was up to mischief, he turned it on and went out to search—they don't like people sneaking into the yard, see.

"Phonse was a few feet away from the shack when he heard a noise behind him, like shuffling feet. Then a soft chuckle, like someone was playing a good joke on him. 'Who the hell is out there?' Phonse shouted out. But he couldn't see no one. Phonse is a pretty big guy, ya know, and he's not afraid o' much." Tom rubbed his hand over his face, shook his head, and scratched his nape as if bewildered.

"But Phonse told me that he was shakin' all over. 'I just knew something was wrong, Tom, b'y,' he said. 'Like every time I turned me back, someone was starin' right at me and gettin' ready to grab me.' He said, 'I was so frightened that I went back to the shed—there's glass all around so I can see outside and still be seen from outside too—and tried to call Cin.' But the phone at the house just kept ringing.

"Then, Phonse says, 'All of a sudden, I saw something comin' outta the woods.' It was so bright he couldn't see a thing."

"What was it?" Finton asked, his whole body tense and his eyes wide.

"Tom, yer frightenin' the poor youngsters to death. Tell me later."

"No, Mom. I wants to hear what Phonse saw. Was it a UFO?"

Tom shook his head. "Worse. Way worse. It was the most awful thing you can imagine coming out of the woods."

"Dracula!" Finton's eyes grew wide.

"Jesus, Tom—go on and tell it then."

"Well, the bright light came closer and closer out of the black woods. And Phonse started to see a little bit of it. And it started to look like a man, but he was covered in orange and red flames on all sides."

"Sure the woods woulda caught on fire." Clancy squinted and grimaced.

Tom paused, scratched his head. "P'raps they did. Anyway, the figure came closer and closer, and just a few feet away Phonse could see him, clear as anything—two big horns sticking out of his forehead!" Tom showed them, using his two index fingers as horns on his head. "And a long, pointed tail nearly touching the ground betwixt his legs, and two cloven hoofs like a goat. Phonse knows 'cause he grew up with goats."

This fact sounded stranger to Finton than all the rest. "He grew up with goats?"

Tom grimaced. "His father had goats."

"Oh." Even though that was the answer he'd expected, Finton was disappointed, as it would make a great story to know somebody whose siblings were goats.

"Anyway, Phonse realized he was lookin' Satan himself right in the face."

"The devil, Tom?" Elsie's face turned pale as she covered her mouth with her hands. "Jesus, Mary, and Joseph, Amen." She blessed herself three times, faster than Finton had ever seen her do it before. It was the devil, after all. "Did he say anything?"

Tom shrugged. "Phonse never said. Phonse could hardly talk. He's off tonight—called in sick and said he don't know if he can go back."

"I s'pose not." Elsie shook her head. "It wouldn't be me goin' back there by meself in the middle o' the night."

"What made the lights go?" Homer asked.

"The *devil*," Tom said, as if he should have seen that fact for himself. "The *devil* made the lights go."

"Well," Elsie said, "I'm lockin' the door and saying a novena."

"Good idea," Tom said as he stood up and plucked his coat from the back of his chair.

"And where are you goin'?" Elsie asked.

"Down to Jack's to tell the b'ys that the devil is come to Darwin."

"Lord God have mercy." She blessed herself again. "I'm half afraid now to let Finton go out for Hallowe'en." Hands clasped in front of her, she appeared to fall into a trance. "Do what ya wants to do," she said. "If the devil is anywhere it's down at Jack's. I'm gettin' down on me knees and praying to Jesus to save us all."

"That's a good thing, Else. To each his own saviour." Tom nudged his youngest son aside and departed, leaving his family praying to keep the devil away.

In bed that night, Finton couldn't take his eyes off the picture of Jesus exposing his bleeding heart, looking so weak and tired. "Mom!" he called out. "Mom!"

Elsie Moon came running as fast as she could. "What is it, b'y?"

"Nudding," Finton said, regretting that there was nothing his mother could do to save him. "I was just wonderin' about something."

She sat down on the bed, one hand shutting the flaps of her tattered robe.

"Do the devil got stronger powers than Jesus?" he asked.

"Of course not. Everyone knows Jesus is stronger than the devil."

"But why is Jesus stronger than the devil?"

"'Cause Jesus is the son of God, that's why."

"Then what's the devil?"

"He's NOT the son of God. He's just someone who thought he knew better than God, and one day challenged God, and God kicked him out of heaven and he landed on Earth."

Finton frowned. "Why would God send the devil down to Earth with us? I thought he was s'posed to be in hell where the bad people goes."

"He is, Finton. Now will ya stop asking so many questions."

"I can't go to sleep with Jesus lookin' at me like that."

"Jesus is there to protect you."

"But he can't protect me if he's lookin' so tired with his heart hangin' out all over himself. Jus' look." He pointed at the picture, and his mother regarded it for a long time.

"You just have to trust in Him, Finton."

"Even though He don't look like He could lift a pail o' water to save Hisself?"

"Looks are deceiving. Put your faith in Jesus, and He'll never let ya down. Okay?"

"Okay."

"Good boy." She reached for the light switch.

"Don't!"

"Don't be so cowardly, Finton. I thought you were big now."

"I am. But the devil is bigger, I'spose."

With a withering smile, she flicked off the light, leaving him in the dark, where he waited half the night for the devil to steal to his window, crawl in through the cracks and take him away from his family.

The next morning when the rooster crowed, he wondered if his father had come home last night. Finton had been awake until four a.m., listening for a sign of Tom's return. Life in Darwin had changed, as if a long, wide shadow had been cast upon all their houses from some horrible monster that had come from the sky.

Dreams of the Lost
(1972)

For a long time, nothing seemed any different. Mary remained distant, though Finton sometimes went out of his way to wish her a good morning or say "See ya!" at the end of a school day. Skeet kept getting into trouble, with or without Finton at his side. Someone broke into the snack bar one Sunday night, and all they took was a carton of cigarettes, a box of Crispy Crunch bars and another of red licorice. The RCMP had parked outside of the Stuckey house Monday morning and stayed a long time. Furthermore, Skeet didn't show up at school that day or the next, but, for a week afterwards, he seemed to have an endless supply of cigarettes and red licorice, which he willingly shared.

Tom went to Taylor's Garage every weekday, and spent most weekends working on cars, drinking beer, napping occasionally, and going for drives on Sunday afternoons. Finton didn't go along for the tour anymore. He'd begun craving his independence and was more likely to walk five miles than to ask his parents for a ride.

Elsie spent her days scrubbing floors, washing clothes, baking bread, and keeping the house tidy. She always seemed tired and yet never took a day off. Finton would observe her relentless cleaning from some corner of the house or the yard, wondering how she found the energy. Most times, though, he just wondered why.

Nanny Moon continued her vigilance over the family, usually from the rocking chair in the kitchen, reading her Bible and commenting with sage disapproval on the state of the world. Sometimes she could be heard after supper, kneeling at her bedside, imploring the Lord to forgive her family's sins. After surviving Grade Eleven, Clancy had enrolled in a mechanics course at the trades school, but Nanny Moon still treated him like an impudent child and, once in a while, ordered him to be respectful to his mother, much as she'd recently warned him about his need to root for the "Godless Russians" when they played Team Canada. She would also advise Homer, who likewise struggled in school, to wash his hands before eating or to say his prayers before bed.

It was a rare occasion when she needed to admonish the youngest Moon, who was always respectful and said his prayers nightly. Once in a while, though, he would express an opinion that gave Nanny Moon concern. In Catechism class one day, the teacher had told them the story in Matthew's gospel in which Jesus had said, "Don't be like the hypocrites who love to stand in the synagogues and on the street corners so that they will be seen by people." When the teacher asked what the parable meant, Finton raised his hand and said, "That we shouldn't go to mass or pray where people can see us." The teacher tut-tutted and told him the Bible would never say that. "But what's the point?" Finton asked. "We should just pray to ourselves and not show off. Shouldn't we?" The teacher explained that he should do both, but Finton insisted: being seen as holy wasn't all that important, at least not to God. When he repeated the incident at the supper table that evening, Nanny Moon looked at Elsie and said, "You're gonna have trouble with that one, and we all knows why." The words stung, and Finton continued to argue the point, but there was no getting around the fact that his mother and grandmother wanted him to go to mass, regardless of what the Bible appeared to say.

While Finton remained a small, freckled boy with a crescent-shaped scar under his left eye, the other two boys were growing up fast. Their increasing maturity was too quick for Finton because it seemed he would never catch up. At seventeen, Clancy bought his first car—a red 1963 Galaxy that mostly sat in disrepair in the front yard while he played at fixing it up. But mostly the eldest boy used it as a place to sit with girls at night and listen to the Top Ten. Homer often said, "The only working part on that car is the radio." But that was enough for Clancy, since his three great loves were cars, girls, and music, his favourite bands being KISS and Black Sabbath.

Homer, on the other hand, had taken to building houses with a local contractor. The homesteader of the family, he wanted everyone to be together on Saturday nights, preferably watching hockey and munching homemade popcorn. Except for Finton, everyone in the house was a Toronto Maple Leafs fan and, while the youngest Moon's allegiance to an American team was irksome, Homer truly only cared that the family did something as a unit. He was a good-looking fifteen-year-old who'd already had a string of girlfriends, each of whom was a bit on the hard side and intimidating to Finton. Recently, though, Homer had taken to his bedroom a lot, where he would play his Rush and Trooper records so loud that everyone else in the house had to shout to be heard. When their father stomped into the bedroom and bellowed, "Turn it down!" Homer would comply, but gradually unleash the volume as the evening went on. As the bass and drums thrummed in his head, Finton figured something was wrong with his older brother.

At twelve, Finton struggled to maintain a sense of self-assurance among this testosterone-heavy bunch. His individuality wasn't in question, since people knew him as "the strange one" of the hilltop-dwelling Moons. He was the one who spent most of his time with his nose between the pages of a book or wandering around solo, showing little interest in girls or people in general. When he wasn't in school or in church, he often found himself alone, either on the shore or in the woods, or sometimes lying in a tree branch watching the world go by. He barely slept at night for worrying about his teams, preferring instead to lie awake listening to Bruins or Expos games through the earplug on his transistor radio. When he did sleep, he dreamed about things he wished would leave him alone—of yellow-eyed wolves chasing him through a predawn forest, of hormonal girls who ran after him, begging a kiss, and various townspeople who wanted to hug him. In order to escape their clutches, the dreams always ended in some sort of falling.

Sundays, he attended mass at 9 a.m., even though other members of the family chose to go Saturday night or later on Sunday. Nine o'clock was when Mary Connelly and her family went to mass, and Finton would sit somewhere behind her. He rarely allowed himself to peek in Mary's direction, as he preferred to dole out such moments as rewards for his self-restraint. The best view he had of her delicate, small frame was when everyone was either rising, sitting down, or starting to kneel. She would turn her head as she tugged the hem of her skirt to keep it from getting tangled, giving him a sacred few seconds to gaze at her with longing. His admiration for Mary was a secret, however, for he would be mortified if anyone knew he went to mass just to see her dressed up.

Everyone thought he attended mass early and often because of his sincere devotion to the teachings of the church. It seemed a foregone conclusion among family members that he would someday become a priest. And, truthfully, Finton didn't mind going to mass. It was quiet there. He liked the singing, particularly on special occasions when a few kids from the high school choir played their instruments and sang hymns in a country and western style. He thought mass should be fun, but it usually wasn't, mostly because he hated being told what to do. The constant sitting, kneeling, and standing on cue, along with the recitations, left him feeling like a trained, and slightly confused, monkey. But it was the only hour of the week when he could watch Mary as she whispered the prayers and sang along with each hymn. The parting of her lips and the quavering of her throat with every note was mesmerizing, and he gladly endured mass just to be in Mary's company. Besides that, his mother insisted on his attendance, and there would be no arguing the point. But, if he were to tell the truth, Finton did not enjoy mass nearly so much as the holy feeling he got from having been there.

One Sunday morning, just past the Darwin fairgrounds, they saw Phonse Dredge, strolling along, dressed as if he were going to church. "Strange to see Phonse walkin'," Tom said, as if to himself. He pulled the car over to the side of the road. "Looks like you needs a ride, me buddy. Hop in." Phonse seemed to think nothing of it as he didn't look surprised, just opened the car door and, with a grunt of exertion, climbed into the back seat. "Lovely day," he said, and so the conversation went—normal, yet strange, considering Phonse had his own car and rarely went to mass.

"Wife's not too happy with me," he said.

"Did you say where you were goin'?" Tom glanced into the rearview mirror.

"B'y, she knows. I can say what I like, but she always knows."

As Phonse was speaking, and Finton was wishing they hadn't picked him up, they passed by Bilch's, then a little further on, a pathway on the left where Sawyer Moon was just coming out of the woods, wearing his familiar khaki green Army jacket and baggy, brown trousers. Tom blew his horn and started to slow down. Sawyer raised his hand in greeting, but Phonse said, "Don't you stop for the like o' that."

"Why?" asked Tom. "What's he after doin' now?" But he kept going and soon the slouching figure had faded from view.

"Oh, if only you knew," Phonse said as they rounded a bend. "I knows you're friends 'n all, but he's a dirty blaggard, that one."

Tom peered with narrowed eyes into the rearview mirror and held Phonse's gaze. "Speak plain, b'y."

"You mean you never heard what he does? Oh, my son, he's vile. He's after the young ones, ya know. Not just the girls, but the boys too." Phonse fell silent for a moment. "Your own, sure."

"What are ya talkin' about, Phonse? What about me own?"

"I'll tell ya about it when we gets there. But not while he's here."

A deep, troubling silence settled over the car, and Tom, in particular, seemed to grip the wheel more tightly and didn't speak again until, a few minutes later, they pulled in front of the church and were parked in their usual spot, halfway between the church and the tavern. "You go on in," he told Finton, "You knows where I'll be."

Finton went to mass, but all through the service, even the stunning sight of Mary Connelly in a short, yellow dress couldn't distract him from thinking about Phonse's words and his father's quiet anger in response.

That night, Finton went to bed his usual time. His father had gone out after supper and, while it was past ten o'clock, he hadn't returned. Finton fell asleep quickly and dreamed he saw a man in the woods, encrusted in ice, lying face down in the marsh. His eyes were open and staring, his mouth forming words that Finton couldn't decipher. In the dream, Finton waded through bog that was filled with floating chunks of ice. With every step toward the fallen man, Finton sunk deeper into the marsh, fearing the man would drown if he didn't reach him soon. As he slogged closer and felt the ground give way beneath him, he sank to his neck in frigid water. He gazed, shivering, into the eyes of the man. "You shouldn't run away," Finton told him, and the man's face dissolved and reformed as Sawyer Moon's. Finton, meanwhile, was sucked deeper into the muck. When he awoke, he was curled in a fetal position, arms clenched around his body, tight to his chest. He'd awakened in the midst of praying a "Hail Mary."

Two days later, he still hadn't told anyone about his dream. Tuesday morning, all through breakfast, he kept replaying in his mind the parts he remembered. No one would notice if he didn't talk during meals, since Tom insisted on complete quiet unless he chose to announce something or regale them with a story. So Finton kept to himself, noticing only that Homer was missing, probably still in bed.

"They're getting a search party out," Tom said while buttering his toast. "No one's laid eyes on Sawyer since Sunday night." Finton stopped chewing and stared at his father.

"Minnie called the hospital." Elsie hoisted a fork loaded with scrambled eggs towards her mouth. "The morgue too." The nurse on duty at the hospital had alerted the police of the potential missing person.

"I dreamed about this," Finton said softly, looking at his plate. But no one heard him. They never paid much attention to you when you were being good.

The rumours swirled as Finton scrambled onto the yellow school bus. Now that he was attending the school in the heart of Darwin, Finton was the first one picked up by the bus driver each morning. He beelined for the last seat so he could peer out the back window and revel in the vision of the houses of Darwin, and especially Moon's Lane, slipping past and fading in the distance.

Minutes later, the bus grunted to a halt and idled in front of the Stuckey place. Skeet flung himself up the steep black stairs, scrambled down the aisle to where Finton sat, and collapsed into the seat across from him. Skeet was always running late and had often confessed both his hatred for school and his plan to quit on his fifteenth birthday. He nattered so often about committing violence towards one of his teachers that Finton wondered if Skeet would graduate to the penitentiary one day. Skeet stretched out his legs and laid his books on his lap, rocking and rolling with the jittery bus.

"They can't find Sawyer," Finton said. The bus sputtered and rattled up the hill.

"Took off somewhere, I'd say—up in the woods." Skeet reached inside his jacket and pulled out a foot-long piece of red licorice. Finton couldn't help notice that his friend's hand was shaking. The bruised knuckles weren't so unusual, as Skeet seemed to be always into a racket with someone. But something seemed off about him this morning. "Piece?" he said, offering him a string of licorice.

"No, thanks." Finton looked out at the passing woods. The trees glistened with melting frost. "Another fine day—but it was some cold last night, I tell ya."

"Got that right." Skeet paused thoughtfully, clamped his teeth around the licorice, bit off a piece and gnawed on it. "Mudder even took Jakey in last night. She said it weren't even fit for a dog out. Mudder's a case, b'y." He jammed the licorice into his pocket and pulled out a Marlboro, which he stuffed into his mouth. "I was out for a while, but had to get home out of it. Freeze the balls off a brass monkey."

The bus driver glared into his big, rectangular mirror and yelled, "Put that fuckin' cigarette away or I'll tell your mother!"

Skeet gave him the finger—the one adorned with a wide, copper ring. "Fuck off," he muttered. "I'm not in the mood for you today."

Finton fell quiet as they passed through Laughing Woods. Nighttime in the woods was darker than anywhere else, especially this time of year when the days were warm and dazzlingly bright, while the nights seemed colder and more foreboding. Sawyer had probably stumbled a lot, tripping in roots and stones. The branches would have scratched his face and tortured him as he called out to his mother.

"What's wrong wit' you?" Skeet stuck the Marlboro behind his ear.

Finton blinked, realizing he'd drifted off. He could smell the turpentine and 10W-40 off Sawyer Moon's jacket, but Skeet seemed far away. "Just thinkin' about Sawyer."

Skeet shrugged and gazed out the window. "Poor bugger's better off dead."

"Nobody's better off dead."

"Sawyer is."

Finton wrapped himself in silence as the bus squealed to a stop for Dolly. She strode to the back of the bus in cloppy high heels, clasping her books to her breasts and propping them up, presumably to make them look bigger. "You guys heard? Sawyer Moon's prob'ly dead."

Al Kelly followed behind her; because Al was an albino, everything he said carried extra weight. He calmly sat down, taking up a full seat, as they each did. "Dad says he's gone to St. John's on a drinkin' spree."

"So how come no one knows where he is then?" Dolly blew a bright pink bubble the size of a plum, popped it, cracked it, and renewed her vigorous chewing which gave Finton a weird, gushy feeling just below his stomach. He watched her intently until she glanced at him. When he looked away, she smiled to herself. While the bus stopped at the Connelly house, he waited breathlessly for Mary to get on board. When he saw her, his brain slipped into a sort of alternate space from where he watched her every move but was unable to sense anything around her except vague images and muffled noises. When she finally took her seat near Dolly, Finton gradually began to breathe again, and the world returned to normal.

"I bet he's after callin' Fanny Fukuto and he's in gettin' laid," Skeet said.

Finton squirmed. He didn't exactly know what "gettin' laid" was, but he had heard some of the boys talking about finding Fanny "Fuck-you-too" in the phone book under "Escort," then calling her and hanging up, giggling among themselves.

Al shrugged and pushed up his glasses on his nose so that they squared with his face. "All I know, he was at Jack's Sunday evening, and Jack gave him a beer. He asked Lance for one, but Lance wouldn't because Sawyer's not allowed to drink. They say Tom Moon bought himself two Black Horse and gave one to Sawyer on the sly." Al's information was pretty reliable, since Lance, the bartender, was Al's older brother. "Sawyers's not supposed to be at it at all, sure. His medication'll kill 'im."

Dolly took her compact out of her big purse and dabbed her cheeks. Finton tried to look away, but couldn't. She reapplied her lipstick, smacked her glossy lips together and bit benignly on a lacy white handkerchief with two other sets of pink lip marks already on it. Finton's head felt woozy. Dolly did not acknowledge his interest in her cosmetic touch-up, but there was something self-conscious in the way she looked at no one as she performed. "Either way," she said, "I wouldn't wanna be the one that liquored him up—'specially if he turns up dead."

"Maybe he just don't wanna be found," Skeet said, squinting out the window at the passing woods. Finton stared into woods as well, but found himself mesmerized by the November sun.

Dolly shook her head. "Someone woulda seen him by now."

"Not if he don't want to be seen," said Finton. "You can hide forever if you don't want anyone to find you." Chewing worriedly on his bottom lip, he sneaked a look at Dolly applying makeup in her compact mirror.

"Why do you even care?" she asked. "What'd Sawyer Moon ever do for ye?"

"I don't care about ol' Sawyer Moon," Mary said. "I'm glad he's gone."

"Me too," said Finton. "We're all better off."

Skeet assessed him warily. "For someone who don't care, you sure seem to care a lot."

"I just don't think he's dead. Probably saw his chance and got the hell outta Darwin."

"What are you—psychic?" Dolly asked.

Skeet poked Finton's shoulder as the other two laughed. He noticed that Mary had taken to gazing out the window.

"No." Finton spoke softly, almost to himself.

That same night, in his dream, Dolly chased him through the graveyard—naked, her boobs bobbing gently. "Give me a kiss, Finton. I won't bite you, my darling!" Her pink lipstick and white pearls glimmered in the moonlight. Finton ran as fast as he could, leaping over headstones and panting. He felt Dolly's hot breath on his neck as she drew closer on her long, spidery legs.

She was almost upon him when he started crying—deep, wretched sobs that rolled down his cheeks and caught his breath short. "Lemme alone!" he cried out.

"Just one kiss, my love." She captured and hugged him, kissed his face all over.

"No! Get away!" Hands flailing, legs kicking.

His left hand fell under the curve of her right breast, and suddenly he seemed to lose control of his mind and body. He broke from her grasp and scurried away again.

"Finton!" He heard a raspy female voice—not Dolly, but Miss Bridie. "You're going the wrong way," she said. He turned around to see her standing at a distance, like a bride of Dracula in red lipstick, a black wig, and a large, blue, cleavage-bearing dress. She strutted towards him, and he was trapped, struggling to breathe.

Backing away from her, Finton turned around in time to feel his feet give way beneath him. He plunged into a shallow grave, face down in the dirt, with Dolly on top of him, kissing and stroking him. When he woke up in his bed, his right hand covered his hot groin and a sick, smelly feeling of guilt filled his head. Jesus looked down on him with sorrowful eyes that followed him all the way to the bathroom at the end of the hall.

A light was on in the kitchen. He could hear murmuring—the whispered words: "…not sure what to do." That was his father. The second, more hostile voice belonged to his mother. Hand pressed to his cold, sticky groin, he leaned forward and strained to hear.

"We're all better off," his mother said. "Some things are better kept to yourself."

His father sighed, followed by a scrape of the chair across canvas. "Sometimes, I don't even know what's right anymore. I mean what if—"

"Just stop it, Tom. Forget about it. That's what's right."

"Right for who?"

There was a pause before his mother spoke. "It never gets easy, does it?"

He couldn't hear what she said after that, for his mother had lowered her voice. But his father's response was, "He's all right. He's a Moon, after all."

Finton felt his nose running and had to swipe it with his sleeve, but he still resisted the urge to run to the bathroom. The voices hushed, as if the speakers had heard something. "I wonder how much he knows," Elsie said, then she rose from her chair, her shadow shifting towards his hiding spot behind the chimney. As his mother's chair was scuffed aside, Finton slipped into the bathroom and locked the door behind him. After cleaning himself with a wet face cloth, which he buried in the hamper, he climbed back in bed, where the eyes of Jesus still judged him.

It was a long time before he fell back to sleep.

The Devil's Greatest Trick

The next day, he stood at the roadside, gazing across the gate at the newly snow-brushed landscape. A rotted, white picket fence half-heartedly protected the property, most of its palings were dead or dying, some buried in tall grass that had laid down and surrendered to the oncoming winter. The shiny, black shingles of the new roof glistened in the sunlit frost and edging of snow. Meanwhile, the sweet smell of fresh-cut lumber drew him in. A busy silence droned in his ears, while the aroma of mildewed sawdust tickled his nose. Finton was seduced forward by the resurrected, but chronically ill house, with its painted yellow windows, sunbeaten clapboard, and newly painted bottle-green door. At that moment, he was keenly aware of the inadequacy of his youth, his relative newness to these strange surroundings.

Peering through the key hole, he saw no sign of life. Miss Bridie appeared to be out. He knocked anyway and was shocked when the quietude surrendered to the sound of shuffling feet. While he considered running away, the door opened.

Miss Bridie cocked her head sideways and regarded him as if he were prey. Her unwashed hair hung about her face, traces of orange whispering of the redhead she once had been. The lines around her blue-black eyes made her look tired, and yet those same eyes contained a vivacity that the rest of her lacked. They looked right through him as if to read his thoughts, even though she seemed to be thinking about something else. Because her head was slightly too large for her neck, it seemed to float above her gaunt body that was draped in a sack-like dress sprayed with grey and black flowers. Finton couldn't swear he wasn't seeing a ghost, nor did the odour emanating from Miss Bridie discourage his suspicions. If she had, indeed, been good-looking once, from this close up, he could see little trace of her former glory, except in those remarkable eyes that suggested intimacy with such horrors as he couldn't imagine. Perhaps it was the result of being bedridden for so long after the fire because of damaged lungs. Maybe because she had never fully recovered, emotionally or physically, from being stabbed by her own daughter. Or maybe there was some other reason that had long ago sprung something vital loose within her. But, regardless of the reasons for her rapid deterioration, she had looked much better from the distance of a high tree branch.

"What do *you* want?" She did not demand so much as inquire disinterestedly.

Barely able to breathe, Finton spoke sporadically, in short sentences. "Don't know if you know me." She stared at him. "Finton Moon," he said.

He looked past her uncertainly and into the dark house.

"Tom's boy." When she spoke, it was the same futile sound like deadened air an accordion makes when it squeezes shut without fingers holding down the buttons. Her words came heavy and slow. "He's a good man, that Tom."

"Yes, ma'am."

"Are you like him or your mudder?"

Finton chose the answer he knew would gain him entry. "Mostly father." He felt guilty about having to choose, so he added, "I got Mom's height."

She appraised him up and down, then turned and hobbled back into the house. "Yer mudder haven't had an easy—" she breathed with difficulty, holding onto her side where he knew she'd been stabbed "—life." She sat at the kitchen table. Assuming he was expected to follow, Finton reluctantly closed the door and took a seat.

The table was large, pure Newfoundland pine, painted chocolate brown to match the chairs. A steaming, brown teapot sat in the middle of the table. There were two cups and saucers, as well as two plates, and everything seemed coated in a layer of fine dust. She reached for the pot and poured for them both. "Drop o' tea—good for what ails ya."

He thanked her even as he watched the leaves floating at the top. He asked for milk and sugar, but she laughed and said she liked it black. "It'll clear ya out better."

Finton didn't really think he needed to be cleared out and certainly didn't crave anything that would perform that task.

"Why'd you come?" she asked after she'd poured the tea.

Finton shrugged, unable to find the words to explain that everything seemed crazy and that he had seen her in a dream last night.

She blinked as if refocusing and, in that moment, he became absolutely enthralled with her eyes, how much lovelier they were than the rest of her. "I was expecting you." Taking advantage of the long silence, he lifted the cup to his face. When he saw all the unsavoury green things floating around in it, he pretended it was too hot.

"Do you know what happened to Sawyer?" he asked.

While she slurped from her tea, he looked around for signs of both humanity and monstrosity. His gaze lit upon a recently dusted object that was set in the middle of a white doily atop a chocolate brown hutch with glass doors: a black-and-white picture in a plain wooden frame. In an old-fashioned, knee-length dress that looked to be her Sunday best, her light hair coiffed to be nearly glamorous, the face of the slim, but sturdy, young woman in the photo shone with the splendour of innocence. Glancing from the woman before him to the one in the picture, he satisfied himself that they were one and the same. Due to the ravages of time and neglect, they didn't look much alike, but there was enough similarity in the length of hair, those dark eyes that even then were slightly troubled, and a thin, pointed nose that Finton was certain of the relationship between past and present. The only difference was that the eyes of the younger woman were even more full of life, the nose not so prominent, and the hair, while untamable, had been subjected to an attempt at styling.

"'Course I do." As he listened to the wheezing of the house, he realized there was no clock ticking. Nor was Miss Bridie wearing a watch or any jewelry, except for a silver chain that disappeared down the front of her dress. Her eyes had followed his, and she fished it out for him to see. "It's a little crucifix." She displayed it for only a couple of seconds before returning it to its safe place. "Gordie gave me that when he brung me here. Same year he left me here, just meself and Morgan."

Finton watched a black fly—unnatural for this time of year—climb out of his tea and onto a tea leaf. Empathy tugged at him, but he wasn't about to rescue it or drink the tea. "I never knew you had a husband."

"Not me husband, b'y. Almost, but not quite." Her eyes flickered with emotion, which she seemed anxious to smother. "Drink yer tea like a good boy."

Finton watched the fly still trying to conquer the leaf, which kept floating away from the drowning insect. "I'm not allowed to drink tea." Unable to stand the guilt any longer, he finally reached into the cup and used his index finger to push the leaf towards the fly, allowing the tiny beast to save itself.

Miss Bridie sighed. "Wasteful child. What grade are ya in?"

"Eight." Despite himself, he couldn't help letting his eyes wander over to the picture beside her. Bridie, he decided, had been an attractive young woman. But his brain had difficulty bridging the gap between Beautiful Young Bridie and Plain Old Bridie. It was as if they were two different people with a common ancestry.

"Smallest one, I s'pose."

"I'm bigger than some people."

She smiled thinly without showing teeth; he could tell by the unyielding cracks at the corners of her lips that she didn't often smile.

"Gordie wasn't right," she said. Finton felt as if he was watching one of those Japanese movies where the dialogue is a sentence or two behind the action. The effect was enhanced by the fact that he kept stealing looks at the old photograph, even while she was talking to him. "I'm prob'ly better off without 'im. But dis is not me home. I was practically a girl when he brung me here, then he knocked me up and left me. Drowned." Her eyes shimmered as she nodded at the painted window. "Went off the road one night down by the fairgrounds. Dark ol' stretch, I tell ya. He was there half the night before someone found him." Miss Bridie sighed, rubbing her legs as if she were suddenly chilled. "Now here I am, forty-one years old, never married, a crazy daughter, and—"

"Where'd you come from?"

She grew thoughtful for a moment and stared at him, her gaze landing somewhere just beyond him. It was then that he realized what bothered him most about Miss Bridie: even though she was right there with him, she always seemed to be somewhere else.

"My people are from the down the Shore," she said. "That's where I was when Gordie came puttin' in the road. Mudder told 'im we already had a road, but they said that was only a cow path and the government sent 'im to widen the cow path and make it a real road for cars." She seemed to resist smiling and clucked her tongue instead. "We didn't have no cars, sure. Didn't know what a car was."

She talked at length about horses and buggies, and long, long walks through the knee-deep snow until Finton became bored and restless.

Nanny Moon was from the Shore as well and often told similar tales. "Gordie knew I was interested in his truck, so he took me for a ride one morning." She halted abruptly and sat straight up in her chair. "Drink yer tea, b'y, before it gets cold as the devil's tit."

Finton heard the smooth hum of a pickup as it zipped along the road in front of the house, but he couldn't see through the painted windows. "Where'd you go?"

She looked straight at him with her luminous eyes.

"A place I'd never been," she said. "Lotta miles away—too far. I never told me mom. But she found out. And now here I am. Dead boyfriend that woulda been me husband. A daughter in the mental, another took, and a burnt-out home in a place where ever'one thinks I'm a witch." Finton's eyes grew wide; he nearly lost his breath. Miss Bridie smiled without opening her mouth. "You think I don't know what you and your friends say about me when yer out on that road?"

"I never said nudding, Miss Bridie. Some people did, but I never."

She stood up and walked over to the stove, muttering mostly to herself. "If they don't like the look of ya, they judges ya not fit, the unchristly sons o' bitches." Finton watched nervously as she plucked a piece of driftwood from the meagre pile beside the stove and held it over the bright, licking flames that nearly singed her arms. He felt the heat from where he sat and couldn't take his eyes off the flames or the stick.

"I gotta go."

She chuckled softly. "Good luck in that."

The door was jammed tight, too large for its frame.

"Ya gotta pull real hard, b'y."

He did. He tried using both hands, with his feet planted on the wet floor.

She laughed—a throaty, hoarse sound—as if she enjoyed his terror. "Ya'll tell your friends I tried to put you in the stove, I s'pose." She tossed the wood onto the flames, and orange sparks crackled gleefully upward. She shuffled over to Finton and took his chin in one of her leathery hands. He smelled lye.

"No, ma'am. Promise. But I gotta go now. Mom said for me not to stay long."

She squeezed his chin, smiled briefly, then released him. "Go on then. Get home." She took a step back and laughed. "Don't ya wanna hear about yer second cousin Sawyer? Don't ya wanna hear what happened to 'im?"

Again, his eyes grew wide.

"Oh, they didn't tell you that part. Never knew you wuz related, did ya?"

"I don't care."

"Oh, I think you do." She stood up straight, hands planted on her hips, no longer paying attention to the knife. "His mother was a Crowley that married a Moon—long time ago. And that Moon's brother was your grandfather Ned. See? So you're not only related to Sawyer, but to the Crowleys too."

"No, I'm not!"

"Yes, b'y. And I'd say you're dyin' to know what the old witch knows. I can tell… and she do know stuff. She really do. And she'll tell ya some more stories that'll break yer perfect little heart if ya'll give her a kiss and a hug."

Finton couldn't move. He thought he might pee in his pants.

"Come on, b'y. Wha's wrong with ya?" She smacked her lips mischievously.

"Un-unh. Let go o' me." Finton wriggled free and wrenched the door open with a two-handed tug of the rusty door knob.

Miss Bridie sighed and clamped a hand to her left side—a reminder of the night he wasn't even sure had really happened. "Go on then. Guess ya don't care if he's dead or alive… or how it involves yer father. I knows more about your father than any one of ye, I do. Stuff I'm sure you'd like to know. Stuff about you too, sure."

Finton wheeled around and peered into her eyes, transfixed by the humanity peeking out from the madness.

"Oh yes," she said. "There's lots you don't know about folks 'round 'ere. Small places got the biggest secrets." She ambled to her seat at the table and wrapped her hands around the tea mug. "Yup. Lots to know. Where do people go, you must wonder," she said, mostly to herself. "And where do everyone come from?" She appeared to lose interest in her captive audience and commenced gazing out the window. "I wasn't always like ya see me today. I used to be good-lookin' once. Yer father thought so. Still do, I s'pose, in spite of it all." She coughed and stared at the crackling stove, her back turned so that he couldn't see her face.

Finton edged towards the table, maintaining a distance. "What about Dad?"

She glanced sharply towards him, though not right at him. "No kiss nor hug, no information." She patted her lips with two fingers—the

70

same two that had just been fishing down the front of her dress—and then spread her arms wide to embrace him.

No, Finton thought. *Nothing is worth that.* But who would know if he kissed the old hag? Surely she wouldn't tell anyone. She had no friends.

"Thinkin', are ya? Well, don't think too long. On second thought, I don't think I'll tell ya anyway. You don't seem like ya wants to know."

"I do." Finton scrambled forward, closed his eyes and thrust his lips towards her. He waited. Then he heard her cackle as if she was in on a private joke. Thinking he was safe, he just opened his eyes in time to see her pale cheek press against his lips. *Chalk that was in the freezer for a month.* She set her hands upon his shoulders to draw him in, but he only touched her arms and drew aside to avoid capture. Dizzy, he steadied himself by grasping the back of a chair. "So tell me."

She smiled. "Tell ya what?"

"About Sawyer and Dad." His voice trembled. "The secret stuff."

"Nudding to tell." She sipped her tea and fell quiet, her lips formed a mocking grin. "Yer a fine kisser, though."

"Shut up!" he shouted, and he kicked the table, spilling her tea and washing the black fly onto the floor where it struggled to lift off. After a few seconds of broken-hearted wing-flapping, it seemed to solidify and congeal, becoming as one with the sticky liquid that surrounded it.

"Watch yerself," she said calmly, sitting up straight.

"*You* watch yourself. You tricked me. You're not s'posed to tell lies. My mother told me that."

"Yer mother, eh?" She sighed patiently and gazed out the window. "You don't wanna know what I know." She glanced to his left. "Yer too young."

"Tell me."

She eyed him suspiciously, looking as if she was withholding much more than she was about to tell. "Sawyer's waitin' for ya."

"How do you know?" He sat down, feeling dizzy again.

"I just know."

"But how?"

She paused. "Ever think about a song and then it comes on the radio?"

Finton nodded. "So?"

"That's how I know." She tapped the centre of her forehead. "Ya don't have to believe me. But it's true." She looked out the window as

71

if seeing beyond her garden of death and decay. "Face down and cold as the grave."

"Stop," said Finton, suddenly standing. "Don't talk about it no more." Not only did the details remind him of his disturbing vision, but the look on her face was frightening. Her eyes had narrowed into dark slits, her face both hard and inhuman.

"Yer father," she said, suddenly straightening, shaking her head, and remembering where she was. "Yer father can tell you the rest. Maybe someday."

"Tell me now."

"Forget about me, sure. I've heard things about *you*. Things that make me wonder what in God's name you are." The way she looked down at him over her chest made him feel even smaller than he was. Then her eyes softened, becoming almost kind. "I believe I owe you a thank-you."

He knew the incident she was referring to, but he wondered what she'd heard.

"You needn't say anything," she said. "We both know what you did." She leaned forward and partly whispered: "If you ever wants some help with that stuff, you knows where to come."

Petrified at first, Finton suddenly understood what she meant and he ran from the house as fast as he could, slamming the door behind him.

The Cathedral

It was Clancy who had introduced him to his first love. His older brother had opened the passenger door of the Valiant and said, "Get in." Finton was six at the time. Clancy had convinced Elsie to drive them to the library, with the understanding that he and Finton would walk home after. "You're gonna love it," Clancy had promised. Six years later, Finton still felt indebted to his oldest brother for showing him the portal to an alternate universe, as well as to the world outside Darwin. By the time he was twelve, the library had become his cathedral, a place of sanctuary from the hardness and confusion.

The bright and spacious Darwin Public Library was divided by an inch-wide strip of wood into two distinct rooms. One room, also the librarian's reception area, was marked "Children's Books" and the other was marked "Adult Books." The former was a place that welcomed him; the latter remained a forbidden country. On that first day, with Clancy watching over him and Finton trembling with excitement, Finton had selected a dozen books. When he'd brought them to the checkout counter, Miss Patterson, the young librarian, had laughed and said, "You shouldn't take more books than you can read in two weeks." Finton promised to read them all, but she still called his mother, who assured the librarian that Finton had, in fact, been able to read since he was two. While she obviously considered the claim dubious, Miss Patterson stamped the books and gave Finton his first library card, which, to him, might as well have been a key to the kingdom of heaven. With a willing heart, Clancy, who only went to the library for *Hot Rod*, *Hockey Illustrated* and *Popular Mechanics* magazines, had helped his youngest brother carry home the bulk of the booty. From that Saturday forward, the library became Finton's refuge from the world of Darwin, all books connected to one another in a single, unified universe. It was with great pleasure that, within five days, he'd returned all of the books and informed Miss Patterson that he'd read them all and was back for more.

As the years went on, Saturdays became sacred because that was the day he trekked the two and a half miles to the library, found a good book and curled up to read on a bench in the children's section. There, you were only allowed to whisper, and Miss Patterson would shush anyone who spoke too loud.

Recently, however, he had developed a problem. In the course of six years, he'd read nearly every book in the children's section and now he was bored. For several months, he would, on occasion, gaze wistfully at the "Adult Books" sign, peer inside the forbidden zone where, most of the time, the three comfy leather chairs sat empty, and wish with all his heart that he could enter and embark on the new set of adventures it offered.

One particularly rainy and windy Saturday, he explained his wish to Miss Patterson, asking if he might be permitted to "go into the adult section," but she was concerned that he was leaping too soon.

"You've read all the books in the children's section?" she asked.

"Yes. Every one that I want to."

"Well," she said, with a tinge of worry. "Let me call your mother."

While the sweet librarian was on the phone with Elsie, the front door opened, and Mary Connelly strolled in with Dolly and another girl, Willow Lush, who had recently resettled to Darwin from Labrador. Willow had long red hair and thick-rimmed glasses, but she was taller than Dolly, with slightly smaller breasts, and she was twice as pretty, despite her freckles. They talked among themselves and barely noticed Finton at first.

"Well, I talked to your mother."

"Did she say I could go into the ADULT section?" It was for Mary's sake that he raised his voice on "adult," and, sure enough, she glanced his way, smiled and waved as she passed by with the other two girls.

"She said it was up to me. But I have to say I'm concerned, Finton. What kind of books do you like?"

"I don't know. All kinds." Truthfully, he didn't know what to expect in the adult section. For all he knew, there would be pictures of bare breasts and blood-drenched murder scenes, with more swearing per page than he'd hear in a year on the playground.

"Do you like Westerns? Mysteries? Travel? Books about life? Philosophy—"

"Yes," he said, nodding for each genre. "I want to read it all, Miss Patterson. I'm bored to death with all the children's books. Some of them I've read two or three times."

It was true. He'd already been through every Hardy Boys book and even the Nancy Drews, although he didn't let his brothers catch him reading about a girl's adventures. He'd devoured the Enid Blytons, the Freddy the Pig Detective series, the Doctor Doolittle books and the *Tintin* comics, as well as *Carbonel, Peter Pan, Alice in Wonderland, Bambi, The Wizard of Oz, Return to Oz, Black Beauty, My Friend Flicka, Man O' War, Brighty of the Grand Canyon* and every book the library had on horses. From various books, likely rarely read, he'd learned about Houdini and magic, mask-making, handicrafts, storytelling, weather forecasting, and judo (most fascinating chapter: "How To Fall"). In short, he really had read every juvenile book he intended to read and was more than ready for something more challenging.

"Well, I see we can't hold you back any longer," she said. "But you will need another library card." Every couple of months, when his card was stamped full with return dates—one for every book he'd borrowed—she issued a new one. He kept the old ones as a record of all his adventures in reading. This would be card number sixteen.

"Somebody likes to read an awful lot," he heard a female voice say. It was Willow, leaning on the far end of the desk, waiting to ask the librarian a question.

He couldn't tell if he was being made fun of, so he simply said, "I do."

"Me too," she said. "Do you like *Alice in Wonderland*? That's my favourite. I've read it, like, eight or nine times."

"I read that a long time ago. I'm in the adult section now." He gulped hard, thinking how pretty she was and that he'd never talked to a girl in the library before.

"Adult? Wow. You must be special."

The words made him feel good, but he still wondered if she might be teasing him. Her face was earnest and kind, though, and he thought he might be able to trust her. "Naw. This is my first day. I haven't even been in there yet."

Miss Patterson smiled as she gave him his new card. "Welcome to the adult section. And if you read anything you don't understand, just skip over it. You don't need to know yet." She winked at him, his sign of initiation.

"Well," he said to Willow. "I better go."

"Yeah," she said. "Those books aren't gonna get read by themselves."

Looking up at the big sign in white letters—"Adult Section"— he felt a slight thrill as he crossed the threshold. For the next half-hour, he browsed through the stacks, finding most of the books too advanced or uninteresting. They were all about sex, adultery, murder, and war—subjects he was pretty sure he wasn't allowed to read about. He tugged at the spine of A *Spy in the House Love* and browsed through it. The title promised excitement, and the author was Anaïs Nin—which, in his mind, was pronounced "Anus Nine." The words drew him in, like a hungry animal devouring unexpected food: "Moonlight fell directly over her bed in summer. She lay naked in it for hours before falling asleep, wondering what its rays would do to her skin, her hair, her eyes, and then deeper, to her feelings." As intoxicating as the words were, he was embarrassed to be reading them in public, so he put the novel back. Emboldened and intrigued, he opened *Lady Chatterley's Lover*, knowing by the title that its contents were forbidden. "She lay with her hands inert on his striving body," he read silently, "and do what she might, her spirit seemed to look on from the top of her head, and the butting of his haunches seemed ridiculous to her, and the sort of anxiety of his penis to come to its little evacuating crisis seemed farcical. Yes, this was love." Softly, hands trembling, he put the book back on the shelf, promising himself that, one day, he would read it all. As thrilled as he was by the appearance of words like "body," "penis," and "spirit" he didn't understand what the author was saying.

Finally, he settled on one called *Great Expectations* by a writer he'd heard of. He decided his first adventure in the adult section would come courtesy of Charles Dickens, and he sat in the big chair in the corner, in front of the big picture window, to get cozy with his book. He quickly became engrossed in the adventures of Pip, Estella, and Miss Havisham, but he was particularly appalled by that strange Mr. Magwitch, whom Finton didn't trust any further than he could throw and, given the heft of the volume in his hands, that likely wasn't very far. It didn't surprise him that this Charles Dickens person was so famous, even though he was dead. He knew a lot of different words and wrote entertaining stories. It was stimulating to encounter new and exotic words, for his teacher had recently told his mother that Finton was "reading at a high school level." Now, at last, he was expanding his brain towards limitless possibilities. The weighty book kept him tethered to the chair, but, as he read, his imagination soared.

"Hey, Finton—enjoying your book?"

The voice startled him, and when he looked up, he saw Mary Connelly's freckled face hovering over him as if she'd been reading over his shoulder. He'd been so enraptured by the story, he hadn't seen her shadow.

"It's really good," he said. "I can't wait to read every book here."

She glanced around, surveying the tall stacks that were stuffed with books. He took the moment to notice how perfectly like a hippie girl she looked in her shapeless, long dress with the floral green pattern, like leaves, all over it. Her hair was tied back with a pink ribbon, and she wore brown platform shoes that only emphasized her smallness. "You're really smart, aren't you?" she said.

"Not really. I just like to read."

"Me too. There's nothing like a good book on a stormy day."

"I read every day—" He stopped himself, remembering that girls didn't like boys who read books. "That is, when I'm not up in the woods or playing hockey 'n stuff."

"Anyway," she smiled, "I just wanted to say hi."

"I'm glad you did. I really like—" He stopped himself from saying the truth, even though, suddenly, he just wanted to keep talking. After all, he might never have this chance again, to talk to her this way. But, somehow, the library made it easier. It was as if she'd come into his home—his *real* home. It was comfortable here, and they suddenly had things in common—interesting things, above the mundane interests of the classroom or schoolyard where everyone was just trying to survive or look cool.

"—the library," he finished. "Do you come here very often?"

That simple question led into a conversation that was still going strong twenty minutes later. She told him about how her father worked and her mother spent all her time working around the house, and how she couldn't wait to go to Paris someday and learn how to paint. He listened intently and encouraged her dreams, and even confided to her that he would like to be a writer someday, a goal that seemed to impress her.

"You're not at all like I thought you were."

"How did you think I was?" he asked.

"Shy and quiet—not interested in girls. That's what everyone says about you." She glanced toward the children's section where Dolly and

Willow were enrapt in their own discussion. Occasionally, they would glance towards Finton and Mary.

He was about to say he really was interested in girls and hardly shy at all, when the front door opened and Alicia Dredge came in, shaking the rain from her coat and wiping water from her face. Her glance immediately fell on Finton and Mary, and she turned away to ask the librarian a question.

Hardly anyone ever talked to Alicia. Still, no one was ever intentionally cruel to her. But Finton figured it must be awful being her. Even though she had dark skin and enormous eyes, like the squaw Dean Martin (and Finton Moon) loved in *Texas Across the River*, he didn't think of her the same as Mary. No one wanted to sit next to her in mass. Boys would often scoot out of the pew and sit several rows away from her if she happened to sit next to them. At lunch, she sat alone in the cafeteria. At recess, if Willie wasn't there, she sat on the steps by herself, awaiting the bell so she could slip back inside, unnoticed.

"Do you know her much?" asked Mary.

"Not really," said Finton. "She never speaks."

"Well, neither do you—and you're okay."

He beamed at the sound of her praise. "I think she's just shy."

"She seems nice." Mary lowered her voice. "But it's hard to tell when she keeps to herself."

Finton swallowed hard. He didn't want to discuss Alicia Dredge. He would much rather talk about Mary and things pertaining to Mary, which included himself. "I'm sure she's nice," he said. "She's the best looking one of the Dredges."

"No contest there." Mary laughed. "She *is* pretty."

"Yeah, she sure is." He felt his cheeks burn with the sudden realization that he'd been staring and gossiping. But those activities felt natural with Mary.

"Well, I gotta go," she said, starting away. "It's been nice talking to you."

"You too. See you Monday at school."

As he watched Mary walk away, he also observed Alicia and wondered what her business in the library might be. Miss Patterson led her to a stack of books in the farthest corner of the library, behind a long, wooden shelf that comprised one wall of the children's section. She almost ran into Mary, who was taking a seat with her two friends.

They exchanged words, but he couldn't say what they were. But as Alicia disappeared around the corner, Mary glanced up and observed her briefly.

Finton tried to sink back into *Great Expectations*. But he found himself reading the same lines repeatedly, gazing out at the raindrops splashing the pavement, and glancing around to see what either Mary or Alicia was doing. Gradually, however, he realized he had the adult section all to himself and shouldn't be so concerned with the activities of those who still inhabited the children's domain.

In his state of distraction, he turned a page of *Great Expectations* and immediately felt its edge slice his finger. He winced and dropped the book to the floor while he held his right index finger. He watched as blood seeped to the thin, white line that separated inside from outside. Blood accumulated around the wound and, eventually, trickled down the sides of his finger. He stuck the finger in his mouth and sucked on it, noting the salty, sweet flavour of his blood.

"Cut yourself?" While he wasn't looking, Alicia had entered the adult area.

Cheeks reddening, he pulled the finger from his mouth and wrapped the fingers of his left hand around it. "Yeah. No big deal." When he unfurled his fingers and observed it again, the blood had stopped flowing and the cut was merely a fresh, white scar. Only the smeared blood on his fingers suggested there'd been an injury at all.

"Looks like a flesh wound," she said, but before he could answer, she was peering over his shoulder to catch a glimpse of his book.

"*Great Expectations*," he said. "It's pretty good so far."

"I still haven't read it all," Alicia said. "I read nearly all of it in one week last summer and then got distracted with fifty pages left. Maybe you can tell me how it ends."

"Sure." He forced himself to look up at her and marveled at her large, bright eyes. "It might take me a while, but I'll let you know."

She was about to walk away, but halted. When she turned around, he was still looking at her, assessing her as a person, both body and spirit—although, to him it meant appreciating both her slender waist and her pleasant personality. Alicia smiled. "I like people who read," she said.

"Me too."

"Nobody reads in Darwin."

"Well," he swallowed hard, unsure of his response. "We do."

"Yes," she said. "We do, don't we?"

After she'd gone, Finton was unable to focus on the book and could barely remember the lines he'd read. As he carried his novel to the counter to be stamped by Miss Patterson, he felt that his life had somehow changed. It wasn't just Alicia, Willow, and Mary, though; it was Charles Dickens, Anus Nine, and D.H. Lawrence. Because of meeting them all in this place, this one afternoon, he knew he'd never look at the world the same way again. As he was getting checked out, he waved at Mary. She nodded to him before returning to her conversation with Willow and Dolly. He saw Alicia in her corner, behind the bookcase, searching among the hardcover books with the olive green covers, and she smiled warmly at him.

Walking home, he stuck his hands in his pockets, supporting the book that he'd tucked under his jacket. He wondered if he could always stop himself from bleeding and how he could apply his skill to stopping the blood flow of others. Despite the fact that he'd always known what he could do, he'd never explored this strange ability to any great degree. Such a talent—and such nonchalance—was simply a part of being Finton Moon.

"Hey brudder!" a voice yelled at him, and he recognized it as Homer's. He glanced up to see his older brother dashing by on his black banana bike, waving and grinning as he left Finton far behind.

The Sunday Dead

"Now don't you tell yer mother where we were." With a careless hand, Tom wiped the foam from his unshaven chin, making a sound like buttering toast, and clunking the empty brown bottle onto the bar.

Finton struggled to keep up as they strode to the tavern door; the boy's legs were short, and his father walked fast. Even at twelve, it was obvious that Finton's growth was stunted, despite his father being nearly six feet tall. In lowered voices he sometimes overheard, it was often suggested that perhaps a fall on one's head at birth could cause height deficiency. Both of his brothers were strapping young men with strong chests and lean, muscular arms, and they had sprouted up like trees. Finton was a disappointment, not only for his diminutive stature, but because his primary pleasure was reading, and he went to mass without complaining. The damning part was that he wasn't ashamed to be seen carrying a book that was not homework related or going to church early on a Sunday morning. People were beginning to gossip that the youngest Moon was a little strange.

Lately, however, Finton's faith had been wavering. Nanny Moon often chastised Finton's brothers for their poor behaviour and bad grades by holding Finton up as an example—a sacrificial lamb, innocent and obedient. Only vaguely did he sense that something between him and them was lost in such a distinction, and he felt increasingly foolish even going to mass.

"Why can't you be more like Finton?" Nanny Moon would ask, glowering at Homer and glancing towards Finton. He would sit on the sofa in his brown corduroys and starched white shirt, buttoned tight to his Adam's apple, and his hands clasped prayerfully on his lap. He didn't mind the pain of the collar; the suffering made him feel good and pure. The pain reassured him he was still breathing, that the moment was worthwhile. As a good Catholic boy, he believed absolutely in the cleansing power of pain. When Finton was at his best, it hurt to be him.

"Finton's gonna be a priest," Nanny Moon would practically sing. Then she would look at Finton appraisingly. Sometimes he had the feeling that his grandmother disapproved of him, as she always seemed to be castigating him. But she had asked him once at supper what he was going to be when he grew up. Seizing an opportunity to distinguish himself, he had responded with what she most wanted to hear and would gain him the most favour, if not a firm place in either her heart or this family. "Isn't that what you said, Finton? That you'd like to be called to holy orders someday?"

As he got ready to be taken to church by his father that morning, Finton had been queried in the usual way, responding only with a slow nod of his head, as if doubting the exact terms of what he was agreeing to. Orders were orders, and he was not fond of restrictions. Also, he had been experiencing particular misgivings ever since Miss Bridie rose from the dead and Father Power had warned him against believing in what he knew was true. And, just recently, Miss Bridie had threatened to bust his entire world wide open. Today, more than anything—especially since the library was closed—he just wanted to go hunting for Sawyer.

"Priests are good," said Nanny Moon, though Finton thought she said, "Priests are God," which is likely what she really meant. It was sort of what Finton believed too. Priests never did anyone harm. They always smiled and blessed your father with a handshake and sent an acknowledging nod towards your mother. When he came to your house for "visitations" your mother scrubbed the floors, told your father to straighten up, and borrowed five dollars from the grocery money to give to the church. Finton liked the idea of being someone who was always treated well, treated others kindly, and would certainly go to heaven. He wanted to be someone his parents would accept and, if possible, respect. Being a priest had its obvious advantages, he thought, even as he chased his father through the tavern after mass.

Because the pub and the church shared the same large parking lot, it was sometimes convenient for his father to visit the bar while the boy attended the sermon —particularly on those occasions when Elsie and the two eldest boys had gone the night before. While Finton preferred the Sunday mass because it coincided with Mary's attendance, the hour-long service also provided an opportunity for Tom to regale his buddies with a joke or two. Mass being over, Finton had entered the tavern in time to hear one of his father's "blaggardly" punch lines, as his wife often called them.

Accepting the signal, Tom finished his Black Horse, wiped his chin and plunked the stubby brown bottle down on the bar. Several of the patrons—including the lone female, a young blonde, who'd been sitting on Tom's knee when the boy came in—cursed and told him not to be so foolish. "Whipped, b'y," said Phonse Dredge with a wink and a scratch of his bearded chin. "Lettin' the little woman get the best o' ya."

Tom only nodded. "You knows better than that." He headed across the floor and pushed open the door, flooding the barroom with daylight and provoking shouts of "Close the goddamn door!" He didn't wait for Finton, for he subscribed to the laws of the jungle which stated that if the boy was meant to go home with him, he would be able to keep up. For the most part, he did keep up. But on those rare occasions when Finton wandered from the herd, no one ever went back for him. "He should at least be smart enough to know where he's fed," Tom said at such moments, and Elsie would suggest that they at least call the store where they had left him.

"Don't tell your mother," Tom said, smacking his lips and slamming the car door on the driver's side. When Finton climbed in and the car was started, he quizzed the boy: "Now what was the sermon about— in case she asks?"

Finton sighed and looked out the passenger window at the cold rain that was beginning to plop from the suddenly dark sky. "God and the devil. Your breath smells like beer, Dad."

"And?"

"And—" a prolonged sigh of boredom ensued as he picked at the discoloured white wool that sprouted from the hole in the blue vinyl car seat "—there's wicked people in the world and the church needs more money to carry out God's word."

"And what kinds of wicked people?" Tom had not yet started the engine, but was staring ahead through the windshield. Raindrops mixed with snow plopped on the curved glass. People were beginning to scurry to their cars, missals and umbrellas over their heads, collars pulled up and hands clutching their lapels. "It's over." Turning the key, he brought the engine to life and shifted the gear stick to the red "D," then blew on his fingers and rubbed them together before he turned the wipers on.

The blade on Finton's side swept across the great plane of glass, like a giant hand wiping out an entire village in one swoop. "Liars and blasphemers and people that don't go to mass."

His father chuckled softly as he eased the Valiant onto the road. "Lovely, b'y, lovely. You tells a good story, like yours truly." He reached over and patted Finton's back, giving the boy a queer feeling. "Loves yer old man, don't ya?"

Smelling the yeast and cigarettes on his father's breath, he was tempted to say that God don't love drunks, smokers, and people who skip mass, but he only said, "Yeah."

"Dad's boy, aren't ya, Finton?"

"Yes."

"Who's boy are ya?"

"Dad's." With the Valiant cruising slowly, Finton gazed out the window at all the families—the complete sets which came with father and mother holding hands and four or five children of varying sizes. He often saw families in church that he wished he belonged to. There were days, admittedly, when he wasn't sure at all whose boy he was. That very thought drifted through his mind just before he saw the Connelly clan scampering towards their car. He'd been disappointed at not being seen by Mary this morning, especially after the incident at the library, and now he watched her and her family with fascination and longing.

"Good boy." With yellow-stained fingers, Tom tousled Finton's dark hair. "And if Mom asks where we were, you say…"

"Dad took me to mass and we stood in the back 'cause it was crowded, and we left before Communion 'cause I got sick." He really had stood in the back for a quick getaway and had left before Communion. But the only sickness he felt was a slight nausea from inhaling cigarette smoke at the tavern.

As they finally departed and left the church behind, Elton John on the radio sang "Goodbye Yellow Brick Road," and within a couple of minutes, Finton was watching the Laughing Woods roll past his window in a grey blur. Father and son didn't speak until they zipped past the Battenhatch house.

Finton noticed the car was straddling the yellow dividing line. "You're over the line," he said, and the car seemed to right itself, spitting rocks on the passenger side. The blinker came on and the car turned right, up Moon's Lane. "Miss Bridie says you knows something about what happened to Sawyer."

The car came to a halt at the top of the lane. The radio clicked to silence, and the two Moon males sat quietly, peering out through the splattered windshield that was becoming obscured by snow and rain.

"Why would she say that?" Tom placed a hand on the door handle, but seemed reluctant to pull it.

"Do you?" Finton gripped the passenger handle, squeezing.

Tom looked sharply at his son, his dark blue eyes appearing... what? Hurt? Angry? Afraid?

"What do you think, Finton?"

"I don't…"

"I'm your father, b'y." He looked straight ahead at the falling rain. "What'n *hell* do you think?" Eyes closed, his head slumped forward.

Finton mumbled, "I don't know," and pulled the handle. He slid out of the car and slammed the door behind him, though he hadn't meant to close it quite that hard.

Before he stepped inside the house, he looked back. His father was still sitting there, gripping the wheel with both hands, forehead leaning on the wheel. Finton felt a pang of regret and considered running back to the car to apologize. But he couldn't.

"Did your father take you to mass or to the tavern?" Elsie didn't even look up from the floor, but kept sweeping, slowly, to take the strain from her aching back.

"Mass."

"Yeah, sure he did. What was the sermon?"

"Liars and drunks and people who don't go to church."

"What about them?"

"They're bad." Rather than look her in the eye, he watched the sweeping motion of the long-straw broom. Elsie was almost religious in her ritualistic gathering of dust, hair, furballs, and bits of lostness to her dustpan, which she had placed on the floor. On the stove, pots boiled with their lids clamped down. "Can I go?" He was already inching away from the kitchen, towards the hallway to the bedroom.

She eyed him warily. "Go on—but don't you be tellin' lies on account of yer father no more, no matter what he tells ya." She banged the dustpan against the side of the garbage can, then pulled hairballs from the broom's mouldy straw. "God sees ya."

He was already shutting the bedroom door behind him in order to throw off his good clothes and climb into his traipsing garments.

"Where are you off to now?" his mother asked as he flew from the bedroom and tiptoed around the perimeter of the linoleum, clinging for support to the kitchen countertop. She didn't look up at him, but remained focused on her purification ritual.

"Out."

"Sunday dinner's in an hour."

He pretended not to have heard her, but closed the door behind him and pulled on his parka as he went. The image of the steaming pots had already begun to fade from his mind. Sunday dinner meant all of the foods he disliked were gathered on one plate once a week. There'd be overdone roast, boiled-to-mush potatoes, and gloppy brown gravy that made him gag. But the worst was the slimy green cabbage that smelled like his father's farts, and the bland parsnips and carrots with turnip greens. The only part he liked was the enormous amount of salt his mother poured onto every food that she cooked to satisfy her husband's dead taste buds. Finton usually managed to force down some of this gunk only if he forsook the gravy and drowned the works in ketchup.

His father was still sitting in the car, staring ahead, an unlit cigarette protruding from his emotionless face. Fighting his guilt, Finton ran for the woods.

The path to the foxhole offered thorny passage, narrowed and cluttered with chaotic brambles and gnarled roots concealed by a thin sheet of snow, already threadbare from the morning's rain. Brown limbs and grey forest flesh poked their way up through the shroud like victims of a mass premature burial. While rabbits and field mice shivered beneath fresh-frosted bushes, juncos, robins and chickadees called from snow-tipped branches. The air was calm, but a ghostly fog had nestled in the woods, requiring the *voyageur* to recall the details hidden in the mist.

After Finton had trudged for half an hour, the trail halted at a clearing where the forest sunk into a spoon-shaped hollow. Perhaps the foxhole had once served as fortification for soldiers. Or maybe, as was occasionally conjectured by Finton and Skeet on hot summer days as flies buzzed around their heads, the hole was the resulting crater from a meteorite that had struck the earth a million years ago and killed tons of dinosaurs. Right now, however, it posed as a gravesite.

Finton's breath caught in his chest as he shuffled forward to view the corpse. Sawyer Moon lay on his stomach in the foxhole, his pants and jacket frozen solid and caked in snow. The small patch of blood on the visible side of Sawyer's skull was congealed like refrigerated partridgeberry jam. His petrified face angled towards the ground and rested in a shallow cavity filled with frozen rainwater and snow.

Finton called out through the fog, his breath billowing, but the clammy air deadened his voice. Even when his foot buckled a soggy branch, the corpse didn't stir. Somewhere above, a robin redbreast offered a long, chirpy song while the boy stood over the body, watching, and Sawyer just lay in the muck with his head down a hole.

Finton lowered himself to one knee and, with the tip of a red mitten, touched one of the corpse's shoulders. It barely moved. As he whispered the dead man's name, Finton caught a whiff of motor oil. For a long time, he held his breath, punctuated by the caw of a crow overhead. Then the silence shifted towards expectation, the feeling that Sawyer would suddenly awaken.

Rain plinked the ragged snow and the corpse alike. Finton felt only a conscious detachment as if he were looking down on himself kneeling by a dead body. He heard the dancing raindrops, the cries of birds, and the world's silence. He thought of his mother preparing Sunday dinner. He saw his father looking lost behind the wheel, an unlit cigarette in his mouth.

He stirred himself and focused on the body face down in the foxhole. Not so long ago, he'd wished that Sawyer was dead. Even dreamt about it. Shame and horror coursed through him while, above him, the robin continued to sing, its joyful noise bordering on sacrilege.

Who killed Cock Robin?

I killed Cock Robin. With my wicked thoughts.

His gaze fell upon a stiffened hand sprawled in the snow. If he stared at it long enough, it might even move. *Live,* he thought. But then he whispered, "Stay dead."

A finger twitched. Finton blinked. Opened his eyes. All was still.

He took a deep breath, then swiveled around and darted into the woods. He kept on running until he reached the bungalow. Without even stopping to beat the snow from his boots, he burst inside to tell the news.

His mother was draining potatoes at the sink while Nanny Moon was setting the table. "About time," said his grandmother. "We almost had to send out a search party."

"I found him," Finton blurted.

"Who?" she asked. But if the colour draining from her face was any indication, she already knew.

Elsie glanced at him over her shoulder, as steam rose up from the colander. "What did you find?"

"Sawyer—in the foxhole. Dead."

The room seemed to spin. But there wasn't time to sit down. His father came out from the living room and studied Finton's face. "Well, that's that."

Nanny Moon blessed herself and said, "Lord have mercy on the poor man's soul."

"Amen," said Elsie, who astonished Finton by likewise casting the sign of the cross and hanging her head. "Rest in peace."

It was Clancy who insisted they immediately call the police. While Tom seemed confused into silence, neither Nanny Moon nor Elsie doubted it was the right course of action. Homer, on the other hand, had slipped down the hall and back into the bedroom. While Clancy took charge, Finton observed, feeling as if he had landed in a dream.

Within twenty minutes, a police car had parked in front of the Moon bungalow. With the afternoon growing dark, Finton, Tom, Clancy, and Elsie, led the two officers to the foxhole. While the policemen tread carefully and marked off the area, Finton stared at the corpse and tried to guess Sawyer's last thoughts. Maybe he'd thought of his mother or the bone-chilling cold. Perhaps he'd thought about bigger things—about God and the devil, or about heaven or hell. There was so much he didn't know.

Although he couldn't erase the image from his mind, he was no longer certain Sawyer's finger had twitched. It was all too easy to convince himself it had moved, just as it was easy to believe it hadn't. But the corpse, he noted with relief, didn't seem to have budged an inch.

As the police conducted their business, the entire scene was all a blur. They asked Tom a few questions, but he was bewildered and appeared to know nothing of how his friend had died. One of them came over to where the boy was standing and asked him if he was okay. Finton nodded, but he felt awful. His world had been turned inside out, and he suspected he would never get past this moment. He didn't like staring at a corpse. Didn't like that someone he knew was dead. Didn't like being surrounded by serious faces and worried eyes. Didn't like that there were questions no one could answer.

"It must have been scary, finding a body." The officer spoke softly while Finton nodded and stared at the ground.

"Why'd you come up here anyway?"

The question made Finton queasy, like he was being accused of something. "I always come here."

"Did you know Sawyer?"

"I guess."

The officer smiled grimly. "Did you like him?"

"Not really. Nobody liked Sawyer."

"Did anyone hate him enough to kill him?"

"Almost everyone."

"Did you?"

Finton looked at him. The officer had a dark complexion and kind eyes, the kind of face he felt he could trust. "I didn't hate him," he said and, as the officer looked perplexed, Finton added, "I was just afraid of him."

The officer asked him only a few more questions, and Finton was left feeling that he had done something wrong. His father came over and said, "That's enough, Kieran. He's only a boy," and it was only then that the officer nodded and said, "Sure."

Finton suddenly realized who the officer was. He'd overheard his mother and grandmother discussing how the oldest Dredge boy had gone away to the police academy. So this must be him. Officer Kieran Dredge. Alicia's big brother.

"Can we go now?" asked Tom.

"Sure, go on and take the boy home. But we'll be in touch."

That night, when things had calmed down and he had gone to bed, his heart still pounded. He couldn't erase the images from his mind. The frozen body. The twitching finger. "I think it moved," he whispered to Jesus, who stared back at him from the picture on the wall. Wind-driven raindrops lashed the side of the house, making it shudder.

Finton's head throbbed.

Ordinary Days

"No," he said when his mother asked if he'd slept well. He'd struggled waking up but somehow finally managed to pry himself out of bed. His brothers were already up, as evidenced by their empty, unmade beds. For the first time since he could remember, Finton neglected to turn back the covers and smooth them over on his own bed. There was no time even to comb his hair or wash his face. It was all he could do to get dressed and drag himself to the kitchen.

The place still looked the same as when he'd gone to bed last night, but somehow it was different. Although the fire was lit, the linoleum was cold. The brown-stained wallpaper with the pattern of red-combed roosters still looked as though it would peel from the walls if he gave it a tug. The black top wood stove with the chipped enamel still squat like an errant spaceship against the back wall, and the hulking, white refrigerator hummed and groaned, its left side hugging the cupboards so that several of the drawers were permanently shut. His father sat at the kitchen table, but as soon as he saw Finton, he stood up, pulled on his coat, muttering about needing to bring in some firewood before going to work.

Despite the sameness, the world looked out of order, sharper than usual. It was more than just the fact that he'd seen a dead body—something bigger was wrong. The difference he saw and felt came from within his own mind. Finton suddenly was more in tune to the edges of things, more observant of the simple, clear lines that separated the floor from the stove, his father from his chair, his mother from the air around her, keeping her upright and present. The oatmeal in his bowl was lumpy and pasty, with bitter, brown flecks. He pushed the bowl away, practically untouched.

He went to school that day with a sense of being different from everyone else. On the bus, he heard Skeet talking about the police finding Sawyer, but was too preoccupied to care, watching his friend's lips mouthing words, a particle of spit forming before he rubbed his lips together and got rid of it. His eyes contained a hilarity that disgusted Finton slightly. No one should be so overjoyed when someone died. When Mary got on board, he watched her eyes for a sign that they now had a bond, but, among the crowd, she didn't seem to notice him. And yet he saw everything about her—that her boot laces were tied too tight, that the front of her slacks had been ironed to a sharp crease, that each of her eyelashes curved gently upwards, that one of her cheeks had six freckles while the other had five, and her small nose pointed slightly upwards. And she seemed sad.

When he lined up behind the other children for entry into the school, he found himself noticing every loose button on every coat, every speck of salt on a pant leg, each individual smile and frown, every emotion in every eye. He sensed a melancholy in Miss Woolfred as she stood on the top step, clanging the handbell. He knew she'd argued with her boyfriend that morning about whether she should take a teaching job in the city. The information caught Finton by surprise; he hadn't even known she had a boyfriend. But he wished there was something he could say to make her feel better.

When Mary and Dolly stepped in front of him in the lineup, he was startled as if jolted from a daydream, but the hyper-reality still pulsated within him. Mary turned and said, "Hi, Finton." But his concentration was divided, and he could only manage to say, "Hey." The thoughts came quickly: Dolly was menstruating, and Mary was anxiously awaiting the beginning of her first time. *Someday.* She was aware of him standing behind her, smelling the No More Tangles shampoo in her hair as the breeze riffled through it. He felt her anxiety and suddenly remembered the math test.

His first thought was to run away. But he resisted the urge, believing that if he departed now, he might find it too easy to perform the same disappearing act every day that followed. No, it was important to stay here today, to remain grounded in this existence. Otherwise, he might never feel rooted again.

As he sat at his desk, staring at the test paper, he doodled some pictures, toyed with writing his name backwards, diagonally and horizontally, and stared out the window from time to time. He wondered what the police were doing with Sawyer's body. He suddenly got the urge to start writing a story, and he jotted the first line: *I'll never forget the day I found the dead body of my sworn enemy.*

"Finton?" His head jerked at the sound of his name. Miss Woolfred stood over him, a disgruntled look on her face. She was still upset after her fight with *Garnett*... yeah, *Garnett*, and was in no mood for a challenge. Her eyes were stormy green, and she had a tiny pimple on the side of her nose, which she had squeezed before coming to work, but its redness hadn't altogether faded. Realizing the gravity of the situation, he quickly put the story away, figuring he would finish it later.

"Are you going to do your test?" she asked.

"Sorry," he said and tried to focus on the paper in front of him.

"Sit up straight," she said, setting her hands on her hips. "And don't give me that tone."

"I never used a tone."

"One more word..." she closed her eyes, inhaled and exhaled, then opened them again. "Just do your test, Finton."

He drew a deep breath of his own and straightened up in the desk, heels clanging against its metal base. He grasped the pen, set his eyes on the exam. He didn't look at his teacher again until the test was done. It was too much to expect that he would figure out the problems, so he just filled in the blanks with made-up answers. Meanwhile, he kept thinking about how to finish the story he'd started.

He didn't relax until the bell rang, ending the first period, and he was able to breathe. Skeet's leg reached over and kicked Finton's heel. "You okay, Moon?"

"Leave me alone."

"It's just not like you to talk back to a teacher—especially ol' Woolfie. I thought you were her pet." His sarcastic grin was irritating. "What's eating you?"

"*You*, okay?" Finton stood up and jammed his books under his arm, then stomped away and left Skeet with his jaw hanging. From the center of the room, Mary turned her head and watched him leave, her brown eyes filled with concern.

Rain fell to the pavement as Finton fled the classroom and then ran from school. It was a couple of weeks before Christmas holidays, but it felt like Doomsday. It was usually a three-mile walk back to the house, but Finton knew a shortcut through the woods. About a quarter mile from the school, he left the road and veered into the trees, slowing his pace only when he'd reached the thicket. He could hear the occasional car zipping by on the wet pavement, but he couldn't see them, and they couldn't see him.

Within minutes he'd found a trail Clancy had showed him a couple of years ago from when the telephone company was erecting poles. It was hard going because much of the underbrush had grown back in, barren as it was this time of year, and the path was muddy. Every once in a while, he'd come to a wide strip of dirty-brown water, and he'd have to criss-cross the whole way to keep from stepping in it.

An hour later and soaked to his skin, Finton broke through the clearing behind the Battenhatch house. He tiptoed across the soggy marsh and crept along the edge of the swollen Moon's River. It was twice as wide and probably twice as deep as normal, with the torrent roaring downstream at a pace that would make it impossible to cross. A dirty, white diaper that had snagged itself in the clutches of a large fallen branch waved at him from the undulating stream.

There was no other choice. Leaving the roar of the river behind him, he turned left towards the Battenhatch house. His sneakers still squished in the soggy grass, and he kept both eyes trained on the dark windows. Finally, as the rain started coming down harder, he ran. His clothes were saturated, but he managed to trot around the blind side of the house. The spruce trees in the front yard stood like sentries. Even though the road was just yards away, he feared he would never escape the Battenhatch yard.

From behind him, he heard the sound he dreaded most.

"Come here!" the voice yelled from the open front door.

Reluctantly, he turned and looked. There she stood, in all her gothic glory, shaking her grey head and beckoning him towards her. "You're soaked to the bone, b'y," she said in her quavering voice. "Come in and get dry."

Halfway between the house and the road, Finton stood, unable to move. He was torn between running and giving in. A glance to his right, through the thin veil of trees between the Battenhatch and Moon properties, showed him an odd vehicle pulling into his parents' driveway—a black cruiser with white doors, a cherry-red light on top, and an RCMP crest emblazoned on the door. Officer Dredge got out and lumbered towards the Moons' front door, soon joined by the second policeman, probably Corporal Futterman. They stood and knocked, but had to stand for a while on the front doorstep in the rain.

"Come in, ya bloody fool!" Bridie fixed him with a threatening glare as she coughed sharply. She stepped onto the front porch, shielding her face with one hand. "Afore you catch your death, luh."

Some combination of obedience and courage impelled him forward, as Finton followed her into the house.

"What in blue blazes were you doin' out there?" Just like last time, she already had the kettle on and two places set. With this weather, he had expected to see buckets everywhere, catching raindrops. But there was a crackling fire in the wood stove, and the air was drier, almost cleaner, than he remembered.

"Nudding."

"Aren't you supposed to be in school?"

"I left."

She didn't respond, but bustled around the table, pouring tea and ripping open a fresh pack of Jam-jams, which she laid on the table in front of Finton. "Have a cookie—good for what ails ya."

"I'm not ailin'." Ravenous from not having eaten yet that morning, he snatched a cookie and broke it in two, taking one half of it in his mouth and staring at the other half as if to ponder its medicinal benefits. Munching slowly, he glanced out at the falling rain, scanning the road for a sign that the police had finished interrogating his parents.

"Oh, I'd say you are. That's what you are, indeed." Miss Bridie sat across from him, cradling a full teacup between her hands, coughing occasionally as if she had a tickle in her throat. "You're soaked from the rain. I got some old clothes, I'm sure—"

"No, thanks."

"Or a blanket."

"I'm not stayin' that long. I got to go home."

She smiled, but with a worried look in her eyes that he had never seen before.

"You know that the fuzz are up in your driveway, don't you?" He nodded. "And you know why they're there."

He fixed his gaze on the painted window through which he could just make out the shape of some trees and, beyond them, the shadow of a narrow, black road. The thumping of his heart marked each passing moment.

"You're in a mess—you and your father," she said. "Old Sawyer really did it this time, didn't he? And there's no comin' back once you're in that particular hole."

He scrutinized her face, wondering, *What makes her so mean? And how does she seem to know everything?* He could count the lines in her face and smell the odour of her unwashed flesh. But he was unable to read her thoughts.

She tapped her right temple with a solitary finger. "You tell more than you think you do. And I listen clearer than most."

Finton shoved the remaining half Jam-jam into his mouth, but struggled to chew. Under her omnipotent gaze, he felt the overwhelming urge to cry, but he held it in.

"He's a goner." She paused and looked out the window, trying to glimpse what he saw. Or maybe she was looking at his reflection in the glass. Or possibly her own. "Doesn't matter." She shook her head as if recovering her senses. "He had it comin' and now he's gone. All we can do is take care of what's left and do what's right." She stopped once more and regarded him closely. "You know what I'm saying, and don't let on otherwise—you know what you have to do."

He looked into her haunted eyes and shuddered. Rain dripped from his hair and nose, splattering onto the plastic-covered tabletop. "What do I have to do?"

"You don't need me to tell you that, child. Just go home and take care of them all that needs taking care of."

Scraping the legs of his chair on the floor, Finton struggled to his feet. He was getting cold and felt a fever and headache coming on. His body ached for something it would never attain. He snatched a cookie and held it carefully as he ran towards the door and yanked it open. Leaping outside and over the steps, he clambered onto the road and took off running. He could feel her watching him as he crossed the flooded culvert.

A muddy brown rivulet flowed down the centre of Moon's Lane. At the lane's pinnacle squat a troubled bungalow and a troublesome car.

The police were still in the kitchen. He tried to be invisible, but they easily noticed him when he opened the front door and slipped inside. Both men seemed anxious, but neither spoke to him at first, as they finished discussing Kieran Dredge's experiences upon returning to Darwin as a lawman.

"It's been strange, indeed," Kieran was saying. "And busier than I would've expected, for sure."

Elsie nodded, sitting by the stove, arms folded across her chest. She turned towards Finton. "Where have you been?" she asked in her telephone voice.

"Out." He scooted past the officers' sharp-creased slacks and shiny shoes with the mud stains on the bottoms. They each held their hats with the shiny brims, their skulls sporting crew cuts.

"Shouldn't you be in school?" Elsie asked.

"I'm sick."

"Why didn't you call?"

"I found my own way home." He paused only for a moment and turned around to face them all. "I'm goin' to bed."

"These fellas want to talk to you, Finton." Elsie opened her stance, laying one arm on the cold stovetop to her right and the other on the tabletop to her left. "Kieran and Officer Futterman are looking into the thing with Sawyer."

"Maybe you heard something at school today?" prompted Kieran.

Finton shrugged. "I didn't talk to no one today."

"You must have talked to *some*one." The older policeman, Futterman, the one with the mustache, was turning his hat over and over in his hands.

"Some people say he got drunk and fell down," said Finton.

"Maybe," said Kieran. "He might have fallen and smacked his head on a rock. Or someone could have hit him and caused him to fall. We won't know for sure till we see the coroner's report, but there's no harm in gettin' a headstart."

"We're asking around to see who knows what," said the older one. "There might be something more to it, ya know?"

Elsie spoke up. "Well, Finton doesn't know anything, Earl. He's just a boy."

"Yes, ma'am. And we do appreciate your time," said Futterman. "But we were hopin' to talk to your husband today. Is Tom around?"

"To tell the truth, I haven't—"

She looked to be about ready to tell one of the biggest fibs of her life when the toilet flushed in the bathroom, separated from the kitchen only by a thin sheet of gyproc. "That would be him now." He'd never seen his mother's face turn so red.

She called out to Tom and, after a brief pause, in which the two officers exchanged unreadable glances, he appeared in the kitchen. His hair was tousled as if he'd just woke from a nap, and he pulled on his belt to insert the metal prong into the correct hole as he intermittently tried to stuff the hem of his white t-shirt into his pants.

"What can I do you for, officers?" He leaned one arm against the stove, standing across from Finton and smelling like beer.

"We're looking for clues regarding Sawyer Moon." Futterman tightened the grip on his hat as he spun it around in his hands. "Just asking around to all your neighbours."

"And all over town," Kieran added.

"Routine, eh?" Tom fished in his pocket for his lighter at the same time that he lifted a cigarette pack from his shirt pocket and squeezed a smoke from the package and into his mouth. He had the cigarette lit and a ring of smoke blown across the kitchen before they even had a chance to reply.

"No," said Futterman. "Nothin' routine about it. A man is dead, and no one seems to know how he got to his final resting place. But everyone knows he was a friend of yours."

"I'm a popular fella." Tom squinted like Clint Eastwood in *Dirty Harry*, one of the movies he and Finton had watched on *Academy Performance* last summer. "Got an awful lot o' friends."

"That's what we hear," said the younger one.

"Been asking around about me, have ya?"

"We're not jumping to conclusions," Futterman said. "But we've heard things."

Kieran coughed and cleared his throat. "Is it true you and Sawyer had an argument on the same night he disappeared?"

Tom's demeanour shifted slightly. He practically became Clint, exuding that same squint and careless swagger in his voice. "Who said that? What lousy prick is talkin' about me behind my back?"

"Can't tell you that," said Kieran "But is it true?"

"We had a few words." Tom spit on the stovetop, his spittle performing a little dance on the iron black top. "But it never amounted to much." Finton observed that his father's lips were wrapped a tad tightly around that cigarette.

Futterman nodded thoughtfully. "What did you argue about?"

Tom reached across the table and tapped his cigarette on the edge of the ashtray. "Just some stuff I heard about 'im. We'll just leave it at that."

"You know we can't do that, Tom."

"Look, I heard he was diddlin' some youngsters, okay?" Tom stared ahead at the wall, studiously avoiding eye contact with anyone.

"One o' yours?"

Tom hesitated, glanced at Finton, then Homer, and finally just sighed. "He said he never done it. I didn't know what to believe. I shoved him a bit and said if I ever caught him doin' the like, I'd come after him."

Again, Kieran coughed. "You actually said you'd kill him, didn't you?"

"Sure," said Tom, "I said it. But that don't mean I'd do it. I only tried to scare him, but that was all. I never had nudding else to do with him after that. Ask anyone."

"That's the problem," said Futterman. "There's no one to ask. A few people saw you arguing, and they never saw Sawyer again."

"So you're accusing me without evidence."

"If there was more evidence, we wouldn't be allowed to share it, Tom." Futterman sniffed, glanced at the floor, then met Tom's gaze. "It could taint the case."

Tom swept a hand through his hair as a cold draught seemed to sift through the kitchen. In fact, to Finton, it felt as if the entire house shuddered. "Case?"

"If there's a trial—you know, after the coroner's report."

"Sounds like ya know what you're lookin' for. Just haven't found it yet."

"Not necessarily," said Kieran.

"But we couldn't tell you anyways." Futterman scowled as he folded his arms across his sizable chest.

"No, I don't suppose you could." Sticking one hand in his pocket and gesticulating with the one holding the cigarette, Tom's nervous habits seemed to be getting the better of him.

"I don't feel so good," Finton said. While everyone was looking at Finton and politely asking if he was okay, he threw up on Kieran's shiny black shoe, causing him to curse mildly and whip out a handkerchief.

"I'll get the mop." Elsie said as she rushed to the porch.

"I'd better put him to bed." Tom placed a warm hand, the one still holding the cigarette between its nicotine-stained fingers, at the back of Finton's neck.

While Finton was still marveling at his ability to vomit on command, both the officers and the parents mumbled their most sincere apologies and mutually agreed that now was a good time to

end the inquisition. There were other houses to go to, other leads—
"or lack thereof," as Futterman added—to pursue.

When they had finally gone and Finton was tucked into bed, amazed
that he now had a fever to go with his vomiting, his mother kissed his
forehead while Tom observed from the bedroom doorway. Their eyes
met each other's, but silence remained their chosen form of commun-
ication. Finton's mind wandered to that Sunday morning when they'd
passed Sawyer as he was emerging from the woods. *I'll tell ya about it
when we gets there. But not while he's here*, Phonse had said. Finton could
only wonder what his father was thinking when he turned his back
and left.

Listening to Tom's grim shuffle down the hallway, Finton imagined
what it would be like to have a father in prison. He could picture it.
Unshaven and scraping a tin cup across the bars, black-and-white
stripes on his pajamas, calling out for the warden and yelling, "I was
framed! It was the kid, I tell you! Get the kid!"

Finton shut his eyes and listened to the rain pattering on the roof.

Finton Moon Lassos Moon

He had something to give her, but she was rarely alone, and he dreaded the thought of being a spectacle.

Everywhere he went, he thought about Mary. Weekday mornings on the school bus, she sat by the window, five rows down, near the window and next to Dolly. Finton sat behind her, watching her reflection in the glass; sometimes, he'd grip the back of her seat so that a strand of her hair might graze his hands. Saturdays at the library, he kept an eye on the door in case she came in. Sunday mornings, he'd attend the early mass because she would be there. In the evenings, he would pretend to need something at the store just so he could wander past her house, gaze up at her bedroom window and imagine what she was doing—braiding her sister's hair, gossiping about boys, doing homework, or watching TV with her family.

Every day, from his desk in the corner, he would watch her. Mary's desk assumed the centre of the room and, while the teacher addressed the class, she and her crowd would exchange notes and giggles. Sometimes they'd chew gum, then plant it under the desktop behind Mary's, which was occupied by Alicia Dredge.

The last day before the Christmas holidays, the mood bordered on hysteria. Somehow, though, Alicia seemed outside of it all. Mary and her friends were the hub of the commotion as the teachers went through the motions of checking homework, asking questions, and writing on the blackboard. Some students feigned interest as they jotted a few notes and laughed extra hard at the teacher's jokes. But no one forgot, even for a second, that Christmas began at noon. Fourteen days of freedom and fun in the snow.

Finton was worried.

It wouldn't be a normal Christmas, even by Moon standards. There would be extra food, such as apples and oranges, but no pantryful of groceries like other families had. And yet it was a special time because the apples would be five-pointed and the oranges extra large, with a variety of cookies and a bucket of hard candy from the States.

Christmas Eve, his father would get drunk. Partway through putting up the tree, Tom would get angry because the lights wouldn't work, and he would take it out on the tree or yell at Elsie or one of the youngsters, usually Finton. Late evening, he would leave the house in search of someone to get drunk with, Phonse Dredge being the likely candidate, leaving Elsie and the boys to decorate the tree. The two older ones sometimes went out with friends while Finton watched *It's A Wonderful Life*. He'd seen it two Christmas Eves in a row and was in love with Donna Reed, with her dark, smouldering eyes and nurturing ways. His favourite part was when the main character, George, tried to prove his affection—"What is it you want, Mary? You want the moon? Just say the word and I'll throw a lasso around it and pull it down"— and when she agreed to take it, he said she could swallow it and the moon would dissolve and "moonbeams would shoot out of your fingers and your toes and the ends of your hair." They were the best lines from any movie he'd ever seen.

The excitement was heightened, both in school and at home, by a snowstorm the day before school closed. In winter, Tom could usually get extra work at Taylor's because so many people needed snow tires installed. This year, however, there'd been no such call until this morning. When Pat Taylor asked Tom to come in to work, he turned it down, saying he didn't feel too good. Finton didn't know how much money his father normally made, but without that extra, it would be a hard Christmas.

But Finton had bigger worries. All morning, he'd watched for his moment. In between lessons, Mary chatted excitedly with Dolly or Willow or another girl. The chances for a shy boy to walk up to her and say, "I have a present for you," then sneak away unnoticed were nil.

Since that day at the library, his love for her had grown. He realized that Mary was popular and friendly: that was part of the attraction. She talked to almost everyone. Every boy—and every girl—wanted to be her favourite and, when he was being honest with himself, he realized they'd barely spoken to each other since that glorious afternoon. He had no reason to think she harboured any feelings for him beyond friendship, and yet here he was with a gift for Mary in his schoolbag, which he gripped with sweaty palms.

All morning, he'd watched both her and the clock as if the three of them had formed an unspoken bond. Finally, the last bell rang and the classroom erupted into whooping and hollering. The chaos was Finton's opportunity.

He noticed some other boys making moves of their own.

Skeet went right up to Dolly, who, despite his recent growth spurt was almost as tall as him, and dangled some mistletoe over her head. "Merry X-mas, Dolly! Let's me and you put the Christ back in Christmas, eh?" He puckered his lips and lingered for several seconds. But, instead of kissing him, she shoved him away, saying, "Get lost, Stuckey!" as her face turned red. Mary hid her face in her hands. Some of the others laughed on their way out the door. Unfazed, Skeet leaned in and kissed her on the mouth. He thrust the small, blue box into her unsuspecting hands and wished her a Merry Christmas. Then he hoisted his trousers up by the belt and huffed out of the classroom amid scattered cheers.

Dolly announced that she had to make a quick trip to the washroom to fix her lipstick, and Finton recognized his moment.

After Willow was gone, only Finton, Mary, and Alicia remained. He fumbled in his bookbag, snatched the package wrapped in red crepe paper, and strode towards her.

"Mary." He sniffled and wiped his nose with one finger.

Startled, she looked up at him. "Hi."

"Hi." He sensed her looking at the package and so he thrust it towards her. "Merry Christmas. It's not much. But I thought you might like it."

"But…" Her big, brown eyes glanced from the package to Finton and occasionally flickered towards the window, catching the light in the loveliest way. "…I didn't get anything for you."

"That's okay."

She smiled and nodded, the sight of her slightly uneven teeth warming his heart. "Thank you. That's so sweet of you."

Barely able to feel his legs, he stumbled towards the door.

"Can I open it now?"

He halted and turned, one hand resting on the door frame. "I thought you'd wait till Christmas."

"*Can't* I open it now?"

"Sure. If you want."

She smiled and carefully removed the red bow and peeled back one corner of the red tissue paper.

Dolly returned from the bathroom. "What's that? Did he give you a present?" She huddled with Mary as if they were in on a secret. "He did—didn't he?"

While Mary pulled the object from its wrapping, Finton moved closer, his heart pounding. She might adore it. She'd probably loathe it. She'd probably laugh and tell her friends what that stupid Moon boy had done. He imagined himself reaching over and snatching it from her grasp. But as she unwrapped the gift with her tiny fingers, she smiled faintly.

"Thank you, Finton. It's very thoughtful."

"Wow." Dolly nodded, obviously impressed. "A jigsaw puzzle."

"It's Paris," he explained, hands thrust in his pockets and cheeks blazing. "You said you wanted to go there sometime."

"I did say that. I really did." Standing up, Mary leaned in and kissed his cheek. She smelled like roses. He felt ill.

"I gotta go," Finton said. "Skeet's waiting for me."

"Speaking of which," said Mary. "What'd Stuckey get you?"

Dolly fished the gift from her pocket and showed her. "Earrings. Nice ones too. I expect he'll want something for that." The earrings looked almost a little too rich and Finton couldn't help wondering where Skeet had come up with the money—or if he'd stolen them outright.

"Hmph!" said Mary. "Imagine—earrings from Skeet Stuckey! He must have the hots for *you*, Doll." She laughed and tossed her head so that her long brown hair swished from her shoulder to the middle of her back.

Fidgeting more every moment he stood there, Finton wished them "Merry Christmas!" and dashed out the door, gulping in the late-morning air, grateful to be alive. It was Christmas at last. Except for his parents fighting and a vivid memory of the corpse he'd found, absolutely nothing lay between him and complete bliss.

Just when he thought it would all come true just as he'd planned, he heard the footsteps of someone running behind him.

"Finton! Wait up!"

He knew the voice, but he kept on walking. *Please God, no. Not her. Not now.*

"I got a present for you!"

He halted and turned, snowflakes lashing his face as he watched her approach, her hair bouncing, a nervous smile on her face. Her cheeks were blotched red. She looked unbearably cold in that thin black jacket that he was sure he'd seen on Willie last week and that short brown skirt with the black tights and a small hole below one knee that exposed her dark skin to the elements.

"Alicia?"

"I tried to give this to you in the classroom, but you left too quick." She smiled, her teeth straighter than he thought they'd be.

"For me? Why?" Her smile flickered briefly. "I mean, I didn't...uh"

"It's okay." She shrugged. "I saw this and thought of you."

She sort of leaned towards him as if to kiss him on the cheek. He stiffened just before she punched him on the arm and backed away. "Have a good Christmas."

"Yeah, you too." He stared at the package as she walked away. "Hey!" She turned halfway around even as she kept walking. "Did you want me to open it now?"

"Naw." She waved dismissively. "It's better to keep gifts till Christmas morning."

Relief flooded his entire being. "Thanks—thanks a lot." He was smiling brightly, even though he could see Dolly and Mary strolling towards them. "See you in January."

"You too."

Then she ran to the yellow bus and, after letting a couple of other people come between them, he followed slowly behind. Climbing aboard, he watched Alicia scoot to the back, and he took the middle, behind the seat usually occupied by Dolly and Mary. He sucked in a breath as he shielded the present with one hand and ripped the brown paper away from one corner.

An orange hardcover of *To Kill a Mockingbird*.

She'd just seen it and thought of him.

"What did maggot-breath give you?" Dolly snorted.

"A book."

"A stupid old book?"

"Cool," said Mary under her breath.

"Yeah," said Finton, suddenly feeling the world grow lighter and bigger.

Silently, he began to read. *"When he was nearly thirteen, my brother Jem got his arm badly broken at the elbow..."*

And just like that, he was hooked. By the end of the first chapter, although he didn't know it yet, he was already in love with Scout Finch.

Christmas flew by as if on wings. He read *To Kill a Mockingbird*, but he told his parents it was for school.

"I heard a girl gave it to him." Homer would always say things like that to get a rise out of him. He and Clancy were playing matchbox hockey at the kitchen table while Finton read by the kitchen stove.

His mother stopped running around and tidying up. "What girl?" She straightened a piece of tinsel that had stretched too far and was dangling from the tree.

"No girl," said Finton. "Homer's a shit disturber."

"Alicia Dredge," said Homer.

"A Dredge? Finton?" She darted him a look, but he kept on reading.

"Your little boy is growin' up," Clancy said. "Did you give her anything?"

"Like herpes?" Homer laughed.

Finton slammed the book shut. "Why don't you all just shut up and let me do my homework?"

"Homework over Christmas?" his mother asked.

"Leave me alone!" Finton scrambled from the rocking chair, stomped to the bedroom, and slammed the door behind him.

That was how he often handled their mocking. He didn't understand their need to make fun of him, just to make themselves feel important, to have their say in his life. More and more, Finton wished he was old enough to get as far away from Darwin as possible. But he was deathly afraid it might never happen; there were so many things that could go wrong between now and high school graduation—and the worst possible example was his own father who got married, settled down, and never left. Lying on the bed, looking up at the ceiling, Finton suddenly found he could barely breathe. Tears seeped from the corners of his eyes, and he hated his brothers for making him feel so weak. But, most of all, he hated Alicia Dredge.

He realized the inherent danger in admitting that Alicia had good taste in books, but Finton savoured each sentence of *To Kill a Mockingbird* like the individual bites of a well-cooked meal. Atticus Finch was such an understanding man who would do anything to protect his family, always had wisdom to convey to his children, and always stood up for what was right. He wished his own father was more like Atticus. Lately, every time he thought about his father, he remembered the frozen face of Sawyer Moon. He wondered how long before the police came back and accused Finton of killing him. It wasn't that he lacked rationality about the whole thing. He knew you couldn't kill people just by wishing them dead. But neither could you raise the dead by imagining them revived. Of course, he'd never told anyone about his premonition of Sawyer's death, but he also hoped no one would put the pieces together. He was even more worried about his father. He didn't want to believe his father was lying, but the coincidences—the mysterious conversation between Tom and Phonse, as well as the argument between his father and Sawyer on the night he went missing—were hard to ignore. Thing was, if a person was capable of killing someone, they wouldn't get too hung up on lying about it.

All during Christmas, it seemed, every night there was a knock on the door—a troupe of boisterous mummers, a lone friend or an entire family from down the road, a long-lost acquaintance—someone was always coming around, looking for a good time, a drink, and a bite to eat. Phonse Dredge had dropped by and stayed for several hours, and Alicia had come with him. She sat across from Finton and would occasionally glance at him and smile as she toyed with her fingers.

"What did you get for Christmas?" he asked.

She shrugged and smiled bashfully. "Kieran came over for Christmas dinner with his girlfriend." Her response astonished him, but he merely nodded. Neither of them spoke again after that, just listened to the adults discuss the hard times they were living through and the better days of long ago.

Winnie and Francis Minnow also stopped in for syrup and fruitcake, and even Father Power came around for a cup of tea. At night, there was constant drinking and laughter, and the inevitable moment when someone would play a song on the guitar or accordion, which always led to a full-blown kitchen concert. Even Skeet stopped by with Mr. Stuckey, and each of them played a song. Skeet was a strong singer, and he belted out "The Boston Burglar" with heartbreaking conviction, while his less talented father sang "Folsum Prison Blues." It seemed that good times were finally returning to the Moon household. And yet Finton cringed each time someone came to the door, anticipating the moment when the RCMP would come to drag him away in handcuffs.

On the morning of New Year's Eve, with a light dust of snow falling and his spirit full of the sociability of the season, Finton stopped by the Battenhatch house, figuring Miss Bridie and Morgan might be lonely with only each other for company. The house looked much the same on the inside as always, for they hadn't bothered with a Christmas tree. Morgan had tacked some scrawny green garland on the wall over the stove, but that was the only decoration. He was welcomed by the older woman first and then by the younger one, as if they were truly glad to see him, both smiling from their eyes as well their mouths. There remained something reticent in the behaviour of both, perhaps because they just weren't used to company. Of course, some electricity would have helped alleviate the gloom. But by the time he'd left, with a bellyful of Jam-jams and tea, after more than an hour of Miss Bridie reflecting on her days on the Shore and Morgan, with her arms crossed, wisecracking at the wood stove, Finton was thinking he might make Miss Bridie's a place of regular visitation, or at least on occasion.

That same night brought another happy moment when the three Moon brothers were sitting around in the bedroom, listening to records—which was one of Finton's favourite things to do. Because of their age differences and divergent interests, it was a rare occasion when the three of them spent time together, but music could overcome such obstacles. He wasn't fond of their music, but he was able to overlook such differences in the interest of brotherly bonding.

The Rush album had just finished, and Homer was pulling a new one out of its sleeve. "Would you believe Laura Connelly tried to set me up with her little sister?" he said, almost as if it were a casual thing.

"Mary?" From where he lay on the bottom bunk, Finton instantly felt moved to commit violence on her behalf.

"She's cute enough," said Clancy as he cranked up the volume on the turntable; tapping his feet and playing air drums, he was obviously bored with talking and just wanted to hear the new KISS album his girlfriend had given him.

"What did you say?" Finton demanded.

"I told her she had to be jokin'."

Homer was boasting, of course; no matter how he really felt about Mary, Homer wanted Finton to know Laura had chosen a real man for her little sister. To Finton, the very thought of Mary and Homer together was absurd. She was the smartest girl he knew, and Homer was not only repulsed by books, but was perpetually on the verge of failing school. All the more reason to rip his brother's eyes from their sockets. But he refrained.

Homer went on talking over the annoying music. "I wouldn't be caught dead with a girl that wears pink ribbons. She's a little girl. She wears a ponytail, for fuck's sake."

Finton breathed a sigh of relief, but it bothered him to think that someone else had noticed her. On the other hand, Homer was a cretin for not seeing past the innocent façade to understand Mary's true personality. She wasn't a little girl—she was a lady.

"Heard that Dredge one's got her eyes on you," Homer said.

"Shut up," Finton said.

"She's cute too," said Clancy. "You could do worse."

Homer snickered. "Pretty hard up when you starts dredgin' Dredges."

Finton just looked at him and said, "You're an arsehole." Homer's only response was laughter, tinged with meanness. As far as the older brother was concerned, his mission had been accomplished.

He went back to see Morgan the next afternoon, New Year's Day. She was wearing a swirly, red dress that came to her knees; she was just finishing a cup of tea with her mother. "I can see he wants to talk to ya alone," said Miss Bridie, and she took her tea to the living room. Since she didn't read and had no TV, Finton couldn't imagine what she would do in there by herself. Most likely, she just eavesdropped.

Morgan yawned and leaned forward, showcasing her cleavage. Some days it felt, for Finton, like the world was full of things he shouldn't look at or listen to. And, increasingly, his world was full of boobs. Being a gentleman, he averted his eyes most of the time. "Only got a few minutes—what's on yer mind?" she asked.

"You're a girl," he said.

"Thank you for noticing." She smiled smartly and winked at him.

"What I mean is, there's this girl I like."

"Mary Connelly. Lives just up the road."

He nodded, feeling his cheeks flush. Everyone seemed to know about his crush on Mary. "So, should I tell her I like her, or should I not? I don't know what girls like."

"Keep it to yourself," she said as she lifted the cup to her lips. "A good girl like that likes a little mystery. Know what I mean?"

"Not really."

"Well, maybe that's a story for another time. But trust me, okay?" She suddenly stood up. "I gotta go. Got a hot date."

"With who?"

"That, dear boy, is none of your business." With that, she was gone up the stairs to make some last minute adjustments to her look, and, though Finton waited for Miss Bridie's return, she never came. So he let himself out, more confused than ever.

The remaining days of Christmas vacation were filled with sliding, reading, and watching TV. Gradually, the days faded backwards into a river of endlessness, and Christmas receded like a repetitive dream. Just before he fell asleep on the last day of the holidays, he breathed a sigh of relief and drifted off to sleep, secure in the knowledge that school started tomorrow and at least he would be occupied.

Of course, that also meant he had to face Alicia Dredge. He would have to thank her for the gift, and people would see him talking to her. Bad enough she was a girl, but she was also a Dredge, so there was an excellent chance his reputation would suffer.

The night passed slowly and darkly. Finton tossed and turned. He tried listening to the Bruins' game on his transistor radio, under the covers with the bud in one ear, but mostly he got static and the announcer's voice fading in and out.

Eventually, morning came and he was summoned out of bed by his mother: "Time to get up! Everybody! Clancy! Homer! Finton! Get out of bed! Toast is ready! Oatmeal's gettin' cold!"

Finton managed to heave himself off the side of the bed and get dressed. Entering the kitchen, he marveled at how his mother managed to do it all. His powers of perception were as sharp as ever, but he had gradually adapted to them and no longer allowed them to distract him, or at least not so often. Still, it was as if he was noticing for the first time that every morning his mother put five plates on the table (Nanny Moon most often opting to fend for herself), each one stacked with four thick slices of homemade bread, alongside a small bowl of porridge. Most mornings, they all had seconds—Finton's record was ten slices of bread and two bowls of porridge. But today he could only manage two slices and gave away one each to Clancy and Homer.

Skeet was on the bus, beating out "Me and Julio" on the back of the padded seat in rhythm with the radio blaring from the tinny speakers.

Alicia Dredge sat in the back, as usual, gazing out the window. Dolly sat across from Finton, scanning *Flight Into Danger* while she cracked her bubble gum. She spoke to him once in a while, but he paid little attention. She was asking questions, such as, Why didn't the pilot just take Tums or make himself vomit after he ate the poisoned fish? "The poisoned *poisson*," she said.

Mary didn't get on the bus that morning, which made Finton worry about her. But he kept his concern to himself.

Rolling around the turns and past the various beaches, along the side routes and back roads, the bus driver picked up kids all over North Darwin. All Finton could think about, besides Mary, was that inevitable meeting with Alicia. When they arrived at the school, before she'd even gotten up from her seat, he fled the bus and hung out by the swings, turning his head away as she entered.

When he came into the classroom, she was sitting in her usual spot. Except, she looked different. At first, he couldn't quite put his finger on it, but occasionally he would glance in her direction when he figured she wouldn't notice. She'd washed her hair for sure. But her clothes seemed better—cleaner and more carefully chosen. She was also wearing makeup, her cheeks being rosier and her lips redder.

He wondered whatever made her buy *To Kill a Mockingbird* for him, especially when he hadn't bought anything for her. It was an amazing story, full of ideas that could hardly fit into his head. The author had written things that Finton had often thought about the world— especially its injustices and the way some people, Negroes in particular, are ghettoized because of the way they look or their lack of money. And Scout's father was a good man, the kind of man every child could be proud to call "Dad." He wondered again whether there was something about him that made her buy it for him. Or maybe it was something about her. He had decided over the holidays that any girl who would even think of reading a book like that, let alone give it to him, was probably a girl worth knowing. The problem, of course, was that that girl was Alicia Dredge.

The book had also made him wonder if he could write a story like that. Over the Christmas holidays, he finished the one about the corpse in the woods, and he wondered if one of his teachers might like to read it. That, however, would take the kind of courage he wasn't sure he possessed. The very idea of someone reading his secret thoughts was terrifying because, chances were, they would mock him—his inadequate vocabulary, his poor attempts at storytelling, and, worst of all, his all-too-obvious vulnerability.

"Hi, Finton." He awoke from his reverie to see her waving and smiling at him. "Did you have a good holiday?"

"It was all right." His tongue felt swollen and thick in his mouth. Out of the corner of his eye, he saw Bernard Crowley, a few rows over, nudge Cocky Munro, both of them eavesdropping and grinning. *Arseholes*, he thought.

"Did the usual," he said in a lowered voice. "You know—games, hockey, food. How about you?"

She appeared crestfallen, looking up at him with those big *Texas Across the River* eyes, and something in his heart stirred for her. It wasn't love or lust or anything romantic. He just felt sorry for her. And ashamed of himself.

"It was okay," she said. "Lots of drinking at our house. You know what it's like."

"Yeah." He nodded earnestly, desperate to deter the subject from the gift she'd given him.

"Did you happen to read any good books?" The hope and sadness that commingled in her eyes were almost enough to make him blurt out the truth—to profess his undying devotion to Scout and Atticus, Jem and Boo, and Calpurnia, too, and to pour out his gratitude for the privilege she'd given him.

"No," he said. "I didn't have much time."

She nodded and lowered her head. "That's too bad."

He felt his heart leap to his throat, and this time, he managed to speak the right words. "I did… actually… read one… actually. I loved the book you gave me."

"Really?" Her cheeks beamed rosy and her eyes twinkled with a happiness he'd never seen in her before. Her entire body seemed to levitate from the desk and, suddenly, she seemed twice as good-looking as before, nearly as pretty as Mary. "I thought you would. I figured you were just the kind of boy who would love it."

The final bell rang just as the teacher came in, smiling pleasantly, and said she hoped they'd all had a chance to read ahead in the curriculum over the holidays.

Finton sneaked the occasional peek at Alicia, who was still glowing, practically vibrating. Once, she caught him looking, and her face burst into a pleasant smile as she blinked slowly and averted her eyes to the blackboard.

As gratified as he was to have made Alicia smile, Finton was disconcerted to see Mary Connelly's empty desk. Most likely, she was just sick. But he wondered if she'd pieced together the Paris puzzle. Somehow he doubted that she'd spent any time thinking about him, let alone laying her hands on something he'd given her.

The day would be long, as most days would be. But tomorrow forever brought reason for optimism. Tomorrow, Mary might be back, and the world might look brighter. But at least he'd made Alicia smile, which felt better to him than he'd thought it could.

Questioning

That evening, just after supper, Finton was scribbling a new story at the kitchen table when the telephone rang and startled him. Clancy and Homer were watching a *Happy Days* rerun, Nanny Moon was in her bedroom, and Elsie had gone to the bathroom. His mother banged on the wall and yelled, "Get that, please!" The voice on the telephone raised the hairs on his neck.

"Put your mother on."

"Are you all right?"

"Put your mother on *now*."

He called out to Elsie, who immediately came running.

"It's Dad." He handed the phone to her.

"Tom, where are you?"

Finton could hear only a small voice coming from the receiver. But his mother's complexion suddenly paled.

"Come home," she said. "Just come home."

She listened some more. The tone of the small voice was sharp and abrupt, trailing off at the end of each sentence. "I'll be there as soon as I can. Just—just hang on." She hung up and called the other two boys to the kitchen. When they'd all gathered, she told them, "Get down on your knees and pray."

"What for?" Clancy whined.

Nanny Moon appeared, wielding her Bible and giving a small cough. Her limp was unusually prominent. "What in the name of Jesus, Mary, and Joseph is going on?" She looked to the children's mother for an explanation.

"Just pray, Nanny. Boys. On your knees now. Finton, start us out with the first round of Hail Marys."

The first round of Speed Rosary began, with each Moon taking a turn, and each round quickening and quickening until Finton could feel the room spinning into an otherworldly realm, propelled by a fuel of desperation and fear. When the rosary was done, and they'd all stood up and rubbed their knees, Elsie cleared her throat and said in a shaky voice, "That was your father."

"What's wrong?" Clancy and Homer both asked at once.

"I'll explain later." She took Finton into her arms, tousling his hair in a demented way, seeming to draw comfort from his smallness. She pulled away then and gazed out the window, appearing lost. "He's at Jack's, but the police are looking for him."

They all nodded, but the two older ones were more concerned about what he'd done. "He didn't do anything." Elsie was pulling on her coat and boots. "It's just a big misunderstanding."

"It's about Sawyer, isn't it?" Nanny Moon looked directly at Finton, almost accusing him. "The bloody fool said something he shouldn't have."

"Why would you say such a thing?" Elsie had stopped in the porch to fumble for her car keys.

"Where else would such a mess come from?"

"Unless he's after beatin' someone up at Jack's." Clancy nodded as he said it, convinced of its truth.

Homer raised his fists in combat mode. "Dad wouldn't let no one off with nudding." Then he roared and raised his arms, punching the air and dancing around until Elsie slapped his face, which stood him up straight, bewildered and speechless. Finton felt sick and just wanted to crawl into a hole someplace no one could find him.

"Stop it!" Elsie said, her face tight with fear. "Just behave for Nanny Moon until I gets back." Then, she departed, coattail flying behind her as the door slammed shut.

Within moments, Nanny Moon knelt at the kitchen table and said, "Let's say the rosary again." Finton knelt with the others, but said no prayers. He imagined his father slouched in the dark corner of the tavern, his mother speeding through the dark streets, racing around turns, tortured by thoughts of raising three children alone.

Nanny Moon coughed through much of the rosary, which got him to wondering who was worried about *her*.

Just past eight-thirty, the front door opened. They must have driven under cover of darkness, headlights off, because, even though he'd been watching out the window for a couple of hours, they took Finton—and everyone else—by surprise. His mother looked haggard, while her unkempt husband smelled like beer. He propped himself up by grasping the doorknob.

"I'm home," he said, stomping the slush from his boots onto the doormat. "Those lousy bastards are lookin' for me, but I'm too smart for the fuckin' works." Elsie and Clancy helped ease his backside into a chair, and he leaned his right arm on the table. Spittle flew from his face as he ranted, his eyes feral like those of a cornered mountain lion. "None o' the Moons have ever gone to jail, and I'll be goddamned if I'll be the first."

"Tut-tut." Elsie shook her head. "Not in front of the boys, Tom."

"Who are ya goin' on about, Tom?" Nanny Moon looked worried, scrolling through her rosary beads.

"I'm sorry," Tom said as he covered his eyes with both palms. "I'm so sorry."

"What have ya got to be sorry about?" Nanny Moon asked. "You didn't kill him sure… did ya now?"

Finton was still marveling at the strange scene when a knock came on the door.

"I'm sorry, Tom. Just doing our jobs." That's what Futterman said as he took their father by the arm and hoisted him to his feet. Tom passively resisted and called him a "lousy mainland fucker." But it was the same pair of officers who'd been at the house several times before, and they didn't seem to take Tom's comments to heart.

Futterman tried again. "Easy now, Tom. We're just goin' down to the station for a talk, see if we can straighten out this mess, okay?"

They talked to him as if he was a wounded animal that might attack if they made any sudden moves. Kieran Dredge gently lifted Tom's opposite arm. "We're not gonna cuff you, Tom, but you gotta be civilized, okay?" His reassurance seemed directed more to the family than to the man being arrested. "Just take it easy."

Tom seemed to calm down after that. He hugged Elsie and kissed her cheek, and he nodded to his mother. He said to the boys, "Watch out fer yer mother."

"They can't take you," Finton said, and Tom bent down on one knee in front of him, his eyes drunk and tired, full of surrender—

the boy, for once, looking down on the man, as if they'd swapped places.

"I'll be back soon, b'y. They can't keep an innocent man in jail." He squinted and cocked his head to one side. "That better not be tears I see."

"It's not," said Finton, turning his face away.

"Hmph," said Tom, a hint of sarcasm in his grin as the policemen pulled him to a standing position. "Imagine that."

They all followed as the officers escorted their prisoner to the cruiser. A cool January breeze ruffled Tom's hair as he stood by the open police car door to observe his family one last time. He seemed to be trying to commit their faces to memory. Elsie cried and fell to her knees in the snow, despite the physical support from the two older boys, one at each of her elbows. "Please don't take him! Please, please, God!"

Kieran came over and removed his cap. "It's just for questioning, Mrs. Moon. If he's innocent, he'll be back in no time."

They all just watched him as if he'd read from the Good Book. He put his cap back on, returned to the car, slammed the door shut and rolled backwards down the lane without flashing lights or siren.

"Proclaim release to the captives and recovery of sight to the blind!" Nanny Moon said, blessing the night air with the sign of the cross, clouds of breath billowing from her mouth. "And let the oppressed go free. Jesus, have mercy on us all." It was a queer thing to say since Finton wasn't sure his father was oppressed or would even go free. But maybe the old woman was right to believe it.

Futterman was certain of Tom's guilt. Over and over the corporal said, "We got the body. We got witnesses that say you gave him liquor. We even got motive."

In the end, however, they couldn't charge him, a purported argument and a beer at Jack's being insufficient evidence to try someone for murder or manslaughter. Officer Dredge brought him home the next afternoon, dazed and angry, but no worse for wear.

Tom clearly wasn't in the mood to talk about what had happened. After he'd relayed Futterman's accusations, he departed to the living room, where he spent the rest of the afternoon on the couch, gaping at the TV, gazing vacantly at the soaps and after-school specials. He didn't eat supper with the family, just sat and stared. After finishing his own supper quickly, Finton sat and watched with his father in silence. One of the big stories on the suppertime news was that President Nixon was in some kind of trouble for withholding evidence in a scandal that was making him look terrible in the eyes of the American people. When the newscast was over, Tom got up and turned off the set. He stood in front of the TV and watched the screen darken, the bright dot in the centre fading away. "They got no proof," he said, then sat down again and stared at the screen.

Things just got worse as the week progressed. Wednesday morning, he rushed from the house and barely caught the school bus. But there was no Mary. As the week progressed, the classrooms got emptier because of a flu that was going around.

"Mary's got pneumonia," Dolly told him, and he figured he should buy Mary something to keep her mind off her illness, to help her pass the time alone. He imagined her lying in bed all day in great pain, unable to move and wanting something to do.

After school on Thursday, he got off the bus at Mary's place and walked up to her front step. The Connelly house was the nicest in that part of Darwin, standing out from the landscape by virtue of its pristine beauty. Although better kept than most houses in Darwin, Mary's home was a modest two-storey with pink trim to highlight the white clapboard. Despite the brown muck of a false spring that debased the rest of the town, the Connelly front yard was flawless, looking as if it had been puritanically swept.

Mary's mother answered the doorbell in a pink track suit and sneakers. He'd seen Sylvia Connelly around town, but she was always at mass or the grocery store, or some school function where she always wore a dress, high heels, and pearls.

"Hi, Mrs. Connelly. Is Mary here?"

She glanced with bewilderment from his face to the present in his hand. "Mary can't come to the door. She's sick."

"Can you give her this, please?"

Smiling, she took it from him. As he was leaving, she called out to him. "Mary's very ill, and she's contagious. Maybe if you came back next week."

He walked home in a weep of falling snow, consoled that there was a reason he didn't get past the front door and resolved that he would return next week, and every week thereafter, until he saw her. Maybe he could even help her get better.

In late January, Kieran Dredge dropped by the house and gathered everyone together in the kitchen. It was fairly obvious that Clancy and Homer were clueless about the whole affair. Homer seemed uncomfortable even talking about Sawyer and simply said, "I'm glad he's dead." Nanny Moon and Elsie weren't able to contribute much either, but they listened with a mixture of fascination and dread.

Tom repeated the few facts that were known, and Kieran kept tapping his fingers on the table as if something didn't quite make sense. At one point, he leaned back in his chair and pushed his shiny-billed cap back on his head, impressing Finton with how confident and wise he appeared.

"I've got to admit, Tom, it doesn't look good for you." Kieran stood up, obviously wanting to pace, but since there was no room, he stuffed his hands into his pockets and leaned back against the kitchen counter. "There's not enough to convict you for murder, obviously, and the coroner says he died of exposure. But there was a blow to Sawyer's head that probably played a role. Either way, you're our only suspect. A man was killed and, sooner or later, according to Futterman, we're going to have to arrest somebody. Make no mistake."

The speech might have been impressive, but the message was terrifying.

"The evidence is all circumstantial," Kieran added, addressing the entire family. "That's not to say Tom did nothing wrong. He shouldn't have given Sawyer a beer, knowing full well it would have a bad effect on his medication. And people are talking, beyond that—stuff that makes you look bad."

"No matter what they said, I'm not a killer," Tom declared, leaving Kieran just as mystified as when he'd arrived.

Following that afternoon, every now and then throughout the winter, Kieran would come over and corner one of the boys for a chat, and Finton supposed he asked all of them the same questions. One warmish day in the middle of March, he got Finton alone on the front step and sat down beside him, Kieran's long, gangly legs spread wide, nearly pointing East and West, while his policeman's hat, with the shiny bill and the broad yellow strip around the band, hung from his long fingertips. The pose reminded Finton of the graceful way his father would handle a fishing pole.

"Did Sawyer ever touch you in a certain way, Finton?"

"Once," he said. "In the woods by the school. Nothin' serious."

Suddenly, he recalled the exact moment. Coming upon Sawyer sitting on a stump. The crazed look in his eyes. The crow cawing. He remembered going to the Planet of Solitude, a detail he kept to himself. Then Skeet had come back for him, but Sawyer was gone.

"Did your father know?"

"I never told him."

"What about either of your brothers?" Finton shrugged. Kieran cleared his throat and seemed a little edgy, squirming his backside on the concrete until he was good and settled. "What I mean is, did either of them start acting *different* at some point?"

He immediately thought of Homer that summer when he, all of a sudden, seemed to be spending more time on his own, barring himself in his bedroom and turning the music up loud. He wondered if it would get Homer in trouble if he told. It occurred to him that Kieran knew the same thing he did—that motives for killing Sawyer Moon were so plentiful they practically grew on trees.

But Kieran spared his dilemma. "I already talked to Homer."

"What did he tell you?"

"Well, now, I can't tell you that. But if you can think of anything else…"

With a shake of his head, Finton drew a curtain of silence between them. He stared straight ahead, trying to convey that it was time to move on.

Mary's seat on the bus remained empty. The ride to school was long and boring, for there were no other girls he loved nearly as much. There were a few whom he considered good-looking, but they weren't reachable like Mary, or nearly as pretty. They had looser morals and ways he didn't approve of.

He had learned from his teachers and parents that women weren't supposed to smoke, drink, or say bad words. They didn't talk back to anyone, and they didn't make loud or rude noises. They didn't romp in the grass with boys or play boys' games. And they always went to mass, carried a prayer book and recited every word of the priest's service. They certainly did well in school while they waited for a boy their own age to ask them to the school dances, then later the prom, and then finally to be engaged and married. Although it was fine if they wanted to be teachers, nurses, and secretaries to earn extra money for the household, they didn't need to aspire to careers and would certainly give up working as soon as the first baby was coming. That was the woman's main job—to stay pure for her husband until she could bear his children.

Mary could be all that and more. Even though she was smart, she was traditional in ways that he liked. Finton wanted an old-fashioned girl and, while Darwin had quite a few of those, it also had more than its share of skanks and streels.

So he focused on a girl he would be proud to have.

When the weekend came, however, he still hadn't seen her.

"Jesus, your girlfriend's not here again today," Skeet pointed out to him on Friday. "She must really be dyin' or something."

"She's not my girlfriend." But Finton was beginning to wonder just how sick Mary was. His worst fears were confirmed when Miss Woolfred started out the morning prayer by asking everyone to remember Mary Connelly because she was sick and her mother requested that they pray for her.

Sunday morning, she wasn't in church, nor was her family. When Father Power dedicated the mass to "the Connelly's dear little girl, Mary," Finton felt a lump in his throat and a ball of gunk at the pit of his stomach.

He went home after mass and went straight to the bedroom to pray. Kneeling on his bed and looking up at the crucified Jesus, he repeatedly asked God to save her. He was still kneeling when Homer and Clancy crashed into the room, laughing and roughhousing.

"Didn't you get enough o' that in mass?" Clancy asked.

Homer asked if he'd heard about Mary Connelly. Finton stopped praying and looked at his brother, who actually appeared sombre. "I can't believe she's that sick. I mean, she's only your age, isn't she?"

"She's in my class."

"She's cute too," said Clancy. "I'm surprised you're not after her."

He felt his heart grow tight in his chest. "Me and Mary are friends."

"Better her than that Dredge streel." Homer chuckled. "Anyway, it don't look like you'll be friends for much longer."

Finton launched himself towards Homer's throat, knocking his brother onto Clancy's bed. "Shut up!" he yelled. "Just shut your goddamn mouth!"

Homer was able to fend him off, and it didn't take long before Clancy managed to peel the younger away from the elder. By then,

Nanny Moon and both parents had come rushing in to demand an explanation.

"He's pissed at me because his friggin' girlfriend is sick." Homer straightened himself up and sniffed, touching a couple of fingers to his nose. Then he smirked at Finton. "You swore."

"Never."

"I heard you." Homer looked to their mother. "Finton said the g-d word."

"Finton, you didn't." The disappointment in his mother's eyes hurt him as much as any words or hitting could do. But Finton locked his lips tight, for fear he might incriminate himself—advice he'd gotten from watching *Perry Mason*.

"Jesus, you're bleedin'," said Elsie, frowning in Homer's direction. "Let's get you cleaned up." Before whisking Homer to the bathroom for repairs, she turned back to Finton. "And you, I'd suggest, better get your act together. Good boys don't hit their brothers and make them bleed. And they certainly don't take the Lord's name in vain."

"He started it," Finton yelled.

But his mother was clearly frustrated. "Don't you think we got enough to worry about around here without the likes of you actin' up and startin' rackets?"

"I'm not just gonna let him—"

"That's enough out of you," said Tom. "One more word, and you'll be grounded to your bed for the rest of this day of Our Lord."

"I don't care." Even as he said the words, Finton felt the anger welling up inside him, and all eyes turned to him. "You won't even listen to me."

His father had no choice. He knew that.

"That's it," Tom said. "Stay here till you rot. Clancy, leave him alone."

They all filed out of the bedroom, one at a time.

"I hate you," Finton said. His father halted and wheeled around, simultaneously removing his belt.

"Just say it again," he warned as he twisted the belt into a weapon and wrung it tight until the leather creaked.

Finton squared his shoulders and glared into his father's eyes. "I hate you."

Tom pulled off and slapped Finton's face with the belt. The boy fell backward and smacked his right ear against the wall as he felt the thin leather belt strike his ribs. He knew by the burning sensation on the flesh of his stomach that the belt had raised a welt.

"Say it again, ya little bastard. Say it again and I'll strike ya down!" His father was panting, eyes blazing with anger, the belt poised and ready to relaunch.

Finton knew he should stop talking, if only for his own preservation, but he couldn't help himself. He had to stand up for what was right or no one ever would. His father had become the enemy of truth. "I hate you... goddamn you."

Tom lashed out again and walloped him in the stomach, engraving his skin with a deep, red mark. Over and over, they replayed the same scene as Finton uttered the words he knew would hurt his father the most—and the father, with his leather belt, meted out justice. Several blows later, panting harder, Tom's tone shifted from angry to pleading. "Say you're sorry, and I can stop hurting you." The hand that gripped the belt was quivering. The eyes that glared at him were deep set and red.

"No," he said softly but as firmly as the first time.

The belt hit him again. And every time his father asked, Finton refused, and Tom would wallop him. "Had enough?" Tom arched the belt, prepared to strike another blow.

Finton could hear no other voices. Everyone must have left. He'd closed his eyes, but he wouldn't cry. Wouldn't allow him the satisfaction. His entire body sang with the sting of the many lashes, but the words that could save him would not rise to his throat. "I said, did you have enough, or do I have to hit you again?" Tom sounded tired—if not quite defeated—as if he, too, had had enough of the senseless torture.

Finton was tempted to just give in, to just say the required words that would signal his repentance, but also his insufficiency. Finally, he managed to open his eyes and look up at his father, tears on the brink of falling forward. He knew his father would show no mercy. But mercy was neither what he wanted, nor needed.

"I love you," Finton said.

For a moment, Tom stood and stared at his youngest son. Then he wrapped the belt around his trembling palm and left without a word, shutting the door behind him.

At first, Finton just lay on his bed, dazed, damaged, and confused, wondering how everything had spun out of control so fast. While Tom waited for some word about a police investigation in which he was the only suspect, he was under extreme duress. So Finton already forgave him. Nonetheless, Tom seemed to be afraid of his own son and, while demonstrations of emotion had never been his father's specialty, lately something had driven a wedge between them.

Finton nearly wore out his brain thinking about it, but his thoughts eventually turned to Mary Connelly, lying on her own bed in her house up the road, barely able to breathe. Sad and afraid, he closed his eyes and the room fell dark. Ripples of colour quivered like sound waves—radiant splashes of orange and violet, inflected by occasional ink-blot splashes of candy apple red and blueberry blue. His soul soared upward, rocketed through the air and thrust forward, up and away, until the heavens turned black, then suddenly exploded in an infinite plethora of colours. All around him danced ten thousand points of light—stars and planets of every shade, both subtle and vibrant. Round and colossal, they were so close he could almost touch them. He soared upward slowly, purposefully. Looking down, he realized he was gravitating towards a hunter-green surface, alive with tendrils of waving grass—at last, his Planet of Solitude. Before him the universe lay apocalyptically bare—extravagant, exposed and divine. Stars zoomed past and exploded in the dark midair, crashing into nothingness, while manifold comets roared arbitrarily overhead.

At last, his feet conquered the luxuriant surface of the planet, and he found himself sitting beneath his tree. He'd sat here before on this same patch of grass with his back against the towering apple tree, which sprouted red fruit hanging low.

He channeled his thoughts towards Mary, how sick she was. How congested her chest was. She coughed now and then, but it hurt so much that she forcibly held back. Her skin was pale, her face rashed. All around her people gathered to pray while her mother sat beside her, holding her hand, and her father stood by the window, looking out. Above the bed hung a large crucifix. Mary was speaking, but he couldn't hear the words. He focused hard, leaning towards her, nearly touching her.

But her lips didn't move.

What are you trying to say?

I'm ready to let go.

But you can't.

Don't wanna be sick no more. Just wanna feel better.

I can help you. I can come to you.

He tried to imagine her with him beneath the tree. But he could no more conjure her there in his lap than he could invoke himself into her bedroom.

Understanding what he needed to do, he opened his eyes, startled by the shift into mundane reality. He concentrated on the bedroom window, but the light hurt his eyes. He wondered how long he'd been gone.

A sound arose from outside his bedroom door. "Hello?" he asked.

The door opened a crack. "I just came in to see if you were all right."

"I'm okay."

"I was in my room, and to be honest, I didn't want to get in the way of your father's wrath."

He watched Nanny Moon step inside and close the bedroom door behind her. She perched on the edge of the bed, her back turned partially towards him. "I don't know what's going on between the two of you, Finton. But you're going to have to be more careful around him. Your father is under an awful strain. Don't talk back so much." She looked at him as if guessing his thoughts. Her eyes were softer, moister than he'd ever seen them. But then, Nanny Moon wasn't usually the effusive type. "I know it's hard for you." She chuckled. "You're the one they said was going to take on the world some day."

He blinked, shocked at this reference to his first days. "Who said?"

"We all said. You came in through the front door practically ready for a battle. For hours, you did nothing but cry, and we all wondered if you were gonna bawl yourself—or us—to death. We were ready to kill either you or ourselves. But I thought you were crying for the state of the world you'd found yourself in. It was like you didn't belong here, and the next thing you knew, here you were."

Finton suddenly felt embarrassed for the tears he'd almost cried earlier. "Nanny Moon?"

"What is it?"

"Are the stories true?"

"Most stories are lies, but I s'pose they're true just the same."

"The ones about when I was born." Finton drew a deep breath and wondered if he dared to ask. "Did it really happen the way they said?"

"Well, I s'pose that depends on who's doin' the telling." She paused, then seemed to sober as if realizing she wouldn't get off so easily. "I could tell you not to mind any of it. It don't really matter, ya know."

"But…"

"But the fact is, you were born. Isn't that all that matters?"

"But it feels like everyone is just making stuff up."

"Yes, b'y. I s'pose it does. But the truth is, your mother and father loves you very much, and if there's anything you needs to know, then they're the ones who should be sayin' it—certainly not the likes o' me."

He wasn't comforted by her words. In fact, they made him more confident that his past was a door which he needed to open and walk through. Someday.

"Don't worry," Nanny Moon said, patting his ankle. "You've always been the toughest of the Moons. I think they're afraid of what you can do."

"What can I do?" he asked, his heart thrumming. "I'm the smallest one."

"The smallest, but the biggest." She smiled weakly.

"I don't understand."

His grandmother sighed and patted his leg. As she got to her feet, she groaned as though she were lifting a thousand pounds. Finton was suddenly aware of how old she was. Turning towards her, he noted the lines on her face, the bend in her back.

"You don't have to understand, darlin'. Just believe."

"Believe what?"

She smiled wistfully and leaned down to kiss him on the cheek with her soft, cold lips. "You'll know when the time comes. Meanwhile, be careful. No matter what you think, you're not invincible. Do what you think is right and the world will come to you."

She asked if there was anything she could get for him. But, as there was nothing he wanted, she departed, shutting the door and leaving him alone.

She was no sooner gone than he stood up and dashed to the window. Then he pushed back the curtains, forced open the latch, hoisted the window and clambered out.

The Turning

The Connelly driveway was crammed with cars, which made him wonder if he was too late. Even as he strode up the front step and rapped on the wooden door, he fought the urge to barge in and bolt past everyone, fly up the stairs and find her.

He didn't recognize the person who opened the door—probably some relative—so he asked if he could see Mary.

"It's not a good time." The young woman's voice quavered. "Mary's not well."

"I need to see her."

"I'm sorry. Come back another time." Her eyes were distant, brimming with tears, as she started to close the door.

"I can help her."

"Only God can help Mary now." The door was shut in his face, and Finton found himself on the outside, looking up at the brass knocker.

He grabbed hold of it and again banged on the door. There was only one entrance, and it was the one he needed to go through.

"I've got to see her," he demanded, more forcefully than he thought himself capable of.

"Well, you can't. Now please go away." The young woman, whom he'd thought pretty, was becoming less attractive.

"No one can help Mary the way I can."

She'd been about to slam the door again, but she paused, appraising him with her big, sad eyes. "What can you do? You're just a boy. And an ignorant one at that."

"I can—" He hesitated, unsure of what to tell her that wouldn't sound naïve or insane.

"You can what?"

"I can comfort her. I'm her friend, Finton Moon, from down the road. We're in the same class. Can I just see her? It won't take long. She'd *want* to see me."

Something softened in the young woman's face, and she glanced behind her. "Just a minute." She left the door ajar as she turned to talk with someone. Finton was tempted to sneak inside, but he remembered what that kind of brashness had earned him from his father. One false word or move, and the whole enterprise would be jeopardized. He had to do it right, for Mary's sake. *Be calm and be careful*, Nanny Moon had said.

At last, the young woman came back to the door, shaking her head. "Mary can't see anyone. And her mother said for me not to let anyone in, especially a Moon."

"But if I can't see her, I can't help her."

"You need to go home. This family's had enough upset without you coming along and making it harder. No one here even knows who you are—but we knows your father, and that's enough."

"That don't matter." He summoned the strength to disobey, despite his trembling legs. "*I* know Mary—that's what matters."

"I'm sorry—" she started to explain again, even as she averted her eyes and began closing the door. He bolted past her and dashed up the stairs.

When he arrived at the entrance to the bedroom, she was lying in bed, the covers pulled to her chin as she shivered uncontrollably. Near the window, her father gazed out at the backyard, barely giving Finton a glance.

"What do you want?" Her mother appeared startled, sitting beside Mary and holding her hand. "Oh, you—didn't Teresa send you away? Who do you think you are?"

"Finton Moon," he said as he sniffled and swiped at his nose. "I'm here to save Mary."

The room smelled like mothballs and vomit, with a hint of Lemon Pledge. The earth-brown curtains were drawn shut, and Mary's body was swaddled in quilts, the top one an embarrassment of butterflies. Finton stepped forward as if treading on thin ice, careful of breaking through to the other side. No one spoke to him, but they all observed Mary as if by ignoring the boy they could wish him away.

He was vaguely aware of how he'd done this before. Just laid his hands on the sick part and... did something. Wish? Pray? He couldn't remember.

Somehow, he hoped, it would come to him.

He forced his way among the strangers and stood beside the bed, gazing at Mary. Despite the blotches on her sallow cheeks, she looked peaceful with her eyes closed. Stepping forward, he leaned down and kissed her forehead. Her skin was cool and clammy. Glancing around, he realized they were all watching him and waiting for something miraculous to happen, even when they didn't believe it could.

"I need space," he said. No one moved, but they all regarded him with quizzical expressions. He looked to Mary's sister, Laura. "I can't do it with everyone watching."

"Do what?" she asked. "There's nothing to do. Let God take His course."

"Maybe God's busy," he said.

"You mean to say you think God sent you?" A general sense of unease invaded the room as people began to squirm in their seats.

"I just came to see if I could help." Finton shrugged. "I've done it before."

"What have you done before?"

"Helped sick people."

"I've heard about you." Sylvia Connelly cleared her throat and stared at him. "Bridie Battenhatch."

Finton nodded, certain she was now going to toss him out.

"The doctor says it's useless. And I never put no stock in that nonsense with Miss Bridie." But she nodded towards her sick daughter. "See what you can do."

He knelt on the floor and folded back the covers from the side of the bed, slowly so as not to disturb her. Fumbling around, he at last found Mary's cold hand and clasped it in his own. He closed his eyes and focused.

He saw the room go dark. The myriad colours. The flashes of red. The white apple tree on the Planet of Solitude.

But it didn't feel real. He wasn't there. The images were inventions of his conscious mind. When he opened his eyes, they were all looking at him, simultaneously expecting and doubting. If the situation wasn't so grave, they might have laughed at him.

"Say the rosary," he said softly.

"What?" Laura's eyebrows were raised in skepticism.

"Hail Mary full of grace, the Lord is with thee." Finton started it himself. The words tumbled from his mouth like pebbles—heavy, clumsy, and useless. *If God doesn't save her, there is no God.* That's what he kept thinking while he was praying. When a couple of other voices joined in and blended with his, he sped up the words. Gradually, they accumulated a force of their own and began to traverse the air around them, spinning about their heads like pixie dust from the wands of mischievous fairies. That was how he imagined it—the words circumnavigating the room like a purple streak of light, weaving in and out between them, pinging off the walls and occasionally flitting upon Mary's upturned nose.

"Blessed art thou amongst women and blessed is the fruit of thy womb, Jesus."

Over and over, they said the words, led by Finton, whose mind disengaged and started to wander, not to the Planet of Solitude, but to Mary's mind.

WakeupwakeupwakeupsweetMaryLordiswiththeehailmaryfullofgraceilove you

please wake up

They were still reciting the rosary when he felt a tingle in his hands, then a tremor. He opened his eyes. Mary was looking at him.

He heard a gasp from Sylvia, and the rosary stopped.

"She's awake!" someone whispered.

Someone else repeated it, louder. Then someone shouted it.

The room fell silent.

"Mary?" Sylvia shuffled closer to her daughter and swiped her hand over Mary's glistening forehead. "Mary, are you awake?"

But Mary made no sound and neither did she move. Her face lacked any expression. What he'd seen and heard might have been one last gasp.

On the window ledge outside, a robin sang.

The next few minutes were a blur. Sylvia Connelly fell prostrate across her daughter, weeping and wailing, while Laura sank to her knees and thanked Jesus. Mr. Connelly turned from the window and, upon seeing his daughter awake, he fell to his knees beside the bed, arm around his wife's waist, and sobbing. The others seemed too stunned to know what to do, let alone comprehend what had happened.

"A miracle!" one old man whispered, gazing at the picture of Jesus and blessing himself. "A miracle!" most of the others echoed, and they, too, looked at the picture and made the sign of the cross on their bodies.

Finton squeezed closer to the bedside, but Sylvia was blocking Mary's face. When at last he was able to glimpse her features, the blotchiness was still there, but she didn't seem quite so pale. Her eyes were open but uncomprehending.

The moment she blinked, he became aware of a sharp twinge in his right temple, and his head started to pound. As he rubbed the side of his head, she blinked again and it was as if her vision began to clear, as her pupils reset and focused. And finally, she coughed, sending everyone into a frenzy of thanks-be-to-Jesuses and hallelujahs!

"Some water!" someone said, and within seconds, the young woman who, earlier, had blocked the front door, scurried in with a filled glass.

Once he realized that no one was paying him any attention, Finton slipped out the bedroom door and crept down the stairs. He felt nauseous as he stumbled down the last few steps and banged his shoulder against the railing.

By the time he'd opened the front door, they were all praying another rosary, sounding like an Easter mass in the throes of joyful gloom.

"Where are you going?"

He halted in the open doorway and looked behind him to see the same family friend at the top of the stairs, arms folded across her chest and tears on her cheeks. She tried to dry them, but couldn't stem the tide.

"Home."

He stepped out and pulled the door closed, but not before he heard her yell out in a quivery voice. "If you're not the devil's imp!"

It wasn't thanks, but it would do.

When he got home, his mother was on the phone.

"I will," Elsie said, her face tight with anger. "Where were you?" He suddenly remembered that he'd left by the bedroom window and should have returned that way.

"Out."

"That was Laura Connelly. She says there was quite the goings-on over at their place." She regarded him closely, but Finton gave nothing away. "Says you were at the centre of it."

"I went over to see how Mary was doing." He left her in the kitchen with an unreadable look on her face. As he lay on his bed, he stared out at the afternoon sky. The sun had arrived, and the shadows of trees had lengthened and deepened. His head pounded, with thoughts pinging like a pinball as he tried to comprehend what had happened. He couldn't rid himself of the feeling that he'd had little to do with Mary's recovery, that somehow it had actually been Mary herself who simply had used Finton as a lifeline to pull herself out. Still, it would do no good to tell that to the rosary-sayers.

"Finton?" His mother, after some hesitation, had followed him into the room. "Are you all right?"

He said he was fine, but she sat on his bed and pushed up each of his sleeves, then ordered him to roll onto his stomach while she pulled up his shirt; then she did the same for his back. "You don't have no scars," she said, her voice trembling. "No bruises. No cuts."

"I don't get many cuts—or bruises. You know that." He saw no point in mentioning his headache.

"I knew it." She nodded vaguely. "But I didn't… think about it."

His father's heavy footsteps came down the hall, and he peered around the doorway. "What's goin' on in here?"

"Nothing," Elsie said and held her breath. "Just comforting him after what you put him through." She seemed grateful when he retreated wordlessly to the living room.

"You can't tell anyone about this thing with Mary, okay?"

"Why?"

"Because they wouldn't understand."

He said he wouldn't, but he couldn't help thinking about the witnesses at the Connelly house. It might not be so easy to silence them.

The Days After

It turned out that no one who'd been at the Connelly house cared to keep the story to themselves. After Finton had left, Mary gradually awakened more and more, and began to recognize her surroundings, as well as the faces of those who had gathered. A short time later, her fever returned, but her mother placed cold cloths on her forehead and gave her water, and the fever quickly receded.

When the real change happened, it was radical. "Miraculous" was the word most often used. "I don't care what his father done or didn't do—that little Finton is a miracle worker," Sylvia Connelly told anyone who would listen. The next day, she was at the grocery store, shopping for ice cream and any food she thought might tempt her daughter. Each time someone asked about Mary's health—which was nearly everyone—she told them the story of how this young fellow from up the road had come to the door asking to help, and the next thing they knew, Mary was sitting up and drinking chicken soup.

"What was wrong with her?" they'd ask.

Sylvia would just shake her head and shrug her shoulders. "The doctors never said. Could have been a virus, some kinda new disease. It started out as pneumonia. But she don't have it no more. Young Finton cured her."

"But how did he do it?" they would want to know.

"He put his hands on her hands—and said some prayers."

"Amazing!"

"He's a little saint, is what he is. I'll be singing his praises to the rafters for the rest of my days."

"Don't blame ya, girl. If it was my young one saved from death's door, I'd be singing the glory hallelujahs too!"

"It was the strangest thing, though," Sylvia would say with a perplexed look on her face, as if the mysteries of the universe were threatening to unfold in her brain.

"What's that?"

"Well, when he took to saying the rosary, he was like—I don't know—his eyes were all fluttery, and he started saying it faster and faster. None of us could keep up with him."

"The rosary!"

"That's what he did."

"He must be one o' them what-ya-call-its? Prophets. That's it. He's a messenger from Jesus!"

"Well, I dunno." Sylvia would start to walk away then, talking over her shoulder and laughing. "He's something, for sure."

And she'd go off a few feet, only to be stopped by someone else, inquiring about Mary, and she'd start the same dialogue again.

Elsie Moon happened to be in the supermarket that Monday morning, with her green bandana tied around her head, getting checked out as fast as she could. It must have scared her, Finton thought as she told the story at suppertime, because she looked as if the worst thing in the world had happened.

"You'll have to be extra careful from now on," she told him.

"Careful?" Tom wiped the gravy from his chin using the back of his hand. "What in hell's name for?"

Finton glanced back and forth from one parent to the other.

Elsie wouldn't even look at him. "People might not take it the way he means it."

"People!" Nanny Moon guffawed. "People can go to hell if they don't know how to take it. Finton's a child of God, plain as the nose on their face. If they can't see that, they can kiss my arse and Finny's." She hoisted a half potato towards her mouth, paused and added, "And they can kiss Jesus's arse too."

"Nanny Moon!" Elsie's knuckles whitened around the fork handle.

"He held hands with Mary Connelly. Big, fat, hairy deal," Homer said. "I would've at least got a feel out of 'er while I was at it."

"Shut up, you!"

"Finton, that's enough." Tom cast him a glare that made him lower his eyes and pretend to eat. "Homer, go to your room."

"Say a round of the rosary while you're at it," said Elsie while Tom sighed and shifted in his seat.

"For God's sake," said Tom. "This is gone too far. She just got better. That's all. She obviously wasn't as bad off as they thought."

"You know what I'd like to see." All eyes turned to Clancy. "I'd like to see Finton scare the shit outta the works of 'em. Start making the beggars work and the blind see."

"Beggars *walk*," said Finton.

"Who says all beggars are cripple? Anyways, you could make a fortune. You could make more money than Doctor Kildare."

"I don't think I want to make money that way. I'm gonna be a writer."

"A writer?" His mother scrunched her face as if she'd tasted something sour.

"I thought you were gonna be a priest." Nanny Moon blessed herself. "That's what you always said, wasn't it? And I don't see what's changed now. If anything, you should be more likely to become a boy of the cloth."

"I don't want to be a boy of the cloth. I want to write stories."

"Writers are smart," said Clancy, "And they knows big words."

"I know words," he said softly. But Clancy had struck a sensitive nerve.

"*Big* words," his brother said. "Besides, who do you know that's a writer?"

Finton fell silent rather than perpetuate the argument. Fact is, he didn't know any writers. Didn't know if just anyone could be one. But he would rather dream big and become disappointed than allow himself to be bullied into accepting his limitations.

That night, he wrote another story, this one with the premise that Jesus was born in Darwin in 1960 as a redheaded girl named Evelyn. People didn't know Evelyn was Jesus reincarnated, and they treated her with great cruelty; ultimately, Evelyn was killed by a bunch of bullies, who stoned her to death, and they all watched in the end as she ascended to heaven. He finished the story in one sitting and wrote "The End." After he'd read it over one last time, he stuck it between the pages of his English grammar book, determined to show it to Miss Woolfred.

The shouting began as soon as he got on the school bus. "Hey, there he is!" they yelled. Some ordered him to sit down with them; others shoved their books to the seat beside them or scooted over to occupy two places. The headache he'd gotten after healing Mary—or whatever he'd done—had subsided, but he was physically drained and slightly dazed, even so many hours after the incident.

He automatically scanned for Mary, but, of course, she wasn't there.

Dolly in her usual seat, looked out the window, disinterested. Skeet was at home, apparently with the same illness that had affected Mary.

"Don't let him touch you!" someone shouted. A few others started chanting: "Coo-dees! Coo-dees! Finton Moon's got coo-dees!"

Two reached towards him as if to poke him. But he didn't flinch. His best chance for survival was to assume a seat as quickly as possible. Alone in the back of the bus, Alicia was surrounded by a moat of empty seats as she, too, gazed out the window. Just glancing at her would get him severely taunted.

Amid the din, Bernard Crowley cupped his mouth and yelled, "Aren't you gonna sit with yer girlfriend?" Finton wanted to shout back at him, but didn't see the point. Instead, he thought, *Forgive them, Father, for they know not what they do.*

Overwhelmed, he wheeled around and sat on the floor, behind the driver's seat.

At school, Finton wasn't normally the centre of attention, but this day they all stayed clear of him. In the classroom, he kept his head down or, alternately, stared out the window, incapable of focusing on work. Now and then, he'd catch someone looking at him—with either curiosity or disdain. Even Miss Woolfred occasionally glanced his way.

Only Alicia came up to him at recess. "They're all talking about you," she said.

"What are they saying?"

"They don't talk directly to me—you might've noticed." She tried grinning, but he saw the hurt in her eyes. "But from what I can make out, they thinks you're strange. They says you thinks you're Jesus."

"I'm not—" He caught himself in midsentence and actually grinned, remembering the story he'd written the previous night. "I don't think anything like that."

"Some of them heard you could raise the dead and heal the sick, and they thinks that's pretty cool," she said. "But that's only a few. The rest, I'd be careful of."

"Thanks."

"Oh, and Finton." She gazed right into his eyes. "You probably shouldn't have talked to me."

"Why not?" He knew why not, of course, but saw no reason to be rude.

"Just watch out for Bernard Crowley." Alicia was the only other person he knew who referred to Bernard by his real name.

"Always do," he said, standing straighter and trying to look brave. "But why in particular?"

"He's a Crowley," she said wryly. "What more reason do you need?"

Her warning haunted him for the rest of the morning. At lunchtime, he sat by himself in the cafeteria, but now and then, he noticed Bernard and the redheaded twins, Cyril and Gerald King, along with the mayor's son, Cocky Munro, talking as they looked at him. He wished he could read lips, but, on second thought, was grateful he could not.

The entire day, Alicia was the only person who talked to him. But as he was leaving for the day, he stopped and gave Miss Woolfred his reincarnated Jesus story. She actually appeared pleased and promised she would read it. He was just about to leave when she said, "I heard about what happened at Mary's place—is it true?"

Finton paused in the doorway. From his experience, teachers paid special attention to you only when something bad had happened and they thought you might "need to talk." But he was certain she meant well. "What did you hear?"

"That you put your hands on Mary and healed her."

He looked out the window—all those carefree children, walking together, conversing happily, on their way to normal homes where these kinds of questions never had to be asked. "I just thought I could help her," he said. "I don't know if I did. But she did get better. Dad says that's all it was—she just got better."

She furrowed her brow, looking slightly perturbed. "Well, I guess if your father says so. But then again…" she leaned in closer, and he was struck by how clear her eyes were, how kind her face was. "…I'd like to believe it was a miracle. Wouldn't you?"

Her eyes moistened, and she laid a hand on his shoulder. Although the gesture shocked him, the next thing he knew she opened her arms, and he just fell into them. He wrapped his arms around her waist and nestled his head against her chest. Her perfume reminded him of a flower-filled meadow. Three times, she ran her fingers through his hair. He wanted to stay there. Just a few seconds more. Then a little while longer. He didn't think he could actually make himself let go.

"I gotta catch the bus," he said finally.

"All right," she said as she touched the crook of a finger to the corner of her eye and wiped. "I've just noticed you were having a hard time of it lately. And I don't want any hard feelings between us. Okay?"

"Okay." He edged towards the door. "Gotta run."

"Go," she said. She waved him on. "Catch your bus."

Deciphering what it all meant was more than he could do.

Wishing to avoid a repeat of the awkward bus trip, he trekked home through the woods, two and a half miles, even though the ground was soaked and muddy.

He decided to detour to Skeet's place, to see if his friend was all right. Coming out near Moon's River and behind the Battenhatch place, Finton cut through the backyard and took a shortcut to the road. It didn't matter who saw him now. His secret was out, and he didn't care to hide.

Finton quickened his step as he passed through those woods, especially the spot where he realized that, if he just kept going straight, he'd wind up at the foxhole. The memory of the frozen corpse got him thinking about Judgment Day, on which, according to his catechism, Jesus would return from heaven and raise the dead, dividing them according to the nature of the "secrets in their hearts." Those who'd been good would enter heaven, while those who'd been wicked would go with Satan to the fires of hell. Finton could picture it all in lurid black and red images, and what he always saw at the end of his daydream was the living body of a boy being torn apart, with a flaming, red Satan grasping his left arm and a brilliant, white Jesus pulling on the right. The boy was himself, of course, and it seemed lately that the devil was winning.

He wondered if anyone would struggle for Sawyer's soul. Or his father's. Or Mary's. Or Skeet's. In his mind, Finton drew up a chart with three columns:

HEAVEN   **HELL**   **IFFY**

One by one, he went through a list of friends and family, assigning each of them to their appropriate category. His mother, unquestionably, would go to heaven. His father had once been safe, but recent events had cast his soul in doubt. His two brothers, who were always tormenting him, were "iffy." Nanny Moon was always praying, and if someone like that couldn't go straight into heaven, what was the point? Skeet was a thief; he swore and smoked; he had committed violence and probably would do so again. But there was a goodness inside him that gave Finton pause, making it impossible to relegate Skeet to hell. Neither could he designate Sawyer for eternal damnation despite the certainty that he deserved such a fate. His teachers, Father Power, some of the nuns, and all of his classmates—he decided to put them all under "iffy" and just keep a close watch on them. In future, if any of them started going more towards "Hell" than "Heaven," he would just pray extra hard for them, send them positive thoughts, or, as a last resort, take them, one at a time, to the Planet of Solitude for a good talking to.

"Skeet's sick," said his mother. The time had ticked by as he went through his mental list, and Finton barely realized he had knocked on the Stuckeys' door.

"How sick?"

Mrs. Stuckey planted her hands on her hips and sized him up. She was not an attractive woman. It wasn't just that she weighed nearly three hundred pounds despite being only five-foot-six. Nor was it just that she dressed like a "streel," as his mother said, in dresses that were raggedy, soiled, and way too small. Her grey hair was a perpetual birch broom in the fits. But, most of all, Finton didn't like her attitude. She always seemed suspicious, sizing people up as if she suspected them of trying to steal from her. He knew some overweight people and some who were untidy, but none of them gave him the heebie-jeebies like Phyllis Stuckey.

"Not sick enough to need your friggin' mumbo-jumbo or whatever you calls it."

"I don't call it anything," Finton said.

"Oh, don't give me your lip. I knows all about you and that young Connelly one. Puttin' yer hands under her bedclothes and doing the voodoo on 'er. There's something wrong with you, that's what I think. Oh, I'll be prayin' for *your* soul, that's for sure. And you'll be keepin' away from Skeet too from now on, Buster Brown."

She was about to close the door in his face when Skeet called out in a hoarse voice: "Is that me buddy?"

"Never you mind—yer too sick for company, or so ya said."

"Tell 'im to come in!"

Trying to ignore Mrs. Stuckey's eyes boring a hole through his back, Finton went into the living room where Skeet was lying on the couch with a pile of blankets over him. "You look pretty sick."

"I'm all right." Skeet coughed and rankled his nose as if to suppress a sneeze. "I'll be best kind soon. Nuttin' like a few days off from school, eh, b'y?" He winked at Finton, who thought his friend was putting up a brave front.

"You're not missin' much."

"Didn't think I was."

"Do you want me to bring you any homework?"

"Jesus, b'y—you're bringin' homework to a sick man?"

"I just thought you'd like to keep up."

Skeet started to smile but coughed instead. "I'd rather just feel better. Rotten flu."

"Can I do anything for ya?"

"Like what?" Skeet eyed his friend warily. "You're not doin' anything like ya did for Mary."

Finton struggled for the right words. "What if it helped? What if you got better, but you could stay home for a few more days, and no one would know?"

"Jesus, Moon—I'd love it, but—" He paused to cough, but suppressed the urge and just lay his head back instead. "Maybe you should go now."

"I'm sure I can do it, b'y. Have some faith."

"What are you—a preacher now?" As Finton reached to lay his hands on his friend's forehead, Skeet squirmed and brushed Finton's hand away. "Lay off, b'y. I don't want none o' that queer stuff on me."

But Finton clamped one hand on Skeet's forehead and the other on his chest.

"Fuck's sake, Moon."

"What's going on in there?"

"Nudding!" said Skeet, then lowered his voice. "Now leave me alone, luh."

But Finton wasn't listening. He closed his eyes and pictured himself soaring upward, towards the open, black sky, surrounded by stars and colorful planets and streaking comets. The voices were muffled at first, and then he couldn't hear them at all.

He wasn't sure how much time had passed before Skeet began to snore. His fever had abated, and Finton was hopeful that his friend would rest easier. He'd done all he could. He just wished it wasn't so hard to get them to listen.

When he arrived home, there were three people waiting for him, sitting on or around the front step. Finton considered ducking into the woods, except one of the visitors was Mary's sister, Laura. With her dark hair, brown eyes, freckles and slightly upturned nose, she looked like a taller, older version of Mary. But Laura seemed more devilish, in her own way, as if she was always smiling at the world, holding a secret.

"I seen what you can do." She smiled up at him from her perch on the concrete step. Something in her manner made him suspicious. Pretty, older girls like Laura Connelly didn't just show up at his doorstep without a good reason. "Mary was dying."

"Is she all right now?"

"Yesterday, I'd have said we'd be burying her this week. Today, she's sittin' up and eating." She stood to her full height and wrapped her arms around Finton, whose face was buried in her bosom. "Thank you for saving my sister."

"No problem," he said as he pulled away from her and drew a deep, life-affirming breath. "I like Mary."

"I got warts." She tugged at her sleeve and thrust one of her hands towards him. Careful not to touch her skin, he scrutinized the spot of discolouration on her thumb to which she pointed, as well as another on the knuckle of her middle finger.

"They're big," Finton said as a cold breeze whistled through the trees in the surrounding woods and whipped up through the legs of his pants; it also blew Laura's skirt so that it twirled slightly and exposed her white panty hose.

"I thought you could maybe do something about them."

He looked at her curiously, slightly alarmed by the casualness of her request.

"You know," she urged, thrusting her hand towards him. "Cure my warts. You probably could do that without blinking."

Frightened by the look in her eyes, he took hold of her hand and spread his palm over the aggrieved area.

"Now kiss it. Like you did for Mary."

Finton did as he was told, though it disgusted him to touch his lips to her clammy warts. He couldn't wait to get inside and wash his mouth, but the other two visitors had already stepped forward by the time he let go of Laura's hand.

"My mother sent me." A pasty-faced girl with brown hair sauntered forward, her arms wrapped around herself. He knew her from religion class as Sarah Wilson, the girl who always breathed through closed lips and made weird noises in her throat. "I have emphysema."

"What's that?"

"It comes from my father smokin' too much. And my two older brothers and my sister." She shrugged. "I smokes too. But we never knew it could make us sick as all that." She coughed without covering her mouth and wiped her lips with one hand. "Mudder says you're able to help me get better."

He looked at Laura, who was examining her hand. "Still got the warts?"

"Still got 'em," she said. "But they kinda seem smaller."

Finton shook his head and told the Wilson girl, "You need to go to the doctor."

"Been there. He can't do nudding. But you can—can't you?" The way she looked at him with those big, sad eyes—and then coughed again—was too much for him to bear.

"Where does it hurt?"

She placed her hand in the center of her chest and rubbed. Hesitating, he reached forward and pressed his hand atop hers. Unexpectedly, she slipped her own hand away and clamped it down over Finton's. She gazed into his eyes and smiled as tears streamed down her cheeks. He could feel the pain she'd endured and knew that it had been very hard for her these past few weeks.

In his mind, he soared to the Planet of Solitude, and sat with her under the apple tree, rocking her back and forth with his hand on her chest. Only a few seconds later, he returned, startled to be standing in front of his own house with his hand on the breast of a strange girl. "That's all I can do," he said. After he'd stuffed both of his hands into his pockets, she grabbed him by the ears and kissed him on the lips.

Finton rubbed his temple as he looked to the third visitor, a boy slightly older than himself, who stood up and limped towards him. "Put your hands on me laig, b'y."

"What's wrong with it?"

"My smallest wart is nearly gone!" Laura emitted a squeal and threw herself at Finton, wrapping him in her arms and twirling him around like a rag doll.

"I'm getting dizzy." His voice was muffled against her jacket.

Just then the front door rattled open and Nanny Moon stood there, squinting. "What's goin' on?"

"Finton cured my warts!" Laura squealed as she released Finton and began squeezing her own hand in disbelief. "You don't know what this means!"

"Oh." Nanny Moon chewed worriedly on her bottom lip. "I think I have an idea. Finny, come in to your supper."

Without a word, he tromped towards the step.

"Hey! What about my laig?"

"Oh. Sorry." Finton whirled around to face him. "What's wrong with it?"

"I hurt me knee playin' ball, and now I can't walk on it."

"Well," Finton placed one hand on the boy's thigh and the other on his knee. He closed his eyes and immediately felt the earth shift as he seemed to leave his own body. Within seconds, he was back, opening his eyes. Bending down, he gave the knee a peck. "You won't have that problem no more," Finton said. Then he spat on the ground and wiped his mouth.

"You're shittin' me." The boy stood up straight and shook his leg, twirling his foot around until the feeling appeared to come back to it. "Goddaim."

"You shouldn't take the Lord's name in vain," Nanny Moon said. "Now get on home and leave poor Finton alone."

The boy took a cautious step forward, planted his right foot on the ground, took a deep, quivering breath as he moved his left foot forward. He did this again, wincing in anticipation of excruciating pain. Instead he turned towards Finton and shook his hand. "Goddaim," he kept saying over and over. "Goddaim."

"Go home," said Finton, feeling truly great and terrible, his head throbbing.

"And don't tell anyone!" Nanny Moon shouted as she bustled her grandson inside.

"I'm tellin' everyone!" Laura shouted, then sent a "whoop!" to the sky as she ran down the lane.

The brown-haired girl smiled and blew him a kiss.

The slightly older boy took hold of his crutch and threw it with all his might into the meadow alongside the Moon house. "No more crutches!" he yelled as he strutted away, hobbling slightly. "Goddaim!"

By the time the door was nearly closed, there were five new visitors coming up the lane, and suddenly Finton was afraid.

"Heaven's floodgates are after been opened now," Nanny Moon said, and she took him inside. They had barely sat down when a knock came on the door.

Elsie answered it. "It's a man who says he fell off a ladder and broke his arm."

"It'll wait till after supper," Nanny Moon said, instructing Finton to sit.

Another knock came and this time it was a woman whose child was sick.

"Let her in," said Finton.

"Are you serious?" Elsie's face was pale. "Are you saying you can help her?"

Finton nodded. "Think so."

That was when Nanny Moon took him by the hand, and he could swear he felt an energy coming from her, though he couldn't decide if it was good or bad. "Don't ever doubt what you can do," she said. "It is what it is, and all you need is your faith. These people believe in you, and that's good enough. Isn't it?"

He thought only for a moment. Nodding, he looked to his mother and told her to let the woman in with her child.

The baby girl's face had a blue tinge and the child was clearly having trouble breathing. Finton took her into his arms and rocked her gently, speaking to her of how beautiful she was. He hummed a few lines of a Dean Martin song he remembered from childhood, then kissed her forehead and gave the baby back to the distraught mother.

"She'll be okay," Finton said and made the sign of the cross over the baby.

"Thank you," the mother said over and over, but she wouldn't take her gaze from her baby's face. "If this works, b'y, I'll owe ya the world."

Finton nodded thoughtfully and went back to eating his dumplings and pea soup.

When they'd left, his mother and grandmother stood staring at him, looking back and forth to each other.

"You're spooky," Homer said. He dashed to the living room and, within seconds, returned with the Bible. "We need an exorcism!"

"Leave 'im alone." Clancy just gazed at Finton with awe, resting his head on his arms on the table. "Finton's got a gift. We all got something, and Finton's is making people feel better."

Another knock came on the door. This time, Homer answered it, with the Bible in his hands.

"Who was it?" Nanny Moon asked.

"Some guy saying he was hearing voices. Thought Finton could fix his head." He looked at Finton as if half wondering if it were possible. The youngest Moon just sheltered his eyes with one hand as he ate and considered the possibility of running away.

"I told him we're eatin' supper," said Homer.

Just then, the telephone rang. The voice on the other end sounded panicked. "My daughter is having a seizure."

The next time, someone's grandmother was dying of old age.

"I can't help that," Finton told his mother, who relayed the message. He noticed an aching and trembling in his fingers, as if someone had stepped on them and ground them into the earth. So he held them between his legs to ease their throbbing.

Around ten o'clock that night, things finally settled down. The telephone hadn't rung in nearly twenty minutes, and no one had come to the door in the past half-hour.

Finton decided to go to bed early, dreading the next time the phone would ring. His entire body was tingling, with a tightness in his chest as if he were wearing a shirt two sizes too small. He slept for a couple of hours but woke up with a cough that racked his chest and exacerbated the persistent pressure at the back of his skull. He crawled out of bed in his pajamas and went to the kitchen. His father was sitting at the table in the dark, his left hand cradling a glass of whiskey.

Neither of them spoke, but sat on opposite sides of the table, letting silence reign. Above the stove, beside the crucified Jesus, the ticking clock punctuated the quiet. Finton finally asked, "Where were you?"

"Out." Tom swallowed the last of his whiskey. As he lowered the glass, his eyes met Finton's, exuding something indefinably forlorn. At times like this, Finton felt he could study those eyes forever and never understand the man who was his father. Other times, he felt he'd always known him, had always been with him and had witnessed every smart and stupid thing Tom Moon ever did. Simply put, he was a good man who had lost his way.

"Can I do something for you?"

Tom smiled sarcastically. "*You* do something for *me?*" He plucked a cigarette from his shirt pocket and stuffed the filter between his lips. "That'll be the day I die."

"I could do something. I really could."

"Don't you go startin' to believe your own press, laddie. All you can do is keep your head down and keep your mouth shut. Go to school, get a trade, and get the hell away from here. Understood?"

The words lashed his soul far worse than the sting of the belt. It was as if his father had been saving up those words his entire life, waiting for the moment when he would show his son he was only a guest and when the time came and his passport was stamped, he was expected to migrate to another country. He went back to bed, leaving his father sitting alone, with an unlit cigarette hanging from his mouth.

Confirmation Redux

"Confirmed?" Elsie read the notice from the school twice and, each time, asked the same question.

Just then, the telephone rang—for about the twentieth time that day—but no one answered it. They just waited for it to stop ringing before resuming their conversation.

"They said I have to be confirmed before I can take First Communion." And to be confirmed meant he had to take classes. "There's always bloody classes," he said.

"That's because there's so much to bloody learn." Nanny Moon peered up from her Bible, her eyes smiling.

"What if I don't wanna learn it?"

"Of course you want to learn it. What kind of priest will you be if you don't know how to be a good Catholic? Do you think Jesus was born knowing it all—or the Pope—" She made the sign of the cross. "Do you think His Holiness was born with the Scriptures emblazoned in his brain?"

"You mean he wasn't?"

"No, he wasn't. You can be born with the Holy Spirit in your soul, but sometimes it takes a Good Book and the sacraments to beat Jesus into ya. Sure, you knows you wants to be a soldier for Christ, b'y. Who wouldn't?"

Finton sighed, sensing that he was engaged in a losing battle. He'd already told them of his plans to write, but no one took him seriously. One day in school, Miss Woolfred took him aside and said, "Your story is really good, Finton. You have real talent for making stuff up."

He puffed up with pleasure, lapping up her words of praise. "Thank you," he said. "I'm going to be a writer when I grows up."

The teacher pressed her hands to her mouth to stifle a laugh. "My, but you do have your head in the clouds! You're still going to need a trade or a degree or something. It's sad but true—you just can't make any money at writing."

"But I like writing."

"You can still write," she said. "But someone as smart as you should be a teacher or a doctor. Something realistic. I mean, you can't feed a family with stories."

As he left the classroom that day, his cheeks burned with shame. He was used to his family saying he couldn't be a writer. But to hear it from his favourite teacher was heartbreaking. For the first time, he thought that maybe he was deluding himself, that maybe he needed to forget about his dreams and just be normal.

After that, he didn't tell people what he wanted to be. When Nanny Moon talked about being a soldier for Christ, he just let her go on, pretending to listen.

As the days went by, people were always wanting something from him. They'd want to be touched, blessed, or prayed for. They'd come to the house any time of day or night. The phone was always ringing, and he'd come to dread its shrill cry. He did his best for people, thinking that if they believed, then who was Finton Moon to deny them some relief? It shocked him that they almost always went away satisfied and, usually, healed. He didn't know how or why it was happening—and didn't know why it centered on him—but he tried not to worry about the results. If the worst he got for helping people was the occasional headache, it was worth the price.

But it was getting harder and harder to live an ordinary life. Few people would talk to him unless they had a sore throat or a nasty cut. He'd lay his hands on them and say a few words of prayer. They always insisted on the kiss, which he didn't like. But he couldn't deny its effects after, time and time again, witnessing the change come over them. Usually, they'd thank him and run off. Sometimes, they didn't even look him in the eye. He knew some people were calling him "Freaky Moon" or "the murderer's son," spewing unkindnesses about him behind his back, but there was nothing he could do about it. Most times, all he wanted was to be left alone.

It was Kieran who sat with him on the front step one day during one of his visits and told him, "You need to protect yourself, Finton. Learn to protect your own interests."

"What do you mean?"

"You're too open all the time. You don't always have to give them what they want. I had an aunt who won the lottery—she was up in Ontario, and it was a couple of hundred grand. Nothing too much, just enough for herself really. But she made the mistake of giving some money to her favourite sister, and a little bit more to a poorly off family back home, which was us. Next thing she knew, the whole family, most of her friends, and every charity from here to Burlington was asking for what she had and some even thought she was the meanest woman alive because she didn't give them enough. She never said no to anyone. Well, you can guess the rest of the story."

"She gave it all away?"

"Every red copper—and she died a pauper, far too young."

"So what you're saying is I shouldn't do everything people asks me to do."

"Exactly. Just because you have it, doesn't mean they deserve it more than you. You need to take care of yourself. No one—not your friends, not your family, or anyone else will do it for you."

Kieran's words struck Finton as true, and he resolved to try and implement the advice.

Confirmation classes were a great excuse to get out of regular class. For a month prior to Easter, twice a week, he and most of his classmates would get on a bus to go down to the Sacred Heart of Mary church where the old spinster, Miss Wyseman, would lead them through the paces. There were lines to learn, procedures to practice, and hymns to rehearse, like "Make Me a Channel of Your Peace" and "Daily, Daily, Sing to Mary," which was the only part he enjoyed. It gave him a special thrill to sing such devout lines to Mary while no one knew he was thinking of Mary Connelly when he sang. Except for that, he hated every minute of the Confirmation training, but he didn't want to embarrass his mother or himself, so he endured it.

Mary still hadn't come back to school, and she hadn't attended Confirmation classes. Skeet and Dolly went, though, and so did Bernard, Al, Cocky, and the King twins.

He envied the two Protestant kids who were allowed to stay behind and do school work. Not that it was easy being a Protestant in Darwin. There were only a couple of non-Catholic families in the entire town, and Finton's mother had often warned him against being infected by their hedonistic beliefs. "They don't believe in the infallibility of the Pope," she'd told him once, meaning they were wicked to the core. Still, Billy Bundy and Trish Gacy didn't seem so bad to him, and they actually seemed cleaner and brighter than most. "That's because the Anglicans have money," Nanny Moon told him. "Makes them arrogant, like that adultering King Henry the Eighth."

"Why don't Catholics have money?" Finton wanted to know.

"Because we're God's chosen, b'y. With faith in the Lord, you don't need dollars."

"But what if you needs to buy stuff. What if I needs to buy chips and bars for watchin' the hockey game?"

"You don't need it. It's Lent, anyway—you should be givin' that stuff up."

"Why?"

"Because Jesus never had potato chips. And if he did he would have given them to the poor, starving children."

Finton considered the likelihood that if he didn't have any money, he might *be* one of the poor, starving children. He looked up at the crucifix over the kitchen table. Maybe that's why he looks so miserable all the time. But he didn't say any of this aloud. In fact, gazing at the crucified Christ made him feel depressed, so he told Nanny Moon he would sacrifice chips and bars for the rest of Lent.

"That's nice," she said. "But it's too late now. Lent is already started. But you can begin now and make up for it by doing the stations."

The stations meant he had to walk around the perimeter of the church's interior, stop at each of the fourteen Stations of the Cross, contemplate the significance of each one, and say a brief prayer before blessing himself ("spectacles, testicles, wallet, and watch," as Skeet had taught him). He'd never done them before and actually looked forward to the arduous "journey." He'd never known his father to do the stations, but his mother did them once a month, to remind her of how Jesus had suffered for her sins.

"What sins?" he asked.

"I don't have any sins," she would answer.

"Then why do you need to do the stations?"

"Because Jesus wants us to. He died for all our sins."

"What sins?

"Shut up, Finton, b'y. Yer givin' me a mortal headache."

"Well, what sins do *I* have?"

"You've got your Original Sin on your soul, like everyone else."

"How did I get that?"

"You didn't *get* it, b'y. You were born with it. It's what ya gets for bein' born."

Thus, when the time came for Finton to do the stations, he found out that he also had to endure Confession. He already went once a month, but only to sit outside while his mother and brothers confessed.

"Bless me Father..."

"For I have sinned."

"For I have sinned. And... I don't remember."

The priest sighed patiently on his side of the confessional, and Finton wondered if he had somewhere more important to be. "It's been how long since your last confession?"

"This is my first confession, Father."

"Excellent. Well, have you any sins to confess?"

"I've got Original Sin on my soul, Father."

"That's true, my son."

"But Mudder says there's nudding you can do about that."

"I can give you a penance, but your Original Sin was absolved at Baptism."

Sitting in the velvety darkness of the confessional, he felt relieved. Then he thought hard about what other sins he was going to confess. He didn't think he should tell about his premonition of Sawyer's death, partly because Father Power hadn't believed him about Miss Bridie being dead a few years ago, and partly because he feared being implicated. Still, his mother and Nanny Moon had told him to confess everything to the priest and to trust in his forgiveness. "The parish priest talks directly to God," Nanny Moon had said. "If you tell Father Power, then God hears it at the same time." When he asked why he couldn't just tell God his own sins, she told him not to be so saucy. "Only the priest is God's vessel—that's one of the mysteries."

Still, he was afraid to tell everything for fear that God might punish him. On the other hand, God probably already knew what was in Finton's heart. Maybe he'd even feel better if he confessed about his part in Sawyer's death, but he didn't know if that was a good reason to confess. The only good reason, really, would be to purge his soul and thereby avoid purgatory when he died. He also wondered if it was a sin to think his father might have killed Sawyer. But he decided he shouldn't say that aloud to anyone.

Unsure of the course that would reward him with the most redemption, he relied on the list of sins he'd compiled in his head, thinking he might just go with that—unless the priest asked him specifically about whether he'd killed anyone with his thoughts.

"I told a lie and had bad thoughts about someone. I talked back to my mother and father. And Nanny Moon too. And my teachers. And Mrs. Sellars because she gypped me fifty cents. She was mean to me too. She told me to get her something to hit me with, but I told her to kiss me arse."

An extended silence, and a sound which could have been mistaken for laughter came from the other side. "Is that all, my son?"

"No, Father. This is my first confession, and I've been alive nearly thirteen years, so I've got lots more. Do you want to hear them all?"

"Just the highlights will be fine."

"All right. I looked at Mary Connelly with lust, Father. And I had a dream about her and Dolly. I couldn't help it. Then I lied about that. I had bad thoughts about Bridie Battenhatch too, and Sawyer Moon, and my mother and father. I had bad thoughts about Bernard Crowley too. And Cocky Munro. I called him an arsehole, and he is too. But I'm sorry for saying it."

The priest seemed to be smiling, though it was hard to tell through the wire. Finton thought he smelled cat's pee.

"You've been a busy little sinner, haven't you?"

"Yes, Father."

"I tell you what—just say a whole rosary, and all your sins will be forgiven."

"But I got more."

"That'll be fine." He raised his hand and made the sign of the cross. "I absolve you of all your sins. Go forth and sin no more. Father, Son, Holy Ghost, Amen."

That was the hardest part. He could recite the rosary like his own name, but going forth and sinning no more wasn't going to be easy. He felt better about himself when he left the confessional, for it was as if God had personally taken his sins away and cleansed him, like taking a toilet scrubber to his soul and scouring it clean.

Go forth and sin no more. He liked the sound of it and thought he might be able to do it. But he wondered if he should have told the priest about Sawyer Moon if only to alleviate his guilt. "To be secretive is to sin twice over," his mother used to say. "And every time you don't confess, you're committing the same sin again." It was when he visited the Twelfth Station that his mind was made up. "Jesus died for your sins." How many times had he heard that? Nanny Moon often said that every time he lied, especially at Lent, he was driving the nails deeper into Jesus' hands and feet. He didn't think he could handle being responsible for something so horrible.

So he lined up again and waited. Finally, after what seemed like forever, he sat with sweaty palms and shallow breathing in the same Confession box, anticipating the sliding open of the small wooden door and the appearance of the priest's perspiring face.

"Bless me father for I have sinned. It's been twenty minutes since my last confession."

"You sin quickly, my son."

"No, Father. I mean, there's one I didn't tell you before."

"But you told me an awful lot."

"Not this."

"Why not?"

"Because I was too afraid."

There was a pause. "Go on."

Although Finton's hands were clasped, his body trembled. He kept seeing that image of the crucified Jesus being nailed to the cross and, suddenly, the Confession box seemed deficient of air. "Can you keep a secret, Father?"

"My son, I have no choice. I am bound to forgive and forget. I can tell no other living soul what you tell me in confidence. Speak freely and all will be forgiven. That is the Church's promise, as well as God's."

Finton breathed easier, but his voice quivered. "I wished for a man to die…" He hesitated, feeling the tiny confessional spinning and closing in on him. "…and he did."

"Which man was this?"

"Sawyer Moon."

"The man they found dead just before Christmas."

The priest made a whistling sound as if sucking in a breath. "Killing a man is a serious sin, as it goes against one of God's commandments. But—" the priest hesitated as if to weigh his words. "You can't kill a man by thinking about it. I mean, it's *wrong* to think about it—and for that you should do penance and ask God's forgiveness—but his death is hardly your fault."

"But I dreamed about it, and he went missing right after."

"My son, you give yourself far too much credit."

Finton didn't feel like arguing. He had confessed and that was all he could do. "Do you have penance for me, Father?"

"Yes, of course."

He offered Finton a blessing and further penance of ten Our Fathers. The boy hurried out of the confessional, tripped in the threshold, and swore under his breath as he ran out of the church. The whole way, he felt the eyes of his fellow confessors on him, and he wondered how many of their souls were stained as black as his own.

The hardest part about Confirmation was choosing a name. He'd been given one at birth, but he was too young then to know the difference. Now that he was older and about to become one of Christ's soldiers, he was old enough to pick out a name that suited him. Finally, the chance for individuation had come.

Secretly, Finton feared excommunication more than anything else. His mother and grandmother were always telling him stories about people who were excommunicated, the idea being that if he didn't stay on his best behaviour, banishment from the church would be his ultimate fate. "Fidel Castro was excommunicated and so was that baseball player that married Marilyn Monroe." They would tell him tale after tale of people being excised from the church for not going to mass, for questioning the Pope's infallibility, and for embarrassing the Holy Mother Church in some way. Finton didn't want to be like Castro— "The In-Fidel," Nanny Moon called him—so he felt the pressure to do everything right. Picking the right name was paramount because the bishop himself was going to be there to hand out the sacrament.

"Have you come up with a name yet?" His mother was ironing his new white shirt. Confirmation was tomorrow, Palm Sunday, and he was getting anxious.

"I thought about John or James or something like that."

"Those are nice names."

"But I was thinking Scout."

He noticed his mother's ironing became more methodical as if she was pressing down on the shirt hard enough to make an imprint of the iron in the material. The iron hissed, sputtered, and made bloated sounds, as she pushed it across the white landscape of the shirt. "Is that a saint's name?"

"I like it."

"Surely God, Finton, there's another name you like."

"I like Scout."

"How about James? He was Jesus' brother."

"It's all right. But Scout is better."

"Jesus, Finton, you might as well call yourself Judas and write a big scarlet J on your forehead. The bishop won't allow it."

Nanny Moon, who'd been sitting with her eyes closed, opened them and watched Elsie perform her ironing duties. "The name should be appropriate for a soldier of Christ," she said. "But it should also be a Christian name."

"How about Arthur, then?" He knew how it was spelled, but they all pronounced it *Arder*.

There was silence as the two adults looked at each other. "Is there a Saint Arder?" Nanny Moon asked, looking mystified.

"There's a King Arder."

"Go ask your father what he thinks," his mother said at last.

His father was watching *Hee-Haw*, and the fat girl with the big breasts was just popping up out of the cornstalks when Finton asked his question. Tom lit a Camel and blew a smoke ring. Finton wondered if Lulu's parents were proud of her for being on *Hee-Haw*.

"Arder?"

"Or Scout. Either one."

"As a Confirmation name?"

Finton nodded. "It's tomorrow."

"Jesus, b'y, you're gettin' up there. Next thing, you'll be old enough to get a job and help out around here."

The thought pleased Finton and made him puff out his chest a little. Maybe this Confirmation thing wasn't so bad after all.

"If I were you..."

Finton waited, watching as his father sucked another draw of smoke, opened his mouth to a perfect "O" shape, and blew the white smoke into the air.

"You should be called... Thomas."

He felt proud that his father would bestow him with his own name. Finton went back into the living room with the news, and Elsie nodded as she kept ironing. Nanny Moon had opened her Bible and rested her glasses on the tip of her nose while she looked up names for Finton.

"Thomas," he repeated, but they didn't appear to hear him. At length, Nanny Moon spoke as if under her breath, though she never took her gaze from the Bible. "Do you know the story of the doubting Thomas?"

"No."

"Well, you should. Thomas was the one that doubted Jesus' resurrection—had to be shown proof before he'd believe it. That's hardly good Catholic faith now, is it?"

"Not really," he said, beginning to feel uneasy.

"Some say he was Judas's twin." Beads of sweat were rolling down Elsie's forehead and dripping onto the shirt she was ironing. "And he was also the only apostle to witness Mary's ascendance into heaven."

"But it's my father's name," Finton protested. "Nanny Moon, you gave it to him."

"That'll be enough backtalk, laddie-o." The old woman burrowed deeper into her Bible, her mouth clamped shut. Elsie rolled her eyes towards the heavens as if to say there was nothing she could do.

As far as Finton was concerned, the decision had been made. On the form the teacher had given him, he wrote: "Thomas." Choosing it had been harder than picking out a Halloween costume, but he liked it enough to take it for the rest of his life.

The next morning, he got dressed in his Confirmation suit, feeling fluttery in his stomach, and went to the bathroom to run a wet comb through his hair. Normally, when it was in need of cutting, it was curly and looked like a wasps' nest, but it was better behaved when he wet it down and pressed his hand against it for several minutes. By the time it dried, however, it would spring right back up again like a freshly risen bun.

He was nervous about meeting the bishop, whom his father always referred to as "His Holiness, Arch the Bishop." Finton had strong memories of being five years old, and Arch the Bishop had come to Darwin to administer Confirmations. Finton and Tom had to stand at the back of the church, so far away from the altar and surrounded by so many taller people that Finton couldn't even see the famous bishop. During Holy Communion, his father lifted him up high so he could see. The bishop was wearing a high, golden hat and red vestments;

with a sceptre in his left hand, he resembled a king. Finton was very impressed and realized that Arch the Bishop was not only very holy, but also rich, famous, and powerful. The thought of meeting him was terrifying.

The Confirmation ceremony was structured and simple. The "celebrant" and his "sponsor" would sit side-by-side in a pew with all the other celebrants and sponsors; the families sat behind them, no doubt gazing on in wonder. Nanny Moon, Elsie, and Tom sat back there; Morgan Battenhatch was Finton's sponsor, and so they sat together.

His grandmother disapproved of the boy's choice of sponsor. "Another one dancin' with the devil," Nanny Moon said. "That girl's after doin' some terrible things." But, to Elsie and Tom, despite Morgan's spiritual failings, the choice seemed appropriate. After all, when he was a baby Finton had nearly ruined Morgan's Confirmation Day because they had to take him to the hospital. "Besides," Elsie said, "it's Finton's choice." Furthermore, Morgan had been mending her ways lately and had moved back in with her mother. They even seemed to be getting along. Finton had a fondness for his all-time favourite babysitter, and he'd never forgotten her many kindnesses when he was a child. It was time, he said, to let bygones be bygones, and Morgan would be his sponsor. If his parents even considered arguing the matter, they did so in private.

"It's going to be okay," Morgan assured him. "If the bishop gives you a hard time, we'll beat the hell out of him."

Finton felt queasy about the idea of committing violence on Arch the Bishop. As if sensing his uneasiness, Morgan squeezed his hand. "Just kidding," she said.

She looked unusually pretty that morning. Where she found a dress at such a late stage, he had no idea, for he had only asked her the day before if she would be his sponsor, and he was certain she didn't own a dress already. It was a red, strapless number that showed a hint of cleavage. Looking at her made him blush, so Finton gazed straight ahead at the throne upon the altar to which the bishop would soon ascend.

Regardless of her reputation, Finton was glad Morgan was there, especially since he felt every eye in the place looking at him as he proceeded down the aisle, towards his destiny. She was an anchor in his chaotic world, plus she was smart and rebellious. The fact that she had once set fire to her mother's house—and another time stabbed her—to voice her frustration only made him admire her more, even if she did frighten him a little.

During the hymns, which the choir and congregation sang together, Finton scanned the pews for familiar faces. He knew a lot of them, although they had come from various schools in the greater Darwin area. Mary Connelly looked ashen and frail in the front row with her adult sponsor. Her hair was clasped in a sky-blue ponytail clip that matched her dress. Being confirmed was probably a big deal to her since he hadn't seen her in public since she got sick. Next to Mary sat Dolly, gnawing a wad of gum, yet looking very adult in her long, white gloves and white satin dress, with her makeup lending her skin a pinkish glow. Directly behind the two friends, Alicia Dredge sat with her dark hair wrapped in a loose bun and wearing a frilly white dress that she must have borrowed from some relative. Skeet was seated to Finton's right with his Uncle Curtis, wearing his best white shirt tucked into his best pair of jeans. He was pale, but otherwise healthy. Somewhere behind them were Bernard Crowley and Cocky Munro, who were also getting confirmed, along with the twins, Gerald and Cecil King.

When the time came to be touched by the bishop and transformed into young soldiers of Christ, the children and their sponsors filed side-by-side towards the front of the church, where Arch the Bishop was sitting. One by one, the children knelt before him and the sponsor presented them by their Confirmation names, saying, "Here is James, and he wishes to be confirmed," or "Here is Cabrina, and she wishes to be confirmed." Then the bishop asked questions, to which there were set answers, anointed them with oil on their foreheads, then lightly tapped one of their cheeks—a reminder to be brave in spreading the faith—and said they were now confirmed Catholics, "soldiers of Christ."

When Finton's turn came, he suddenly found himself standing before the bishop, while Morgan cleared her throat and announced, "This is Thomas. Thomas, this is the bishop." She paused as if she expected them to shake hands. All went well until the bishop, finished with the skill-testing questions, slapped Finton's cheek a little too hard, initiating the boy's backward sprawl into the arms of the girl behind him. People laughed as he lay on the floor in Alicia Dredge's lap with his head cradled in her slight bosom. Morgan tried hard not to smile as she extended her hand to the boy and pulled him up. "Jesus falls for the second time," she whispered in his ear.

Finton could barely hear her or anyone else because he suddenly felt sick to his stomach. He hadn't slept last night and had just managed to force down some breakfast, but only because Nanny Moon had insisted he eat the rolled oats she had cooked for him. When he stood up and his knees felt wobbly, he immediately realized he might fall again.

"Are you okay, young man?" He looked up to see the blonde-haired bishop lean forward in his chair and reach towards him with his sceptre. He happened to point it in the very direction in which Finton staggered, and the boy smacked his forehead on the sceptre's pointed end. Morgan grabbed him by the waist, keeping him from falling again, but she couldn't keep him from vomiting at the bishop's feet.

"A gift," Morgan said as she sidestepped the deposit and escorted Finton to his seat.

Miss Wyseman rushed forward with a roll of toilet paper, but the church carpet was "stained irreparably, like the Shroud of Turin," as Nanny Moon said later. They tried to leave, but Nanny Moon insisted that he and Morgan had to finish the ceremony; otherwise, the whole thing would be tainted and he would have to be confirmed at another time.

"At a time to be confirmed," Tom said. But nobody except Morgan cracked a smile.

The change, for Finton, was instantaneous.

"He threw up on the bishop," Tom announced as soon as they were home. Clancy and Homer begged for details, but Nanny Moon was quick to discourage sideshows on such a big day.

"So how do you feel?" The old woman gazed at him with a strange combination of pride and awe as she brushed back the shock of hair overhanging his bruised forehead.

"Do you feel any different?" his mother asked.

They swapped stories about their Confirmation experiences, each when they'd been at the age of between twelve and fourteen. "Everyone is different," Nanny Moon said, knitting by the wood stove. "Confirmation is a time for awakening. It's like the Apostles all gathered in one room at Pentecost—they all started speakin' in tongues, sure. Couldn't understand a single word anyone was sayin' except themselves." She stopped knitting for a moment and looked up at him. "Their hearts opened up to Jesus."

Finton didn't know if his heart would open up to Jesus, but he did feel different. Maybe it was because his heart was already open to the son of God—his stomach certainly had—or perhaps it was because of the tiny mark on his forehead. He told Nanny Moon, his mother, and everyone else who asked that he felt a bit of heartburn, which made them look at him with concern. But really what he felt was more complicated than that. He just didn't have the words to explain it. In some ways, it was as if something vital inside him had fled, like he'd lost an organ without having surgery.

After the Confirmation dinner—which was actually the same dinner they had every Sunday—Finton opened his Confirmation gift. It was a pair of brown wooden prayer beads. "They came from Peru," his mother said, a trace of sadness in her voice. Her sister Connie, who was a Presentation Nun and named after Connie Francis who sang "Where the Boys Are," had gone to Lima "on the Mission" about two years ago and occasionally sent gifts home to the family. Usually, they consisted of local handmade art, like alpaca rugs and seashell ashtrays. "These," the note said, "were made by one of the local girls who's a convert to Sister Constance's mission."

He stared at the wooden rosary beads in his hands and prayed for the strength to be silent. After a minute in which he must have seemed to choke up with emotion, he finally said, "Amen, Sister Constance," then retreated to his room to get changed.

Not long after, wearing his everyday pants, sneakers, and homemade Bruins sweatshirt with the hand-drawn logo, he charged through the kitchen and dashed through the front door. When his mother asked where he was going, he pretended not to hear.

Miss Bridie was glad to see him. She opened her front door and ushered him inside. "You're some boy," she said with a wink as she poured tea. "Comin' to see poor ol' me on the most important day of your life. What a lad."

"I get sick of questions—Nanny Moon telling me I'll be in the priesthood soon, mother givin' me rosary beads from Peru—"

"Rosary beads?"

"To make me pray better."

She smirked. "Hopin' for something a bit more expensive, wuz ya?"

Finton shrugged and watched the tea leaves swirling around in his tea. They were still disgusting, but he'd gotten used to them. "It just makes me wonder about things, that's all."

She leaned forward, hands cradling her cup, her eyes much kinder and wiser than he'd realized in those years when he'd been afraid of her, and yet they still retained something indefinably dangerous, and just a bit off. "What kind of things?"

Since Christmas, he'd been coming to see her every few weeks or so, and she always seemed pleased to see him. She made tea and talked about everything he wanted to discuss. Usually, it was about school or his parents, about his father's skirmishes with the law. And, although he always refrained from disclosing too much, today was different. He felt like talking to someone about all his crazy thoughts.

"Priests are not allowed to have girlfriends. But I *like* girls. I'd like to have a girlfriend someday."

"Priests can have girlfriends."

"They can?"

"They're just not allowed to tell anyone."

"Oh. Well, why does God expect us to pray to Him on our knees? Why do we have to go to Confession? And why does the Bible have to be the truth? What if it was written by some men just telling stories, making it all up as they went?"

"Well, now, you might be on to something." She rubbed her chin and sat back with her arms folded across her great chest. "You've been doing some thinking, I see."

"I can't talk to that crowd about stuff like this. Nanny Moon would have me excommunicated."

"Big deal! I haven't been inside a church in ages and it haven't harmed me none."

"Well…" He hung his head, unsure of how to respond. "I *have* to go to mass."

"Why do you have to? What did mass ever do for you?"

He couldn't tell her the real reason he went, which was to see Mary Connelly all dressed up and sitting in the front pew. Sure, he went for religious reasons, but they weren't his main goal. "Mass brings us closer to God." He looked defiant at first, but then hung his head, realizing he'd been caught in a lie. "That's what Nanny Moon says."

"Nanny Moon has been brainwashed. And she's doing the same thing to you."

"Anyway, I don't know what to do about any of it. As long as I live in Darwin, this is the way it's always going to be. Tomorrow will be just like today because that's the way it always was. Everyone goes to Confession on Saturday, Communion on Sunday, and goes home and sins for the rest o' the week. Then they do it all over again."

"You're a wise man for such a small boy."

"They're just hypocrites, that's all."

"I know what you should do." She reached into her apron pocket and pulled out a blue and white package of Rothman's. "You should try one of these."

He shook his head solemnly.

"Ah," she said, waving a hand disgustedly. "Too puritan for your own good." She stood up slowly, holding her left side, and went to the cupboard, where she extracted a forty-ounce bottle of rum. "Drop o' this will fix what ails ya."

"I don't drink." He found his gaze transfixed by the way the sun illuminated the copper-coloured drink through the thick glass. It looked so beautiful and harmless, like fairy juice. His mother and grandmother had been warning him away from liquor since he was old enough to know what it was.

She pulled down two shot glasses and filled both, setting one on the table in front of him. "Drink up." She sat down and lowered down her drink, sucking in hard and hollowing her cheeks as if her lungs were on fire. She exhaled like a dragon. "Your turn."

He stared at the glass, caressing it with one doubtful finger.

"Pick it up."

Before she could say another word, he picked it up and brought it to his lips. He could feel her dark-blue eyes urging him. "Drink!"

He tipped up the glass until the warm liquid touched his lips, washed over his tongue and slid down his throat, on its way to the coils of his stomach. The explosion of heat radiated his entire being, inside and out. Immediately, he wiped sweat from his forehead. Encouraged by the originality of the experience, he sipped again and sat quietly, waiting to be struck by a bolt of lightning or for his mother to come bursting through the door, screaming eternal damnation.

"It's good," he said when it was all gone.

"I told you."

He could barely hear what she was saying. The room looked slightly fuzzy around the edges, and the ceiling seemed to have lowered to within his reach, while the floor had risen to meet him. He felt he had outgrown the room, with a body too large for the chair and arms too long for his body.

"Whenever you wants another drop, you just come on over and Bridie'll fix you with a drop o' the devil's cure. Okay?"

He nodded. Meanwhile, he continued to sit and talk to her about everything he thought was wrong with school, his parents, the whole time wishing he could have another drop of the demon rum. Somewhere along the way, he picked a cigarette out of her pack and lit it. His first drag inspired him to start hacking, but he managed to stay seated and to let it burn down between his fingers while he occasionally inhaled.

Then Morgan came in, still wearing that red dress that made her look like a girl from the Sears catalogue. "What are y'all talkin' about?"

"Life," said Miss Bridie. "Siddown and have a drink with us."

She studied her mother's face, the cigarette between Finton's fingers, and then the bottle, which she snatched from the table and carried with her as she turned and bolted upstairs. She halted on the second step and called out, "Finton, can I see you in my bedroom for a few minutes? I have something to show you."

The boy and the older woman exchanged glances. Miss Bridie just waved her hand dismissively. "Go on, b'y. We'll catch up later on."

Up the staircase, Finton followed the red dress.

"Close the door," Morgan said when they were inside her bedroom, which smelled like lavender perfume.

There was only a small single bed and a white chest of wooden drawers with a mirror. Beside the bed sat a white chamber pot that reminded him of the one his grandmother kept by her own bedside. Along the ceiling were several wooden beams. He couldn't help imagining her swinging from one, eyes wide open as she tried to die.

Because the sunlight didn't reach this part of the house, Morgan's room was darker than downstairs, the only brightness emanating from the window beside the bed. He stood with his back to the door, watching her and surveying the backyard. Outside, he could see the marshy bog alongside the swollen river and the dirty, white diaper waving from a branch.

She stepped out of her shoes, then turned around and pointed to the zipper of her dress. "Come help."

Legs suddenly numb, he stumbled forward and seized the tiny zipper between his fumbling fingers. A pang of nervousness seized his stomach. He hesitated.

"What are you doing?" Morgan asked.

"Nothing." He sniffed once and licked the dryness from his bottom lip. He pulled the zipper down slowly across the curve of her spine so that she seemed to spill out of it like a ripe fruit. Her flesh was the whitest he had ever seen.

She reached up to her shoulders and stripped the red dress to her bony hips, then skimmed it the rest of the way to the floor. She gently stepped out of the garment and, with one bare foot, shoved it aside. Sensing the immorality of his gaze upon her nearly naked body, Finton focused on the pool of scarlet fabric lying on the floor, gleaming and empty.

She wheeled around to face him, a strange, beseeching look in her eyes that he'd seen only in black and white movies starring Ingrid Bergman. "Well." She planted her hands on those alluring hips, and again he licked his dry lips. "What do you think?" There was a smile in her voice that frightened him. Her belly was white, so soft-looking that he yearned to reach out and touch it, run his fingers down over it, lean forward and kiss it. She was standing before him in only her white bra and underwear, and he felt himself changing. Embarrassed, he turned towards the window.

"Finton?"

He forced himself to look at her again and was glad of his willpower, for he'd never seen anything like her before. In some ways, he had always seen her like this—she'd merely adapted to his daydreams. And yet, there was something changed in her too, as if she was no longer the Morgan who had once been his babysitter or the girl next door, nor even the one who had tried to burn her mother's house to the ground. This was a brand new Morgan—one who would not be contained or put back in the box when he was done with her—or, more to the point, when she was done with him. "I shouldn't be here," he said, surprising himself with the ability to speak.

She stepped forward and took his hand. She kissed one of his fingers, then took the same finger in her mouth and slid it in and out between her lips. She pressed his other hand to her left breast and, at the very same moment, he felt something let go inside of him—as if his soul had popped out of his body. At first, he thought he had peed in his pants, but quickly recognized it as something else, warm, sticky, and messy. "Oh God," he said, backing away, taking his hands with him. "I got to go."

"I won't hurt you," she said, reaching towards him with naked arms like branches of the whitest, rarest tree and luring him back inside. He shut the door gently, worried that Miss Bridie would hear the sound of his acquiescence. He didn't like the idea that she was down there at the kitchen table, laughing to herself at the frailty of his soul.

"Stay with me." The young woman spoke in a comforting voice that weakened his knees and rendered his flesh pliable, his spirit malleable. "I'll make a man out of you."

Her words reminded him of the difference between them—she twenty-four and he almost thirteen. Lying on top of her, with her hands down his pants, he felt like a little boy, and he knew he would never want to leave this bedroom or her.

He quickly discovered that Morgan was hungry and that he—his flesh, his cock, his very breath—was her sustenance. When he was inside her, she grabbed his bum and pulled him deeper, never getting enough, needing more from him than he was able to give. She wrapped her legs around his, pulling him tighter, bringing him further than he thought was possible. For him, there was plenty of Morgan—she gave him life, restored his soul, made him feel as if all that existed before this moment was vacant and dull. When he entered her, the world expanded and contracted all at once. When he pulled himself from her, he felt empowered, ready for battle.

When they were finished, he was energized and hungry. He had done what she'd asked, been what she commanded. But when they were lying together in the grey afternoon light, she'd started to laugh. Her face had changed, too, and her features had hardened like clay, with thin cracks appearing at the corners of her eyes and mouth. He touched her right breast, drawing a finger gently around the curve, allowing his thumb to stray to her nipple. She didn't flinch, but laughed again. "That was fun," she said. "Bet you can't wait to tell your mother about this." She'd instantaneously transformed from a goddess into a wicked girl who had torched her mother's house and stabbed her—a thought with a certain reality attached, which suddenly appalled the most decent part of him. Even as he scrambled out of her bed, he was uncertain of the nature of what they'd done, but he knew they could never do it again.

Fortunately, Miss Bridie was in the living room, probably snoozing, so he scrambled out the door as quick as he could. As he ran home, tucking his shirt into his pants, Morgan's laughter still rang in his ears like the most awful church bell he could imagine, signaling the funeral for a friend who'd been indispensable to his survival and sanity. The laughter dissipated as he came closer to home, but all he could think about was how ashamed of him his mother and grandmother would be, particularly in light of the fact that he'd forgotten his underwear. There was no doubt that leaving his shorts tangled up in Morgan Battenhatch's bedclothes would get him excommunicated.

Trying to master his panic, Finton ceased running. Tried to breathe. He gazed up at the bungalow atop Moon's Lane, drew a long, deep breath and resolved to complete the walk with dignity. He'd barely begun strutting up the hill when he tripped on a rusted fender that had been lying on the same spot for so long it had become part of the environment and now seemed deliberately placed there to punish him on that day. Blood spilled from the cut like wine from a chalice and, even in that moment, he recognized the necessity for sacrifice, even if he wished it were otherwise. Falling to one knee, he tried to press the gash closed and cried out for his mother. But no one heard him. No one came running. He clamped both hands around the wound and tried to imagine the Planet of Solitude. He focused hard on comets, stars, and the apple tree. But when he opened his eyes, he knew he hadn't gone anywhere. Disappointed, he stood up. Blood trickled down his leg, drenching his sock and tainting his shoe as he limped up the lane.

When he finally got inside, he could barely contain his tears. His mother was on the telephone. Her eyes widened as she gazed at his bloody leg. "What did you do?" She clamped a hand over her mouth, the other over the receiver. "Father Power is on the phone. He wants to see you."

Finton groaned, suspecting trouble. After a few more words to the priest, Elsie hung up the phone and dashed towards her son, swearing over and over, "My sweet, sweet Jesus." She pushed up the ripped leg of his trousers to reveal his wound. "Oh Jesus, Finton—what are you after doin' to yerself?"

"What does Father Power want?" he asked, all the while thinking that all of this was God's punishment. Although Morgan could certainly bear some of the blame, he should have been able to resist temptation. Jesus was in the desert forty days and forty nights, and, despite hunger and thirst of the highest order, still managed to spurn the devil. Finton Moon was confirmed by the bishop one minute and the next minute lying naked with the girl next door. Some prophet. Some priest he would make.

While his mother retrieved supplies from the bathroom—ointment, gauze, and white hospital tape—his grandmother haunted the entrance between the kitchen and living room, shaking her head while stringing the rosary beads through her hands. She wasn't speaking, but her lips kept moving.

Elsie came back with a pan of water and laid it beside the chair. "Take off your pants and put your foot in this while I clean your leg."

He remembered his mislaid underwear. "I can just roll it up."

"That'll cut off your circulation." As she squat down and waited for him to undo his pants, for reasons only a mother would know, she also sniffed his shirt. "Why do you smell like smoke?"

"That's why." He motioned his hand toward his father, who had emerged from the living room, smoking a cigarette.

"What's going on?" he asked, but the way Tom scrutinized Finton made him wonder if he knew.

"I cut myself on an old car part." Finton motioned towards his bandaged leg.

"Why don't you just heal yourself?"

Everyone looked at him then. Even his brothers had emerged from playing records in the bedroom to lay eyes on the unexpected scene that posed disturbing questions. "Yes, come to think on it," said Nanny Moon. "Why is the healer not healed?"

He was grateful for the distraction, but Finton was unable to think of an answer.

His excommunication would happen on the same day as his Confirmation. Anyone could see it and know he deserved it.

Father Power had mentioned to Bishop Connor about the boy who was rumoured to heal the sick and make the lame walk. "If so many people are talking about it," the bishop had said, "it's time for you to have a talk with him." The priest asked Elsie if it would be all right for Finton to join him for supper that evening.

"I'll go with him," Tom said. "One of us has to."

Nanny Moon had argued until her face was a faint shade of purple that it was her right to go with Finton because she was the most churchgoing of the Moons, as well as the oldest. But Tom had countered that he was the boy's father and that was that.

"Well, Jesus *did* go among the sinners," Nanny Moon mused and reluctantly agreed, but she still spent the rest of the afternoon sulking.

Meanwhile, Finton couldn't guess why he'd been invited, but he was suspicious it had something to do with the Confirmation debacle.

"I don't know what to wear," he said, his foot still soaking.

"Father Power won't care as long as you're clean." His father lit a cigarette, puffed and squinted. "Are your underwear good?"

"These are the only pants I got and they're all bloody." Finton then proclaimed what everyone had been waiting for: "I'm not going."

"But the parish priest is expecting you!" Nanny Moon scowled. "You wouldn't put off supper with the Lord if he asked."

Finton stood up in the pan of water, sloshing it enough that it threatened to overspill its plastic sides. "He's not the Lord. He's only a priest."

"Jesus have mercy on your soul." Nanny Moon blessed herself furiously. "You used to be such a good boy." She glanced at Elsie and murmured, barely loud enough for Finton to hear. "I expect that's his other side comin' out."

"That'll be enough o' that kind of talk," Elsie scolded as she urged him to lift his foot out of the pan and into the towel she held forth. He slipped, but his mother caught him and patted his foot and his leg dry one at a time. "Finton, you're just gonna have to wear the pants you got on."

"I could wear my jeans," he said hopefully.

Even as she murmured the "Our Father," Nanny Moon's eyes bulged as if she might have a stroke, although she constantly amazed Finton with her skill at upholding her part in a conversation while praying. "Jesus didn't wear jeans when he gave the Sermon on the Mount. Or when he turned the money-lenders out of the temple."

"No," said Tom. "He probably wore the same ratty, old robe he always wore. No shoes either."

"No shoes, no shirt, no service," Clancy laughed from behind his father.

"You're all going to hell." Nanny Moon shook her head sorrowfully, still counting her beads.

"I'll just wear these," Finton announced, unrolling the hem of the pants he was wearing. He winced as he pulled the cloth down over his injured leg, wondering why, indeed, he hadn't been able to heal himself.

As they cruised along in silence, Finton found himself thinking about the morning and afternoon he'd had—a strange confirmation, followed by his first taste of sex. His body still thrummed with the memory of his orgasm, an ejaculation that had taken just a few seconds. They didn't have to wait long for his second coming either, or even his third. Each time, Morgan had looked as if she was both doing him a favour and devouring his soul. Only now in the quiet of the car, alongside his father, could he recall the details, and the more he thought about it, the prouder he was. He had been so scared, both during and after, but now he wanted to scream to the whole world that he'd lost his virginity.

"Doin' okay there?" Tom asked.

"Yup."

"Don't be too nervous now. He's only a man."

Finton was relieved that his father couldn't read his mind. "So why did you want to come with me?"

"Be serious, b'y." Tom smiled mischievously. "Sending you down there with religious people, with either your mother or Nanny Moon to protect ya? That'd be like sending the wolves to guard the lambs from the lions."

As Finton pondered what his father meant, Tom turned on the car radio, and "Superstition" blared at them. They both reached for the volume knob, but Tom smiled and relented as Finton turned it up. The same song was still playing when they pulled into the driveway. The evening was darkening, so the lights were turned on in the priest's house, which had been built adjacent to the church, down a long, straight driveway a couple of hundred yards from the beach. The huge white building was three times the size of the Moon bungalow, with an extra story and a massive foundation. It was a spectacular sight, rising up from the rocks with the mountains as a backdrop and the ocean practically bordering the front yard. The priest's door boasted a brass doorbell—a feature lacking from most other houses in Darwin. Finton had seen them only on TV.

Millie, the middle-aged housekeeper with her hair in a bun, answered the door and greeted them warmly before leading them into the parlour where the priest was watching television in denim jeans, powder-blue short sleeves, and a thin white collar. The casualness was startling, like seeing his mother in her underwear.

Father Power rose quickly and extended his hand to Tom, who shook it heartily despite being surprised by the gesture. *Nanny Moon would be proud*, Finton thought.

Father Power asked what they thought of the cold weather they were having.

"Makes me want to go someplace warm," Tom said and cleared his throat.

Finton squinted as he assessed the priest's face, not seeing much in the way of lines or wrinkles. "How long have you been a priest?"

Father Power's cheeks reddened as he looked helplessly to Tom. "He's an inquisitive little fellow, isn't he? Does he get that from you?"

"Oh, I'd say so, Father. He's always asking questions, that one. We just tell him to be polite and mind his own business, but he just keeps on asking. Might have to lock him up one of these days just to shut him up."

The priest laughed again, with genuine enjoyment shining in his eyes. Finton thought he appeared rather lonely and was suddenly glad he had agreed to come for supper. "I hear you've had your own experience with prison," Father Power said.

"Just a bit." Tom seemed suddenly deflated. "It was all a big mistake."

"Yes," said the priest. "No doubt, it was." He nodded towards Finton. "Meanwhile, I wouldn't worry too much about the boy's curious nature. I'm sure he'll grow out of it—you know, with the proper instruction."

Tom ran an agitated hand through his hair. "He's all right. Just a bit, what was it you said? *Inquisitive*."

Millie appeared from the kitchen to announce that the cook had finished preparing supper. To Finton's relief, as they followed her to the dining room, no one had mentioned the bloodstains on his pants or inquired about his underwear. Father Power sat at the head of the table, while Tom assumed the seat on the priest's left, and Finton sat on his right.

Even with the gigantic table, oversized chairs, and a hutch full of dishes on display with rich, colorful patterns, the dining room easily could have accommodated another set of furniture of about the same size. The towering white candlesticks rose up like miniature skyscrapers from the enormous candelabra in the centre of the table, and the heads of the fresh-cut jonquils loomed over the table like floating faces. Gazing into one such flower, Finton half expected it to talk to him while he dined. There was more cutlery than he'd ever seen, each piece plated in silver and larger than Finton could comfortably grasp. Three silver vases filled with small, simple flowers sat beside a different bottle of red or white wine.

After Millie and a pretty, young redhead who appeared to be her assistant, brought the meal out on silver trays, everyone filled their own plate. But no one spoke, perhaps out of discomfort because they were strangers to each other, or maybe from a sense of awe. There was enough food to feed a Peruvian village: steaming potatoes and assorted colours of vegetables, a gravy boats with a long-handled ladle, a turkey and a ham, as well as stuffing and peas pudding. On a subconscious level, Finton was plotting how to bag some of it up to bring home to his perpetually hungry brothers.

"I hurt my leg today," Finton said as he chewed on a thick slice of ham. The mere mention of that incident reminded him of his time with Morgan earlier that day, and he felt his cheeks burning. He hoped no one else could see his embarrassment, but the yellow-faced jonquil seemed to be staring at him.

Father Power peered questioningly at Finton, causing the boy to stop eating and put down his fork. "I was thinking my young guest would honour us with grace."

Finton hadn't realized all eyes had turned to him until Tom cleared his throat. "Finton?" Startled, the boy looked up. "Father Power asked if you'd like to say grace."

"No, thanks."

"Finton."

There seemed to be no escaping this horrible moment without some casualty, and so the boy sighed and clasped his hands. "Dear God." He paused to assemble his thoughts, aware that, except for a cat meowing in some other room, there was no other sound in the entire house. He thought it best to pretend he was addressing an actual being, and so he directed his speech to the invisible puss. "Thank you for this meal and for bringing me and Dad to eat with Father Power. God bless us all. Amen." He blessed himself and peeked for reassurance at the holy man, who nodded mirthfully. His father, with glistening eyes, had forgotten to unclasp his hands and was gazing blankly at a wall full of paintings and dark furniture.

"So," Father Power said, clearing his throat. "You've become quite the celebrity."

"I dunno. I'm just me." Finton suddenly felt terribly uncomfortable, especially since he could feel fresh blood seeping from beneath the bandage on his leg.

"The rumour these days is that you can heal the sick." Father Power fixed his eyes on Finton, reminding him of the shady-looking actors he'd seen portraying Judas in those Sunday afternoon religious movies. "There are stories going around about how you helped a boy walk without his crutch, and another girl came to life when she was, for all intents and purposes, dead. And then there's the incident you told me about yourself—Miss Bridie Battenhatch, I believe."

"But you didn't believe me," said Finton.

"That's irrelevant now." The priest chewed slowly, despite an apparent lack of interest in his food. "The point is whether it's true. Do you think you possess this… power?"

The boy squirmed, feeling the heat rise in his cheeks. "I'm not the one who says it, Father. That's what everyone else says."

"They're just stories, Father. Hearsay and rumours." Tom cleared his throat again and unconsciously patted his shirt pocket for a smoke. "Finton never claimed any such thing. They just started comin' around, knockin' on the door and ringin' the phone like there was no tomorrow. Finton fix this, Finton heal that. It's to the point where we don't even go out anymore. People are always asking him to do stuff."

"So it must be true." Father Power leaned forward, hands clasped. "You really can heal the sick."

"I'd rather not talk about it," said Finton.

"But you should talk about it. Anyone who can do what you do…" The priest paused, his eyes taking on a faraway, serious look. "It must make you very *proud*."

Finton angled his fork towards the mashed potatoes and dug a hole through them that went all the way down to his plate. "It makes me sad."

"Sad?"

"Yes. All those people who are sick. Sometimes I can't even give 'em what they need, and it makes me wish I could. But mostly I wish they'd just stop it and go away."

"But surely you understand what a gift you have."

"More like a curse. The family never gets a minute's peace. Mom can't even go to the store without being pestered. My friends don't even hang around much no more." The words felt true, but he sensed that he shouldn't have said them aloud, as an uncomfortable silence entered the room. The flame of one candle quivered as if a breeze had swept in.

"Finton's always been a loner," Tom said as he fumbled with his breast pocket. "He has friends, but they don't come to the house."

"You're an unusual sort of boy." The priest picked up his fork, thoughtfully and methodically. "You have to be very careful about these kinds of things, Finton. Only Jesus can raise the dead and heal the sick. Read your Bible. Or maybe you already did. Perhaps that's how you know these stories. You're obviously quite a good student."

"I'm not making it up," said Finton.

The priest smiled. "But I'm sure you can understand why the church would be interested. The bishop wanted me to remind you that there's a penalty for claiming to have the same powers as God."

"Excommunication?" said Finton, the very word causing a sudden pang in his chest. He glanced at his father, who seemed lost in thought.

"Unless," said the priest, "you can perhaps show me these miraculous healings. I'd like to see that."

Father Power pushed his plate aside and nodded to the young redhead to come take it away. "I burned my arm yesterday on the stove." He blushed deeply as he rolled up the sleeve on his right arm. "I sometimes like to fry up some hash from leftovers if I have the time. Gives the women a break." He showed them the angry, red scar on his forearm, wincing as the sleeve was pushed all the way up.

"Looks pretty bad," said Tom.

"The very fact that I'm asking you this isn't to be repeated outside these walls, if you don't mind." The priest smiled halfheartedly. "It might be construed by some as a bit hedonistic to ask for an act of magic, as it were."

Tom leaned back and folded his arms across his chest. "You could go to a doctor."

"It's not much of a burn, as far as burns go. It'll heal on its own in good time. But I thought, since Finton has these powers, why not ask? Give the boy a chance."

"I can't," said Finton, stuffing his clasped hands between his legs.

"Please, Finton." Father Power stood up, his hands folded as if in prayer at his waist. "You'd be doing your church—and me—a great service."

"No," said Finton. "I can't. I don't know why, but I think I lost it."

"Can you at least try?" The priest sighed heavily, furrowing his brow. "I'm not saying I believe, but—"

"You don't understand." Finton pushed himself away from the table and let himself down from his chair. He slipped in a spot of something on the floor and had to grip the table with both hands; the entire table shuddered and clanked. One candle went out, sending white smoke wafting upward. "I can't do it."

"That's all right." Tom cocked his head and winked. "You'd do it if you could, right?" He turned to the priest and gave a quick wink. "You have to understand, Father—I never really believed he could do anything special. Everything he did can be explained. You said so yourself: Miss Bridie was never dead. I'd venture to bet the young Connelly one was gettin' better on her own. And I never saw anyone really get healed." Tom pulled a cigarette from his pants pocket and stuffed it between his lips. "I don't think there's anything to it."

"Fine," said Finton, suddenly feeling challenged by his father's doubtfulness. "I'll try."

The priest immediately stuck out his arm, holding back his sleeve, while Tom gave him another sly wink. "What do I have to do?" Father Power asked.

"Nothin'," said Finton. He grasped the priest's wrist and took a deep breath. "This might hurt when I put my hand on the blister, okay?"

Father Power held his breath and nodded quickly. "Just get it over with."

Quickly, but gently, Finton placed his palm over the burned area and closed his eyes. He heard a gasp as the priest shuddered and swore, "Jesus, Mary, and Joseph."

But Finton wasn't feeling anything. In his mind, he tried to reach for the Planet of Solitude. Tried to envision himself leaving the earth. Conjured an image of a white apple tree, but it wasn't the same one. He even tried praying a "Hail Mary" out loud. But when he opened his eyes, Father Power still winced in pain, eyes shut, looking as if he were about to pass out.

"You can open your eyes, Father."

All three of them gazed at the wound, which was just as angry and raw as before, perhaps even more so. "It didn't work," said Finton. "I don't know why."

"It's fine," said the bishop, shaking visibly as he rolled up his sleeve. "I'll just have Millie put something on it. "Go with God, my son."

Father Power saw them to the door. "Your grandmother once told me that you were hoping to join the priesthood someday." He gazed into Finton's eyes. "You'd make a fine priest."

"Thank you," said Finton. He considered admitting his recent doubts, but didn't see the point of making things worse. They were standing in the open doorway now, the chill of the night enveloping them all. "I'm sorry I couldn't help you."

"It's unfortunate." The priest rubbed his arms and began to close the door. With a touch to the father's shoulder, he said, "But at least now we know. Of course, if your circumstance changes, please apprise me. I'll tell the bishop what had happened, and that'll be that. No miracles for Darwin. At least not tonight."

"You go ahead, Finton. I wanted to talk to Father Power for a minute." Tom gave him a nod, and Finton did as he was told. Sitting in the car, he watched the two men converse, their figures illuminated by the light above the door. Considering his father wasn't religious, he wondered what Tom could possibly have to say to a priest. It might be a confession of some sort, but somehow he doubted it.

By the time his father said goodnight to Father Power and got in the car, Finton forgot all about it. He was simply relieved that the show was over.

On the Run

For Mary, the road to wellness was long and fraught with setbacks. Shortly after her Confirmation, she relapsed and became too weak to get out of bed. At the request of Mary's mother, Finton went to see her again.

She was awake, but barely and, in fact, she hardly seemed to know he was present. He didn't perform any special ritual, just sat and talked to her. He told her about school, that Dolly and Skeet seemed to be getting along, and that he was a little worried about Bernard Crowley. She didn't offer much of a response, just nodded once in a while and tried to smile. He considered telling her about Morgan. *Not that Morgan could replace you,* he would have said. But he decided it wouldn't help much to go blabbing to the girl he loved about his sexual encounter with another woman. Instead, he said, "I brought this great book," and he opened his copy of Harper Lee's novel and read from the beginning. Before he'd finished the chapter, she'd fallen asleep.

"Thank you for coming," Sylvia said when he was leaving.

He didn't tell her he could no longer heal, didn't want to explain. Finton was used to feeling different, but his power to heal people was the only thing that made him feel special. His one gift had left him on Confirmation Day and now that it was gone, it was highly possible it might never return, especially since he didn't know where it came from.

"You're welcome," he said, feeling sadder than he'd ever been. "I hope Mary can come back to school soon."

"I don't know about that." Sylvia shook her head. "There's times I'm not sure anything can help her, except maybe time."

"Hear about what happened at Bilch's last night?" Skeet stared down the orange metal hoop and lined up his next shot. Ever since his father had installed a hoop onto the Stuckeys' garage door, basketball had become the latest fad. Now and then, a bunch of the neighbourhood boys assembled for a game, but most evenings throughout the spring and summer it was just the two friends, bouncing the ball on the hardpacked earth and shooting twenty-ones. It was a simple game of follow-the-leader—when one player made a shot, the other one had to follow with a shot from the same location.

Finton found himself in the position of following. "Heard about it?" He laughed bitterly. "I'll probably never hear the end of it."

"I was there," said Skeet, who delivered his shot, the ball boinging off the rim and falling to the dirt. "We were all playin' pool—a bunch of us, including your brother. I was just rackin' for another game and in she comes, sir, like the friggin' wrath of God. Says, 'I'll give ya smokin'! I'll give ya girls 'n goddamn pool!'" Skeet wagged his finger and put his hands on his hips as he acted out the infamous scene. "'Get yer arse home out of this den of iniquity!' she said." Skeet pretended to grab Finton's collar and he was dragging him out a make-believe door. "Friggin' priceless. I'll never forget it."

"Neither will Homer," Finton said.

"What did he have to say about it?"

"Not much, b'y. Homer keeps that stuff to himself. He don't let on to anyone, but I'd say he's embarrassed."

Skeet laughed. "Well, he should be. If my mother did that, I wouldn't show meself anywhere again."

"Wasn't his fault." Finton picked up the ball, arced his arm, and swept the ball into the hoop. "Mom just don't like him going to Bilch's."

"It's still pretty funny." Skeet spat on the ground, lunged for the ball, grabbed it and faked a layup. He was a little scrawnier these days, but had recovered well from his illness. And he was still bigger than Finton by far. "You know, you still haven't told me what you did to me that time when I was sick."

"You said you weren't all that sick."

"Well, I lied. What did you do to me?"

"Nothing. I just… I don't know, okay? Just leave it alone."

"What about what you did with Mary—was that nothing too? And Miss Bridie?"

"I can't explain it, Skeet. I just can't. I laid my hands on you and just imagined you getting better."

It wasn't the first time his friend had asked for particulars about those incidents. Furthermore, it had been two weeks since dinner at the priest's house, and Finton still hadn't divulged any meaningful details. But he didn't know how to explain either the healings or the fact that he couldn't do them anymore. Furthermore, to divulge that the priest had asked for a demonstration would feel like a small betrayal since Father Power had asked him not to.

And yet, despite the lack of details from the source himself, many in Darwin viewed Finton as a celebrity. He wasn't even sure why, or when, his life had changed so dramatically, but he'd come a long ways from when no one wanted to sit with him on the bus. Perhaps Sylvia Connelly's praise of him had softened some hearts. As well, Skeet had told Dolly about his quick recovery from "certain death," thanks at least in part to an afternoon visitor—and confiding in Dolly was the surest way to spread news.

One day Finton got on the bus, and Albino Al and Dolly immediately squeezed in beside him, while a few more gathered around. Initially, he was flattered, but when the scene was replayed over and over, he grew tired of the constant attention. At school, as well, lots of people desired some favour, blessing or a simple touch, but even those who asked for nothing retained the right to gossip about him—or so he'd heard from Skeet, Dolly and sometimes one of his brothers. Most kids had grown accustomed to his extraordinary facility for healing, and some had begun shadowing him around the school grounds, hoping to catch proof of his supernatural talents. He'd come to think of them as akin to those pesky little birds that perch on the arses of rhinos and chew on their scabs. According to Marlin Perkins on *Wild Kingdom*, they were called "oxpickers," a name that bore a certain ring of truth.

Every day, Finton clambered onto the bus and a few people would wave their hands for him to sit beside them. If he sat alone, someone would join him. More and more, he began sitting in the back beside Alicia Dredge, comforted by the secrets they shared—their moment in the library and the book she'd given him. She expected nothing from him and, in fact, was one of the few who had seen fit to give something to him. He'd read *To Kill a Mockingbird* again and kept it under his mattress; occasionally he took it out to reread certain passages. On the bus, in such close proximity, they exchanged greetings and the occasional bit of chatter about the inhabitants of a house they passed by or some animal on the side of the road. He felt as if he was getting to know her a little, but mostly he took comfort in the knowledge that she was even more of a social misfit than he was.

One day, she had been quieter than usual and barely raised a smile as he approached and sat beside her. After a couple of minutes of staring at the passing landscape, he asked her, "Are you okay?"

With obvious hesitation, she admitted that her father had come home from drinking the previous night and wreaked havoc upon the Dredge household. "Nights like that, I can't even sleep," she said. "I stay up to make sure he doesn't hurt Mom, but there's not much I can do."

"Does he hit you?" Finton asked.

"Not unless I really deserve it. But Mom gets it regardless."

Finton nodded, wanting only for Alicia to keep talking, which she did. "I went to bed, but he was shouting and throwing stuff around. I heard him kick the TV, but he only hurt his foot." She smiled faintly. "I don't know what he did to Mom, but she didn't get up this morning. I checked on her, but she just told me to go away."

"Pretty rough," said Finton. "Dad only hits me when he's trying to teach me something… most times."

"Oh, mine is teaching me something, all right." She didn't finish the thought, but Finton was pretty sure of what she meant.

"I can't stand the cruelty of this place sometimes," he said as they rolled past Bilch's where the chestnut brown horse was grazing behind the fence.

"I know," said Alicia, and he could tell she was pretty sad about her mother. "Everybody drinks. You're nobody if you don't drink with them."

"It's the beatings, too," said Finton. "The fights. The names people call ya. The way they treats ya, like you're not even on the same level as them. But most of the time, they're just ignorant. They wouldn't know a good thing if it came outta the toilet and bit 'em on the arse." He raised his head and nodded towards the skyline on the left. "That salt water out there is filled to the brim with drowned cats and dogs, sure. The woods got more rotten carcasses than a cemetery." He hung his head and sighed, wondering if he'd gone too far. He lifted his gaze to see if Alicia felt the same.

She nodded slowly, as if coming to a sudden realization. "Darwin is a strange little place. Sometimes, I don't know how we live here."

"Or why," said Finton. "All I know is sometimes I feel I've got to get out of here so bad, I think I'll die. I don't know if it's better anywhere else, but I got to try."

She shook her head. "I'll never leave. I want to. But I think some of us are just meant to stay where we are."

"That's just foolish," said Finton. "You can leave whenever you want."

"Yeah, well, maybe you can." Alicia turned back towards the window, leaving Finton feeling as if he'd pushed her far enough for the moment. Apparently, it was harder being a Dredge than even he had known.

It occurred to Finton he'd left briefly, in his mind, and hadn't spoken to Skeet in quite some time. It was the bounce of the basketball upon the ground that brought him back. But Skeet was used to the long silences between them, and used to Finton being in two places at once. He hardly missed a beat. "Heard you were spending time at the Battenhatch house," he said.

"Who told you that?" Finton roused himself with a shake of his head.

"Morgan told me."

"When did you see Morgan?"

"Don't matter." Skeet rolled the ball around in his hand, focused on the net and made his shot. "Seen Mary lately?"

"Few days ago. She's doin' all right."

"Aren't you worried about her?"

"Kind of."

Finton had been about to take his turn when Skeet snatched the ball from him and said, "Why don't you ever talk about what's goin' on with you?"

"I tell you stuff."

"Yeah, right." Skeet plucked a homemade cigarette from behind his ear and popped it in his mouth, then whipped out his lighter and lit up. After a long, wistful draw, he underhanded the basketball to Finton. "You got more secrets than the Pope." He waited for Finton to miss his shot, then snatched the ball and slam-dunked it—not so difficult, considering the net had been rigged a foot lower than regulation. He returned to the shooting line, rolling the ball between his fingertips, and meditated his next shot.

"I don't like to talk about myself, that's all."

"I get it." He released the basketball, arcing it perfectly into the hoop. Finton chest-passed it back to Skeet at the line. "You're not the only one with secrets."

"Yeah?" said Finton. "Like what?"

Skeet paused, seemed as if he wanted to say something, then shook his head. "Never mind." His shot banked off the backboard and would have smacked the side of Finton's skull if he hadn't ducked.

Finton retrieved the ball and carried it to the line. Even as he was readying his shot, he found himself disturbed by Skeet's confession. He'd always thought of Skeet as someone without secrets or complexity. With everything else so messed up in his life, he'd come to depend on the simplicity of his only real friend.

"You can tell me," he said. "I wouldn't tell anyone."

Skeet smirked. "Shoot, would ya."

Finton launched the ball towards the net, but missed competely. He groaned, not because of the bungled shot but because he was worried about Skeet.

"If you change your mind—"

"Just fuck off, okay?" Skeet's choice of words was shocking. His swearing was notorious, but he'd somehow always refrained from directing such crudeness towards Finton. "There's nothing wrong. It's just school. Mudder. Fadder. Life. It's just all a big fuckin' joke, okay? I'm just sick of everything." He stepped to the line and appeared to consider his next shot. Then, without warning, he reared his arm back and lashed the ball at the side of the shed and made the clapboard rattle.

Finton threw his arms in front of his face as the ball zinged past him. It rolled behind them both and into the road. He hung his head, afraid to look at Skeet, fearful of this tantrum just as he dreaded those fights between his parents. If it were possible to do so, he would have gone invisible.

There was nothing he could say.

"Gotta go," Skeet said, taking a final draw of his cigarette and flicking it to the ground near Finton's feet. Then he strode away and into the woods.

When Skeet was worked up like that, there was nowhere for Finton to turn. He and Mary weren't exactly friends, but they at least had history. So he strolled the couple of hundred yards to her house, thinking it would be nice just to see her, to be in her presence, or to catch a glimpse of her.

She was actually sitting on the front step, sipping a cup of chamomile tea. Her complexion was so pale that even her freckles had faded somewhat, but being outdoors gave her more of a semblance of health than he'd seen in a while.

"Good to see you up and about," he said as he strolled up to her. He stuck his thumbs in the loops of his belt, hoping to look more casually confident.

She smiled as the sun beamed down on her face and rendered it buttercup yellow, nearly translucent. Just seeing her made his body thrum and his heartbeat quicken. "Hey, Finton. It's good to see you, of all people."

"Really? Why me?"

"Why not you? I hear every day about how 'that wonderful Moon boy' made me feel better."

"But you still seem kinda sick."

"Oh, this is definitely an improvement, believe me. I sit out here now and then, and I can feel myself getting stronger."

"Do you know what was wrong?"

"Started out as pneumonia," she said, shrugging. "Grew into something worse. I dunno. Anyway, thank you. I don't know what you did or how you did it, but everyone says I owe you my life."

Although he was certain she'd spoken figuratively, he liked the sound of her words. "You don't owe me anything. I just wish you'd come back to school."

"That's sweet of you to say. Sometimes I don't know how I got so lucky, to have such good friends as you and Dolly."

"And Skeet."

"Yes," she said, a flicker of trouble in her eyes. "How is Skeet?"

"Haven't you seen him?"

"He did drop by—I'm surprised he didn't mention it to you."

"When was that?"

"A couple of days ago." She lifted the cup to her mouth, her hands trembling from the exertion. "He seemed agitated. I was sitting here just watching the cars and people, tryin' to get used to the world again. He went by and I waved. He came over and sat. We didn't talk about much important, but he did say one thing that I thought was strange."

"What was that?"

"He looked me straight in the eyes and said, 'Do you ever wish sometimes you could say something to someone, but you know you shouldn't because it would change everything?'" She looked at Finton as if she were reading his thoughts. "Do you know that feeling?"

"I think so," said Finton. "What did you say to him? What was his big secret?"

"I had to practically beat it out of him—with words, I mean. He tried to take it back and almost left without telling me, but I threatened to run after him. Skeet's a hard one to figure out."

"Don't I know it."

She lowered her gaze. "He said you had a thing for me, but have always been afraid to say it." She looked directly at him in such a knowing, honest way that he couldn't escape the glare of exposure, nor could he lie. "Is it true?"

"I can't believe Skeet would say that to you." The world slowly slipped from beneath his feet. He jammed his hands deep into his pockets. "I mean, why would he?"

"Did you say anything like that to him?" she asked.

Here was the moment. If Finton lied now, he could never tell her the truth. This was an opportunity. Maybe he could have what he wanted. Maybe some stories had a happy ending. "Maybe," he said, starting out uncertainly. "The truth is… I've had a thing for you since Grade One."

She seemed stunned. Then she nodded, and kept nodding. "I should've guessed."

"I tried not to make it obvious."

"The Christmas gift," she said, still nodding. Not smiling and her eyes with a hint of pain. "I thought you were just being friendly."

"I didn't give one to Dolly, or Skeet." His voice faltered and faded. "Just you."

"Maybe I was just hoping," she said. "But why me?"

"You're the most beautiful girl I know. You're kind. You're smart. I can't wait to see you every day, and when you're not there, I want to go looking for you." He stopped, unsure of how much he could say, pretty sure he had ruined everything. "I think I'm always looking for you."

Her eyes brimmed with tears, and he wished he could erase the last three minutes from the world's history. "That's really, really… nice," she said. "I mean, wow. I never… I mean, what do you say to something like that?"

"That you like me too?" he said.

She shook her head sadly. "I can't say I feel that way for you when I don't. If I led you on, I'm sorry, Finton. I appreciate your friendship and all you've done for me. I probably wouldn't even be here if it wasn't for you." She wiped tears from her eyes, sniffled, and drew a deep breath that she exhaled slowly. "I'm glad you told me how you feel. I'm sure it's good for you, not to keep those feelings bottled up inside you. But…"

"You don't love me."

"No. I don't."

"Do you feel anything for me at all?"

"Not love," she said. "I don't want to give you false hope. Besides, I'm only fourteen. I haven't even dated yet. I've been sick—and my parents think I'm too young."

"Is there someone else you wanted to date?"

She thought for a moment, averted her eyes and said, "No."

"Well, that's it then." Finton looked away down the road, then once more at Mary. She seemed paler and weaker than when he'd arrived.

"I have to go inside," she said. "I don't feel well."

In one quick motion, she stood up and turned to go. At the last second, she swiveled and laid a hand to his face. She kissed his cheek, just beneath his scar. "Someday, you'll find someone who loves you and appreciates you. In time, you won't even remember me."

"I doubt it."

"I don't," she said. "You really are a wonderful boy, Finton Moon. Don't ever believe otherwise."

Then she turned, went inside, and was gone.

Something Wicked

"Now—" From her familiar spot at the rickety kitchen table, Miss Bridie plunked down two tumblers and a bottle of Five Star. "Tell ol' Bridie what ails ya."

As she poured the drinks, he deliberated on where to start. At first he said nothing as he avoided her haunting gaze. He stared at the comatose clock above the heat-blasting wood stove. Miss Bridie turned her head away, the glass raised to her parted lips, but not before he observed the moistness in her eyes.

"Sometimes," he said, "I just want to get the hell away from here and go where no one knows me."

"What about the girl?"

Her implied familiarity with Mary was unnerving, but he dared not show it.

But Miss Bridie pursued him to the darkest corner of his mind. "The little one you're always chasin' after—Mary, I believe. Does she even know you're alive?"

"She knows. But she don't care."

"Pretty harsh stuff," she said. "Not nice being unwanted."

They each fell quiet then and waited for the other to break the silence. She, being older and more practised in patience, outlasted him. "I just wish I felt at home somewhere, where people loved each other. That's not asking too much, is it?"

"Oh, you'd be surprised."

Morgan emerged from the bedroom in her cut-off blue jeans. There were large, ugly bruises all over her calves, thighs, and shins. "Hey, buddy."

"Morgan, be a good girl and put on the kettle. Poor Finton's had hisself a day."

He watched discreetly as she flicked her blonde hair behind her shoulders, picked up the kettle and brought it to the sink. While she turned on the tap and ran the water into the kettle, she stole a glance towards him, winked mischievously and smiled.

"Are you listening to me, lad?" Miss Bridie laughed and shook her head. "No, I don't suppose you are with the likes of that runnin' around half naked. Yer not so far off from yer father, are ya?"

He thought it was better not to refute the accusation. Meanwhile, Morgan eased the tension by announcing that she had to wash her hair.

"Goin' out again, girl! Can't ya stay home a single night with yer poor ol' mother?"

"There's more people in the world than you, Mudder."

Once again, Finton wondered who else she was seeing, though he tried to redirect his thoughts. No more rejection today. He just didn't think he could handle it.

Morgan ambled from room to room, grabbing a towel and a Balsam Plus bottle. She turned the water on, tested it for warmth, and thrust her head under the tap, letting the water anoint her. She chattered continuously with them as she scrubbed her scalp and massaged the shampoo into her long, blonde hair. Despite his better judgment, Finton found himself sneaking the occasional peek at her backside.

"Did you get anywhere with that advice I gave you about the Connelly girl?" Morgan was rinsing the soap from her hair.

"Depends on what you mean by 'anywhere,'" said Finton.

Morgan smiled as she turned off the taps and wrung the water from her hair. She bundled her hair into a towel, making her look like a Hindu goddess. "You're so sweet. I can't believe some bitch hasn't snatched you up yet."

"Believe it," he said. "'Cause it's true."

"Come on upstairs and we'll talk—Mudder don't mind, do ya?"

Miss Bridie cast a suspicious gaze at her daughter, furrowing her brow. "I hope talkin' is all yer doin'."

"Now, Mudder, he's only a child, sure. I'm just helpin' poor Finton with his girl troubles."

"That better be it." Miss Bridie jerked her head and coughed, a raspy sound that caused Finton to worry she might have something seriously wrong. "Go on then. I'm goin' for me walk." Miss Bridie had already removed the kettle from the burner and was pulling on her boots and coat, coughing occasionally, as Morgan shifted past him. As Morgan ascended the stairs, he scrambled to keep up with her. Two steps at a time, he followed those naked legs that promised sanctuary.

His face was blazing red, and the crotch of his pants had grown uncomfortably tight. Still, he liked this feeling of becoming. It was a pleasant sort of torture that he would gladly endure for as long as he had to. There was something delicious in the dark, musty air of the Battenhatch house that held him captive, intoxicated and yearning. In his own home, and in the world outside, he felt a perpetual hunger. But here he had the reasonable expectation that his cravings would be satisfied. Out there, he was forever foraging and never finding. Here, he'd discovered something tangible and comforting, however forbidden.

He took one last look at Miss Bridie. "Enjoy your walk," he said. He heard Morgan giggle from just above him. Turning towards the steps, he caught a glimpse of those legs and the trailing, white hand with its beckoning index finger. As he fled up the stairs and followed close behind her, she dashed into the bedroom. Shutting the door, Morgan twisted her body and fell onto the bed, clinging to Finton's shoulders. As the front door slammed shut, she pulled him on top of her and kissed him, snaking her tongue nearly to his tonsils. It felt as if she were pulling his soul forward and into her own.

This time was different from before. With their clothes off, rolling around on the bed, they fought for positioning, torsos taut, legs outspread, arms outstretched, grasping for something unattainable. He pulled the towel from her head and dropped it to the floor, causing her wet, blonde hair to caress his chest. Clinging to her hips, he licked her skin, nibbled her neck, and tasted her essence, memorizing the nuance of every part of her, gripping her like a faith object he was afraid would disappear. She played the starving animal, as before, but he was discontent with being prey. Each time she pushed, he pushed right back; whenever she tugged, he twisted, escaped, and landed on top. At one point he sat on her stomach and pinned her by the wrists, splaying her arms apart. He stared at her breasts, thinking how beautiful and full they were while he enjoyed a moment of unsatiated lust. He faced a choice—to maintain control of her or to let go of her wrists and touch her perfect, brown nipples. Having momentarily tamed Morgan, he feared to unleash her, certain that she would turn on him and make him her pet. He let go of her arms and reached for her breasts. But, in a matter of seconds, she flipped him onto his back and sat astride him, writhing, moaning, and satisfying herself at no one's whim but her own.

Not that he minded. It always had to be Morgan's way. Always had to be carried out in the manner conducive to her liking. Fortunately, he was thirteen and easily satisfied—satisfaction, however, was a temporary phase.

After he'd come twice, once as she straddled him and once as she lay beneath him, he was still descending from his great emotional height, on the brink of exhaustion, when he found himself gazing at her sated face, closed lids, and lips squeezed shut—and he suddenly became curious about what she needed, what made her lose her mind in the best of ways. He said, "How do you like it best?"

At first, she looked startled. It was a look she'd never given before. "You're not ready," she said. "You might never be."

It occurred to him then that she must have another lover, one who was ready. "I think I love you," he said. Despite the feeling that he had somehow betrayed Mary with those words, he was confident in his intentions.

She laughed, touched his face, and pushed him away. "You've lost your mind, b'y. It's only sex."

It was nearly an hour before he emerged from her bedroom, needing tea and a couple of Jam-jams. At some point, Miss Bridie had come in and had fallen asleep on the couch with a ratty blanket pulled over her. He sat at the kitchen table and watched the setting spring sun spill orange over the distant mountains, where the sea blazed the colour of hellfire and the sky reflected the blackness of his heart. If this was what it felt like to be a man, he wished he could have remained a boy. There would be a cost for falling in love with Morgan, or even just for loving her. But he didn't care. He only wanted the truth she offered. She had even told him, when he asked if she was on the pill, "You needn't worry about protection. I'm covered." It was a little too late for such concerns, he realized, but he was nonetheless relieved.

In the days and weeks that followed, he found himself obsessed with Morgan—or what she offered. Some days, he got lucky and found her home and willing, but most of the time Miss Bridie was there. He managed to kill time until late in the afternoons—school on weekdays, library on Saturdays, and mass on Sundays, or walking in the woods. But she was forever on his mind. Mid-afternoons, he would knock on Miss Bridie's door and she would usher him inside for a cup of tea. She never seemed suspicious that he was coming around so much, didn't seem to draw the connection between him and Morgan. On rare occasions, he would find Morgan at home by herself, and they would spend a few minutes or an hour, naked and having sex. If Miss Bridie happened to come in, he would go downstairs afterward for a yarn and some tea. But it didn't happen often enough to arouse her suspicions— or so he hoped. Perhaps she was simply good at keeping her misgivings to herself in the absence of proof.

Some days Morgan herself was out—likely babysitting, but he didn't know for sure. One day, Miss Bridie told him she was upstairs with another boy who'd arrived before him. "That's no odds, sure," she said. "I'll put the kettle on."

"No, thanks," he said, backing out the door, his gaze traveling up the stairwell. "I'll come back later. I needed to talk to Morgan." As much as he wanted to run upstairs, he didn't want to know the identity of her other lover. The age difference between him and Morgan meant she would have others; he'd already figured that out. He would have been deluded to think she cared only for him.

Deluded, even, to think she could really care about him. It hurt to think of such things, but there was nothing he could do. Just as Morgan knew he would, he kept coming back. He was addicted to her and didn't want a cure. She made him feel good, but she made him crazy. She gave him confidence, but filled him with self-doubt. He came alive in her bed, although she usually left him numb. Leaving her was like a resurrection—rising like Lazarus, more undead than alive.

On the morning of his fourteenth birthday, he got up early, determined to shake off the heaviness of recent events and do something great with the day. Nearly the whole family was gathered at the table having breakfast. No one mentioned his birthday. There were no presents, no confidential whispers. He gobbled down some oatmeal as fast as he could, burning his mouth when he forgot to blow on it.

"Homer said he saw you go into the Battenhatch place yesterday," his mother said. "I don't like gossip, you know."

"I saw you." Homer had his mouth stuffed with toast, while Clancy worked on a crossword puzzle and chewed his food.

Elsie was buttering her own toast, paying it close attention. "I don't want you going there, Finton. There's nothing good there for you."

"Happy birthday!" Nanny Moon said as she entered the kitchen. She'd been sleeping later in recent weeks and rarely had breakfast with the rest of them anymore. She crossed the floor and hugged him, gifting him with a peck on the cheek. "My, you're getting to be a big man now, aren't you?"

"Birthday?" Elsie's eyes grew wide. "Why didn't you say it was your birthday? You're always so secretive about things."

"Happy birthday, stinko!" Clancy didn't look up from his crossword puzzle, on which he often worked while eating.

"Yeah," Homer chimed in through a mouthful of toast. "Better watch out—you're gonna get the bumps today."

He regarded them all for a moment and took a mental snapshot. Leaving a half bowl of porridge, he dashed to the porch and out the front door. He leaped down the steps, taking all three at once, and nearly stumbled over a young woman who'd been sitting on the middle one.

"Sorry, Ruth. Didn't see you there." He recognized the young, shorthaired brunette as an older friend of Clancy's. She was one of the Crowleys, although distinct from Bernard and the rest of her family. Her clothes were hand-me-downs, but they were clean and well matched. In her early twenties, Ruth Crowley was more mature than Finton's oldest brother, with whom she occasionally consorted. "Clancy's having breakfast. Go on in."

"I came to see you," she said, standing up to her full height.

"Me? Why?"

"I've heard what you can do."

"But I haven't done it in a long time."

Her expression struck him as serene and sad, like one who'd endured much suffering. There was something else about her he couldn't quite touch.

"I'm going blind." She lowered her head, but lifted it again as if remembering her pride. "They told me all I had to do was touch your sleeve."

"There's more to it than that." He came forward and regarded her more closely. Her eyes were normal except for a thin, pale film that appeared on the upper half of both eyeballs. Without warning her, he covered them with his palms. But the pain in his hands was excruciating, and he jerked them away. Blood trickled down her cheeks. He instinctively held his hands in front of his face and, when he saw that his palms were smeared red, he emitted a sharp cry.

"What is it?" she asked. "What's wrong?"

"I can't help you—I just—" He blinked and opened his eyes. Ruth was fine, not a trace of blood on her. He'd just been imagining. "I'm so sorry," he said.

He heard the front door open and tore away down the lane like a youth possessed, away from that house, wondering if he was really hearing someone screaming behind him. Hands clamped on his ears, he ran for the woods and stopped only when he reached the landwash, where the stench of rotting seaweed made his eyes weep. He ran to the water's edge and knelt in the sand. He dipped his hands in the sea and scrubbed them clean, then splashed his face and rubbed his eyes. A wave rolled over his legs and backside, soaking his pants. As the imaginary blood dissipated, he peered to the sky where the seagulls laughed. Panting hard, he fell backwards onto the rocks and sand. The next wave rolled in and shot cold through his body like an injection of a powerful drug.

Without thinking, he said out loud, "Don't believe anymore," and he liked the sound of his voice, though the salt water gagged him. He said it again, his voice strengthening with each repetition until he was shouting and crying at once. "Don't believe anymore!"

The seagulls screeched while the ocean rolled over him.

Minutes passed. The sun soared overhead. Two gulls and a crow hopped about on the beach rocks, foraging for shellfish. The crow got brazen and pecked on his sneaker, even plucked his lace.

In time, Finton picked himself up and trudged, wet clothes and all, to the Battenhatch house. He knocked on the front door, but didn't wait for a response as they were getting pretty used to his visits.

Stepping into the porch, he was relieved that Miss Bridie wasn't sitting at the table. "Hello?" he called out. "Anyone home?"

"Just me," came Morgan's voice from upstairs. "Come on up, Romeo!"

He rushed up the steps to where she lay on the bed with the curtains drawn, listening to strange music. For a moment, he stood in the open doorway, until, perceiving his hard state, she rushed towards him, clasped his head on both sides and demanded to know what in Christ's name had happened to him. As she led him to the bed, he could only murmur, "I think I'm dead."

She stripped off his clothes and wrapped him in a musty towel. He shivered as she pulled him into the bed and under the covers. She slid beside him, hugged him tight, and rubbed him all over. "It'll be okay," she kept saying, over and over. He figured she was wrong, but he let her believe it. "Mudder won't be back for a while," she added, although, for once, he didn't care where she was. He was tired of secrecy and small town games, wanted out of his own head and out of this place, never to return.

When he was warm enough, they made love—urgently, gently, and wordlessly.

As they lay together afterwards, she said, "Happy birthday."

All he could think of, gazing up at the ceiling, was the hallucination he'd had of the bleeding, blinded woman.

"When did it all go wrong?" he asked.

"What?"

"I used to be able to heal with my hands."

Morgan hesitated as the shadows of late morning fed the room's darkness. The only sound was his beating heart. "I've never seen you do that," she said. "What do you do?"

"I made people feel better. I put my hands on them, and it made them better."

"How did it make you feel?"

"I don't know."

"Don't say that. You do know."

"It made me feel worse."

"In what way?"

"Like I gave them something they couldn't handle. That I couldn't even handle myself. I got headaches. Nosebleeds, sometimes. But it wasn't just that. It was something inside me. Not good or bad, just different. And maybe I shouldn't be doing it. Ya know?"

"Yeah," she said. "I know what you mean."

"Where did it come from?"

"I don't know."

"Maybe it's better that way."

He rolled over, kissed her on the lips, and awaited her reaction. He studied her face, so small and perfect, despite the lines he'd never noticed before at the corners of her eyes and mouth. "Why did you pick me?" he asked. His breath lodged in his chest.

"The same reason we all did," she said.

"I don't know what you mean."

"You'll figure it out."

"Why can't you help me figure it out?"

"That's not my job," she said with a sigh.

"What is?"

"Oh, I think we both know," she said as she traced a line down his chest and towards his pubic hair. He closed his eyes and focused on drawing his next breath. "You need me. I need you. We use each other. We both get what we want."

"What do you need me for?"

"Will you stop asking so many questions? What's wrong with you today?"

He didn't answer. "What do you need me for, Morgan?"

"Well, if you must know…" She cleared her throat. "I just wanted to see if I could corrupt you."

"I guess it was pretty easy."

"Sort of," she said in a mysterious way, her eyes taking on a troubled look. "But, in some ways, not so easy."

"What do you mean?"

"More questions?" She sighed dramatically and swept her hair from her face. The creaking of the bedsprings was intimate, comforting. When she realized he wasn't going to relent, she continued. "You're changed since we first did it. But you're still you. You know what I mean?"

He shook his head.

"You're still good," she said. "You still care about people. That's what I like about you." She propped herself up on one elbow. "Anyway, enough serious talk. Did your parents give you anything for your birthday?"

He lay back on the pillow, gazed up at the ceiling and marveled at the cobwebs that looked like a bride's veil, hanging from the ceiling. "They never do."

"You mean you've never had a birthday gift?"

"We can't afford it."

"You mean *they*. *They* can't afford it. You can do whatever you want if you make your own money."

He didn't speak for a few seconds. The thoughts and questions tossed in his head until, finally, he blurted one out. "Do you love your mother?"

"What kind of question is that?"

"I want to know. You seem to get along most of the time."

"Now we do. But we still fight. Let's just say we called a truce." She rolled over and leaned her head on one hand, her elbow propped against the pillow. With a finger, she traced the faint scar above his cheek—the one she'd given him when he was a baby on her Confirmation day—and then allowed her hand to wander, absently caressing the promise of chest hair that showed signs of becoming a bumper crop.

"Why did you hate her?"

"Oh," Morgan laughed bitterly, "where do I begin?"

"Wherever you want."

"Well, I don't owe you an explanation—or anyone else. But... she was mean to me. In the worst way. She'd call me names. Bitch. Slut. Cunt. Whore. Every time she saw me with a boy." Morgan's eyes glistened with a faraway look. "She can be pretty spiteful, my dear ol' mother."

"Enough to make you burn the house down?"

"Oh, that." Through Morgan's attempted smile, he saw a hint of nervousness. "I was messed up. Partying for days—came home for some peace and all I got was attitude. Same old names. Same old hatred. I brought up something I shouldn't have, and she threw a junk of wood at me. 'Do it again,' I said. 'I dare ya!'" Morgan laughed for real this time. "What a pair we were. I tell ya. She threw another one at me head. And another one struck me in the chest. I told her to stop or I'd fuckin' burn her out."

Finton could barely breathe. Never in his life could he have made up such a thing, and he was reasonably sure Morgan hadn't done so either. On the other hand, he could barely fathom that every word was true. "What made you stab her?" he asked, though he wasn't sure where the courage came from to ask such a question.

The coldness of her smile belied the merriment in her eyes. "That was a fuckup," she said. "She was bitchin' at me, as usual, for staying out drinking, accusing me of doin' drugs, screwin' around. Here I was, *trying* to get my act together. And there she was, half soused. She wouldn't let up." Morgan shrugged casually. "The knife was just lyin' there on the table. You wouldn't believe how much I was tempted—how hard I tried not to listen to the voice in me head telling me, 'Go ahead and stick it in her. Gut her like a trout.'" A flicker of regret appeared in her eyes. "Been best kind ever since. But if I hadn't fought back, I don't think we'd be even talkin' to each other these days, let alone livin' under one roof." She smiled languidly, seeming to realize Finton hadn't spoken in a while. "What are you thinkin' about?"

"You." He ran a hand through the shock of blonde hair that hung across her forehead, thinking how beautiful she looked when she wasn't wearing makeup or putting on an act. He found himself wondering if he loved her. *Enough.* That was the word that came to mind. Suddenly, he realized that, yes, he loved her in a certain way. But did he love her *enough?* "I always thought I had it hard, being so different," he said. "But I've had it easy compared to you."

He lay back, eyes closed, and enjoyed the warmth of her hand upon his chest, wanting to stay there, doing just that, for the rest of his life. That would be enough.

"You haven't had it easy," she said. "You and me are the same."

It was a lie, but he didn't tell her that. She needed it to be true, as much as he needed it to be false. He didn't want to be the same as anyone in Darwin. Acceptance here would also have a cost, and he wasn't willing to pay it.

"Happy birthday," she said. "You're one step closer."

"To what?" he asked.

"Everything," she said sadly.

In her eyes, there was a truthfulness he saw nowhere else in his world. Sometimes Morgan could be as artful as the most money-starved prostitute. But once in a while, her face possessed the most plain-spoken honesty, no price demanded.

It was only a few minutes later that they heard the front door open and shut, followed by the unmistakable sound of Miss Bridie coughing. It was the first time Finton had ever paid serious attention to it, as the coughing, for Miss Bridie, was as constant as her cigarettes or her cups of tea. They were all just a part of her. But the way she seemed to nearly gag with her hacking made him wonder if she was going to be all right.

"She went to the doctor," Morgan half-whispered, as if she'd read his mind. "She saw blood this morning."

Trembling, he immediately pulled on his clothes and, as casually as possible, went downstairs. "Heard you come in," he said. "Me and Morgan were talkin'. She said you went to the doctor."

"Nothin' to worry about, b'y," she said, barely glancing up from the table. He noticed she'd already put on the tea. "The bad news is that I'll live."

Crowley

As he stepped into the close confines of Bilch's snack bar, Finton's first thought was that he didn't belong. It wasn't a sudden realization so much as a remembrance—the recognition of an eternal truth.

It was the beginning of summer, and school was over for the year. The sun was just beginning to set on the streets, hollows, and hills of Darwin. It had been another rough day. Homer had brought home a failed report card, and neither parent had reacted well. Elsie cried briefly; Tom struck Homer on the backside with his hand and sent him to bed without supper. Finton tried to make his brother feel better. "Not everyone's good at school," he told Homer. "You can build things. I wish I could do that." Clancy, too, tried to cheer Homer up, but it was no use. The crisis simply needed to run its course.

After supper, when things had calmed down, Finton sat on the front step, still tense, but relieved that the school year was done. Mary never did come back to school, but he hadn't stopped looking for her on the bus. Now, he was relieved to be able to quit waiting. The police rarely came around their door either. Futterman would drop by to ask Tom questions about the Sawyer affair, trying to dig up forgotten information. But it had been weeks since he'd seen either Futterman or Kieran Dredge. Even Skeet was starting to come back to himself, though he was still pretty moody at times.

But none of that mattered now. There were only good days ahead; all he had to do was imagine them. He'd even decided to stop seeing Morgan. It took a few days after his birthday to make up his mind, but it seemed like the best thing. He didn't like being addicted to her, or to anyone else. Besides, he didn't get to see her very often, and he was tired of sneaking around for something he knew was for the short term. He yearned only for the freedom to do whatever he wanted this summer, no strings attached—no one to hurt, and no one to hurt him.

Then, after supper, Skeet came along. He seemed to have forgotten about their argument. Finton could hardly remember what they'd fought about, but he recalled that Skeet was dissatisfied with life in general. But, then, Skeet had a talent for getting over such things, and Finton was skilled at forgiveness. The one thing he couldn't forget, however, was that Skeet had blabbed to Mary about Finton's feelings for her.

They sat together on the Moon's doorstep, musing about the school year and the oncoming summer, favourite girls and comic books, as they gazed out at the meadow and the surrounding woods. Mosquitoes danced before their faces. Chickadees, robins, and sparrows sang. The setting sun cast trees and rocks in a blood orange veil. For the first time in weeks, Finton felt good and free.

"Did you tell Mary I had a thing for her?" he asked.

"She dragged it out of me," Skeet said. "Besides, someone had to tell her."

"Me," Finton said. "I should have told her."

"Yeah," said Skeet. "You should have."

"It wasn't up to you."

"Sorry."

Skeet looked sincere enough when he apologized, and so that was the end of it. Finton still felt the dual sting of Skeet's betrayal and Mary's rejection, but there was nothing he could do except swallow the pain, which was preferable to losing two friends over the same incident. He resigned himself to the likelihood that everyone had meant well; but, for some reason, Finton was the one who had gotten hurt.

Skeet suggested they go to Bilch's and play pool, a rite of passage Finton had yet to endure. While he occasionally wondered what went on inside of Bilch's after dark, he would gladly have ended his days in Darwin without ever having known.

"There might be girls," Skeet had said.

"I don't need girls."

Skeet had shook his head impatiently. "You're just a scaredy-cat."

"I don't see any reason to go to Bilch's, that's all."

"Don't you ever get sick o' being inside your own noggin? There's a world out there, Moon, and you're missin' it all with your nose stuck in a book half the time."

"You're tellin' me there's a world at Bilch's?" Finton had smiled sarcastically. "I don't think so."

"There's girls."

"You said that already."

"Well, then, lots o' girls—and they're nothing like Mary Connelly."

"Girls are the last thing I need."

"Because…"

"Because I plan to leave this shitty town, and I don't want to get some girl knocked up."

"Jesus, b'y—lighten up. It's only a friggin' game o' pool."

"Then leave the girls out of it."

"Fine." Skeet stood up. "You comin' or not?"

"I don't know."

"What's wrong now?"

"You know what happened with Homer."

Skeet laughed roughly. "So it's your mudder you're afraid of."

"That's not it." Finton jumped to his feet and stuck his hands into his pockets. He'd kicked at a rock beside the step, but his feet merely scuffed its surface, and the rock had gone nowhere. "She made him look like a tool in front of everyone."

"I know—I was there."

Finton sighed and squinted at the sun. "If she did that to me, I'd run away for good."

"Ah, b'y." Skeet clapped a friendly, big hand on Finton's back, leading him down the lane. "What's life without a little adventure?"

Bilch's was about a mile from Moon's Lane walking along the dusty shoulder of the road. By day, the Bilches ran a convenience store, where they sold every item known to Darwin—from shampoo, Corn Flakes, and hockey tape to Campbell's soup, ABC detergent, and louse combs. There wasn't much that Mudder Bilch didn't carry in her store, which was sometimes tended to by one of the younger Bilches. The father spent his time either watching TV or up in the woods, far from the prying eyes of the welfare officers. He had a bad back whenever they were around, but most times he was the picture of good health.

In reality, the snack bar was the rectangular west wing of a medium-sized, tumbledown bungalow a mile down the road from Moon's Lane. Aside from the dire need of a new paint job and the stench of manure from the fenced-in, chestnut horse in the side yard, the exterior was passable. But the insides fell a few shades below respectable.

As he pushed open the door and made the bell ring, Finton stood in the doorway, one foot inside and the other on the step. Already, those wood-paneled walls were closing in on him. Blue cigarette smoke hung over every piece of furniture and drifted above each head. A pinball machine was pressed against the back wall, with a large deep freeze to its right and a jukebox—blaring "Tin Man"—to its right. To Finton's left as he entered was a long, wooden countertop laid with a strip of red-and-black checkered linoleum. On the near edge of the counter sat a bubble gum machine, two-thirds filled with balls of various colours, the red ones being the most entrancing to Finton. Behind the counter, in front of a Coca-cola sign, Mudder Bilch leaned forward, hands clasped, watching Bernard Crowley and Willie Dredge play pool. Beside her, her son Chosey—a freckled, thirteen-year-old boy with the mind of a toddler—sat on a stool, scratching his head and squinting with puzzlement at the entertainment before him.

"Mom," he was saying in a graveled voice that sounded like a cat in heat. "When are these people goin' home?"

"Don't be so foolish, Chosey. These people gives us money so they can play our games. Why would you want them to go home?"

"I don't like 'em," he said, swiping at an imaginary fly on his cheek. "'cept that one over there." He nodded towards Millie Griffin, with short brown hair and freckles, drinking a Mountain Dew and smiling as she leaned against the deep freeze and watched Morgan play pinball. "I likes Milliegriffin," Chosey said. Despite feeling that he'd entered a madhouse, Finton sensed an innocence in Chosey that was rare in Darwin, at least among teenagers.

The main attraction was the hulking pool table, which consumed nearly one-third of the room. More than a dozen patrons milled about—drinking, talking, playing or watching—and he recognized some of them: Morgan Battenhatch playing pinball, shaking her rear end to the music and tapping the corner of the machine to make the silver balls do her bidding. Alicia Dredge watched her brother Willie line up his next shot, a worried expression on her face.

He glanced towards the only vacant space, near the back of the room, where a thick brown curtain separated the business side of the bungalow from the residential side. Finton wondered what was behind the famous curtain—definitely not the Wizard of Oz, but something more troubling. He heard rumours about the Bilches— how, at all hours, strange noises came from behind that curtain; how the youngsters were often brutalized by their father; how the small horse was brought in at night to sleep on the pool table. He couldn't quite picture any of it and, for that, he was glad.

Drawing a deep breath, Finton tried to quiet the warnings in his head as he timidly stepped forward into "that den of iniquity."

And then he saw Bernard Crowley with a cue stick.

"Well, look who's here." Bernard didn't move except to lift his gaze.

"Hey, Bernard." Finton nodded unsteadily.

"Don't worry about him," Skeet murmured. "We're just here to shoot stick."

"Mommy let you out tonight, did she?" Bernard had a cigarette stuck in his mouth and was bent over the side railing of the pool table. In his denim jacket, black t-shirt, and tight blue jeans, with his hair slicked back, he was a skinnier version of the Fonz. He sunk his shot, then looked up at Finton, who turned his back to his nemesis and went straight to the counter.

"Orange Crush," Finton said.

Mudder Bilch sized him up. "Haven't seen you in here before—not at night anyways."

"I knows you," said Chosey. "Do you know me?"

He shook his head and said "thank you" as she handed him the warm bottle—making him think the electrical cord joining the fridge to the outlet in the wall was a ruse—and he turned to assess his best chances for survival. His instinct was to huddle with Alicia, but she appeared more nervous than him—all the more reason to join her. He glanced towards Morgan, who was surrounded by horny teenage boys and a couple of girls, including Millie Griffin, all watching her slay the pinball dragon with quarters and a lot of shimmying and swearing. The bells on the machine rang out so prolifically that he assumed her quest was successful. It was the first time in a while he'd seen her anywhere but in her bedroom, and she appeared relaxed and enjoying herself.

Although he knew them all on sight, they were mostly strangers. Except for Skeet, Alicia, and Chosey, just about everyone there was older than him.

The next song that came on the jukebox was weird—he'd heard it only once before, in Morgan's bedroom—something about "heat whispered trees" and "two spirits dancing so strange"—and he figured she'd already put coins in the machine.

As he sidled close to Alicia, Orange Crush clutched in his sweaty palm, he could feel Bernard glare at him, grinning. But Finton ignored him and nudged Alicia. "Hey."

"Hey." She smiled, barely removing her gaze from the game.

"Good game?"

"Not so much."

"Bernard's beating your brother, eh?"

"Yeah," she said. "Bad for me."

"Why bad for you?"

She overlapped her top lip with her bottom one, then smacked both lips together. "They're playing for me."

Finton scrunched his eyes together. "You mean Willie's your proxy in the game?"

"No." She shook her head somberly, hair swaying before her eyes. "He ran out of money and Bernard gave him double or nothing—if Crowley wins, he gets to take me out."

"On a date?"

"Yeah." She swallowed hard, eyes glistening, lips drawn tight.

"That's kind of sick."

Alicia didn't answer, just focused on the game.

"How much money does he owe?" Finton asked.

"Twenty-four bucks," Alicia said. "Dad'll kill him if he doesn't win it back."

"Don't you get a say?"

Skeet suddenly moved in behind them and punched Finton's arm. "See? Not such a bad place, is it?" He tilted his Coca-cola bottle upwards and took a long, gurgling draught. When he'd emptied the bottle, he smacked his lips and patted his stomach, belching so loud he momentarily drowned out the jukebox.

Finton shook his head in disgust.

"I get a say." Alicia winced as Willie missed an easy shot to a corner pocket. "But Willie don't have all that money. If he don't pay up, Bernard and his buddies are gonna beat the shit out of 'im."

"You're kidding," Skeet interjected, now fully engaged in the conversation.

"Nope." Bernard suddenly stood upright, jamming the cue stick between his legs and stroking it up and down. "Couple more shots, and Miss Dredge and me are gonna get it fuckin' on!" He whipped around, bent over the table and, without hardly drawing a breath, he called his next shot—"combination, four off the nine, into the side"—and pointed to the pocket. Boom. Just like that. One ball left.

"Wait a minute," said Skeet. "This is not right."

"They're treating you like a piece of meat," said Finton. "Speak up for yourself."

"Too late." Alicia raised a hand to her mouth as if to chew her fingernails.

"It's not too late," he said, although something in her demeanour made him question whether she was really convinced. She seemed more interested in Bernard and, in particular, the way his backside filled out his jeans, than in how her brother was faring. Maybe she wasn't so dead set against the idea of going out with Bernard after all.

"Yer in the way, faggot." Bernard squeezed between the table and Finton, leaning in for his last shot, an easy pick: the three ball into the corner. Even Finton, who'd never played pool in his life, could have made that shot. He closed his eyes. *Don't make the shot*, he thought. *Don't make the shot.* He heard the clink of cue ball against three ball—a quick kiss, and it was done. The soft roll along the green felt tabletop lasted only a moment. There was a sickening clunk as the last ball dropped.

He opened his eyes as Bernard Crowley let out a whoop and celebrated with a pump of the cue stick. Bernard looked at Alicia, almost apologetically, then grinned at Willie and shrugged. "Better luck next time, Dredge."

He reached for Alicia's arm. She jerked back, but he moved quickly and pulled her towards him. He pressed his body against hers and whispered in her ear, causing her to slap his face and try to push him away.

Without thinking, Finton wedged himself between Alicia and Bernard, surprising all three of them and spilling some of his soft drink. "You don't have to go with him, Alicia," he said.

Skeet's eyes opened wide. "Fuck," he said, shaking his head. "This is not good."

Finton turned to Alicia. "Get out," he said. "Go home."

"She's mine," Bernard said as he tugged on her arm. "I won her fair and square." Again she yanked her arm away, but he grabbed it once more. Finton clamped a hand down on Bernard's wrist and split them apart, then gave Bernard a small shove, which made the Crowley boy snarl, "Back off."

"I don't like it either," Willie said, scratching one of his large ears. "But he did win, fair and square, like she said."

"Well, aren't you the man?" Skeet said sarcastically.

Suddenly, the jukebox went quiet. The pinball machine paused. The shouting fell silent. Finton laid down his Crush.

Willie sneezed and wiped his nose in his sleeve. "Not your problem, Stuckey. Stay out of it."

"Finton?" a female voice called from the far left corner. *Morgan.* He cringed as she made her way through the small crowd, pushed Alicia aside and stood beside him. Alicia quickly edged her way back in, however, and maneuvered her way in front of Morgan. "What the hell are you doin' here?"

Here it comes, thought Finton. Gettin' dragged by the collar out of Bilch's snack bar—the new Moon family tradition. But that wasn't Morgan's style. Not at all.

"This arsehole giving you a problem?" She glared at Willie.

"Hey—watch it!" said Alicia. "That arsehole's my brother."

"Not him," said Finton, and he nodded towards Bernard. "This arsehole." He paused, partly for a reaction, partly to give himself time to think. He truly didn't know what he was going to do. But he had to come up with something fast because Bernard already looked as if he had run out of patience, throwing the cue stick aside and raising his fists.

"Alicia, leave." Finton nodded towards the door.

"This isn't your business, Finton. You should go." Even as she said it—despite her obvious anger—she fought back tears. The way she looked at him said she was grateful he'd stepped in. Unlike her dumb brother, at least he hadn't abandoned her.

Bernard grabbed the front of Finton's shirt. "I've been wanting to pound the shit out of you for a long time, faggot." Instantly, Skeet grabbed Bernard's wrist and wrenched it away.

"Outside!" Mudder Dredge yelled. "Don't want no blood on these floors. Take it outdoors, or I'll call the cops."

"Fine." Bernard pounded a fist into his open hand. "Outside is what I had in mind anyway."

But taking matters outside didn't resemble Finton's wishes at all. Bernard led the way, pulling open the door and making the bell ring. Finton thought, with little satisfaction, that an angel had just gotten its wings. The uproar from the mob was nearly deafening as he found himself being propelled towards the exit, despite the fact he had no intention of fighting.

There were two suped-up cars—a blue Charger and a yellow Javelin—in the small, dirt driveway. The two antagonists were thrust together, while the throng of spectators squeezed itself between the two vehicles. Although Alicia remained near Finton, clutching his right arm, and Bernard's cronies, Cocky Munro and the redheaded King twins, retained a close proximity to their hero, most of the ones Finton knew had been pushed to the perimeter. From near the back of the crowd, Skeet shouted, "Leave 'im alone, Crowley!" Morgan jumped up on the Javelin, flexing her bare arms and shadow boxing. In her denim short-shorts and tight, yellow t-shirt, she looked like one of the girls from Clancy's *Hot Rod* magazine covers. "Uppercut, Finton. Your best goddamn friend—uppercut!"

He'd never given anyone an uppercut before and, furthermore, didn't know how to, even if he'd been so inclined. He supposed that if a fight were to happen, Bernard would just beat him up with any combination of two or three punches. It might only take one, of course, and that in itself would be merciful.

Across the road and away to the south, the dying sun had set the ocean ablaze. Even the trees seemed draped in an orange veil that grew denser as the sun sank behind the mountains. Finton lifted his eyes as the sun's last rays painted his skin. The fading heat infiltrated his pores and seeped into his soul. A voice from somewhere said, *Don't be afraid.*

Bernard was waving around his two softball-sized fists like a prize fighter warming up, and Finton was mesmerized by the steady, piston-like motion. Blue and white spots danced before his eyes and inside his head. He'd expected to panic, but somehow, he stayed calm. People were banging on the hoods of cars, screaming for someone to hit someone. "Don't be afraid of him," he heard Millie Griffin say. There was no mistaking the intended recipient. Bernard Crowley wasn't likely to be afraid of anyone, especially Finton Moon.

"Rip his head off," someone else yelled. "Piss down his neck!"

An impatient onlooker shoved Finton towards Bernard, and Alicia yelped. As if he were flicking a crumb from his lapel, Bernard grabbed Finton's shirt and pushed him away. Finton fell to his knees, hands planted in the rocks and dirt.

"Stop it!" he heard Skeet shout.

"Get up!" Morgan yelled from her perch on the Javelin's hood. "Fuck him up good!"

"You gonna fight or not?" Bernard pounded his fists together and managed a slight shuffle despite the closeness of the surrounding mob. Then he ripped off his jacket and flung it aside.

"That's enough," Alicia said, stepping between the two of them as Finton rose to his feet. At the same moment, Bernard took a jab at Finton's face, but instead struck Alicia's cheek, and she fell backwards into a pair of arms.

"Jesus," Finton yelled, and he thrust himself forward enough so that he could place a hand on the small of her back.

"I'm all right," she said, though her eyes were glassy.

Finton rose up to his full height. He glared at Bernard, who shrugged and said, "She jumped in front o' me. It's her own fuckin' fault."

"Someone needs to teach you a lesson in how to treat people," Finton said.

"Come on then, if you're man enough."

Finton dangled his hands loose at his side to show Bernard he wasn't going to fight. "What's wrong with you?" he asked.

"Just shut up and fight." Bernard took a step towards Finton, who felt his first real tremor of fear. His eyes were bedazzled by the setting sun, which had painted the landscape behind Bernard like a vibrant oil painting. A mosquito buzzed at his ear and landed on it. Instead of swiping at it, Finton merely picked it up and tossed into the air between him and Bernard where, it hovered for a moment before flying away. Despite the jolt of adrenaline, Finton felt surprisingly peaceful, as if this moment were no different from any other—as if this was where he was supposed to be, doing precisely what he was supposed to be doing, no matter how awful it probably looked.

"Why do you need to do this?" said Finton. "These people are just using you to spill some blood. They're too scared to fight you themselves, so they like the idea of you beatin' the shit outta me just for fun."

"Fun for me too," Bernard smiled shakily. "So let's get it over with."

"Fine." Finton raised his hands and spread his arms outward. The sun was nearly blinding him. All he could see was the dark silhouette of an oversized high school kid with his upraised fists. Behind him lurked shades of other kids, most just standing and staring in near silence. *They're listening to me*, Finton thought. Hanging on every word between the two combatants. They wanted some blood—it didn't matter whose—but mostly they craved the show. Something to tell.

Bernard came forward, fist raised to strike. Finton closed his eyes and thought, *Our Father, who art in Heaven, hallowed be thy name.* When Bernard socked him, the pain in his stomach was excruciating, and he doubled over, holding his gut. *The kingdom come, thy will be done.* No sooner was he aware of being suspended by both arms when he fell to his knees, vomit burning his throat as his fishcake supper splattered onto the ground.

"Get up," he heard Bernard say.

The voices around him said, "Just stay down." But Finton stood up and wiped his mouth. There was Bernard, standing mostly in shadow, tinged with orange. He looked perplexed, as if he'd never seen anyone get up from a beating before. In fact, Finton's audacity must have made him angry. Bernard rushed at him, wrapped his arms around Finton's neck, and wrestled him stock-still.

From atop the car, Morgan yelled, "Kick 'im in the nuts, Finton!"

Skeet shouted, "Leave him alone, Crowley! He's littler than you," and he lunged across several people to take a swipe at Bernard's head. His knuckles made contact, but Bernard barely flinched.

"Back off," Finton said in a calm voice that seemed to come from deep inside him. "I got this." He didn't struggle against Bernard's chokehold. He chose to remain tranquil and tire him out, figure him out, and wait for the danger to pass.

"You don't want to be doing this, Bernard. It's just because of who you are."

"Jesus, faggot, if you don't shut up, I'll kill you."

"All they wants is for you to entertain them like a circus freak. Like a stupid animal—'cause you're just a Crowley."

Bernard squeezed harder. Finton feared his windpipe would be crushed.

"You won," he rasped. "You proved you could beat me. Just let go."

"I already knew that."

"Well…" Finton coughed. His stomach hurt. He would certainly throw up again if Bernard didn't release him soon. "Then why are we fighting?"

"Because you're a faggot."

Finton struggled to speak, his throat hurt so bad. "Even if I was, you're not proving anything." Coughed again, thought he tasted blood.

"That's enough," Skeet said. Suddenly he was there, pulling them apart.

"No," said Finton.

But Bernard allowed his arm to be drawn away—too easily, Finton thought. Once freed, Finton slumped to the ground, coughing and sputtering, and folded his hands across his chest to hold himself in, hands to his throat and elbows against his stomach. Morgan crouched beside him, cradling his head in one hand and stroking his arm with the other. Alicia hovered over him, looking down on him, the last rays of light setting her crown aglow.

"Wait," Finton said as he struggled to his feet. The earth was unsteady beneath him, the stars above unnaturally close. "Bernard."

The Crowley boy was rubbing his chin as Skeet pointed a serious finger in his face, saying, "Next time, I'll kill ya." Bernard blandly ignored him and looked at Finton instead. He couldn't help feeling it was the first time Bernard had truly seen him. A diminished light stared out from those eyes. "Yeah, faggot?"

"Just 'cause you won don't mean you gotta keep fightin'."

Bernard sighed and looked up to the stars. "Jesus, Moon." He glared at him again and, once more, seemed to see the human being standing before him. "Just shut up, will ya?" He nodded to Alicia, who appeared to be in shock. "You comin'?" he asked.

She glanced apologetically towards Finton. "A deal's a deal," she said, "and ya gotta admit—he earned one date, at least."

"At least," Finton murmured as he watched her allow Bernard to take her by the arm and guide her away.

That's when the police car came, and everyone scattered—everyone but Finton.

Since Finton wasn't being charged with a crime, Kieran Dredge let him ride in the front seat. It was only a few minutes from Bilch's to Moon's Lane, but long enough for his initial sense of shame to become mixed with a sense of pride at riding in a police cruiser.

Kieran glanced at Finton. "So who was involved?"

"Just me."

Suppressing a sardonic grin, Kieran prodded him. "Oh, come on. You mean to say you were fighting yourself?"

"No. There was no fight at all."

"Then why the crowd?"

"Everyone just realized it was time to go home."

"All at the same time?"

"All at the same time. I guess Mudder Bilch was closing up."

"I got a call that there was a fight goin' on between a Crowley and a Moon—care to enlighten me?"

Finton sighed. "I don't want to be a snitch." Too quickly, they chewed up the asphalt. Already, he could see the Battenhatch place. Almost home.

"Look, Finton. You're a good lad. But you're going down a bad road."

"Yes, sir."

"Stay away from there," he said and turned onto Moon's Lane. "More important, stay away from the Crowleys. They're bad news. The worst."

"I know."

"Give me your word you'll keep your distance, and I won't pursue this any further… not with you anyway."

"But Bernard's the one who's after me. I don't have nothin' to do with him, but he's always lookin' for trouble."

"Next time, walk away."

"It's not that easy. You don't understand."

"You don't think so, do ya?" Kieran laughed. "Alicia ever tell ya what a hard ticket I used to be?"

"You?" Finton's eyes grew wide.

"Oh, yeah. I'm not proud of it, but I was a pretty bad case. Ask anybody around here. I won't say what I did, but it's a wonder I got out alive and without a record."

"So how'd you get into the RCMP?"

"I was determined to get away—to clean up my act and do whatever it took. I thought about the military, but this is more my style. I'm a stay-at-home kind."

"Not me," said Finton. "I can't wait to get away."

"Yeah, well, for that to happen, you're gonna have to stay outta trouble—unless you're lookin' for someone to take you away. You get what I'm sayin'?"

Finton nodded. But, apparently, that wasn't good enough for Kieran, who kept on talking. "I'm saying there are other ways outta here— there's handcuffs and there's body bags, and you don't want either one, understand? And neither do your parents."

"Got it." Finton slid out of the car, paused and said, "Thanks." Then he slammed the door on the police car for what he hoped would be his first and last time. Still, there was a part of him that couldn't wait to tell Skeet.

Some Other Place

The only blessing was that neither his brothers nor his father were home when Kieran dropped him off. But the look on his mother's face hurt more than Bernard Crowley's fist or chokehold.

"I was pickin' up for someone," he said, a slight wheezing sound in his throat. He touched a thumb and forefinger to the aggrieved area, realizing that talking might be uncomfortable for a while.

She blessed herself and laid a hand on his swollen cheek. He couldn't remember being hit in the face, but he guessed it might have happened inadvertently during the skirmish. The cut was little more than a flesh wound. "That's the last time," she said. "Don't you ever set foot into Bilch's again, ya hear me?"

He didn't answer, but he figured staying away would not be a problem. He'd had more than his fill of Bilch's and everyone there. As far as he was concerned, Bilch's was the worst of Darwin epitomized. The cruelty. The bloodsports. The pettiness and strange sense of justice. And now, Alicia going out with Bernard Crowley? Who would have thought that was even possible?

Of course, he suspected the real reason she hadn't spoken up for herself. "This isn't your business," she'd said. Secretly, he figured, she really wanted to go out with Bernard, and the pool wager was just an excuse. After all, she hadn't exactly seemed brokenhearted to go with him. If anything, she seemed eager, and that realization stung more than the rest.

"I never thought I'd see the day the police would be coming to this house on a regular basis. First for your father and now you." She shook her head shamefully as she plastered the Band-Aid on his cheek and smoothed the edges. "Where in the name o' God did I go wrong, I wonder?"

That was a question for which he had no response. He wasn't even sure she'd done anything wrong; he just had the sense that he'd been born a certain way, and trouble would probably always follow him. Tom came home at that moment, and the first thing he noticed was the injury to Finton's cheek. "What in the blazes happened to you?"

"Don't start," said Elsie. "I already had me say—and you're in no position to judge. In fact—"

"In fact, what? You're saying this is my fault?"

"Well, I'm not the one he takes after."

"Please stop," said Finton. "Don't fight again."

"Finton, don't talk that way to your mother."

Déjà vu. That was the feeling. But this time, he wasn't having it. He got up from the table and started for the living room and turned on the TV. "Let me know when you're done fighting." For the next half hour, while she told Tom the details of his exploits at Bilch's, and they argued like politicians, he watched *The Dean Martin Show*. He'd seen this one before, with Donna Fargo singing "Happiest Girl in the Whole U.S.A." His mother loved that song, but he turned down the volume when it came on.

Finally, when things calmed down and his mother had retreated to the bedroom to collect herself and cry, Tom came slowly into the living room and sat down on the couch. They watched a skit where Dom Deluise came to the door and Dean answered it, pretending to be drunk. His father even laughed. "I love that Dean," he said. "He's the king of cool. There's nobody cooler than Deano."

"I remember the story from when I was born and everybody sang that song."

"What song was that?"

"'You're Nobody Till—'"

"'Somebody Loves You.'" He chuckled as he lit up a cigarette. "Yeah, sure. I remember now. Always loved Dean. Always did."

"Skeet says Dean is a Negro." Finton didn't know exactly why he said it, but it was true. Skeet had said it, and now Finton wanted his father's impression of the idea.

"Well, sure, he's got dark skin. But Deano's as white as me or you. Not an ounce of Negro blood in 'im. Where the hell would he get an idea like that?"

Finton shrugged. "He's pretty dark."

"I s'pose," Tom nodded, then shifted abruptly as if leading up to what he really wanted to say. "Your mother's not too happy with you."

"It wasn't my fault."

"I know. I just wanted to say… I'm proud of you."

"For what?"

"For standin' up for yourself. Goddamn Crowleys are a no-good bunch. Had my own run-in with Hector Crowley a long time ago, and one of us nearly got killed that night, I tell ya."

"Why?"

"Don't matter. Let's just say he had a thing for your mother, and my thing was bigger." Again, Tom laughed, and Finton cracked a smile in spite of himself. "Anyway, I promised yer mother I'd say something. And I mean it—you did good to look after yerself—'cause in the end, you're all you've got. Remember that. No one else is gonna look after you, so ya got to look after yourself." Tom's eyes flickered towards the TV screen. "Still and all, you don't want to end up like me, you understand?"

"Not really. No."

"I mean, havin' the cops comin' to the door. Beatin' around. Smokin'. Drinkin'. It's a hard road, Finton."

"But I don't go that way. I don't smoke or drink." It was a small lie, but a convenient one, since he'd confined those activities to Miss Bridie's place.

"Well, just don't say I didn't warn ya."

With that, his father left him alone with Dean Martin jumping on a piano, only to fall on his backside to the floor, singing "Everybody Loves Somebody Sometime."

"I'm not allowed to talk to you." Naked from the waist up, Skeet stood in the doorway and peeked behind. He saw no sign of his parents, so he whispered, "Come on."

Summer had deepened in the days and nights following the ill-fated evening at Bilch's. The buds on the aspens and maples were plumping, and a few crocuses and dandelions had sprouted on the neighbours' lawns.

Together, they ran across the tree-dotted landscape until they'd reached the edge of the woods. The Stuckeys didn't have money but owned an enormous piece of inherited property with tall, broad-leaved maples and dogwoods. The two boys collapsed in the shade of a dogwood tree sprouting thousands of leaves.

"How's your face?" Skeet asked.

"All right."

"First time to Bilch's, first fight—nice goin', Moon. Yer old man would be proud." He laughed and added, "Hell, I'm proud of ya."

Finton hung his head at the mention of his father.

"How's things with him?" Skeet asked as he lit a homemade cigarette, his hands trembling slightly.

"Jeez, Skeet. You gotta lay off the booze, man."

"Nothin' I can't handle," he said. "So the cops still comin' around or what?"

"Not so much—unless you count droppin' me off that night."

Skeet laughed. "Sorry about that, ol' man. I split as soon as I saw 'im. Thought you'd have enough sense to do the same."

"I froze, b'y—although maybe I wanted to get caught."

"Why would you want that?"

"What if they saw me? I'd spend the rest of the summer waiting for them to come get me." He hung his head. "Bad enough waitin' for them to come take Dad away."

"Do you think he did it?" Skeet blew a smoke ring in the breeze.

"No," Finton said, and he plucked a blade of grass, considered tossing it away, but kept it between his fingers instead. "He wouldn't."

"What makes you so sure?"

"I just knows, that's all."

"Well, the cops think he did it."

"They don't know anything."

"I heard he got pretty mad at Sawyer that night." Skeet sniffed and hawked in rapid succession, making Finton queasy. Fishing a cigarette from behind his ear, Skeet stuck it in his mouth and lit it, all in one motion. "Do you wanna know what I think?"

"I guess so."

"Well, everyone's sayin' that yer father got Sawyer drunk, then took him into the woods."

Finton closed his eyes and listened to the breeze whistling through the treetops. "He probably did something. But he didn't kill him."

"Your old man was about the only one that had the time o' day for Sawyer. I often wondered why, and now I knows."

"What do you know?"

"That it was all an act, I s'pose. Like, maybe Sawyer had something on 'im."

Finton shook his head. "I don't see that. Everyone here knows everything."

Skeet shrugged and took another draw, his whole body shivering, despite the warmth of the afternoon air. "It just all seems pretty strange to me."

"What about it?"

"Everything about it. Everyone knew Sawyer couldn't drink because of his medication, and your father went and got him drunk."

"He didn't get him drunk."

"Were you there?" asked Skeet.

"No, but neither were you."

"No, I wasn't." Skeet stared at the ground. "But maybe Sawyer had it coming."

"Maybe."

They both fell silent until Finton deliberately changed the subject. "Been to Bilch's since?"

Skeet shook his head, a disgusted grimace on his lips. "Folks won't let me. They only thinks that'll stop me." He spit on the ground. "You?"

"Don't care if I ever go back."

"Scared o' Slim Crowley." Skeet nodded sagely. "I get it."

"It's just not my kinda place."

"Well, what is your kinda place?"

"I don't know," said Finton. "Some place where you don't have to get into a brawl every time you want to go out after dark. And people don't think you're queer because you reads books."

Skeet laughed, but it was an ugly, judgmental sound. "And where might that be?"

"I don't know," said Finton. "But it better be surrounded by ocean, have lots of books and lots of trees."

"Sounds perfect," said Skeet, "for you."

"Where would you go?"

"Me? I'd take off and sail around the world in my own boat. A different girl in every harbour. Not come home no more, just go far away."

Skeet was shaking uncontrollably, as if he were freezing. As he spoke, his yellow-stained fingers fidgeted on his homemade cigarette, and he rarely glanced upward; when he did, he looked away quickly.

"Sounds nice," Finton said, "for you."

Picking at a blade of grass, Skeet peeked over at him, but only briefly. "Yeah, well, we all knows that's not gonna happen."

"It might. Ya just gotta say you're gonna do it and then just go do it."

Suddenly, Skeet looked straight at him. He stuck the cigarette in his mouth, imbuing himself with an extra measure of toughness, then pulled it out and blew a ring of smoke into Finton's face. "Dreams are for losers, kid. I'm not goin' anywhere."

Long after he'd watched Skeet strutting half naked back to the house, Finton sat back beneath the tree and listened to the whispering leaves.

To the Moon
(August 1974)

July crept by in a sweltering haze in pursuit of the perfect summer day—swimming in the ocean at the Darwin Day fairgrounds, splashing and bobbing on a sparkling lake while clinging to a gargantuan inner tube, or sipping an Orange Crush and reading a good book in a shady spot. Nights meant sitting on the front step or lying in the meadow, looking up at the stars and wondering, dreaming, scheming grandeur. Finton and Skeet, sometimes with Homer, would camp out overnight in a tent or a newly built tree house. Finton's favourite evening pastime was sitting in Clancy's Galaxy, turning the radio way up and singing along to the Top Ten. Alone or with Skeet or one of his brothers, it didn't matter. The only activity he religiously avoided was going to Bilch's or anywhere else Bernard Crowley might be.

Early in July, he ran into Alicia as they were both getting checked out at Sellars' store. "How's your summer?" she'd asked.

He was about to tell her about the new book he was reading when a voice from behind him said, "Hey, faggot. Does your mommy know you're out by yourself?" Bernard Crowley slipped from behind a shelf. Finton thought, *You need some new material, buddy.* Judging by the corner of a Caramel Log bar sticking out of his pocket, Bernard had been stuffing his jacket with chocolate bars; a glance at Alicia suggested she knew nothing of her boyfriend's illegal activity.

He ignored Bernard's insult. "Fine," he said, "how about yours?"

Bernard wrapped an arm around Alicia's waist, although she seemed surprised and uncomfortable with the arrangement. "We're just fine, as you can see," he said.

"You're going together now?" He directed his question at Alicia, as he could barely stand to look at Bernard.

"We've gone out a couple of times," said Alicia. "You know—hangin' around Bilch's. Both times."

"Sounds…" he looked at them and wanted to say something appropriate: "strange," he finished.

"What a thing to say!" Alicia looked slightly wounded and, judging by the partial smile, rather amused.

"Whattya mean *strange*, Moon? You sayin' I'm not good enough for her?"

"I just didn't expect you two to go out… together. That's what I meant." *Yes*, he thought, *just go with that. No need to provoke.*

"Well," said Alicia. "we've gone out twice, to Bilch's, like I said."

Finton nodded and paid for his Dreamsicle. He peeled the wrapper off slowly, letting them get a head start. He didn't want to risk having to walk with them.

"See ya," said Alicia.

"See ya, Alicia."

"So long, faggot." Bernard raised his middle finger as he departed.

By the time Finton got home, the police cruiser was just leaving, with Futterman glaring at him as he backed out of the Moon's Lane.

In the living room, his father sat watching the news, hands clasped before him. Nixon again.

"Why are they still coming around?" Finton kept one eye on the television set. Grey-haired men in suits talking into microphones. Now and then, they showed film of Nixon, gazing into the camera with his dark, scowling eyes. Finton glanced at his father's darting, cobalt eyes and wondered what he was capable of.

"'Cause they thinks I did it." Tom sighed and ran a hand through his hair. "Lots o' people think I got Sawyer drunk, got into a fight with 'im and killed 'im." His eyes assumed a faraway look, a familiar mixture of fear and hurt.

"Do you think they have enough to ever send you to jail?"

"No." As Tom averted his gaze towards the window, Finton wondered what he saw through those eyes—if the meadow had looked different these past few months. "I have faith."

"You mean in God."

Tom laughed. "In the truth and the decency of certain people. I never done nutting, and that should be enough."

"Then why don't they leave you alone?"

Tom swept his hands through his bedraggled hair, shaking his head like he was suffering some kind of breakdown. "'Cause they needs to do their job… I s'pose."

"Then they should go after the real killer."

"I wish it was that easy." Tom's eyes misted, causing Finton to be amazed as well as embarrassed. "But things will unfold as they should. Justice will prevail."

Finton shook his head angrily. "What the hell is justice? I don't see much of it around here."

"Justice is when the good go free, and the bad get punished. It's as simple as that."

But Finton wasn't so sure. "Did Sawyer get punished?"

"Some would say so."

"Would you?"

Tom coughed and stood up, unsure of what to do with his hands. He was trying to give up smoking, so he stuffed them in his pockets as if they were the most useless appendages a man could own. "It's too nice to be stuck indoors," he said. "You'll get enough of that when you're older."

It didn't sound so bad to Finton, being able to stay inside all day without anyone telling him what to do. But his father had looked so sad, it made him think that adulthood was a prison sentence from which there was no bail or parole. Kind of like it was for Nanny Moon. And his mother too. It must be hard to grow old, knowing you can never be young again. They all seemed so serious, sad, and angry. He decided he would never grow up in that way. Sure, he couldn't wait to leave Darwin, but he'd never take life so seriously that he only believed in the bad stuff.

He ran out of the house, slamming the door behind him. There was no one around, so he ran for the woods. When he reached a dense part of the forest, he slowed to a walk, barely breathing hard, feeling more alive and scared than he had in a long time. The shadows from the trees were deep and cool. He felt as if he should be able to slip right into them and slide into a secret world beneath the earth.

The best he could do was climb a tree and lie down in its branches. So that's what he did.

In early August, he heard on the radio that the circus was coming to Darwin, a rare event that his mother agreed would be a welcome distraction for him. But she warned he would have to earn his own money for admission and cotton candy, as she simply had no extra. He resented her response, since he hadn't asked for anything, and yet she'd found it necessary to curtail his expectations.

Despite his desire to maintain a distance from girls, Finton found himself more immersed that summer in a world where females held sway over all his senses. They were all he could think about—How's Mary? Who's Morgan with tonight? Did Alicia tell Bernard Crowley to take a long walk on a short pier? For the most part, though, girls seemed unconcerned with him. Maybe it was because his father was suspected of killing a man. No one said it to him outright, but the signs were all there. Tom's work at the garage completely evaporated, and he wasn't able to find a job anywhere. Jobs had never been plentiful in Darwin, and Tom had never worked in the fishery, carpentry, or anything else except mechanics and driving trucks. He had some unemployment insurance coming in, but that too would dry up before Christmas.

Regardless of who his father was, girls had never exactly thrown themselves at Finton's feet. Alicia had always liked him, and Morgan was always there for him, but neither female represented his ideal romance. Only Mary did. But now he adored her from what seemed like a much greater distance, making her all the more attractive.

On Friday nights he would go alone to movies just to feel like he was a part of something. Darwin was growing, with a new mall in the works and a new cinema showing movies like *Earthquake* and *Towering Inferno*. *Earthquake* was supposed to have "sensurround" technology that made you move in your seat when Los Angeles was being destroyed, but the seats in Darwin stayed disappointingly still; plus, he couldn't help thinking of Charlton Heston as Moses, saying, "Let my people go!" Finton stood outside the cinema before showtime and watched the good-looking high school girls goofing around with their good-looking boyfriends, and he wished it could be him with the girl. Once, he saw Alicia with Bernard, and they exchanged awkward greetings, then went inside, where they sat many rows apart on opposite sides of the theatre.

He walked past Mary's house every day, hoping she'd be out front, sipping tea or watering the garden. Occasionally, he saw her, sitting on the step, but he never stopped in. If she saw him and waved, he would wave back and hurry his step. But he was in no particular rush to repeat that hurtful conversation. He wondered if he—or Skeet, really—had ruined things for good.

As the days stretched into weeks, and summer slipped past, Finton began to give up on romance and adventure, except for in his novels. He didn't talk anymore about his intention to be a writer because they always made fun of him when he announced plans for a future. And yet he could feel the difference within him, like that moment when Dorothy awakened to find herself transported to the world of Oz—lately, he saw the world in Technicolor as he strove for new and better ways of expressing his burgeoning understanding of all that surrounded him. In early summer, *Tom Swift*, *Robin Hood*, and *King Arthur* had been his daily companions; through July and into August, they'd been succeeded by Tom Sawyer, Holden Caulfield, and, finally, Jay Gatsby—each more real and inspiring than any person he'd ever known. He wrote a couple of stories of his own, but grew frustrated with the feeling that his ability to express himself was stunted by his lack of knowledge about the world. The books were helpful, his imagination vast. But he craved intimacy with faraway places; he yearned for big cities and the English countryside, experiences like those of the characters in novels. But these desires, too, he kept locked inside himself, hidden from those who would not understand them.

His father was barely speaking and kept mostly to himself, even when they watched TV together. Their favourite shows were *Front Page Challenge* and the CBC news, with a particular fondness for American politics. Finton didn't understand the Watergate scandal, nor did he know much about the Middle East, but his father seemed to care, and that was enough. For Tom, observing the faraway trials of others seemed to replace discussion of the trials and tribulations at hand. Finton yearned to offer his father words of comfort, but he was always struck wordless when the need was greatest. Unemployed and suspected of sinister deeds, Tom would just sit there, watching TV, eyes glazed over as if he'd retreated to the darkest recesses of his mind. Or perhaps he possessed his own Planet of Solitude where he went to escape his troubles. But right here on earth, Tom had surrendered his efforts to give up smoking, and the burning cigarette between his fingers was the only indication that the light inside him hadn't expired.

Indeed, the whole family came to avoid the subjects of jobs and police. While it was a rare moment when Elsie would retreat to her bedroom and quietly weep, most days the tension was etched in her face. Neither of his brothers spoke of the troubles, and Finton spent most of his time alone, writing or reading stories, or hiding out in a newly built tree house. And yet, every day began with hope that something thrilling would happen—that maybe Sawyer's killer would be caught or his father would land a job.

One day at the library, Finton came across an article with sun-drenched photographs of massive lawns and towering oak trees. There were old, brick buildings with ivy climbing the sides and winding across the eaves. But the one picture that made him sit down in one of those big chairs and gape in wonder was of a happy, young man with a wide grin, holding an apple-filled basket and standing in front of several lush, green trees with boughs that drooped from the weight of ripe, red fruit. The caption was: "Migrant Apple Picker in Wolfville, Nova Scotia." For the first time in his life, Finton looked at a photograph and said to himself, *I need to go there. There are jobs and trees.* He loved the photo so much he asked the librarian to make a photocopy for him, which he took home and tucked into his copy of *To Kill a Mockingbird.*

Meanwhile, the spectres of Sawyer, Mary, and Morgan—along with his family—were his daily reality. At night, he dreamt of corpses and killers who resembled either his father, Miss Bridie, himself, or Skeet Stuckey. Finton awakened each morning at the crack of dawn to the crow of his grandmother's aged rooster, perched on a boulder outside his window at the crack of dawn. His mother complained about "that Jesus chicken" but Finton loved being startled to begin the day. He would lie awake on the bottom bunk, watching the broad sky over far-off mountains evolve from blue-black emptiness to a bright orange-yellow, casting long, reaching shadows across the deep, green forest. Sparrows and robins sang and whistled, while blue jays screeched and crows cawed. Lying in bed and listening to the potential of the day was the most perfect peace that Finton felt. It was only after he got out of bed that the day, either quickly or slowly, went downhill.

The day of the circus, August ninth, he leaped out of bed even though he'd hardly slept the night before. He killed time that morning by reading *Toby Tyler, or Ten Weeks With the Circus.* After dinner, with the circus starting at two o'clock, he was getting ready to walk into town when his father appeared in the bedroom doorway, bleary-eyed from watching television. Something big was happening with President Nixon, but with the circus in town, Finton hadn't paid much attention.

"Where you goin'?" his father asked.

"To the circus."

"Where'd you get the money for that?"

"I sold beer bottles."

"Yeah, well, technically, that money is mine."

Finton was silent, his eyes downcast.

"Hand it over."

Finton knew why Tom wanted the money. He reached into his pocket and fingered the two five-dollar bills, feeling their gritty texture. He didn't know what possessed him, but he pulled out one bill and presented it to his father. The other bill remained in his pocket, and Finton couldn't help thinking that something had changed between them forever.

"Yer a good boy." Tom tousled Finton's hair and turned to leave. "You can sneak into the circus, can't you? That's what I used to do when I was your age. Just go to the side of the tent where there's not many people and crawl under the tarp. Piece o' cake."

Tom went back to watching television while Finton snuck out of the house as quietly as possible, his right hand stuffed into his pocket to keep the bill in place.

Singing "Goodbye, Yellow Brick Road" and "Yellow Submarine" made the trek into town go quickly, although he wished he had a bicycle to make it go even faster. The circus was supposed to have pitched at the ballfield, but when he arrived there was only an empty space and a few people milling around. On the galvanized gate was a cardboard sign; the message, scrawled in orange crayon, read: CIRCUS IS MOVED. The sheer random mystery of the pronouncement induced panic in his heart. He noticed a small gathering of the concerned in a corner of the parking lot. When he joined them, he heard someone say that the circus lacked an operating license for that location and, with a softball game about to begin, they'd been forced to move their tents. As added proof, several players were entering the field, carrying bats, balls, and softball gloves.

"Where's the circus?" Finton asked a dark-headed girl who appeared to be his age.

She turned around, smiling. "Finton!"

He glanced at her muddy shoes and managed to smile back. "Alicia!" Her wide, bright eyes were brilliant accessories to her light brown skin. "Going to the circus?"

"We are." She pointed out a swarthy man in checkered pants and a short-sleeved white shirt, chatting with some of the younger men. Three young Dredges huddled around him, hanging on every word. "My father's here," she said. "Is someone with you?" She lowered her gaze, though he sensed it was more out of sorrow than shame.

"I wanted to come alone," he explained, feeling flushed. She regarded him curiously, almost with the air of a non-believer, but she simply informed him that the circus had moved to a location over by the high school.

"I take it Bernard doesn't like the circus," he said, almost breathlessly.

"I wouldn't know," she said with a shrug. "I haven't seen him lately."

"You broke up?"

"We just went out a few times. No big deal."

"But I thought—"

"What Bernard wanted you and everyone else to think." She lowered her voice and leaned in closer. "He got physical a couple of times. Can you believe that? The first time, he said he was sorry and I said okay, but don't do it again."

"Let me guess..."

"He did it again—or tried to. Haven't seen him since. Don't care if I do."

"Proper thing," said Finton, trying to sound confident. "There's no need o' that."

"I couldn't agree more." She offered him a ride to the circus, and he declined at first. But she badgered him until he agreed to go with the Dredges in their black Volkswagen with the putt-putt engine that reminded him of an underpowered lawn mower. Finton found himself squashed between three smaller Dredges, who smelled like a mixture of motor oil and sweat, and kept pulling on their sister's hair. Alicia sat up front, looking cool and refined despite their abuse and her hand-me-down clothes. Her father didn't say much, though, and Finton wondered if his inclusion was resented.

Phonse Dredge had aged greatly in a couple of years, his wavy, black hair having turned completely white. "How's your dad?" Phonse asked, his lips tight and twitchy.

"Pretty good. Bit worried about stuff, though."

"I daresay he's got lots to worry *about*." Without bothering to explain, Phonse resumed his troubled silence until they'd reached their destination. Finton didn't pay him much attention, though. He'd caught sight of the red circus tent, its big flaps flopping in the heavy wind that swept up from the beach across the road.

"Enjoy the circus, Alicia."

"You too." At first, she didn't move away, and he almost felt as if he should stay with her to protect her. But at last she turned to go.

From a safe distance, he watched the five of them buy tickets from a blonde girl sitting at a table and then bustle inside the red tent. Once they were out of sight, he meandered to the less populated side. He sucked in a breath when he saw how the pegs driven into the ground were barely able to restrain the enormous canvas. He was reminded of a large red kite demanding its escape from earth, craving release to the infinite sky. Meanwhile, the impish wind kept flapping the sides of the tent, offering him a space under which to crawl.

He fingered the five-dollar bill in his pocket and reminded himself that he might just be able to afford cotton candy. Checking only once to make sure no one was watching, he bent himself nearly flat, swung his lithe physique inside the tent and, in a dizzying instant, found himself standing at the back of the big top. His senses were gobsmacked by a bejangled elephant giving rides to some children, a yellow-haired clown juggling firesticks for a small crowd, and bored-looking, mangy lions and tigers stuffed into their cages. Most peculiar was an undersized, wire cage with the words inscribed on a wooden plaque:

NEWFOUNDLAND WOLF
(Thought to be extinct)

Inside the cage, a yellow-eyed, dog-like animal with matted, grey fur and a dark strip all the way down its back and tail, lay shivering from either hunger or fear—probably both. Finton glanced nervously around. When he finally crept towards the "wolf" cage, a mustached man in a uniform appraised him, and Finton held his breath, waiting to be collared. Ultimately, however, the security detail moved on, hands clasped behind his back, only to linger near the very spot where Finton had illegally entered.

Finton exhaled and turned his attention to the unkempt animals who, with their mud-and-straw coats and rib-baring skins that hung off them like clothes handed down from a superior generation, were decidedly less majestic than he'd expected. A couple of boys slightly younger and yet bigger than Finton used sticks to poke at them through the bars, trying to provoke a growl from the docile creatures. Alas, they seemed incapable of raising a mewl and barely managed to appear annoyed. "Leave them alone!" Finton yelled. One of the boys turned around and whacked Finton's arm. The attack stung and left a small gash on his skin, but he was vindicated to see the boys run off to their negligent fathers, who drank beer from waxen Coca-cola cups, and leave the animals to seal their crusted eyes in suffering silence. Instinctively, he laid a palm over the cut for a few seconds, but when he lifted his hand to see, the cut was still bleeding.

Trying to ignore his sudden misgivings about the circus, he ambled toward a clearing that appeared an ideal spot for watching the acts. The makeshift bleachers were bursting with people, but dozens stood attentively at the perimeter of the rings, awaiting the start of the show. The loudspeakers blared circus music while the aroma of buttered popcorn thickened the air, but when the ringmaster entered and announced the trapeze act, Finton felt strangely unmoved. He marveled at the beautiful, strong women and lean, handsome men in their sequined costumes as they flung each other into the air like angels engaged in cloud-tossing, and they always caught each other, making the audience gasp in fearful wonder. But Finton's compulsion to keep looking over his shoulder spoiled his enjoyment. He kept waiting to be grabbed by the collar and escorted to the police station and, eventually, to the boys' home in Whitbourne. Much worse, his criminal activity would make his mother cry and Nanny Moon pray for him as she read him Bible passages and went "tut-tut" as she shook her embarrassed head.

He was relieved when the circus was over. On his way out, he presented his five dollars to the blonde girl sitting at the table, selling tickets for the next show. "I snuck in," he confessed when she regarded him quizzically.

Through the mid-afternoon throng, he saw the Dredges bustling to the Volkswagen, gabbing and laughing, as one boy pulled on Alicia's sleeve. He wondered if he should have asked her out. But he thought better of it. They could finally be friends again, as long as Bernard

Crowley stayed away, but to date her was courting trouble. Besides, she might say no, and he couldn't handle another rejection.

When he got home an hour later, he knew something was wrong. His parents and brothers were sitting sombre faced on the sofa and floor in front of the TV. A helicopter had perched on the lawn of the White House. President Nixon was waving, his rubbery, big-nosed face etched in mockery. "They were gonna impeach him," his father said, sucking a vengeful draw from his Camel, then letting it dangle from his fingers like a smoking gun. "The lousy fuckers were out to get 'im."

"Watch yer language in front of the children." Elsie nudged him with her shoulder, but he stared stone-faced at the screen as the chopper lifted off.

Finton desperately wanted to hug his father, but couldn't allow himself that consolation because he knew how such a treacherous act of sympathy would play out in the world of Moon men. "But he's not our president," he said.

"No, but I would've voted for 'im if I could. Goddamn right, I would've. He was a good man."

On behalf of his father, Finton felt the loss. He sat with the family, just as he had done when Orr scored the goal and when Armstrong walked on the moon. Tragedy and heroism came from TV. The Moons might as well have been on television, for it was where their family began and ended. If heroes did not emerge from the screen, they did not appear at all except in books, but he was the only reader among them.

A montage of notable moments in the Nixon legacy flickered on the screen while the president's voice played over it: "For years, politicians have promised the moon; I'm the first one to be able to deliver it." They watched as Nixon flew away to California, which didn't sound so bad, considering they had sunshine, gold, and women in skimpy bikinis, so it seemed natural to believe Nixon had set out for Paradise.

In the highlights of Nixon's press conferences, he always looked so shocked and defiantly saddened to have been accused. "People have got to know whether or not their president is a crook. Well, I'm not a crook. I've earned everything I've got," he said. He was leaving the White House, not because he was guilty, but because the country needed to begin "that process of healing which it so desperately needed."

"Did he do what they said he did?" he asked his father that evening while Elsie was washing the supper dishes.

"If you ask me, he just got caught doing the same thing we all do." Tom blew a ring around Finton's head. The boy lifted his nose and inhaled; the father appeared startled for a moment, then perplexed. "He just wasn't smart enough to hide it, that's all."

"But what did he get caught doing?"

"He told a lie. That's all. Goddamn reporters went snoopin' around where they shouldn't have been."

"Mom tells us we're not supposed to lie, ever."

Tom took a long drag of the stubby Camel. "That's right. And don't ever let me catch ya."

He wondered how long it would be before he stopped expecting the police to come and arrest him for sneaking into the circus.

Lone Wolf

The last weeks of summer raced towards the finish line. Finton read as much as he could, mainly from Thomas Hardy's *Far From the Madding Crowd*, keeping his place in the book with his photocopy of "Migrant Apple Picker." Or, he would go to the library, browse *National Geographic* and read magazines about places he wanted to go.

"Look at this." Clancy had a part-time job cleaning up at the trades school cafeteria and, now and then, he brought home some left-behind novelty, maybe a *Popular Mechanics* magazine or a partial pack of cigarettes, a lighter or a few coins. Today it was a copy of *The Daily News*, dated August 30, 1974. Finton stood behind him, peering over his shoulder. There was a headline: "Circus Animals Escape Overturned Truck." He leaned in closer, but his brother repositioned himself and read aloud that almost all of the animals, including the lion and tiger, had been in cages that, thankfully, hadn't broken open. A couple of cages were damaged, but "nearly every animal was captured quickly."

Finton grabbed for the paper, but Clancy was faster: "A circus spokesman says that, as of Wednesday afternoon, only a lone, grey wolf remains at large. However, they expect to recapture the animal soon."

For the next few days, Finton imagined various scenarios in which he encountered the creature in the Laughing Woods. The highway was a long ways away, but he read that wolves were great travelers. As the season for picking Irish blackberries and blueberries came closer, he overcame his initial skittishness about going into the woods alone and began venturing there every day, wandering through the brush or sitting in the foxhole, hoping for a chance encounter. He went to the public library and looked up books on wolves. There wasn't much available, although one mentioned the extinction of the Newfoundland wolf in 1930 because of a government bounty. The real reason for the demise of the once-large population, however, might have been starvation, as the food sources for the wolf dwindled. The story was a sad one, reminding Finton of tales he'd read of the Beothuks and the Great Auk. Newfoundland had an apparent knack for pushing certain, noble species into the abyss. He hoped to catch a glimpse of the escaped, lone wolf by Labour Day, but his daily woodland treks generated no sightings.

On September 3rd, he got out of bed and put on his only good pants, bloodstains and all. The night before, it took him nearly an hour to iron his only good shirt, the same navy blue one Homer had worn in last year's school pictures.

Monday morning, it rained, and no one spoke to him as he entered the classroom. But every eye turned towards him. He hung his head, stared at the floor, and drew in his shoulders. It had been the same on the bus where the only seat available was next to Bernard Crowley, who had just kept on talking to Cocky Munro and refused to move his bookbag from the seat to make room, supposing Finton had been willing to sit there. Forced to stand, he bounced around between seats like a stringless kite on a breeze.

When the final bell rang, the Grade Ten teacher, Miss Snow, followed close behind him and shut the classroom door. The new teacher, who'd just finished her degree at Memorial earlier that year, was stern as she called the roll. Even in high heels, she was barely five feet tall and quite attractive. Now and then, some boys exchanged mirthful glances, but most students sat quietly, listening and brooding, or just biding their time.

Finton assumed a seat at the back of the room. Most of the people he knew—who were familiar at least, if not actually friends—had landed in other homerooms. But there was one girl he recognized, sitting up front, near the big windows. She'd looked up and smiled as he entered, then lowered her head. Alicia Dredge wore the regulation blue polyester skirt and white, buttoned blouse, but with worn hems and faded hues. With her black army boots and knee-high socks, she looked like a homeless nun.

At recess, he sat by himself on the swings.

He hoped that school would somehow provide a distraction. He could no longer help his father, and his mother had gone out and gotten herself a part-time job at the liquor store. With his wife gone most days, Tom was mopier than ever. He usually sat around, did the occasional crossword, or wandered the meadow. Nanny Moon, as usual, had lost herself in the Bible. She rarely spoke, only looked up now and then, appearing as if she could speak great truths. Ultimately, however, she sighed and pulled her spectacles back on, then retreated to the comforts of the Good Book. Meanwhile, Finton hadn't seen Miss Bridie in weeks, and he was beginning to wonder about her health, physical or otherwise. Morgan had mostly withdrawn from the world, but he saw her occasionally on her way to a babysitting job or on her way to Bilch's or to Sellars' store. But it wasn't strange to go nearly a whole week without laying eyes on her. Perhaps she was merely attending to her increasingly reclusive mother.

"Miss Bridie's got cancer," Elsie announced at supper one evening. The words might have contained a touch of sadness, and maybe deep inside, she felt some sympathy for her neighbour. But if either of those things were true, Elsie was careful not to show it. Finton had an idea of what having cancer meant. He'd heard of some people dying of it and others living with it. When he heard Miss Bridie had it, he assumed she would get better. But it did explain why he hadn't seen her in so long, especially now that he was no longer visiting Morgan on a regular basis.

After supper, he ran to the Battenhatch place, and Morgan answered the door.

"I heard she was sick," he said.

"She doesn't want to see anyone. I'm sorry." Morgan truly did look apologetic. In fact, she looked haggard, which Finton guessed was from spending too much time indoors, taking care of her mother.

"Tell her it's me," he said. "She'll want to see me."

"No." She shook her head. "She said especially not to let you in."

He argued with her, but, ultimately, he knew his efforts were useless. The Battenhatches were stubborn once they'd made up their minds.

After that evening, the couple of times he saw Morgan at the store or out walking, the conversation was awkward and brief. When she laughed, it was with a tinge of bitterness, and he always noticed the deepening of the lines at the corners of her eyes and mouth. Skeet Stuckey's parents, meanwhile, had ordered him to stay clear of the Moons and, though Skeet likely wouldn't obey them for long, at least for now Finton inhabited a new planet of solitude.

Of course, some people were native to this world of isolation. At recess, while the other children were hanging out together, gabbing excitedly or blending in, Alicia Dredge stood unaccompanied on the wooden school step, peering out across the rocky landscape. Clancy had been among those young people hired this past summer to lay sod on the school grounds, but—between the fights, the girl-watching, and the beer-swilling—the job was incomplete. While patchy grass adorned the west side of the school, the east side was a moonscape, covered in boulders and gravel, pitted with shallow holes. Even the ground beneath Finton's swing was concave, and his soles couldn't quite reach the earth.

He considered how different Alicia's life must be from his own. As a teenage girl in a houseful of boys, she was smarter and better looking than any of her brothers, with the ability to do something with her life, go anywhere and become anything. She could be a great artist or doctor, a beloved teacher or an astronaut. But no matter where she went, she would always be a Dredge. Just as he would always be a Moon. But then there was her brother, Kieran, the cop. Finton could only imagine the hope that her brother's lofty achievement must offer Alicia. It must have driven Kieran to distraction seeing his little sister taking after a Crowley, and his relief must have been palpable after they'd split up.

Oblivious to the rain, Alicia just stared at nothing. She looked like an unassuming prisoner, plotting an escape from purgatory. For some people, high school was an unpleasant stopover on the way to something even more unpleasant. That's likely how it was for Alicia. Hardship was her birthright, struggle her fate.

"What's so fascinating about her?"

The voice had the ring of one he knew. The face was startling—and ghostly familiar. He could barely believe she was standing there. "When did you get here?"

"I came in early." Her brown eyes sparkled. Her grin was strong and bright, baring only a hint of the suffering she'd endured. "Which homeroom are you in?"

"Snow," he said. "The new one."

"What's she like?"

"Seems nice. Who you got?"

"McGrath—just like I wanted."

"You're so lucky."

"Good to see ya." Her grin softened her face and eased the tension between them.

"Yeah. Long time." Her body still needed a hug. Her saucy smile would still make everyone adore her. He wanted to ask her what it had been like, being that sick and so far away. For sure, it had been a long, hard road. She probably had bedsores, and no doubt there'd been nights of lying awake, coughing, throwing up, racked with chills, and wishing she could either get better or die. He could almost envy her.

"Are you—?"

"Fine." She held forth her palms for him to see. "The fever broke in early August, and I've been walking a bit, building strength. I can forget the Montreal Olympics, but I can at least come to school."

He laughed the obligatory laugh, but then the silence crept in and choked the moment of its vitality. The profound quiet, with only the shouts of the playground, reminded him of another moment several weeks ago, when they'd last talked.

"I understand if you hate me," she said.

"I don't hate you," he said. But she looked at him doubtfully. "Honest."

"Really?"

He took a deep breath, drawing courage from deep inside. "Really." He knew it was what she needed to hear.

"There's a dance coming up this weekend," she said. "You going?"

"I've never been to one."

"Oh, come on—you should. Everyone's going."

Something about her earnestness, her joyfulness, and her genuine desire for him to do something sociable made him reconsider. "We'll see. I'm just not sure."

"I mean, first dance of Grade Ten. Who'd miss that?"

Elsie wasn't thrilled with Finton's decision to attend the Friday night dance. She washed dishes and piled them in the rack, constantly tut-tutting as she dragged dripping plates and utensils from the hot, soapy water and stacked them in the tray. "Father not working and you're off chasing girls. Nice to be like ya. Sure, go and dance your little feet off."

Then it was Nanny Moon's turn to tut-tut. "God's sakes, Elsie. The poor child hardly goes outside the house. Good for 'im to get out and blow the stink off."

"Hmph." The last fork dropped onto the lid of a pot as Elsie turned around, clutching the dishtowel to her hip. "All right for you, Nanny Moon."

Clancy leaned against the doorway. "It'll be good for 'im to meet some girls."

"He might get his skin," said Homer, who was also going to the dance. "Then he'd really have something to confess."

"Shut up!" Finton punched him in the chest, but Homer didn't flinch.

"Boys! When your father gets home, he'll straighten ya out."

"I'm just jokin' with ya, b'y." The mere mention of Tom was enough to put a damper on their argument. He was over at Francis Minnow's having a yarn, but nobody wanted to give him another reason to be in a bad temper.

"Boys, stop it." Elsie closed the cupboard door, shutting the dishes away. "Finton, I can't stop you from goin' to a dance, God knows. But make sure you gets home early—and stay away from the drugs and liquor."

Finton was relieved, but his mother's warnings always made him feel like he'd already done something wrong before he'd even left the house.

Entering the gymnasium, he felt like an alien who'd forgotten the purpose of his visit to a strange, glittery planet. To think he was missing *The Rockford Files* for this. He felt wholly inadequate in his oversized, hand-me-down clothes—the milk-chocolate brown shirt, matching brown shoes, and checkered plaid pants all had been claimed from Homer, who'd inherited them from Clancy, who'd worn the same outfit five years earlier. He even had on one of his father's belts. In essence, Finton wore nothing of his own except his white socks and underwear. Nervously, reverently, he entered the gymnasium and looked all around at the high-flung ceilings and dangling fluorescent light fixtures, the burgundy and gold "Go Huntsmen!" banners hung above the stage and stapled to the far wall to remind everyone of the boys' basketball team. At three of the corners stood a black-clad Christian Brother, who chaperoned all high school dances because, the perception was, they had nothing better to do on a Friday night. Sister Angela Murphy stood at the fourth corner, beside the double doors that led to the washrooms. There were so many familiar faces—but how many he could truly call his friend? And yet here he was again, traversing that fine line between bravery and foolishness.

As she came towards him, she parted the crowd simply by walking among them. His mouth went dry at the sight of Mary in her blue jeans and pink t-shirt, hair tied back in a ponytail. The DJ played "Smokin' in the Boys Room." He wiped his perspiring hands in the legs of his pants.

As she passed Bernard Crowley—in his usual blue denim—Bernard laid a hand on her shoulder and whispered in her ear. She nodded, and they sauntered onto the dance floor, boogying their hips and shaking their limbs. Finton wished a sniper would appear on the stage and shoot him in the heart so that he could justify crumbling to the parquet floor in a quivering heap.

Song after song, Mary danced with someone new, while Finton stood on the sidelines, hands in pockets, tapping his foot and bobbing his head to the music to stave off the humiliation of immobility. He was loathe to glance in her direction and yet unable to restrain himself from doing so. Out on the dance floor, mingling with her people, she looked so beautiful and happy. Not so long ago, she was closer to death than any of them knew, and now here she was, the princess at the ball.

His face burned. Skeet and Dolly had arrived together, Skeet in a white suit with an oversized lapel, grooving to "Jungle Boogie" beside Mary and her latest partner. Standing on the fringes, a plastic Coke cup in her right hand, Alicia Dredge was wearing red lipstick and looking cute in a navy, flower-print dress, her hair hanging loose at her shoulders.

He felt a pang of envy towards those on the dance floor who were caught up in the moment and oblivious to his anguish. Alicia wasn't even looking in his direction, a lack of mindfulness he took as his cue. Squaring his shoulders and lifting his chin, Finton stepped to his left and cut a line straight for her.

"Would you like to dance?" His voice was breathy.

"Finton—hi!" Alicia smiled sweetly. "I didn't see you there."

A tall rival—Jack Hannigan Jr.—appeared at her left side in black slacks and white shirt with a black, bolo tie. "Alicia, would you, ah…"

Her eyes flickered towards Finton. Tenderly, she placed her hand on Jack's chest. Defeated, he hung his head and started to move away.

"Maybe later," she told him. "Finton asked first."

Finton nodded graciously to Jack and led his damsel towards the dance floor where everyone was dancing to "No More Mr. Nice Guy." He flounced with Alicia on the crowded floor and sang louder than Alice Cooper. Alicia bopped her head and swayed her hips, arms outspread like an awkward bird just learning to fly.

They continued to dance through a KISS song and then another by Carly Simon. He managed not to step on, hip-check, or smack anyone—until he spun around on the chorus of "Mockingbird" and his right arm clouted someone. Turning, he saw his older brother clutching his nose and checking for blood, his eyes brimming with anger.

Mary leaned in to shift Homer's hand from the injured area so she could assess the damage. She cast Finton a killing glance, and he realized that she and Homer had been dancing together. Leading Homer by the shoulder, she guided him past Sister Angela, who checked him over, then opened one of the doors. One of the Christian Brothers quickly followed, probably to ensure that Mary didn't enter the boys' bathroom.

Alicia laid a concerned hand on Finton's arm. "Are you okay?" she asked. He shook his head. Didn't want to explain. He could think of nothing but Homer's offhand remark one time that Mary was childish. His first impulse was to have it out with his brother when he returned to the dance, but his overriding instinct was to run away.

"Finton?" Alicia stared at him, looking worried. "Are you okay?"

"Never better." He grasped her wrist and pulled her close. "The Way We Were" played just for him. She lowered her head to his shoulder and clasped her arms around his waist. He grasped her hips and felt every slow movement. He forgot she wasn't Morgan and let his right hand slip to her backside. When she gently moved his hand to a less offensive body part, he felt chastised but grateful that she hadn't made a scene.

When the song was over, and "Loco Motion" spilled from the speakers, one of the double doors opened at the far corner of the gym. Homer had returned, appearing fine, with hardly a scratch. Mary, beside him, was watching his nose. From across the dance floor, he and Homer exchanged nods. Then Mary pulled Finton's brother onto the dance floor, and Finton resigned himself to the anger and hurt that burned in his gut.

He felt a tap on his shoulder and swiveled around to see Bernard Crowley glaring down on him, imaginary smoke billowing from nostrils and flanked by his usual cronies, the King twins and Cocky Munro.

"Movin' in on my girl, faggot?"

Finton looped his thumbs in his belt. "She's not your girl."

Bernard thrust his face close enough to Finton's that he could smell the sweat from Bernard's underarms. Alicia stepped between the two and placed a firm hand on Bernard's chest. "That's enough," she said. "I'm not your girlfriend."

"We were just dancin'," Finton added. "No law against it."

"Well, see, that's where you're wrong. I got a law against it—me 'n the b'ys here. So maybe you'd be better skedaddle on home."

Finton's heart beat savagely. He blinked slowly, barely able to think. But with each word his enemy spoke, Finton's mind grew more lucid. He saw the spittle on Bernard's bottom lip, the whitehead pimples on his cheeks, the wart on one knuckle of his left hand, the oily hair matted to his forehead, the frayed edges at the cuffs of his jean jacket. These degrading details made Bernard familiar and human, but mostly pathetic. He was a frightened animal that feared extinction, whose only defense was aggression—an unrelenting desire to destroy any threat or perceived weak link that reminded him that weakness existed and, therefore, was threatening in itself.

Although slightly unnerved by these insights, suddenly Finton felt calm. Grounded. Strong.

"I don't need this," he said and turned towards the door. Then he stopped and said to Alicia, "Great night for a walk."

Bernard scowled, and his eyebrows knit together like a mustache. "That's it, coward. Run and hide. But I'll still find you."

Finton shook his head, smiling virtuously. "I'm not hiding from you. I'm just going for a walk."

Bernard rushed towards him, and Finton stood still, ready to knee him in the balls when the moment arrived. But it never did. At the last possible second, Bernard was pulled aside by Homer and Skeet, one on each arm. "By the Jesus, Crowley," Homer said, "you pick on one Moon brother, you take on all of us." He looked at Finton. "Go wherever you goin' to." Skeet nodded. "We got this," he said.

Alicia took Finton's arm and practically dragged him to the door. As they departed, he had a pang of conscience about leaving his brother and friend to fend for him. Worse, he remembered Skeet's long-ago words about dealing directly with arseholes like Bernard Crowley. Bernard wouldn't quit until he was put in his place, but Finton didn't want the torture to go on too long. "I should stay and fight him," he said.

"And get killed?" Alicia was pushing him now, with one hand on his back and the other pulling his arm. "I don't think so. Come on, b'y. Fer God's sake."

Logic like that was hard to ignore, especially coming from a girl in red lipstick.

They wandered home together along the two miles of road where the streetlights were few and the dark was plenty. For the first few minutes, still within range of the light provided by the school and small shopping district, they walked side by side, careful not to touch each other unless necessary. It felt, at least on Finton's part, as if they were strangers, with nothing interesting to talk about.

On the left side of the road, facing traffic—which was scarce in Darwin after dark—it was difficult to see. There was the occasional guard rail, usually in places where a car had gone over the side and someone—like Miss Bridie's boyfriend, Gordie—had gotten killed. In Darwin, guard rails, usually, were grave markers. So, in that vein, thankfully, there weren't very many of them. On the other hand, walking after nightfall in this section of town was treacherous. For much of the way, about four feet from the pavement was a sheer drop. So they stayed close together, occasionally allowing their elbows or hips to graze against each other's.

About seventy yards off, moonlight illuminated the ocean's surface. Each wave roared as it struck the rocky shore, enlivened by a breeze from the east.

"Was this your first dance?" he asked.

"No. First time I've danced, though." She chuckled. "You were the first boy who ever asked me."

"Seriously?"

"Seriously."

The rush of a distant wave swept onto the shore below, sending a shiver through Finton's entire body.

"I never saw you at the Grade Nine dances," she said. "Well, *dance*. Singular. I only went to one. But I went home early because I got tired of holdin' up the walls."

"I can't believe that. You're so—" *Shit. Almost spilled the beans that time*. "Any fella should be proud to dance with you."

"Thank you, Finton." He could hear the smile in her voice. "How come you don't have a girlfriend?"

"I don't want one," he said, which actually felt true.

"Why not?"

"Because I'm not planning to stay here, and I don't want to have a girlfriend making me stay."

"What if your girlfriend—I mean, if you had one—was willing to go with you? Not that I know where you're going. Where would you go?"

"I don't know. Just somewhere else. Somewhere better."

She fell silent for a moment, letting the surf have its time. Finally, she asked, "What if Mary wanted to be your girlfriend—would you still say the same thing?"

"It don't matter who," he said. Then he added suspiciously, "Why Mary?"

"It's kind of obvious," she said with a laugh. "I think you've been after Mary Connelly for as long as I've known you."

Known you. The words suggested familiarity. Intimacy. A relationship. "How would you even know something like that? Have you been spying on me?"

"Noticing," she said. "When you're as quiet as I am, you notice a lot."

"I know what you mean."

They had just reached the street lamp at the top of the hill, a few yards away from Miss Bridie's house. A few yards beyond that was Moon's Lane. Finton was slightly disappointed that their time was almost done.

"Would you like me to walk you the rest of the way?" he asked.

She hesitated. "No, thanks. I'll be fine."

He stood at the middle of the lane and watched her stroll away into the night and gradually disappear.

He hadn't expected anyone to be waiting up for him, but there was a light on in the kitchen—Nanny Moon in her chair, reading the Bible. He was startled at first because his head was still filled with bits of his conversation with Alicia.

All he could think was, *How old she's getting.* The lines on her face were etched like tire tracks on a dirt road, her blue eyes sunk deep in their sockets behind her wire-rimmed glasses, leaving half-moon shadows on the upper part of her sallow cheeks. Her white hair glowed in the light that showered down on her from above. When she finally looked up at him, he was reminded of a person who'd been waiting for something for a long time. Nanny Moon's identity had always been that of the old woman alone—not as "widow" because he'd never known her to have a husband and didn't think of her as having been with someone. But she had been married once and had lost her husband a long time ago, before Finton was born, before Elsie Fyme and Tom Moon were wedded.

"Have a good time?" She pulled the silken, blue bookmark taut between the pages and laid the book aside.

He ambled over to the sink, pulled down a peanut butter glass from the cupboard and filled it under the tap. He was already guzzling when she asked him again if he'd enjoyed himself. "All right."

"That's it? You left here tonight just for that? What's wrong with ya, b'y? You should've had a big ol' time of it, danced with every pretty girl in sight, and you should have come home here tellin' us all about it, makin' us jealous that we weren't there too. Well, I'm jealous anyway. Lord knows I wish I was your age again. I wouldn't be sittin' in this chair tonight, I can tell ya that."

"Where would you be?" Finton pulled up a chair and rested his glass on the table, folded his arms in front of him and laid his head atop them.

The old woman stopped rocking—the effect startling—and appeared defiant, yet sad. For the first time ever, he saw her not as his grandmother—not as old Nanny Moon who read her Bible and rocked, not as his father's aging, ever-present conscience, nor his own moral compass—but as a young girl who had yet to be kissed, had yet to meet that special young man who would woo her, court her, marry her, and bring her to a house where he would eventually leave her. This tough, old woman was once his own age and had a lot more in common with either Bridie Battenhatch or even Morgan, for that matter, than she had with the other old women he often saw around town. They all dressed in their colourful bandanas and long, felt coats, with their panty hose and long skirts, each of them hunched over and clutching the hands of their companions and protectors as if they were life itself to them. All they were concerned about was making it back home again without falling and breaking a hip or having a heart attack. But that wasn't always the case, he realized. They, too, had once run fast through the Laughing Woods. They'd gone to the same school and sat in those desks. They probably played Red Rover in the meadow and swam in the ocean, and mumbled impolite words when their parents forced them to go to mass or kneel for the rosary.

He was struck with an idea—a thought so wonderful—so horrible—so wonderfully, horribly *awful* that the mere conception of it made his stomach roil and his knees weaken. If he could heal the sick and raise the dead, cure everything from warts to chicken pox, was there even a limit to what he could do? Sure, his power was gone, but what if it was just dormant? What if it came back? Could he, in fact, make Nanny Moon young again? She could make her wishes come true—go dancing or work in the garden again. Was it possible, he wondered, to bring youth to the old? And, if he could, what would the consequences be?

"You're awful quiet, b'y. Whatcha thinkin' about?" She licked her dry lips and cleared her throat. She'd been doing that a lot lately, as if she possessed an unquenchable thirst. With her face so wrinkled and parched, he wondered if she was slowly dehydrating, like a crabapple in the sun.

"Just you."

"What would you be thinkin' about the likes of me for?" She chortled. "Did ya meet up with any pretty young ones tonight?"

"I danced a bit."

"Good." She smiled, almost to herself, as if she were harbouring secret thoughts.

"Nanny Moon?"

"Yes, child." She screwed up her face. "What's got you looking so vexed all of a sudden? Did something happen?"

"No," he lied. He just didn't want to talk about Alicia, Bernard, Homer or Mary, not with the sting of those earlier events so fresh on his mind. "I'm just wondering. Do you remember being young—you know, goin' to dances 'n all that?"

She smiled again, more softly, though no less mysteriously. "Oh, the stories I could tell." He waited, sensing that she would come forth with a few wonderful tales to fill his soul, to make him envision her as she remembered herself. But, just as whenever anyone in his family was questioned about the past, she discarded the smile and seemed to think better about divulging too much. "Things I'd rather keep to meself."

It was like having a big fish on a tiny hook, and he was afraid of losing her. He rushed to think up a question. "Do you ever wish you could be young again?"

The sadness returned to her eyes, and she nodded. In them he saw profound regret and he wondered if, even on his strongest days, he could remove it.

"Do you think I could try?"

She laughed, but the look on her face was deathly serious. "What do you mean?"

"You know. What I used to do… with my hands." He held them up, palms toward her. She studied them carefully as if he were promising her the moon and she didn't trust him at all to deliver. "Maybe I can give you back your looks. Maybe I can—"

"No, Finton."

"—make you young again."

"God's sake, Finton, no. Not in this lifetime." She stopped rocking— though her rocking was so natural, like breathing, that he hadn't even noticed she was doing it—and she stood up, leaning on the kitchen table for support.

"But I could try."

"Look here," she said, attempting to soften her tone, but still glaring at him with those sunken, blue eyes and her voice as rough as a scowl. "What you're talking about, even if it was possible, isn't God's work. It's the devil's."

Finton stood up, white-knuckled, clutching the edge of the table. "You didn't say that when I was helping make all those people better."

"You seemed to enjoy helping them—and they had stuff wrong with them—but this… this is going too far. It's goin' against nature."

"You want it." He understood the startled, clear look that came to her eyes. She was afraid to admit it, fearful of its possibilities, unwilling to consider that her smallest grandchild could remove years of aging and hardship, nullify decades of anger and regret, render moot all those hours wasted on prayer. For if her grandson could save her life, restore her youth, what was the point of God?

"No," she said, shaking her head. "It's not possible."

He stood perfectly still, clutching the table as she toddled up the hall and shut the bedroom door behind her. He didn't move until he heard her crying—at least, he thought it was crying, since he'd rarely heard the sound before.

But when he tapped on her door, she didn't answer.

Trials and Tribulations

If August was a whisper that gradually, gently awakened the soul, September was a shout that called his spirit to life. The days were bursting with vibrant sunshine, fleeting warmth and disquieting cool. Finton often yearned for something different, someplace more exciting, and September filled him with a burgeoning desire to see the world that his books told him existed, out there somewhere beyond the borders of Darwin.

Nonetheless, while school was interesting at first, it quickly became a drag. Even though his grades were quite good, the lessons were easy and rarely retained his interest.

Meanwhile, he had underestimated the capacity of some Darwinians to gossip and to pass judgment, particularly in the absence of proof. The first time someone mentioned his father and Sawyer in the same sentence that fall, he was shocked to realize that many people were talking about him and had already convicted him, no matter what the legalities were. In the summer, he was mostly alone and hadn't heard much gossip, except for the occasional taunt. But now that he was back in school and surrounded every day, he heard the rumours constantly. He overheard one of the Donnelly girls asking another girl at recess how any of the Moons slept at night, with a murderer under the same roof. Every week seemed to bring another incident—Clancy in a fight because someone said his old man was a "murderer," Homer raising his fists to defend the family name, or Finton tolerating bullies who called his father a "killer." Even Elsie had to put up with people shaking their heads and whispering when she went for groceries. Nanny Moon had stood on the steps of the church one Saturday evening, leaning on Clancy's shoulder, telling a couple of gossipers to mind their own business. Late in September, Tom was told there likely wouldn't be any more work for him at Taylor's. "It don't matter if you're guilty or not," Pat Taylor said. "Not enough people want you to work on their cars, and I can't afford to lose the business." Besides Phonse Dredge, there were a few people who stood by him—most noticeably Francis Minnow and his wife Winnie, who occasionally dropped by for a cup of tea, as well as Miss Wyseman, the church lady, who didn't mind telling people she still thought Tom was a good man, no matter what he did. But it was shocking how many chose to disassociate themselves from the Moons.

Of course, none of Finton's friends repeated the rumours in his company. He talked to Alicia almost daily now, usually in the morning before school started. Neither of them had asked to have their desks moved closer together, since that particular commitment was beyond the range of their unspoken friendship. He hardly ever saw Mary, although he perked up whenever he caught a glimpse of her in the corridors, the lunchroom, or on the playground. But she was in a different homeroom: thus they ran in different circles. A few times, he saw her on the steps of the school, sneaking a kiss with her newest boyfriend. For both his own sake and Mary's, Finton resolved to let her go. Twice a day, when he and Mary saw each other on the bus, they nodded and said hello, but that was all. Once again, she was slipping away. Skeet, meanwhile, seemed to have forgotten all about Sawyer Moon. Finton even asked him once if he'd heard the rumours, but Skeet just shrugged and said, "I couldn't care less."

On the first day of October, there was a slight change in Tom's usual, quiet demeanour. At the breakfast table, the boys were filled with the exuberance swept in by the cooler days of October. For Finton, it was the turn towards Hallowe'en, the start of the new hockey season with the new divisional alignment, and the Bruins finally getting the chance to redeem themselves for last spring's devastating loss. But he suspected it might be more than hockey that caused his father's anxiety. Elbows on the table, Tom barely touched his food and only sipped his tea once in a while as he tapped his leg nervously. Finton kept expecting Tom to make some grand announcement.

"New hockey season starts today," Finton said, trying to provoke a discussion.

Tom forced a smile. "Something to look forward to."

"Leafs got 'er this year," Homer said. "Stanley Cup this year for sure."
Finton could only shake his head.

"I can't believe it's October already," Elsie said as she wrapped her arms around Tom, who stiffened. "I'm not lookin' forward to the winter."

Tom slurped his tea. "It's been hard, I allow."

"What are you going to do today?" Finton asked, prompting his father to stand up, sweep his hand through his hair and fold his arms across his chest.

"What are you, *The National Enquirer?*"

"I'm just askin'."

"If you must know, I'm going huntin'." A triumphant gleam shone from his eyes. "Job huntin'."

It had been months since Tom's last contribution to the family coffers. The only steady income, besides Elsie's part-time hours at the liquor store, was Nanny Moon's pension—"God love Joey," she said every time the old-age pension cheque came in. Clancy had a talent for finding part-time work, but even that kind of labour was scarce lately. Homer assisted a local contractor with the occasional house. Even Finton felt he should find a way to contribute, but he wasn't sure what kind of job he could get with book smarts.

"Can I come with you?" he asked his father. "Maybe they'll give me a job too."

"You can ride along if you want. Be like old times."

"You should go to school," Elsie interjected, looking slightly worried.

"One day isn't gonna kill me."

"Just for the morning, Else." Tom gave her a wink. "It'd be good for 'im."

She relented more easily than Finton expected, but then, she probably sensed that Finton might have a calming influence on her husband.

They took Clancy's Galaxy because, despite Tom's mechanical talents, the Valiant was too old, with "more problems than Buckley's goat," as Elsie said. In the passenger seat with the window rolled down, cool air on his face, Finton felt like things might finally get back to normal. The sun was shining, the engine rumbled smoothly, they had a quarter tank of gas, and he was riding shotgun for his father. And it had been nearly a couple of months since Futterman had come around to poke at Tom's cage.

Tom turned the radio on and fiddled with the dial. Father and son sang together: "Her eyes they shone like the diamonds—ya'd think she was queen of the land…" Finton didn't even like Irish music, but he tolerated it, and could even enjoy some of it for his father's sake, just as his father had learned to accept that his three sons were maniacs for rock 'n roll. Their common ground was country music; not one of them would pass up the opportunity to sing along with "Your Cheatin' Heart," "Snakes Crawl at Night," or "Folsom Prison Blues."

When the next song came on, Tom turned it up. "This a good one—just listen."

Finton paid close attention to the lyrics and tapped his foot to the beat. It was obvious why his father liked that song. "One Piece at a Time" told the story of a mechanic who worked at General Motors and wanted to own one of the Cadillacs he worked on. His genius solution was to steal it one part at a time in his lunch box. He took the parts home and assembled his new car in the garage, without it costing him a dime.

"I like it," Finton said. Tom turned off the radio during the commercials about MUNN insurance, Caul's Funeral Home, and Good Luck margarine.

"Our first stop," Tom said as the car came to rest in front of Taylor's Garage. "You stay here."

Although tempted to follow, Finton sat and waited. Within a couple of minutes, Tom came out, got in, and slammed the door. "Well, that's that."

"What did he say?"

"Not much." Tom gripped the steering wheel and stared straight ahead. In the open doorway, Pat Taylor cleaned a wrench and stared at the ground. The garage owner seemed sad, which, in turn, saddened Finton. But he didn't have much time to think about it before they pulled in front of Brown's Supermarket.

Tom took a deep breath and exhaled. He glanced into the rear-view mirror.

"I'm coming in this time."

His father's glance showed clear disapproval. And yet he suddenly changed his mind. "Sure—why not?"

Maybe he thought, as Finton did, that his youngest boy would be his good luck charm. But it didn't work that way, not this time. The manager, a nice, balding man named Donnelly, told him the boss wasn't hiring.

"Give him a call," said Tom.

Donnelly did call—and Finton gave him credit for trying—but the owner, Mr. Brown, said he didn't have any openings.

"Where to now?" he asked his father as they got back into the car.

"Everywhere."

They stopped by Jack's Place, but Jack Senior had room for only two full-time bartenders, which he already had, and Jack Junior was now working part-time for free. From there, they drove to the new mall, where Tom hoped he could get a line on something—full or part-time, cashier, security—he didn't care. But no one hired him.

"I'll tell you the truth, Tom." The superintendent of the school board sat on the corner of his desk while Tom sat in the chair, looking very uncomfortable. "I'd be uneasy hiring you as a school janitor—you'd be around kids all day long. Know what I mean?"

"No." The stress on Tom's face was palpable. "I don't know what you mean."

"Well, here's the thing—and you should thank me for being straight with you—there are rumours. And I don't care if they're true or not. I usually don't even listen to gossip. Just hearsay, is all. But, now, how would it look—"

"But he didn't do anything wrong!" Finton blurted.

"How would it look?" asked Tom, hands folded on his lap.

"To a lot of parents, it would look like we hired someone without considering his reputation."

"That's just—"

"Stupid," said Finton.

"Go wait in the car." Tom's fists clenched, but didn't yet leave his lap.

Finton never heard the rest of the conversation. He sat in the car, watching the entrance. When Tom finally emerged, he said nothing about the meeting.

"Next." He backed the Galaxy up and pulled onto the road, the tires squealing in complaint. "He asked why you weren't in school today. "

"What did you tell him?"

"I told him you were helping me."

His father's words suddenly made everything seem hopeful.

Over and over, they stopped at shops and offices, and went in to speak with the respective managers. One said, "Not right now, Tom, b'y. Maybe in time." A couple of people wished they had work to offer. But, in the end, no one was willing to hire the most gossiped about man in Darwin whose name wasn't Crowley.

"Don't you ever feel like fighting back?" Finton stared out the side window, fists clenched in his lap as the shadows of early afternoon encroached. They were parked in front of the town hall, where his father had just applied for two weeks of work on the garbage truck. It was a long waiting list, they told him, and it wouldn't be until the spring, if at all.

"I feel like fighting everybody." Tom lit a cigarette and rolled down the window. "In many ways, I feel like I've been doin' that my whole life."

Finton regarded him doubtfully. "But you're the most popular man in Darwin. Everybody knows you and talks to you—everybody loves you."

Tom laughed, in spite of himself. "You just keep tellin' yourself that little fairytale. Meanwhile, I needs a job."

"Why are they punishing you for something you didn't do? They're just being stupid. Bunch o' backwoods hicks."

"Hey, hold on now. These are our friends and neighbours. This is your place, right here. Don't ever forget it. People can be pricks, but they're still your people."

Finton was stunned into silence, frustrated with his father's refusal to see Darwin for what it was—just a mean-spirited killer of souls. "They only questioned you," he said. "They can't prove anything. And you're just looking for a job! I don't think that's too much to ask." He drove his fist into the dashboard and cried out in pain. The dashboard wasn't even dented.

Tom leaned back his head and laughed. "See where violence gets ya? Don't be a fool, b'y. Change what ya can, and accept the rest—and the rest is just bullshit."

"You're acting like you don't care."

"Just the opposite. I care so much that I feel like givin' up."

"Sometimes I think—"

"What?" Tom narrowed his eyes. "What 'n hell do ya think?"

"I think—I wonder—I mean—for someone who didn't kill anybody, you accept it all too easy." As soon as he said the words, Finton cringed.

"So, after all this, you still think I did it? Is that it?"

"No. That's not what I—"

"Let me say this once—and I don't intend to repeat it, ever again: he was my friend, and I didn't kill him."

"But you bought him a drink—and he wasn't supposed to drink."

"So you're putting me on trial." Tom thrust his head forward, gazed into Finton's eyes. Never before had Finton been so afraid of his father. "All right. I guess that's the way it'll always be. Yes, I bought him a beer. Big fuckin' deal. He was thirsty. Haven't you ever had a friend so thirsty, craving something so much that he couldn't have, you'd do anything in your power to get it for him, no matter the consequences?"

"No," said Finton. "I'd do the right thing."

"Well…" Tom pulled back, giving Finton some breathing room, "maybe that's the difference between us. I'd do the right thing too. But it would be truly the right thing, and not just what somebody told me was right."

Finton was silent.

"I gave him a beer. He thanked me. That was it."

"You told the cops you and Sawyer got into a fight."

"That's my business, not yours or theirs."

"What was it about?"

"I told the police—that's enough."

"Fine." Finton sighed. "I got one more place we can go."

Finton wondered why he hadn't thought of it before.

Father Power was out for a walk when they arrived at the big, white house. They waited on the front step until he arrived, hands in pockets, dressed for the weather.

He was startled to see them and kept looking at Finton with a sad expression.

"We need to ask you a favour, Father," said Finton.

"Strange… very strange… but go ahead."

"My father needs a job."

"I see."

Tom stepped forward and said, "I'll take anything, Father," then blew on his cold hands. Finton was aware of how his father looked with his tired eyes and five o'clock shadow, exuding desperation. His clothes were ragged, his boots worn at the toes, and his hands bare. His shoulders slouched forward like those of a man who'd spent his whole life bent over.

"He's a good worker," said Finton. "And I thought… you could do something."

"Funny you should ask," said Father Power. "Perhaps we can help each other."

"Here we go," said Tom, with a roll of his eyes.

"How?" Finton asked.

"You said you were looking for a job. I just happen to have an opening. It's not full-time, mind you. But it is something."

"Thank you," Finton said, beaming.

By the time they returned to the car for the last time that day, the sky was pitch black and the street lights had come on. They didn't speak to each other. The radio played "Somebody Done Somebody Wrong," and Finton gazed at the Laughing Woods as they passed. His fingers were tingling in a way they hadn't in some time, his entire body filled with a familiar warmth, a sense of possibility and promise he'd thought gone for good.

Meanwhile, part-time or not, Tom had become the family's first gravedigger.

News

Supper was in the oven when they burst through the door.

"Dad got a job!" Finton shouted. Everyone was in the living room, watching TV, and wondering aloud why they hadn't heard from the two hunters. The whole family was ecstatic, and Elsie hugged her husband. They chattered excitedly about how good times were finally returning. There was justice in the sudden turn of events, and they all seemed to feel it. After a celebratory supper of chicken and potatoes, all hands, except for Nanny Moon, returned to the living room where Elsie added to the joyous ruckus by putting The McNulty Family on the stereo.

Finton crept out to the kitchen where Nanny Moon was rocking by the wood stove, humming to the music and tapping her foot, as she read. He leaned in and said softly, "I think I can do it again."

She kept rocking and reading as if she hadn't heard. He held up his trembling hands, so close to her face she couldn't ignore him. "My hands." He raised his voice slightly, yet kept it low so those in the living room couldn't hear.

"What are ya talking about, b'y?"

"That thing... the gift..." He didn't mean for his voice to quiver, but it did.

While she maintained her place with an index finger, she raised her head and looked at him over her glasses. "The gift."

"Something's changed," he said. She regarded his small hands and waited for an explanation. "I think I could make you young again. I can heal your old age." She laughed and pressed the Bible to her chest. "It's not funny, Nanny Moon. I can do it."

Laying the Bible aside, she took off her glasses and grasped the corner of her apron. She smiled as she wiped a smear from her lenses.

"Tell you what, b'y. If I ever needs ya to do that, I'll let you know. For now, though, I think I'll stay just as I am, the way God intended me to be—old as Methuselah and crooked as sin." She laid a hand on his shoulder and squeezed as if to absolve him of some secret offense.

"But I can probably do it."

"I've no doubt you can, child. There's lots you could do. Lots we *all* could do." She slipped her glasses back on and clasped her Bible with both hands. "But that doesn't mean we always should."

While she went back to reading, he studied the flesh of her sallow, lined face. She had several brown spots on her cheeks and the backs of her hands, and sometimes he imagined he could play an endless game of connecting the dots on her skin. Neither of them knew how much longer she would live. Nor did they know if he could actually make her younger and stronger. But if he didn't try, she would never know.

Eyes still focused on the Bible, she suddenly spoke again. "I don't suppose you've given much thought to the priesthood lately."

"Not really."

"And why is that now? A young man of your talents belongs to the church."

"These days, I'm not sure what I think about God."

"Oh? That's a hard thing to say. You'll need to confess that one."

"See, that's the other thing. I'm not too keen on the church lately either."

She didn't respond, just returned to her reading, and so he sauntered to the living room. No one there paid him much attention, being too enthralled by the return of The McNulty Family. Only once did his mother look up and catch his eye. He didn't see what he'd expected to see—a hint of contentment, perhaps, or a trace of love. But, instead, he saw and felt—rising above the accordion's squawk and the raucous singing—a terrifying emptiness, devoid of hope. She never expected to be raised from the stultifying poverty that engrossed every thought and nuance of this family. *Things are never going to get any better. This is it— this is all there is ever going to be. My husband digs graves, but we can pretend it's all right.* The most horrifying words he could imagine, he'd read in his mother's eyes. The thoughts—and those eyes—followed him all the way to bed where he lay on his back, staring into the darkness.

About two in the morning, as he dreamed about some magical place he'd never been that had lots of trees and books and was surrounded by ocean, Elsie awakened him with a gentle shove, the look in her eyes unreadable. "Morgan is here. She's asking for you." Without a thought or a word, he got up and dressed, while his mother wrung her hands and said, "She asked for Finton. Only Finton will do."

Rubbing the sleep from his eyes, he stumbled to the kitchen, with the entire family in tow. Even Nanny Moon opened her bedroom door and came out in her grey nightgown, squinting and rubbing her eyes. Morgan was waiting in the porch, her hair bedraggled, eyes dark and bewildered, her face luminescent like autumn moonlight. Those eyes accused him of having avoided her. "She keeps asking for you," Morgan said. "*Finton knows how.* That's all she says, over and over."

He shook his head, feeling as if he could slip away.

"You don't have to go." His mother stood back, arms folded across her chest.

"I don't want to."

Her face slackened in relief. Nanny Moon patted him on the shoulder and called him a good boy.

"But I think I have to."

"I don't want you to go," said Elsie. "I forbid you from going."

"She needs me," he said, prepared for his mother to stand in his way. But, though her face showed the strain of utter disapproval, she didn't try to stop him.

He left his mother and father, Nanny Moon, and his brothers standing in the kitchen, shocked and bewildered.

All the way down the lane, Morgan squeezed his hand and never spoke. The early winter had injected the night air with a cool vitality. The sky was high and deep above the babbling brook in its icy sarcophagus. But at least the piles of dirty snow standing sentry at the bottom of the lane had withered.

"Is she okay?" he asked.

She wouldn't answer, just kept marching and turned left at the road.

All lights were off at the Battenhatch's. The place never changed. The shadows of night concealed much of the decay. Miss Bridie was nowhere in sight. Morgan pushed open the door and ushered him in. "Upstairs."

The aroma of fried fish nearly gagged him. Morgan hung her coat on the back of a chair, but left on her boots and prompted the boy to do likewise.

With clunking footsteps, they crept carefully up the stairs. The house creaked with every move and breath. Family photographs hung from nails above the railing, their faces buried beneath a veil of dust.

They turned right at the top of the stairs and were confronted by a white door. Morgan rapped and paused. She held her breath, her face morbidly pale as she glanced at Finton, who was shivering. Finally, she cracked the door ajar. Moaning came from within. Morgan took Finton's hand and squeezed it, startling him with the blunt-force cold of her skeletal fingers. "Don't be frightened," she said. But he couldn't speak, could barely move his head. So he said nothing, just waited for her to fully open that awful door. She pushed it further inward to a reverberating screech, revealing the darkened pit within. The stench of decaying flesh was overpowering. To his tired eyes, there was mostly darkness. Squinting, he discerned the bed's edgeless shadow, quilts spread over the central bulge. He clamped both hands on his mouth as bile jumped to his throat and backed down, leaving a bitter taste on his gums and tongue, lips and teeth. Mumbling arose from the bed as several flies buzzed all around.

He let go of Morgan's hand and stepped inside, gradually discerning the gaunt shape beneath the blankets. When the tenuous mass emitted a death-defying groan, he exhaled with gratitude.

Bridie smacked her gums as she muttered a Hail Mary. But her rosary broke off. "Come in," she said in a voice stretched and gravelly like a long dirt road upon which he had no urge to travel. "I want to talk to *you*."

The way she said "you" made him want to turn and bolt, but he managed to step forward. "What do you want?" The flies seemed to thicken and perch on the blankets around her face like a tiny coven, buzzing and praying.

Morgan rolled her eyes. "Mudder's got it into her head that she's dyin'."

"I am." Miss Bridie's breathing was congested, making speech a chore.

"I've seen her like this before. Gets all tired and weak. Don't eat for days. Don't remember the last time she et anything."

"Wednesday, I had a bun."

"She wouldn't eat dinner on Thursday, though I cooked a fine feed. I ate what I could meself and threw the rest out to the cats. Today, she never ate no leftovers, nor none of the fresh cod fillets I cooked up. I expect I'll have to force her soon."

"Damned if you will." Her mother wheezed and hacked, sounding as pained as if she were trying to regurgitate a small, furry animal.

"Damned if you can stop me." Morgan stood by the bedside, arms folded across her chest, her bedraggled, blonde hair casting the room's only light—so bright that Finton could discern some of Miss Bridie's features, especially the haunted eyes encircled by deep lines, like knotholes in a tree, gazing straight at him. Morgan herself was more visible, her mesmerizing face emerging from the shadows in which the room was submerged. She was a fairy come to life, like one of the ancient folk of the King Arthur tales—maybe a sister of Morgan le Fay. Her face was thin and dream-like, seemingly lit from within, skin like a white sheet illuminated from beneath by a flashlight.

"Are you really dying, Miss Bridie?"

"If you never thought so, why did you come?"

"You told Morgan to come get me."

"'Cause I wanted to see you."

"Tell him." Morgan's voice was stern, but softer. Her eyes flickered back and forth from her dying mother to Finton.

Eyes closed, Miss Bridie drew a soulful breath and gradually let it out. She coughed and clamped a hand to her chest as if to keep herself earthbound. "She never told you, did she?"

"Who?"

Miss Bridie struggled to swallow, but finally managed to rasp: "Elsie."

As he stared blankly at her, Miss Bridie coughed, then paused to collect her faculties, and raised her voice as much as she could. "You must have always wondered why you weren't like the rest of 'em."

"I'm just different. That's all."

"No, me b'y. That's not all." She shut her eyes and then opened them to gaze at the ceiling, her breathing tentative and ragged. "I had a baby." She glanced furtively at Morgan. "Another one. A boy. Had 'im right here in this bed. Different times then."

"What does this have to do with me?"

"Your mother was pregnant too, right before that—but she lost it."

"You mean the baby died?"

"And that baby was you—well, not really you."

"Oh, for God's sakes, Mudder, stop torturin' the boy. Tell him!" Morgan said in a warning voice. "Tell him what you told me."

"Gettin' to it, child. Don't hurry me."

"Yes, yes. We all knows yer dyin'." In Morgan's eyes, Finton caught a flicker of emotion, but he couldn't tell if it was sadness or anger. "Just get on with it."

Miss Bridie looked at him and took a shallow breath that seemed to cause her pain, for she winced as she exhaled, then licked her dry lips. "Look at me," she said. "You need to know this." Except for her eyes, lips, and faltering breath, her body was still. She measured her words, speaking without hurry. "They told me I wasn't fit, kept saying so over and over till I was convinced of it. 'You fucked up your daughter,' they said. It was Phonse that said that. Times like that, you don't forget the things people say. Takes nerve, b'y, considerin' the brood he got."

"What did they mean, you wasn't fit?" Finton asked.

"To have you—to keep you. No money, no husband. Didn't know if I was comin' or goin'. There was no midwife—not in them days. Them times were long gone.

"I was skinny then too. No one woulda guessed I was havin' a youngster. Five months into it, I panicked and told Tom I couldn't have no baby. I sent Morgan away to her father's crowd in Halifax for the summer. They were used to that. But you had to come early, ya little devil. Seven and a half months—couldn't wait no longer. No sir, not for another second. Out ya comes! Oh, what a state I was in."

Miss Bridie's voice faltered. Her eyes shimmered. A single tear slipped from each eye and onto her pillow. Finton dared not interrupt, could barely draw a breath to call his own. Morgan laid her hands on his shoulders.

"I thought I might be all right, but that first night I couldn't stand the sight of ya. I bawled like a banshee and you just kept lookin' at me like you wuz questionin' every single thing—and I could tell you didn't like me no more than I liked you.

"I said to Tom, 'B'y, I don't know if I can handle this. If I has to spend the night, and every night after, with that thing lookin' at me… I'm as like to smother it with a pillow as beat it against the wall.' You shoulda seen his face." She started to cough violently, the bed shaking with the strain on her body. Finally, after several minutes of trying to regain her composure, she resumed her tale.

"Tom looked absolutely mortified," she said hoarsely. "But he never said a thing, just took off. Not much longer, they came. They had me on painkillers and booze to take the edge off. Your father was the ringleader, along with Phonse Dredge, that bloody sleeveen. I remember the priest and the nun. Your mother was in the doorway lookin' like she wanted nothing to do with it, and yet there she was. There was one or two more, but I couldn't say who.

"'I'll take care of 'im like he was me own,' Elsie said. Tom took you and handed you off to her, and I can still remember the relief. I wasn't sure it was right, but it felt right. I'm still not sure, though. Anyways..." she paused as if to appraise her options, while appearing to choke back another fit of coughing. "... it's neither here nor there. They gave you to Elsie and the goddamn thing dropped ya. Ya still never cried, mind ya. All she said was 'oops' or some useless thing. The nun picked you up and shoved ya into her arms again.

"They all left then, except for Tom. He said, 'We all agreed this was best, Miss Bridie. You're in no state, and we'll gladly look after him. When he's old enough, we'll tell him what we did. But for now, it's best to pretend he's ours. Best for you. For Morgan. For Elsie. Everybody.'"

I was sobbing like a youngster meself then. I remember touching Tom's face and sayin', 'What about him?' I said, meaning the baby." She looked at Finton then, and he thought his heart would stop. "Meaning you."

"What did he say?" Finton asked.

"'Especially him,' he said. He was on his way out, but he stopped and said one last thing. 'I'll let him come to see you once in a while. But you can't tell him or anyone. Not even Morgan. 'Cause if the boy finds out, he'll never forgive you. Or us.'

"'God have mercy on our souls,' I said, and I bawled my eyes out long after he was gone. I wanted to say something all this time. But I figured you'd hated me and everyone else. And that would leave you all alone, for sure. Worse than meself."

She coughed and looked at Finton again. "I weren't very good after that. I sent for Morgan a week or so later, but I wasn't ever the same. I weren't much good after Gordie drowned, but I been worse since they took you. I knows that much. I knows when I'm not feelin' right. But I got the cancer, see, now. And I figures it's time."

As Finton fell stunned and silent, a gust of wind came up and rattled the window pane. He didn't know what to think, but he had the urge to run home and confront his mother—he needed her to put it right, to tell him Miss Bridie was a lying old witch who only tormented him for pleasure.

"Oh, I s'pose they meant well," Miss Bridie said, as if she'd been reading his thoughts. She coughed again and had to close her eyes, to keep herself from vomiting. "So did I. It was some hard." She reached out and laid a feeble, cold hand atop his young one. "And you wanna know the kicker? Your father is still your father."

The words were like a riddle, the answer all too obvious—but, surely, there must be some other meaning. It felt as if she was consuming his soul, drawing his breath and spirit into her own body. The room closed in around him, and he turned to flee. But Morgan grabbed him tighter. He struggled to wrench himself free, but she wouldn't relent until he had ceased squirming.

Finton looked to his captor. "Do you believe her?" he asked.

An eerie light flickered in Morgan's eyes. "You know as much as I do."

He turned to the old woman, whose eyes were still shut. "I don't believe you."

Her eyes opened and pierced his soul. He tried to bolt again, but Morgan caught him, wrapped both arms around him, and forced him to stand still. There, he felt strangely safe and significant, as if they were part of the same body.

He turned his face away from Miss Bridie, into Morgan's breast, even as he yelled at her. "You could've told me ages ago."

For several seconds, the old woman couldn't speak, though her lips kept moving, attempting to form words. When she licked her lips, Finton could hear the scraping of tongue on dry flesh. "Telling you now, sure."

Tears rose to the corners of his eyes. "Why now?"

"Everything in its time," she said, and as she resumed coughing, her eyes squeezed shut. The bile in her throat seemed to squeeze out from under her lids, and Finton feared they would never reopen. But she did open them. Her face contorted in anguish. "None of us were fit, sure." She gasped for air, licking her lips and wheezing. "That one over there... she belongs to me brother Jacob."

"Morgan's your daughter, Miss Bridie. I don't know what you mean."

"Have mercy on me soul," she said. "It warn't wrong or nuttin'. That's what they told us. What did I know, out there in that shitty old house on the Shore? Sure, who could we tell? How did we know what was wrong or right? There was no one to be tellin' except for the priest, and he was the worst of all, sure." When she coughed, he thought for sure she would die, as each bark seemed to come from the pit of her being, straining to turn itself inside out. Finally, when she'd managed to calm herself and was able to stop coughing, she continued. "That's why I called for you. You can make it right."

He shook his head. "It don't work like that."

"Don't it? You don't even know how it works. Anyone talked to you about it?" Her eyes narrowed as if to slice him with her gaze. "They're all scared of *you*." This time, the way she'd said "you" made him feel accused.

"Ya got the dirt in ya, b'y—and we both knows where you got it from."

Finton nearly choked with indecision. Morgan appeared ready to grab him again, and although he struggled to maintain his distance, he nonetheless fell forward into her arms and buried his face in her bosom. Once there, he wanted only to remain until that crazy woman had died or stopped talking.

"What do you want from me?" he murmured into Morgan's chest, confused by a hideous cocktail of nostalgia and nausea.

"You already know," Miss Bridie wheezed.

"I can't do it."

"Not to make me better, b'y—is that what you thought?"

Lifting his head from its haven, he looked towards Miss Bridie and shrugged, unsure of how to respond. But she saved him the trouble.

"No one loves me." He kept staring at her, fascinated at the things he was hearing. She coughed again. "I need you to do… what no one else could." She trained her eyes towards Morgan and nodded. "*She* don't have it. Destructive little bitch. *You* got it all, sure." Again with the "you" as she stared into his soul.

"I don't know what you mean."

"I'm dying, b'y."

"She's not," Morgan interjected, wringing her fingers.

"Listen to me. Like this." Miss Bridie took his hands and placed them over her left breast; Finton feared he would faint, and yet he allowed it. "See, it's the cancer in me. It hurts so bad I could kill someone." She licked her lips again. "Just think of the pain—of stoppin' it. Then picture me not breathin' no more."

His palms throbbed, suddenly craving the blood inside her chest. "I don't want to." He jerked his hands away and, stepping backward, struck his leg on something sharp.

Morgan stepped forward and pressed a hand to his shoulder, shooting her mother a questioning look.

"Sure, he can always go," Miss Bridie rasped. "I just thought he might like to do me this. Himself."

"I can't."

"Please, b'y—if ya have any pity for me at all."

He closed his eyes, inhaled wearily, and thought about what she was asking. All his life he'd been told it was wrong to hurt anyone. He'd devoted most of his life to healing, not destroying. And yet, he had to wonder, if sometimes destruction was necessary if healing was to truly begin—or maybe destruction *was* healing. Finally, he opened his eyes and tried to sound confident in his choice. "I'll try."

"Thank you." Her smile was unexpectedly radiant. Again, she placed his hands on her chest, above her heart, its rhythm unhurried, the odd beat skipped. He imagined the gradual slowing of her pulse. He heard the last breath leave her body and felt her heart stop, her pulse fade to nothing. Even with his eyes closed, he could feel her gaze. She was inside his head, her mouth bursting wide open like that painting of "The Scream" a teacher had shown him.

Thank you, she kept saying to him, over and over. He could feel the pain leave her body. Could feel her recede, slipping away. He leaned forward and kissed her cheek and, suddenly, he was on the Planet of Solitude, sitting beneath the familiar white apple tree, with Miss Bridie in his arms, her head on his lap. No wind. No light. No breath. Eyes open. Hair fallen to red, closer to the colour of the young woman's tresses in the picture in the hallway. The lines faded from her face, leaving only a peaceful girl with silent features.

As he leaned over and kissed her cold forehead, a tear slid down his cheek.

Lifting his head, he could see what the Planet of Solitude had so long hidden from him. All around, as far as his eyes could see, the corpses were piled high like sandbags in anticipation of a great flood. Unfamiliar, dead faces peered out at him with unseeing eyes. The ground was sand covered, with grassy green knolls rising up at random. Beyond the rotted corpses stretched endless miles of smouldering bog beneath a sky comprised of ink-black clouds racing across a dark, distant plane.

A voice called out to him. His head jerked backward.

"Finton."

He opened his eyes. Morgan was beside him, shaking him by the shoulders. "Let go," she said. "Let go. She's gone."

He pulled his hands away from Miss Bridie's chest and wiped them in his shirt. Eyes wide open, her face was frozen in the shape of a moan. No more wheezing. No rise and fall of her breast.

When the phone rang the next afternoon, it was for Tom, and everyone knew why. "Yes, Father," he said as he wrote down some details on a piece of paper provided by his wife. When he hung up, they were all looking at him—the entire family, united in various forms and degrees of melancholy. "Father Power wants me to dig her grave."

Both Elsie and Nanny Moon complained about the injustice of the request, but Tom said, "I'm lucky to have the work—and maybe it's only right that it's me, after all."

Homer stood up and said, "I can help."

A glimmer of gratitude rose to his father's eyes, prompting Finton to say, "I'll go too." Even Clancy nodded and said, "I might as well go too, I s'pose."

"Fine." Elsie folded her arms across her chest. "It'll make your father's work go faster."

All four Moon men got aboard the Galaxy and made the long drive through Darwin and up the winding, dirt road to Darwin Cemetery. Following the instructions he'd gotten from Father Power, Tom knew where to go and what to do. He stopped at the shack and grabbed four shovels, then they walked for a long time, around hundreds of graves, until they found the spot marked with a white, wooden cross. "Grab a shovel, b'ys." Each young man took a shovel and followed his lead. He showed them where to dig and told them how far down to go.

Finton followed the instructions, but his heart wasn't in it, and his mind was elsewhere. He felt dead inside, his thoughts paralyzed, fixated on imagining what his father and Miss Bridie had done together in her bed. How must Elsie have felt when she found out? Surely, she must have wanted to kick his arse outta the house. But with two youngsters already, maybe it was the prospect of getting another one that caused her to hang on. Either way, he didn't think much of his father. And he didn't care much for his mother's actions either. Whose boy was he now? What place did he belong to? As for his relationship with Morgan, well, he didn't even want to think about that part just yet because the ramifications were horrifying. And now Miss Bridie—supposedly his mother—was dead and gone, and she didn't even have to worry about any of it anymore.

"I don't see the point in this," Clancy said, even as he tossed a shovelful of dirt to one side on a mound he'd created. "She won't know the difference."

"We'll know the difference," said Homer.

"And Morgan," said Tom. "It'll matter to her."

"Miss Bridie don't know the difference," said Finton, looking at no one, even though he could feel their collective gaze upon him. He wondered if Homer and Clancy knew the truth, but, given the family propensity for secrecy, he was almost certain of their ignorance. "But we'd all want the same done for us," he finished.

While the boys kept digging, Tom leaned on his shovel and stared at his youngest.

"Wonder if she's goin' to heaven or hell," Clancy mused.

"I don't believe in either one," said Tom. "So it don't make no difference. All we get in the end is a hole in the ground, a pile of dirt, and a few prayers said over us."

"That don't make sense," said Homer. "That would mean there's no point to anything."

Finton thought about so many possible responses to the speculation that he started to get a headache. But what he finally said was, "You don't know what to believe, so you might as well believe in something as nothing. It's all the same thing."

Again, they all exchanged glances while continuing to dig. Tired of their company and filled with gloom, Finton lay down his shovel and went for a walk among the graves. He read the ancient dates, some going as far back as the 1600s, and he read the inscriptions, every one of them beseeching God or the angels to "take this beautiful soul to heaven," or words to that effect. They all made him sad, but none sadder than the tiniest graves inscribed with dates in months instead of years.

The work was done within an hour, and Tom led the other two boys in a moment of silence while Finton watched from a distance. All three dug the blades of their shovels into the ground and leaned on the handles, with their dirty, white gloves tucked beneath their chins.

When they returned to the car, Finton was waiting in the front seat on the passenger's side. Then they drove home, Clancy, Homer, and Tom making jokes, laughing and breathing easier than they had all day. But Finton only stared straight ahead as Darwin came into sight, his mood growing darker with each passing moment.

Ever After

Week's end summoned a surprise hurricane. Morning afforded rain, but the wind arose in the early afternoon with a violent shout that must have rattled every house in Darwin. When the lights went out in the lower part of town, the school closed early, and Finton walked home. His parents had offered to give him a respite from school, considering Miss Bridie's funeral a couple of days earlier, but he'd gone anyway, sombre and silent, as though something terrible were brewing in his brain. These days he didn't much care what they wanted him to do.

The hurricane had toppled trees that were older than Nanny Moon, and across the doorstep lay a sprawling spruce. The simple act of wrapping his arms around the lifeless tree and dragging it away to a place where it could do no harm was, in itself, deadening. He couldn't stop thinking about what Miss Bridie had said and wondering what he should do. Eventually, he would have to confront his parents, but he dreaded the moment, hated the necessity of it. Gradually, he had retreated into his own mind, detached himself from family, and distanced himself from life. More and more, he felt like an alien who'd been dropped on a doorstep with a note that said, "Please feed my baby," and the Moons had followed the request to its letter. They fed his body, but not his soul. And now here he was, nearly fifteen years old, bereft of connections.

Inside the house, things never changed. Nanny Moon was in the kitchen, reading or knitting while the wind howled outside like a wounded demon and threatened to separate the house from its foundation. He felt every gust that slammed against the bungalow, and he shuddered in the armchair where he was sprawled, pretending to read *The Scarlet Letter*. The family had scattered—Homer watched television; Clancy went down the road to his girlfriend's house; their mother paced the floor and wrung her hands as she gazed out the window. When a particularly bad blow made the windows buckle, she took out her rosary beads. Finton bolted for the bedroom. He wasn't speaking to God these days and, in fair turnabout, the Lord wasn't exactly communicating with him. They'd taken a timeout from each other, but, for Finton, it was more than that. There was a black cavern in his heart that tunneled right to his soul. God had taken more from him than he could ever replace, and, furthermore, didn't seem concerned with making amends; quite the contrary: the Lord seemed intent on absolute, irreparable destruction.

Around five o'clock, Elsie knocked on the bedroom door and opened it a crack.

"Finton, supper's almost ready."

Silence.

"Are you coming?"

More silence.

"Battered chicken is your favourite."

"I'm not hungry."

Insensible to his hope that she would just give up, she slipped inside, closed the door and sat on the bed. Despite the gloomy darkness and the rain that lashed the window pane, she didn't turn on a light.

"Are you all right?" she asked. With her right hand only inches from his leg, she could have offered a consoling touch, but didn't. He was glad. He didn't want her comforting—not now, not ever. His mother had never been good at mothering. Food and shelter, sure. Check those off. Clothes? Always second-hand, nothing fashionable. As for love and affection, well, motherly hugs were hard to come by. She'd never said she loved him, but probably her own mother hadn't said it to her. Finton once craved those things, but now he yearned only for solitude—a goal he approached with every moment that passed. More than a goal, it seemed his fate.

"Are you happy?" he asked.

"Why?" She eyed him closely, trying to read his thoughts. "What's wrong?"

Finton shrugged.

She seemed about to snap at him, but, instead, closed her eyes, opened them and reset. "I'm not *miserable*." She looked away, into the shadows of the farthest corner. Her pupils dilated as if she'd found something solid on which to focus. "Some things will never change as much as we want them to. Even if we think we deserve better."

"Do you deserve better than Dad?"

She looked at him sharply, then softened her expression as if suddenly remembering. "Sometimes, I s'pose. Maybe I do."

"Do you love him?"

She opened her eyes wide. "Why would you even ask such a thing?"

"You never say it to each other. And you're always arguing." It was probably asking for too much, but he hoped she would confide in him, wanted to be someone she would trust.

"Look around you, b'y. We don't argue no more than any other married couple," she said. "And I s'pose I do love him, in spite of his ways." She laid a hand on his wrist. Her fingers were cold. "How are you doing?"

He sighed and stared at the window, wondering if she was lying because, that way, it was easier to get by. "Don't wanna talk about it."

"Did you mind the funeral?"

"No." But that wasn't what he wanted to discuss. He steeled his nerve, gazed at her and tried to make himself spill what was on his mind. He could keep it to himself, but that wasn't really an option. He suspected that Miss Bridie had told him the truth about how he was taken from her, but he needed to hear it from the woman who'd been pretending all along to be his mother—the one who, all these years, had made his breakfast and supper, forced him to say rosaries and go to mass. The one who'd carried the burden of the masquerade and bore it so well. She was looking at him with expectation, as if she knew that what was coming would not be easy to escape.

Finally, the silence between them became too much. The words welled up inside until he thought his head would burst. So he blurted it out: "Miss Bridie told me something before she died."

"What did she say?"

His tongue faltered. "She said I was took from her. She said—"

"Your father and I have always done our best—"

"Is it true?"

"Did you even for one second think we weren't really your flesh and blood?"

"No," he said, and while the relief was still fresh on her face, he added, "For many seconds. Lots of times, I've wondered."

The slap from her right hand stung his cheek, and yet he didn't raise a hand in self-defense. He wouldn't satisfy her.

"How dare you say that after all we done for you? How bloody dare you?"

Already, the sting had dissipated. But he could feel his soul hardening, some essential element escaping the core of his very being. "She said I was took right after she had me, and that Dad warned her not to say anything about it to anyone, especially me."

His mother stood up, striking her head on the ladder that led to the top bunk. As she rubbed her crown, testing for blood, he could see the brightness of her eyes and the glistening on her cheeks. "I don't know what to tell you."

"The truth. I just want the truth, for once."

Sighing once more, she seemed to give in to the inevitability of the moment. She resumed her seat on the bed, clasped her hands on her lap, and stared at her fingers. "I knew we couldn't keep it a secret forever."

"Who else knows?"

"Just a few," she said with a trembling voice. Again, she rubbed her head and checked for bleeding. "Believe it or not."

"But whose son am I?"

Tears welled in her eyes. "You're my son. I raised you."

"But those stories about me being born—was it all just lies?"

"It was mostly true," she said. He could see by the rise and fall of her chest that she was struggling to maintain both her breath and composure. Still, he couldn't help but admire the strength it took to sit there and have one of the hardest conversations she would ever have. "You fell on your head, but it wasn't the nurse. It was me. I felt awful. And you did cry a lot when he brought you into the house. We thought you'd never stop. Everyone tried singing to you, but your father found the perfect song. Or maybe it was the fact that he was your father." She shook her head, obviously close to tears.

"I had a miscarriage after nearly full term," she said. "It would have been a girl."

He was shocked, yet relieved, to hear her say it aloud. In fact, it made him feel slightly better to know some of the details were drawn from fact and that it wasn't all lies.

"I was beside meself, b'y. I can't tell you how hard it was. And the worst part…" She spoke in a flat tone, as if already distanced from the cruel reality she was describing. "The worst was being told I couldn't have no more." Pause. "Here I was with just two boys. Two! I was hardly even a woman, sure, if that's all I was good for. As far as I was concerned, my life was over. What was the point of a marriage? What was the point of anything? I was so young. Back in those days, Nanny Moon was always lookin' at me like it was all my fault, like she hated my guts. It was all bad enough.

"Don't you dare breathe a word of this to no one—I can't believe I'm saying this, but I guess I have to." She swallowed hard and drew a deep breath. "Your father and I got married because I was pregnant." She laughed bitterly as if remembering the details of that thorny decision. "Imagine the irony of that. Pregnant too young. Married too young. And now I couldn't have any more. It was like being trapped with people expecting too much from me. I've always felt that way, really— thank God you're not old enough to know that feeling."

"Wasn't two boys enough for you?"

"For me? I s'pose so… if that's all I could have. For everyone else? Definitely not. You can't even imagine the pressure, b'y—pregnant one minute and neither child to show for it the next. I guess, at some point, the wheels got to turnin'—that somehow it would be okay if I could just have one more. And I prayed for it. I really, really did. I prayed for a boy just like you."

Finton felt himself go a little more dead inside. If he were hearing this story from anyone else, he would have had empathy for the young woman's plight. But this was his mother… or the mother he'd thought was his. And the child was himself. That made all the difference, and he couldn't help but disapprove of her awful choice.

"When your father told me about Bridie Battenhatch being pregnant, I nearly went mental—the likes of *that* having a baby! Not even a husband, sure, and the daughter she had showing signs of wildness, and her brother Jacob, well… I really shouldn't be telling you this." She drew a deep breath. "To some people, the most immoral things aren't wrong, and that's all I'll say about it." She seemed to lose her breath momentarily, but Finton was unmoved. He was afraid of disrupting the flow of honesty.

"I coulda killed someone," she continued in a calm, even tone. "But your father had an idea. He said, 'She's not stable, you know. Look at poor Morgan. Sure, she seems fine. But sometimes the things she does give me shivers. Miss Bridie's on her own and she's talking about doin' away with it!' I'll never forget how he leaned in, with such hope in his eyes, and whispered, 'We could take this one, Elsie. We could love it like our own. It *would* be our own.'"

"Something in the way he said it made me wonder. I'd wondered before, but now I had to know. 'Where is this idea coming from?' I asked him. 'You didn't just haul that rabbit out of a hat.' I'll spare you the details. It took some doing, and a lot of yelling and crying on my part and his, I tell ya, but I finally got him to admit it."

"Admit what?"

"That you were his. That he and Miss Bridie… had a… thing. One drunken night."

"A thing."

"I don't want to say it, Finton. Jesus. You're my son. And that's all that matters."

"I can't imagine," said Finton. "What it took for you to tell me that." She smiled gratefully, but he wasn't finished. "But I don't understand how you could do that to her."

"She was incompetent, Finton. You should have seen her. She wasn't fit. She would've done away with you and probably herself too."

"She was my mother."

"*I'm* your mother."

"No, you're not," he said. "You should've told me."

"Don't act like that," she said. "You're my boy!"

"I'm nobody's boy."

"Finton!"

"Get out!" he shouted. He turned towards the wall and kicked it with all his might, punching a small hole in the drywall. "Just leave me alone!"

"How dare you!"

"Morgan's my…"

As she left, she pulled the door shut, leaving Finton alone in the dark.

"…half sister—isn't she?" he said, in a voice that grew smaller with each word, as if he were vanishing right along with them.

The next afternoon, the boys were gone out, Nanny Moon was in her room, and Elsie was at work. Tom was on the couch, the television muted, and Finton saw his chance.

"I know what happened between you and Miss Bridie—and I know you took me from her when I was born."

Tom looked at Finton, shoulders slouched and a worn expression.

"Your mother said you knew. But I never thought Miss Bridie would tell you."

"Did you love her?"

"I loves your mother. What 'n hell do ya think?"

"But did you love Miss Bridie?"

"Why does it matter?"

"Because it does."

"Yes," Tom said, his hands clasped in front of him. "In a way, I did."

"Why?"

"You don't want to hear this, Finton. This is adult stuff."

"I'm old enough," he said. "This is the only time I'll ask."

"All right." His father wouldn't look at him, just stared at the TV. *Another World.* "I won't say everything, but I'll tell you some. But just remember, you're my son."

"I want to know why you went to her. Wasn't your wife enough?"

"I never went lookin'. We were playing cards and gettin' drunk. Morgan was young, but she was gone babysittin' or something. And we were talkin' about how shitty our lives were. I mean, she wasn't half bad lookin' back then. But I s'pose also... I wasn't the pickiest at times... about anything. I mean..." He laughed bitterly and shook his head. "...look at my life. Not exactly the fruit of good choices, is it?" Finton gave no reaction. "It was one time, and how was I to know what would come of it?"

Finton figured he should have known, but then he considered his own occasions having sex with Morgan without protection—to think... no, he couldn't think about that. It would drive him insane. *You were only twelve,* he reminded himself. *Nobody told you that stuff.*

"One more thing," he said when he figured his father was losing his motivation to keep talking and the pauses had become lengthy.

"One more," Tom said warily.

"Once and for all, did you kill Sawyer Moon?"

"I told you—"

"We're all telling the truth today for the first time ever. So tell me..."

"No," said Tom. "I told you before: I'm never answering that question again."

Lost

On the afternoon of the second last day of October, snow plummeted from the sky and blanketed the countryside. He'd stayed home from school, saying he didn't feel well. But everyone had scattered yet again, and, especially with his father taking Nanny Moon to the grocery store, he saw an opportunity to leave unnoticed. Through an opening he'd cleared on the sweaty windowpane, Finton watched in silent wonder and realized—*it has to be now*.

Now and then, he would glance outside to ensure that the snow was still falling. Then he pulled on his clothes and double-wrapped his long, red scarf around his neck so that it hung like vestments. He soon shut the door behind him, trundled out into the meadow and up the hill towards the woods.

The world was shockingly white, a land without edges or sharp distinctions. On the snow-laden ground, patches of brown grass and brambles poked up through the white carpet, reaching skyward against the rushing, white flakes.

In awe of how quickly the world had changed, Finton trudged the ghostly path. Where once the landscape was brown and drab, all had now turned bright. It was as if he'd breached the forbidden border and emerged into a land enshrouded by snow, where everything blended with everything else. Oblivious to the flakes on his cheeks and bare head, he forged a path into the waiting woods. Twenty minutes later, he stopped on the home side of the cold, dark river, peering into the thicket. Clouds billowed from his mouth. Over there would be darker, colder. The babbling brook seemed to call: "Step over. Hurry up. Don't waste time."

At the edge of the stream, he bent down and slid flat onto his belly. He leaned forward, leveraging himself with his arms, and drank from the river. Every time he thought he was done, he thrust his lips and nose back into the cool water, and gulped until he'd had his fill. Satisfied, he stood upright and sniffed the wind that smelled of spruce, pine, and birch, and the rot of half-frozen bog and damp peat moss.

For a long time now, he'd had the feeling of being watched, and he'd expected to see his observer when he'd lifted his head.

With the back of his hand, he wiped his mouth, tugged both ends of his snow-stippled scarf, then launched himself across the brook, landing with a thud on the other side. The river's song was unexpectedly different—deeper, resonant—reverberating in his heart. Hundreds of times he had crossed that river and never noticed the variance. But the thought was fleeting as the sun skittered behind a cloud, and he plodded towards the ominous thicket.

Except for the shimmering, white flakes that continued to fall, the woods were dark. A brown-coated rabbit hopped across the phantom path, paused to face the traveler, then quickly disappeared into the underbrush. Finton paused to notice the imprints of feathery paws and a furry belly that formed a divergent trail. He expected something magical to happen like in *Alice in Wonderland*, for someone to speak to him, tell him to go back home—or perhaps welcome him back to this place where he once belonged. He hoped not to be scolded, but that wouldn't have surprised him.

He stared at the branches of a snow-laden pine and thought how majestic it was. He marveled at the moment's silent perfection, frozen in time. Then, all at once, the branch bowed down, flicked upwards and dropped its load. The accompanying sound was like a gas stove igniting, jolting and abrupt. As a fine white mist sprayed the air around the tree, he gazed in wonder, blinked, and trudged onward.

At last, he came to the foxhole, where he sat on the rim, dangling his feet, and caught his breath. The snow was falling thicker now, as if it might go on forever. If he lay on his back, they'd probably never find him here—at least not until the spring, and then it would be too late.

He climbed into the hole and lay back, closed his eyes and listened to his own breathing rising and falling. Then he heard a sound—a light, quick intake of breath. His eyes snapped open, alert for an oncoming bear or a circling wolf. He swallowed hard and scanned the woods.

But he heard the sound only once and, after a while, his breathing slowed, and his senses attuned themselves to the woodland scene. The north wind whistled through the tops of the snow-covered evergreens, and a lonesome chill enveloped him. Already, the damp cold had seeped through his corduroy pants, and he wished he'd worn his snowsuit. He wondered how long he'd had his eyes closed, and whether he'd dozed. He kept his eyes shut, despite the cold and the truculent snowflakes that slowly buried him.

He knew how it should end. Jesus had to die for the sins of mankind. The world wouldn't take him back once he'd gone so far and shown them all how badly they'd behaved. Galilee was no place for such an enlightened soul.

All Finton had to do was to lie there and he'd be dead within hours. He was just exhausted. *So much much.*

No one was looking for him—they were all too busy. No rescue party was coming, at least not until it was too late. But it was some cold. Starting to shiver, he was tempted to wipe the snow from his cheeks and eyelids. But the snow felt so right. The foxhole was welcoming.

"Finton?"

Go away.

"What are you doing?"

"God? Is that you? I'm not answering until you explain some things."

"It's not God."

He felt like that fisherman in *The Old Man and the Sea.* How much had he hated that book? Skeet actually threw his copy into the garbage can outside school and set it on fire. A few other guys threw theirs in too. But it stayed in Finton's mind how the old man used to have these conversations with the big fish and the teacher said he was really talking to God. *Bunch of baloney,* he'd thought. He wanted to open his eyes, but couldn't. Something not quite like sleep had overtaken him and resisted his attempts to animate himself. His lips were frozen, but he managed to ask, "Who's talking?"

"It's me, b'y. What the hell are you doin'?" she asked, and he knew her now. "You can't stay here."

"Why not?"

"Snap out of it, b'y. Get yerself up or you'll freeze to death."

Warm hands caressed his face; soft lips pressed themselves to his frozen mouth. He considered resisting. But it was too late. No one could save him. He felt two fingers pinch his nose and cut off his breath. Sputtering and coughing, he bolted upright. "Jesus, girl—tryin' to kill me."

She squat in the snow across from him, her hands red, her discarded mittens lying in the snow beside her. A mischievous grin adorned her face.

Found

She brushed the snow from his face and chest. "Talk to me," she said. But his tongue was too numb for words. By wrapping one of his arms around her shoulder and leveraging him upward, she coaxed him to stand. She shouldered him ploddingly along until the foxhole had receded from view. Gradually, he became more alert and noticed she was dressed all in white except for her brown boots that looked like some kind of animal skin. Her mittens were green like Granny Smith apples. Her pants and down-filled jacket, even her hat, were whiter than the snow and so dazzling he had to shield his eyes.

The longer they walked, her arm around his waist, the warmer he got. Eventually, the numbness fell away from his legs and he was able to lumber solo.

"What in God's name were you doing there?"

"Th-thinking." His teeth chattered, and his breath was visible. "Wh-what are you doing here?"

"I scouted you." She shrugged as if it wasn't a big deal that she stalked him occasionally. And sometimes, like now, it came in handy. "Did you think about the fact that you coulda killed yerself?"

He watched the silent, white world slip past, the snow still dense, though less than before. Gradually, as he observed the same familiar trees and rocks, he began to feel as if he were emerging from a long journey or an extensive sleep.

They weren't following his usual trail. He had always known of a diverging path, and this was the one toward which Alicia steered him, although it had recently been obscured by snow. No need to ask—he knew where they were going.

In snow, the Dredge property looked the same as any other place. When he hesitated on the doorstep, she grabbed his hand. "Come on."

He followed close behind her, his legs still numb—closed his eyes against the dual smells of cat's piss and rotting wood. As they stepped into the kitchen, she pulled a chrome, padded chair alongside the table for him, and then she began stripping him—first his boots and then his socks, revealing his reddened feet. "Jesus," she muttered.

"What's he doin' here?" It was Alicia's brother Willie, in only his underwear, chewing on a red Twizzler, his ears even redder.

"What are you doin' here, smarty-pants? You should be in school."

"So should you, shit-for-brains."

"He got caught in the snowstorm. Help me get him into the bathtub."

"You're off yer head, girl. What are you gonna do—take his clothes off?"

"That's the plan."

"No thanks."

"Arsehole."

"Bitch."

"I should go home." Finton tried to stand, but just as suddenly, found himself sinking until his behind was in the chair. And yet he had the sensation of floating towards the ceiling. Alicia laid a hand on his shoulder, a motion more comforting than anything his mother had ever done, and the next few minutes were a blur as he was lifted and moved. In his dazed and nauseous state, he calculated that if he opened his eyes, he would definitely vomit. Alicia managed to guide him onto the toilet seat and, despite his mild protests, she proceeded to pull off his pants. At some point, she had also begun running water in the bathtub, its hollow babbling making the room small and all other sounds muffled and detached.

A knock came on the bathroom door. The door opened slightly, and Mrs. Dredge demanded to know what in God's name her daughter was at. He clenched his eyes shut for fear of discovering the scene was real—drunk and dazed in the bathroom with Alicia Dredge, pants to his knees, and her mother barging in and catching them in the act. Too strange-headed to care, he was nonetheless relieved when the door closed, allowing Alicia to finish the task.

"Keep your underwear on." She laid a steadying, cool hand on the small of his back. When he was finally soaking in the tub—trying not to think about the peculiarity of the moment—and she was wiping down his face and neck with a cloth drenched in hot water—he inhaled so deeply that the breath caught in his chest as he choked a rising sob. Something about the way she stroked his body with the cloth made him wish his life was better, that he loved his family, that it wasn't all so ridiculous.

"I love you," she whispered. He pretended not to hear.

Meet the Dredges

Watching the Dredges eat supper was like witnessing a dozen exuberant puppies feed from the same bowl. Finton, without his underwear and wearing a black bathrobe that smelled of dog, sat in a corner as bodies bustled around the chrome-trimmed table. Some stuffed food into their mouths, forks grasped in one hand like tridents and plates balanced in the other like shields. Alicia's mother had baked fresh bread to be dunked in the pea soup, but Willie was boiling spaghetti in a giant pot while another baked pizza. Yet another Dredge—a boy of about eight, whose name was Stinky—watched with wide, hungry eyes over a steaming pot of boiling fat that he'd stuffed with potato wedges and a chunk of hamburger meat. An older girl with freckles and copper hair munched an uncooked wiener as she slammed the refrigerator door, then tromped to the living room.

Finton wished there was a polite way to excuse himself, gather up his wet clothes, and go home. But Alicia had already called Elsie Moon to ask permission for him to stay for supper. He imagined his mother had been surprised, yet polite, when she'd said it was all right. In fact, Kieran was at their place and had agreed to stay for supper. So Finton found himself imprisoned, uncertain of a timely release.

Suddenly, as though some signal had been given, everyone who would be eating at the table sat down, while all others found a corner elsewhere in the house. Elbows on the table, all fell quiet. Alicia clasped her hands and bowed her head. Finton pulled his chair close to the table, joined his hands, closed his eyes, and bowed his head. When he opened his eyes, his previously empty bowl was now full of pea soup.

Mrs. Dredge's grace was terse, thankful, and to the point. Then, as if on cue, the kitchen door banged open, and Alicia's father flew in like debris in a storm.

Phonse Dredge appeared exhausted and perturbed, the lines on his face like crumpled pieces of paper around his eyes and mouth, deeper than when Finton last saw him. His disheveled hair, though formerly pure white, was now mingled with a few yellow strands that made his crown look like peed-on snow. Despite the fact that he possessed an air of rushing in at the last possible moment, his deep-set eyes conveyed a weariness, like a man who had been through the holy wars and was ready to lay down his life to the next soldier who pointed a gun at him.

When he saw Finton, those same pupils dilated as if sensing a threat. In an instant, the boy recalled the story his father had told about the night Phonse had seen the devil outside his watchman's shack—he could picture the scene as if he'd heard the story only a moment ago. Now, years later, he looked like a man who'd been living ever since with that image of evil in his head. Mrs. Dredge welcomed him home and a couple of the younger ones cheered, but none of the others looked up from their soup. His gaze immediately fell on the strange boy at the table.

"Finton got caught in the snow," Alicia said. "His clothes are wet, so I asked him to stay for supper."

Phonse grunted and pulled off his coat as he trudged through the kitchen, on his way to the living room. "Get me a beer," he said to one of the girls as he lowered himself into the ragged, brown recliner.

"Your supper's gettin' cold." Mrs. Dredge turned her neck sideways in an uncaring manner. Finton gleaned that this was a daily conversation, with him always late and her battling to keep the meals from going to pot.

The TV was turned up. The news was on, Glenn Tilley's sharp baritone propounding the headlines of the day against the background noise of smacking gums, loud chewing, and the scraping of forks against plates. Even the deep fryer had settled into a cautious simmer.

Finton and Alicia exchanged glances as she shook her head and kept eating.

"The soup is really good," he said. True enough, while the pea soup resembled something a dog might regurgitate, its flavour was unexpectedly pleasant.

"How's your father doing?" The raspy voice from the living room made Finton spasm in fright, but the sound was so distant he didn't immediately realize that Phonse Dredge was talking to him. When Alicia nudged him, he offered the first answer that came to his mind, but the words got stuck in his throat.

"Speak up, b'y. I said how's your father?"

"He's all right." Finton spoke louder and hoped it was sufficient.

The footsteps on the canvas made his heart leap into his throat. Finton cringed when he saw a hard object in Phonse's left hand as he entered the kitchen, but sighed with relief when he realized it was only a beer bottle.

"All right, is he?"

"Yessir."

Phonse laughed, an unpleasant sound that made Finton feel as if a shit storm was coming. "I'm neither a teacher nor a policeman, so you can knock off the *sir*. To you, I'm Mister Dredge."

"Yes, Mister Dredge."

He eyed Finton's empty bowl. "Supper good, was it?"

Only then, in glancing around surreptitiously, did the lad realize he was the first one finished. "Yessir—Mister Dredge."

Phonse's smile revealed his lone, yellow tooth. "You're afraid of me, aren't you?" He swigged from the bottle, maintaining a firm gaze on the boy. Despite the fact that he was obviously attempting to intimidate him, Finton sensed fear emanating from his pores. At first, he couldn't fathom what a man like Phonse Dredge had to worry about from the likes of him, but there was no mistaking that this man desired to beat the living shit out of him. And then, of course, he remembered Phonse's small part in both Miss Bridie's story and Sawyer's as a witness to those matters that should not be spoken of.

"No, sir. My father often says the only two things I need to be afraid of are him and God, and you're not either one."

"Are you saucin' me, boy?"

"No, sir."

Phonse rubbed his hand across his chin, caressing the stubble as if pondering heavy thoughts. He nodded towards the bowl. "Do you want more soup?"

Finton's stomach was nearly empty, and he'd worked up an appetite trudging here in bad weather. In fact, he easily could go for another bowl of soup and another slice of that delicious, warm bread. "Please—" His plea was interrupted by a kick in the back of his leg and a narrowed look from Alicia. "No, thank you, sir. I'll be going home now."

"Come on," said Alicia. "We'll get you something to wear."

As Finton got to his feet, Phonse kept rubbing his hand across his bristle, gazing at the boy. "Well, tell your father… we should have a beer sometime."

"Yessir."

Phonse grimaced, and Finton felt he could read his mind. It was not the soul of an innocent. His black heart pumped thick, oily sludge through decrepit veins like thin, rusted pipes. *This man is afraid of me*, he thought. *He's sure I know something about him.*

"Come on." Alicia tugged Finton's arm.

"Stay, sure. Have more soup." Phonse looked askance at his wife. "Surely to God we can give 'im some more soup. Those poor Moons don't have very much." He blessed himself with the hand that held the bottle.

Hauling on one of his arms, Alicia dragged Finton down the hallway and into a small room stuffed with garbage bags, cardboard boxes, comic books, old games, toys, and clothing—all of it cobwebbed and musty. The room was dank and dark, with a small, fogged window and a white sheet drawn across the door frame. "This is where we keep the stuff we don't throw away."

"Why don't you just throw stuff out?"

"Mom doesn't throw anything out. She says you never know when you might need it."

"I can wear my own clothes," he said.

"They're still wet. You'll catch a cold or pneumonia if you goes wearin' them. You look cute in Kieran's bathrobe, though."

"Kieran… oh, your brother Kieran."

"He's way older than me. Went away to cop school, but he's back here now with the RCMP."

"You must be some proud to have a policeman in the family."

"You have no idea." She seemed about to explain, but simply added, "It's complicated."

Alicia sifted through piles of clothing, mostly of the summer variety. Now and then, she'd pause on a sweater or a pair of slacks, most of it old and smelly.

"Honestly, I can just go with what I have on."

"You'll be a laughing stock in that, b'y." She held up a gigantic brown snowsuit, which looked to have all of its limbs and other vital parts intact. "This is Dad's, but I don't think he uses it no more."

Upon closer inspection, both Alicia and Finton noticed the large, dark stain in front. "Well," she said. "You're not going very far in it."

Finton gazed at the offering and pondered whether to wear it. He'd just decided it was better than walking home in a black bathrobe when Alicia turned towards him with an armful of clothing. "There might be something better here."

Finton grabbed the oversized, green sweater and brown corduroys she was offering. "I'll just put these on." But she didn't let go. He tugged on the garments and Alicia came along with them, pressing her face towards his. Just for a moment, he wanted to kiss her. But visions of Bernard Crowley flashed in his head, so he pulled back and yanked the clothes from her hands.

"You can change in my room," she said. She guided him down the short hallway and waited outside the bedroom door. When he'd gotten dressed—and accepted his wet clothes in a green garbage bag—he hustled towards the kitchen. The fire in the stove was still going strong, but most of the Dredges had already scattered to other parts of the house or outdoors. The dishes were piled next to the sink. "Gotta clean up," Alicia said as she rolled up her sleeves.

He hesitated, wondering what he should do. She swallowed hard, her eyes glistening with unreadable emotion. "What are you going to do now?" she asked.

"I don't know." He approached her at the sink and lowered his voice. "What do you think I should do?"

"I don't know what you mean." She rubbed her arms for warmth, then gently laid a hand on his arm, startling him with the unexpected show of affection. She rubbed his arm, then suddenly withdrew her hand and said, "You should go."

Finton nodded and started to leave. "Thank you for—"

"*Shhhh…*" She pressed a finger to his lips. "Just forget it."

Recovery

Past the saltbox houses where kitchen lights gleamed, Finton strode home in his borrowed clothes, carrying his wet ones slung on his back. The blue-black ocean, beyond the ashen trees, sparkled in the dying light of an early winter sun. As if to belie the oncoming darkness, a layer of snow brightened each lawn, concealing a multitude of landscape deficiencies. With every step, he was plagued by doubts, yet filled with certainty. There was much that the world had decided about him, and for him. But there was also much he'd decided about the world.

"Fancy duds," Kieran said when Finton walked in the front door and lay the garbage bag on the linoleum. The constable stood by the kitchen window, wearing his usual uniform, although the top button was undone, and his white t-shirt showed through.

They were all sitting there, plates already emptied of baked beans. Tom was at the head of the table, Nanny Moon on his right and Elsie next to her. The two boys sat on their father's left, with Homer closest to him. Only Kieran was standing, as if preparing to leave.

Finton had forgotten about his Dredge costume. When Kieran noticed, he merely shrugged and sat down.

"We were just talking about you," Elsie said. "How'd you get your clothes wet?"

"I lay down in the snow," he said.

"Why in the name of God did you do that?"

"Because I didn't care if I lived anymore."

Silence filled the room, an unwanted guest.

"I think we'd better talk about this later," she said.

"I don't want to talk about it at all. I'm over it now."

"That's not for you to say," Tom said. "Your mother and I will decide that."

"No, you won't. I'm sick of everybody else deciding what I can do and what I can't—what I can talk about and what I'm supposed to keep quiet about. As of now, I'm doing things my own way, and everybody else can just worry about themselves."

Elsie's face was flushed, and her eyes flashed with anger. "Finton, go to your room."

"I'm too old to go to my room."

"You'll never be too old or too big for me to handle," said Tom. "Now do what your mother tells you."

"Yeah—like you do."

"Finton!" Elsie's eyes were pleading now. They all knew better than to provoke Tom's temper. "Go to your room now."

"No," he said. "You're just saying that because Kieran is here."

His father rose from his seat and grabbed Finton's shoulder. "Listen here, " he started to say, but Kieran's sharp cough caught the attention of them all.

"Finton, would you mind walking to the car with me? I'd like a word with you."

As Tom's face showed shock, the youth broke free from his father's grip and followed the policeman, who tipped his hat to Elsie and again to Nanny Moon. "Good night, all."

"They've all been worried sick about you," Kieran said as they walked to the police car.

Finton stuck his hands into a pockets and kicked the bumper. "I'm all right."

"Really?" Kieran seemed neither angry nor earnest. It was one of those strange moods that Finton had a hard time pegging. Because of the uniform, everything he said carried extra weight. Kieran never seemed to take anything too serious, and yet everything, to him, was extremely important. "Are you happy, Finton?"

"I don't know."

"Listen." Kieran turned his head slightly, one side of his face catching the soft light of the porch lamp while the other side was captured by darkness. Effortlessly, he opened the car door, reached inside, and started the engine. He turned the headlights to low beam, then closed the door and stood in front of the car. "If you don't know enough about happiness to know when you're feeling it, you need to live your life better. Start on a path that will make you feel good about yourself. I don't know what that means for you—it means something different for everyone. But you're nearly a man now, Finton, and it's time to point yourself in the right direction—before it's too late."

Finton didn't say anything. He wasn't sure where all of this supposed wisdom was coming from. He'd never heard anything like it before, from anyone, except maybe Atticus Finch.

"You're awful quiet," Kieran said.

"Just thinking."

"About what?"

Finton glanced up at the bungalow atop the hill, like a haint in the pale wash of headlights. He exhaled a breath he didn't know he'd been holding. "Nothing."

"Well, make sure *nothing* doesn't eat you alive." The words made Finton feel better, as if Kieran had known just what to say. He still didn't quite have faith in the guy, but his words were often the right ones. Maybe he was just trying to trick Finton into giving in to his parents because that would make it easier for everyone. And easy was how everyone liked life to be. But something about Kieran Dredge invited his trust.

"Why do you care?" Finton asked.

The constable stared fully into the headlights. His face and hands glowed white, almost as if he were a ghost Finton had conjured and clung to, willing him to remain, afraid to startle him. "Because the alternative is just too hard, Finton. It's easy to lose faith. Keeping it is a hell of a lot harder and way more admirable. But let me tell you this—life will beat the life out of you, and if you're not strong enough to take it and pick yourself up now and then, you're just gonna stay down for the count. You can't depend on anyone else to do it for you. There are just some things you've got to find for yourself. And I mean *got* to. It's the difference between living and dying."

"You seem to have given it a lot of thought."

Kieran smiled. "First time, matter o' fact." He scratched his head, pushed back his hat and fixed it right again. "I guess you've got a way of bringing that out in me."

"I'll take that as a compliment, if you don't mind."

"I'd be offended if you didn't." Kieran laughed. "But lookie here— I've been where you are, and I made up my mind to either get what I wanted out of life or die trying. People say when you're at the bottom you got nowhere to go but up. But, let me tell you, there's worse. And you don't want to go there."

When Kieran said goodbye, Finton wondered if he'd ever see him again. To his great surprise, that prospect actually made him melancholy.

"Home" was the word for failure—the place that ensured you retained the emotional perspective of an eight-year-old, filled with people who presumed to know you better than you knew yourself and who presented every obstacle to your attempts to rise up in the world, to become who you truly are.

Don't go back. His heart beat the words in a primitive rhythm. *Don't go back. Don't go back. Don't go back. Don't go back.* He wanted to scream, the primeval breath urging and plunging behind his rib cage, threatening to explode its marrow and bones. So he followed the taillights of Kieran's car down to the bottom of the lane, where he turned left and walked a short distance.

Ascending the steps of the Battenhatch house was like coming home—as decrepit as it was, despite the bad habits he'd acquired there, the memories were comforting, the creak of the rickety steps reassuring. Despite the snow packed in front of the door, with no footprints leading in or out, the darkness of the front porch welcomed him.

After he'd knocked, he heard no sound from within. But she was in there. He'd seen the silhouette of her watching him from the kitchen table as he ascended the steps. She'd sat in the dark, the glow of her cigarette a sign to the world.

When she finally opened the door, there was no light inside except the glow from a candle atop the cold wood stove. She stood in the entrance like a banshee bride, dressed in her white nightgown, her blonde hair gone limp and dark. He expected some kind of welcome or an acknowledgement of all that had passed between them and beyond them. Instead, she merely turned to one side and went back inside, leaving him standing in the doorway. He followed her in and shut the door behind him.

"What the hell kind of costume is that you got on?"

"Oh, these aren't mine. I had to borrow some."

"Should I ask?"

He shook his head. "I just came over to see how you were."

She wheeled around and looked at him, her colourless face imprinted with cruel lines. She tapped her cigarette on the handrail of the stairs and poked it back into her mouth. "Good as can be expected, I s'pose."

He nodded and watched her hands, sensing that to say little was wise. "It feels strange here without... your mother."

"I s'pose it does." Puckering her lips and sucking inward, she drew fire from her cigarette until it glowed angry orange. She withdrew her lips from the butt, a long sliver of ash protruding from the filter tip. "People die. Life goes on. Then you die too." She assessed his silent stance, hands in pockets, staring at her with his head cocked, and she squinted. With a clump of her bedraggled hair overhanging her right eye, she looked like a wild animal. "Got something on yer mind?"

"Mom said Miss Bridie told the truth."

She laughed—a cackle, really—that was slightly unnerving. "That woman never told the truth about anything. Surely to God, ya knew that much about her."

"She said..." He swallowed hard and licked his lips, cleared his throat. "She said I was hers—" He felt something pop in his chest and wondered if he was going to have a heart attack. Suddenly, he felt lighter than a late-October leaf wavering on its stem, a freakish holdout caught between worlds. "—that they took me when I was born."

"Jesus, b'y. Get a grip." She took another draw and the cylinder of ash lengthened, threatening to break off. "That's some fairytale in that head o' yours."

"Did you know?"

"Christ, b'y, I don't even know now what to think. I was only a youngster in them days. I didn't know what anyone was up to and, furthermore, didn't care. All I know is Mom never fit in here from the first day. Never belonged no matter where she was." One more draw; the ashen line got longer and weightier, closer to falling. "Some people never belong anywhere, I s'pose. She said people were cruel to her nearly every day." She lifted her head and squared her gaze at him. "But not your father."

"He was good to her. She said that."

She nodded. "The only one."

"What do *you* think?"

She grinned, a far less natural, and much more disturbing, expression. Although still young, Morgan had become a creature just like her mother, supplanting her in that house that his father had rebuilt. Where, not so long ago, she had been his haven in an endless storm, now she was on her way to becoming a bitter hag, a face that bore only memorial lines of the beauty she'd been. In her eyes, he still saw some of the girl he'd known. Beneath the nightdress, her body was slender, but not nearly so taut or supple as before. In time, he knew, that girl would be gone for good.

"Your father loved my mother—and he never stopped." She winked at him and blew an "O" in the air above her head. "The only ones that knew it was Sawyer and Phonse Dredge."

"You don't know that."

"She told me one time—not that he loved her, but other things. He liked her 'cause she was different from your mother. Too uptight and religious, he said. And a baby belly. My mother was a heathen, and your father liked that. Men usually do." The wink she gave made him lower his head.

A truck rolled down the road and baptized them both in a lurid white light. If she was telling the truth, Finton knew the rest: Sawyer kept the secret, but his loyalty came at a price. That secret had bought his father's friendship. He could easily imagine how Sawyer had known—maybe saw Tom and Bridie together one day, a peck on the cheek or a harmless hug, and Sawyer's silence could be bought fairly cheap, no doubt. Phonse was uncomfortable around Finton because he'd been there the night they took Miss Bridie's baby and gave it to the Elsie. Who else was there? he wondered.

"Sure, come in and sit down. Have a yarn with me." Morgan sashayed her shoulders, trying to be free and easy as she used to be. "Old times' sake 'n all that?"

He thrust his hands deeper into his pockets and nodded. "I gotta go."

"Afraid of me now, aren't ya?"

"No, Morgan. Not afraid. Just came to me senses."

"You can come around now and then if ya want," she said, a twinkle in her eyes. "Just talk. You're good for that."

He smiled, grateful to see a trace of the old Morgan—the young Morgan, the one who didn't care about the rules or what people expected of her. She did things the way she wanted to, regardless of who got hurt. Mostly it was herself or Miss Bridie. Everyone else was afraid to come near. The wildness in her eyes. That's what drew him in, and he could almost see it returning. Almost. It was enough of a glimmer to make him think she would be okay, once the grieving days were done.

"Sure," he said. "Whatever you want." But he knew he wouldn't be coming back around. There was just too much history between them.

She followed him to the door, holding it open as the night breeze wafted inward and swayed the hem of her nightdress to expose her pale thighs. "I never thought I'd say this, but I miss the old girl… ya know?" She wiped a single tear from the corner of each eye, and forced herself to grin. In that same motion, the finger of ash broke away from her filter and dropped onto his leg. He brushed it away as if it were a loathsome spider. He jerked away, trying not to offend her, but her eyes betrayed a mortal wound.

He leaned in closer. His lips found the whorl of her ear, and he whispered low, but clear: "We were innocent." He raised a hand to her cheek, tender and tentative, as if touching her for the first time. Her flesh was clammy, her cheekbone hard. "No matter what we did—that was then. But we didn't know."

She pulled away, her eyes full of sadness. "Get home out of it, b'y. And don't come back till ya can talk about something sensible."

"Take care of yourself, Morgan. It's not too late," he said. "It never is."

The smile she attempted warmed his heart and made him smile back. "What you're talking about is hope," she said. "I don't even know what that means anymore."

"You need to get out," he said. "This place is no good for you. You still got time."

She started to object, but he leaped off the step and started to run. At the last moment, he turned his head to catch her in the act of squeezing the door shut. A cluster of hair had fallen over her face, rendering her virtually unrecognizable. He would never know what it felt like to have a sister, or what that meant. It would probably take years to extract her from his brain, especially those summer afternoons upstairs in her bedroom.

Turning up Moon's Lane, he slowed and regarded the hilltop bungalow. He studied it hard as if its secrets would unfold in its size and shape, the projection of its heart light from the kitchen window to the ground below, the front door that was barred tight like a medieval drawbridge, or the ruinous nature of its concrete doorstep. Perhaps there was a welcoming somewhere, a place to lay his aching and tired head. But, for all its familiarity, he was a relative unknown there, a place where he'd never lived.

The Time of Survival
(1976)

On the fifteenth of May, Finton stood at the counter of the Darwin post office and asked for a stamp. He reached inside his jacket for an envelope, which contained a letter he'd composed the night before in a moment of great hope but low expectation. After affixing the stamp, he glanced at the envelope and gave it only a moment's reflection before dropping it into the slot.

Now there was nothing to do but wait.

In the months that followed his "resurrection," Finton tried to remain interested in Darwin life. During the short, cold days of winter, he renewed his dedication to books. Most Saturdays, he went to the library where he curled up in an armchair by the window. His companions were Faulkner, Stoker, Shelley, and a new guy named Stephen King, whose *Carrie* had become one of his favourites.

All of these authors were suggested to him by a teacher—a lanky, young Christian Brother named Murphy Regan—who saw "a creative spark" in the lad and wanted to encourage him. He convinced Finton to enter a short story contest sponsored by the school board authority, and when he got second prize, he couldn't wait to tell Brother Regan, who told him, "You're a natural, and I'm sure there's more where that came from. Just keep going." Buoyed by his one success, Brother Regan tried to interest Finton in school council, the photography club, or any of the school's sports teams. None of that mattered to Finton, but in late March, he became curious about cross-country running and showed up for tryouts. He discovered that he wasn't the fastest, but had by far the most endurance. He sprained his ankle along the way, but it didn't cost him much time. He still finished first. Already done, he waited over a minute for his nearest competitor to emerge from the fog and cross the finish line. By that time, he'd already decided to quit the team. The trial itself was enough. Sometimes a trial is necessary for clearing the air, moving forward, healing the wounds.

Sometimes, if he cut himself—by paper or the jagged edge of an opened can—he watched the blood flow for a few seconds, just to reassure himself that he was normal. Then he would kiss the wound and press his hands together and, always, within moments, the bleeding would stop. Likewise, a bruise would heal or a sprain would dissipate.

As he kept more to himself, people had stopped asking him to heal their ailments, and he gave them no reason to start up again. His father didn't dig many graves over the winter. The parish invoked a new policy that January, saying they would have to store all bodies until the spring because the ground was too hard for digging. Tom got unemployment insurance, but Elsie got a raise and an increase in her hours at the liquor store, making more money per hour than either of them had ever seen.

They didn't talk about events of the previous fall—Miss Bridie's passing, or her deathbed revelations. These matters had been discussed and now they were buried, like Miss Bridie herself. Sawyer Moon, likewise, had become a memory, his death a mystery enshrouded by the days that passed, the way a lost bike can be plastered by falling leaves, and then covered up by the snows of winter. No one missed Sawyer, and if someone had done away with him, there was likely a good reason that might never be known.

If he had any thoughts about digging deeper into his father's involvement, they were banished for good when, one evening in May he overheard Tom say to Elsie, "Meself and Phonse are goin' for a few beer—ya know, it gets pretty dreary without a friend or two." That evening, his father was in the best mood Finton had seen since before Sawyer's disappearance. It was as if springtime had come for Tom Moon, and when Tom was happy, the Moons were happy.

Elsie had found salvation in her job. She didn't drink, but she hoped her good Lord and saviour would see her new occupation as a necessity, for the sake of her family's survival. Even Nanny Moon and Tom had new respect for her. Her mother-in-law cooked supper on evenings when Elsie worked until five o'clock, and would clean up afterwards, with help from the two youngest boys. Elsie complained, of course, about the difficulty of going to work, but Finton could tell she secretly enjoyed the money it brought and the sense of purpose she'd gained.

The entire family was getting along better than ever, but, if anyone noticed Finton's increased detachment, no one mentioned it. Occasionally, Tom shook his head and said, "That boy always was a lone wolf." But nobody seemed to worry about him or, if they did, they kept it to themselves for fear of raising the spectres of the past. Their mistake was in assuming that he never thought about his origins or the lies he'd been told to cover it up. As the weeks accumulated, he simply became more disconnected, since nothing could change the way he felt. Simply put, he had never belonged here. It wasn't a matter of blood ties, neglect, or even cruelty, but an innate sense of his own difference.

Although he read more books for enjoyment, Finton put hardly any time into his homework. His grades dropped from A+ to B, still superior to Homer's Ds and Fs. Homer, meanwhile, was desperately trying to finish high school, but he intended to quit school altogether if he didn't pass this year. "No big deal," Homer said. "It's not like I need Grade Eleven to get a job."

Still, one evening, when he saw Homer wringing his fists and pulling his hair, Finton sat at the table beside him and said, "Let me help." Together, they figured things out that, in a classroom setting, had been beyond Homer's comprehension. By the fifteenth of May, when Finton mailed his letters, Homer was scraping by, but nevertheless passing. Finton was earning brownie points with his own Lord and saviour by coming to the aid of the brother who had danced with Mary Connelly.

Clancy and Finton didn't see each other much, as the age difference meant even more as they got older. The oldest Moon boy had a steady girlfriend and spent most of his time at her house. She was a good Darwinian, with a strict Catholic mother, and a household full of girls—she had four sisters. Finton had always thought Clancy could have been something more academic or artistic, for he possessed an intellectual curiosity of sorts. But his brother had succumbed to the subtle rural pressure to accommodate and imitate the known way of life, to reject creative and literary pursuits that didn't involve financial gain as a waste of valuable time. Besides, his love of machinery was so obvious that it was hard to imagine him any happier than he was.

A few days after he'd mailed the letters, Alicia called and asked him to meet her at the old schoolhouse.

"What's up?" he asked. But she wouldn't drop a hint. Twenty minutes later, they sat on the step together, side by side, staring out at the woods. He wondered if her memories were like his—full of bright, vibrant colours, incomprehensible violence, and a lot of running, with swirling moments of beautiful faces with wide, open eyes.

"Listen," she said, "do you have a date for the prom?"

"I'm not goin'." He'd made up his mind long ago that it would cost too much for a single night of playing pretend. More importantly, he didn't have anyone to ask.

"Would you go with me?"

"What about Bernard?"

"Oh, he still stalks me. But I'm not goin' to the prom with someone like him."

"But why me?"

"Because you're the best friend I have," she said.

Despite his misgivings, there was no good reason, except for Bernard Crowley, to disappoint Alicia. He told her he would love to go, which was only a slight lie. But as the days went on, it felt much like Confirmation, an emotionally useful rite of passage, a signal to the brain that it was time to move forward.

At school, he took part in two official prom rehearsals, in which he practised walking into the gymnasium with Alicia, holding her hand. He actually enjoyed that part, as well as sharing some laughs with his classmates. Skeet and Dolly practised together, while Mary's prom date was an older boy, Pete Lundrigan, who'd graduated the year before, and so she practised walking in with one of the teachers. Bernard, apparently, had declared that if Alicia wouldn't go to the prom with him, he wouldn't go at all.

In early June, Finton bought a brown, polyester suit at the mall for forty dollars. On the fourth of June, he bought a corsage at the flower shop. On the fifth of June, Skeet and Dolly picked him up in Skeet's lime green Gremlin, then stopped for Alicia, and they all arrived at the prom together.

On a sultry June afternoon, there was a church ceremony during which the valedictorian, Mary Connelly, in a long, red strapless dress, praised everyone and thanked their parents, spoke earnestly about having endured and enjoyed their time together, but now it was time to go forth and enjoy all that life had to offer. It was a pretty speech; she meant every word. Finton even felt a little nostalgia to go along with his nerves. That was important to him. Feeling something meant it was right, that he'd gotten something from it, that he'd actually been there.

The dance began at 7:30 p.m., and the decoration theme was "Dreams," with fluffy clouds made of cardboard painted white and a wishing well swing where graduates, including Finton and Alicia, posed for the official prom photograph. As the graduating students entered the gymnasium, paired off and holding hands, the song on the sound system was Diana Ross's "The Theme From Mahogany (Do You Know Where You're Going To?"). To his surprise, Finton got sucked in by the bittersweet nostalgia. All his life, he'd never felt as if he'd belonged at this school, and now he could almost believe otherwise. These people said such comforting words and played such sweet songs that suggested they'd all experienced the very same things in exactly the same way.

He knew it wasn't true—it had been different for everyone. But the high school committee had done its best to represent the student body and, in a way, they had achieved their mission. None of them really knew where they were going to, what doors would open or close, or what life would offer. But they had each survived high school in their own private, yet inescapably public, way.

Once the hoopla was over, it was a dance like any other, except it was far better than Finton's previous experience. No one grabbed the front of his shirt, and he didn't accidentally strike anyone's nose and make it bleed.

Alicia was beguiling in her simple, green dress and he danced with her most of the night, to fast songs and slow. "Go Your Own Way," "More Than a Feeling," "Tonight's the Night," "Turn the Page," and "Blinded by the Light." He danced with Dolly to a couple of fast tunes.

When the first few notes of "The First Cut is the Deepest" played, Finton instinctively looked for Mary. They had barely looked at each other all night, and he couldn't help but feel that, if there would ever be a perfect moment to dance with her, this would be it. He knew where she was, for he'd kept one eye on her all along. Her boyfriend, Pete Lundrigan, was leading her by the hand towards the dance area, so he rushed. "Mary!" he said breathlessly. "Would you like to dance?" Deep down, he suspected she would turn him down. But she smiled brightly and offered her hand. "I'd just about given up on you," she said.

"Nice dress," he said.

"Thanks. You look nice too."

"Thanks," he said. He suddenly couldn't think of anything else to say. "Oh, I really liked your speech today. Very nice."

She smiled and thanked him again. "You seem nervous," she said.

"I'm just having a good time. No nerves for me tonight. One of the best nights of my life."

"Alicia seems to be enjoying herself too."

"You think so?" He glanced towards his prom date, who was standing by herself near the punch table, sipping her drink from a plastic glass.

"Yes—and she looks amazing."

"I'll tell her you said that." The song was ending way too fast, and he hadn't come close to saying all he wanted to say to her. "I'm glad you're feeling better," he said.

"Honestly, Finton, I never thought I'd be here tonight."

"You look amazing. I mean, I know I said that, but you really do. You seem really happy now with Pete too—and I'm glad. I'm just glad for you."

"Thank you," she said, smiling sweetly. She laid her head on his shoulder to finish the song, and Finton thought life could get no better, nor sadder, all at once. After that, they barely spoke to each other. There wasn't much more to be said, for it had all been said a long time ago. The emotions of a deeper discussion would have been crippling, so he just kept dancing—the loud music and constant motion being the best method of keeping the darkness at bay.

His head was still buzzing when he and Alicia, as pre-arranged, left before the last song. Everyone else had plans for private parties after the prom. Some guys had procured ill-gotten booze, and more than a few carried rubbers in their wallets. A few girls, according to Alicia, were planning to lose their virginity that night. He assumed she'd lost hers to Bernard, who didn't seem to be the patient type. Finton couldn't help thinking about his own lost innocence to Morgan Battenhatch when he was just twelve. Maybe it was better that way—satisfying his primal needs early, getting them out of the way quickly so they wouldn't land him in trouble. Maybe he owed Morgan gratitude, after all.

They walked home, not holding hands, but laughing wildly and touching each other occasionally when the moment called, or allowed, for it. The moon was waxing, nearly full, and, when it wasn't hiding behind a cloud, it shone upon the ocean and afforded meagre light upon the road where they tread. On rare occasions, a car passed by, headlights blinding them as the two graduates clung to each other to keep from falling.

With some light from the moon, the mood was playful. Prompted by the memory of a song the DJ had played, they sang a few bars of "Only

Sixteen" by Dr. Hook, and giggled when they grew conscious of their mutual giddiness.

"You're good for me," he said. "I feel like I can be myself with you."

Her eyes glistened when she stopped and stood in front of him, impeding his progress. He laid both her hands on his shoulders. "That's the nicest thing you've ever said to me. I mean… that anyone's ever said to me."

"I could kiss you," he said.

"That would be nice," she said with a smile.

He leaned in and touched his lips to hers, and then they both laughed.

"It was nice," he said.

"I thought so."

She slipped her hand into his. "We should get going."

His head was spinning, his rational side telling him that his feelings were just the product of a successful prom and a romantic walk in the moonlight with a beautiful girl. The kiss alone wreaked havoc with his hormones. But, of course, he was already in love with her, and so it would break both their hearts when he had to leave.

Alicia said something about her plans for the summer—she'd found work at the fish plant, starting next week—but Finton wasn't listening. He was fearfully watching the car, with its lights on high beam, slowing down as it came towards them.

"What's this jackass trying to prove?" He pulled Alicia away from the road, towards the gaping maw to their left—a treacherous plunge that could cause serious injury. The pitch darkness made it impossible to determine the drop off point, and so they halted breathlessly, clinging to each other, and stood completely still while they waited for the danger to pass. But the car accelerated and veered straight for them.

"It's Bernard," she said. At the last possible moment, she pushed Finton to the ground and fell on top of him. Alicia yelped as the car zoomed past, blaring its horn.

"Did he hit you?" Finton shouted above the roar of the engine.

"Yes," was the only part of her response he heard.

A few yards away, the driver tried to guide the car back onto the pavement, but just as Finton was imagining the worst possible outcome, the vehicle skidded off the pavement, with screeching tires, crashed into a guard rail and flipped. It rolled over once more as it tumbled down the embankment, filling the air with ghastly noises:

crunching metal and a heart-stopping scream. On last impact, its headlights went dark; the whole world fell still, except for the whirring of spinning tires.

As they stared at the black space where they'd last seen the car, neither Finton nor Alicia were sure of what they'd just seen. "Did that just happen?" Alicia asked.

Stirring themselves at last, though it had only been a few seconds, together they lumbered towards the wreckage. Alicia had looped her arm around Finton's neck, and she was hobbling slightly. "I've got to get down there," said Finton, although he couldn't see the edge where the shoulder ended and drop off began. "Are you all right?" he asked.

"I think so." Alicia lifted her hands and, in the feeble glow of moonlight just emerging from behind a cloud, he saw that her palms were coated in blood.

"You're bleeding," he said.

"Just go—he might be seriously hurt."

"Or dead."

"Don't even think it." Alicia's voice quavered. Although he argued that she should stay on the roadside to wave down a car, she insisted on going with him. "If anyone passes, they'll see us in their headlights," she said.

More and more, it felt as if they were delaying the inevitable and so carefully, together, they maneuvered towards the railing, figuring a guide post would provide them with something to grasp and, therefore, their best chance of scaling the steep hill. But they quickly realized that, even below the railing, there was no solid ground, only loose rocks and gravel.

"It's too dangerous," Finton said. "I'll go on my own."

"You'll kill yourself," Alicia said.

As they gazed into the darkness at the bottom of the hill, the returning moonlight produced a glint of metal that revealed the wreck's location. There was, at first, no sign of Bernard, but as the light grew stronger, Finton realized he'd been staring right at him—an anonymous mass just a few feet from the upturned car. "That's him," he said, pointing. "It *is* Bernard."

"Oh, God." The strain in Alicia's voice was agonizing.

"I'm going down." He spread his arms wide and bent his body slightly. Then he dipped the toe of his shoe, searching for earth but finding air. He tilted himself forward like a downhill skier at the top of a mountain. "Leap of faith," he said in a trembling voice. "If I don't land safely, I'll call out, and you'll have to flag someone down."

With a deep breath, he let himself fall. He focused on the car, assessing the distance, as his feet struggled to keep in contact with the shifting gravel. The scuffing noise and the pressure on his soles were his main reassurance that he was standing upright. Stomach in his throat, heart thumping madly, Finton hurtled downward in a seemingly endless dive.

Suddenly, his feet couldn't feel the ground. He felt the twinge of a twisted ankle, the crunch of a jammed toe, the wrench of a knee. And yet he kept plummeting until he reached the car and collapsed a few feet away from Bernard Crowley's lifeless body.

His first thought, upon realizing he'd safely landed, was whether it was truly possible for an overturned car to ignite and explode. The thought was interrupted by much grating and squeaking, as well as the unnerving sound of tires slowly spinning. A few seconds later, the tires fell silent, and the only sounds remaining were the distant roar of pounding surf, and the odd pops and pings of metal cooling.

"Are you there?" Alicia shouted.

"Yes!" he called back. "I'm here!"

"Is he alive?"

"Good question," he said aloud, but only to himself. Thankfully, the moonlight was now at its peak, although it would soon duck behind another cloud.

He scrambled to where Bernard lay sprawled, face down, a few feet from the car, recognizable by his denim jacket. The image of another face, from several years past, an unburied ghost, flickered before Finton's eyes. He could swear he saw Sawyer Moon, face down in the foxhole.

"Please, God," he muttered as he rolled the body. "You can do this," he said. "You've done it before."

But that was a long time ago, yish it was.

"I can do this," he said. "I can."

Why go saving the likes o' him? Won't get no medals or thanks for that. Yer new girlfriend's better off without 'im—'n you'd be better off too.

Finton struggled for breath. He didn't know but the car would blow at any second. It continued to make strange noises—pings and cracks, the disconcerting grinding of metal against metal. Helping his enemy wasn't really a choice, for, in reality, Finton knew it was his instinct and calling. He tapped Bernard's face and yelled. "Wake up!"

But the eyes didn't open. No limbs twitched. No breath seemed to come from Bernard's lungs. Finton had seen dead before, and this was it.

But then, he'd also solved death before, though never quite like this, and never with any sense of reluctance. The worry and doubt, he knew, were natural.

"Bernard Crowley—you arsehole—open your goddamn eyes!" He slapped Bernard's cheek, then, seeing no results, took hold of Bernard's face and shook it. The smell of alcohol almost made Finton puke. For a moment he thought the eyes might open, but seconds passed, and finally he gave up.

"Goddamn you!" he said as repositioned himself. "Goddamn."

Scanning the body, he spied a gaping wound above Bernard's left eye. Finton quickly placed one hand on the injury, trying to ignore the blood beneath his fingers. The other hand he placed on Bernard's chest, above his heart.

Then he prayed out loud. "Our Father who art in heaven, hallowed be thy name. Thy kingdom come, thy will be done. On earth as it is in heaven."

He heard Alicia call out to him: "What's going on? What are you doing?"

He was vaguely aware that another car had stopped beside the guardrail, headlights on. Alicia called out his name, her voice fading.

"Hail Mary, full of grace, the Lord is with thee…" He felt as if he were leaving his own body. He soared upward, toting the gruesome cargo into the blue-black sky. "Now and at the hour of our death… Amen."

After what seemed a long time, he stopped praying and opened his eyes. The earth was receding. Below, he saw the Darwin Day fairgrounds and just beyond them, a small car pulled over by a guard rail, headlights on, Alicia standing beside a youth. He knew the young man. Couldn't see his face, but knew it just the same. *Skeet Stuckey*. And that was Dolly standing with them.

Shockingly fast, he jetted upward and found himself bedazzled by bright, stars of varying hues. A long-tailed comet dashed through the sky, instantly followed by two more.

There, just below, was his Planet of Solitude. Breathing deeply, he allowed himself to descend, the weight of his load growing heavier. All around him, the planets were clustered, blazing brightly in myriad, deep colours.

Beneath him, the white apple tree had come into view as he descended towards the planet's grassy surface. And then he touched down. Quickly, he scurried—somehow walking-floating—to the tree and lay beneath it.

Immediately, he heard a voice say, *This is what you brought?*

Yes, he said. *I hope it's not too late.*

This one's not fit for your concern.

Maybe not...but who am I to say?

It's your gift to give. It's always your say.

Then I say, he lives.

Silence greeted his proclamation, and Finton looked down at the face of Bernard Crowley, lying in his lap.

The dark eyes opened and looked up at him. "Am I dead?" he asked.

"Yes," said Finton. "You are."

"Good." Bernard spoke softly as if all the meanness had drained out of him.

"It was your own fault," Finton said. "I should leave you here."

Bernard's eyes flickered—sadness, perhaps, and some regret and resignation.

"But I won't," Finton finished. "Now open your eyes."

Bernard's lids flickered open, and Finton knew he was back in Darwin. His hands ached. His arms practically screamed with pain. But Bernard was stirring. He still had that ugly gash, and he was covered in scratches, cuts, and blood. But he was alive.

For better or worse.

Last Leaf

The first official on the scene was Kieran Dredge, who had quickly called for paramedics, checked the extent of his sister's injuries and draped her shoulders in a police jacket. With the aid of a high-power flashlight, he negotiated the steep embankment and, within a couple of minutes, he reached the overturned vehicle. Finton was sitting, head between his knees, beside Bernard who lay on the ground, bleeding and gasping for air. "Son of a gun is alive," Kieran told Alicia, when he and Finton had clambered to the roadside. "Someone up there's looking out for him, for sure."

She nodded vaguely and turned to Finton. "What did you do?" she asked. The breeze played with her hair while the moonlight cast her features in a soft, ethereal glow. The attendants had inspected her wounds and applied bandages to her arms, as well as a Band-aid to the palm of one hand that was scraped and bleeding. But the worst of her injuries was a flesh wound on one elbow where Bernard's side mirror had grazed it.

Finton was trembling and dazed, but relieved to be back at the top of the hill, leaning against the police car, with its red lights flashing.

"I just helped him," Finton said. He considered telling her what he'd done, but decided discretion was best. "I just stayed with him. That's all."

"Thank you," she said. Alicia fell silent then, her body quivering as she started to cry. Finton understood: they'd both been traumatized by the accident—not because it was Bernard, but because they had almost been killed. It was just one more example of Darwinian violence wherein the supposed strong fall victim to their own instincts.

It took more than an hour to load Bernard into the ambulance. Getting him up the hill was an arduous task, especially in the dark, without a street lamp nearby. Eventually, the two attendants, with Kieran and Futterman, managed to pull him up to the side of the road. By that time, Finton had answered every question he could about how Bernard had come from out of nowhere, how he'd been tormenting Alicia for a long time, and how he'd flipped over his car without any help, or taunting, from them. Thankfully, there were no questions about Finton's voodoo. They didn't suspect and didn't need to know. Bernard, if he survived, would never know how.

As spring moved on and summer closed in, Finton kept his own counsel and rarely sought wisdom or companionship outside of himself. He had been removed from the family into which he was born—perhaps, in some way, he'd even been rescued—and taken into a household to which he would never truly belong. On some level, he was grateful, but that didn't justify his parents' actions. He was developing an interest in history and, in the library, he read articles about how Newfoundland was railroaded into Confederation—some kind of trickery performed by the "Father of Confederation," some cloak and dagger maneuvering that allowed certain politicians to justify their skullduggery. The Canadian government would never admit their own greed, that they acted not to save the "youngest province" from a horrible fate, but to enhance their prestige and to spare themselves from feeling incomplete with each glance at the map that showed a detached, lone wolf in North Atlantic. In the end, they'd created artificial ties with an entity who'd never truly assimilated with a family that had merely kidnapped it.

A few weeks after the accident, on an unusually hot day, Finton was reaching for a Dreamsicle at Sellars' store when he heard a familiar voice. "What's up, Moon?" He looked up from the freezer and saw Bernard Crowley peering down at him. While it looked like Bernard, his skin was pale, he was thinner, and he leaned on a cane. The image was startling.

"Hey, Bernard… Slim… how've you been?"

"Few stitches here and there. Nothin' serious." Grimacing as he spoke, Bernard rubbed his right thigh. "Taking a few pain pills. But I'm on the mend."

"That's good," said Finton. "Glad to hear it." He started to move towards the counter. "Well, my ice cream's gonna melt if I don't get checked in."

"Yeah, it's hot all right." Bernard limped alongside him, using his cane, and Finton couldn't help feeling sorry for him. As Finton paid for his ice cream, Bernard kept talking. "You know, I was only trying to scare you that night."

"Forget it."

"I mean, I wasn't trying to run you over. I'm not that kinda guy."

Finton ripped the wrapper from his Dreamsicle and took a small bite. Immediately, the pain shot to his forehead. Brain freeze. "I don't care anymore. If you're trying to apologize, fine, I accept. But I don't buy what you're saying. You could've killed us, and you knew it."

Bernard hung his head, then forced himself to look into Finton's eyes. "It was stupid. I don't know what came over me. I saw you and her together, and I went nuts. There's not much more I can say."

"Just leave Alicia alone. She's had it hard enough." Finton took another bite; it didn't hurt so much this time. "Not because I told you to—because that's what she wants. Hell, Bernard, you're bigger than me, always will be." He grinned sheepishly. "Although I'm pretty sure I could take you now."

"I'd beat you to a pulp with my cane." Bernard raised the metal stick in a feigned show of aggression. But he was grinning, which Finton took as a healthy sign. "I thinks the world of Alicia," Bernard said. "But I'll leave her alone."

Finton was stunned. "Really?"

"Really." Bernard nodded and extended a hand for Finton to shake. As Finton reciprocated, he noticed a red and raw five-inch scar; it looked as if Bernard had narrowly missed severing an artery on his right arm. Slightly unnerved, he shook the proffered hand and said, "See ya 'round."

The chittering of robins, sparrows and jays heralded a new dawn, waking Finton and drawing him forward into a world of promise. Their songs and sounds were harbingers of a life to come, rumours of a past that had died. He smiled to recall that the day before, a letter had arrived with good news.

When the rooster crowed again, he snapped fully awake. Clancy was coming around, but Homer lay in the top bunk, presumably asleep, harder to read.

A woodpecker perched on the windowsill, pecking away like a jackhammer. When Finton stirred, the bird lifted its head and peered through the glass. They read each other's thoughts until Finton's gaze flickered and the woodpecker flitted away. Further afield, the crows were calling-and-answering while a soaring seagull cried out its misery. Underlying the cacophony were the peeping of a peppy chickadee and the nearby trilling of a joyous redbreast.

When he could no longer bear to lay still, Finton slipped out of bed and padded down the hall in his underwear. He crept outside and wandered to the far side of the house where the birds had congregated. He sat beneath the bedroom window, back against the wall, watching and listening, feeling as if they were singing for him—the universe in tune with his rising optimism.

For a long time, he sat there, pondering the magnificence of what lay before him.

Long before he arrived at any conclusions, he went back inside and got dressed. From beneath his mattress, he pulled a rectangular package wrapped in brown paper. With the package tucked under his arm, he crept outside once again and meandered down the lane while birds in the branches of trees all around performed their orchestral tune, and the aged rooster cracked the air with its third raucous call. By now, the whole house would be waking up. But he was long gone from its oppressive gloom.

The further he strolled away from Moon's Lane, the lighter he became, the ebb-and-flow pain he'd endured for so long had finally receded to a low-level ache with which he could function. In a vain attempt to reconcile his pursuits and intentions over the past few months, he mulled over the faces and names he associated with certain moments. Most days had begun with the lethargic sense that his life was a lie, that his parents were imposters, that his family was not a family but a row of beads collected on a piece of fragile twine and named for something presumed to be holy. For many months, he'd endured high school, did his homework, attended mass dutifully—yes, sir—no, sir—kneel down, stand up—thank you, ma'am—bless me, father, for I have sinned. In no way did he invite scrutiny into the darkness of his heart. He ate his supper, said hardly a word, never caused trouble, talked to no one, didn't fit in.

Then he'd opened himself up—he went to the prom because Alicia asked him to, and then a version of hell broke loose right in front of him. For nearly two weeks, the questioning stares persisted. While he'd told no one of what he'd done for Bernard Crowley, the expectation of magic seemed ever present. The certainty that he would never have a moment's peace—the very concern that he would never have a life within the smothering confines of Darwin, Newfoundland—had become inescapable. It stared at him every time he looked into a mirror, or when he looked into the face of a friend or stranger that provided a mirror to his thoughts. The faces all said, "Get out while you can!" even while they, themselves, remained imprisoned by their fear of the unknown, their love of the familiar, or their natural acceptance of the *status quo*.

He went to see Skeet, and they hung out by the tall, swaying conifers at the far end of his parents' property. Skeet smoked, and Finton rubbed his eyes as he told his comrade of his plan to escape. "It's been good," he said. "You've been a real friend."

Skeet shrugged and said, "Ditto, buddy. Well, you come back now and then, all right? Remember where you was made."

He was just about to get up when Skeet said, "If you're goin' for sure, I got something to say." Finton assured him this was his last chance to make any dire confessions. He'd meant it jokingly, but Skeet turned serious. "I can't bring myself to say it out loud or say exactly what." He scrubbed his hands over his face. "But I been carrying around an awfully big secret for a really long time."

"Don't torture yourself," said Finton. "I know what you're gonna say."

"You do?" Skeet appeared gobsmacked. "How?"

"After that night, you changed—at least for a while. You came back to yourself after a bit, but I could tell—somethin' was wrong. But I got to admit, no one's got a poker face like Skeet Stuckey."

Skeet hung his head. "I couldn't tell anyone. I didn't want to go to jail."

"Did you kill him?"

"No," said Skeet. "We had a fight. I struck him on the side of his head." To demonstrate, he leaned over and placed his powerful fist against Finton's temple. Finton could see how the copper ring on Skeet's middle finger could do some damage. "I mean, he was drunk as a skunk. So it was pretty easy. He said some stuff—mouthin' off about Dolly. 'Nice tits on that young one,' he said. I told him to go home and sleep it off, but he kept at it. I finally got mad enough, and I clocked the old bugger. He fell down, but then he got up and he staggered off. But I gotta say he didn't look too good." Skeet scratched his head as if piecing it all together for the first time. And maybe he was, since he'd likely never mentioned it to anyone else, including Dolly. He'd been just shy of thirteen at the time—big for his age, but little more than a scared kid. Until now, there was no one he could tell. Finton was glad to give him the chance, especially since Skeet had looked out for him since they were kids. "I didn't think I killed him," Skeet said, "but I didn't want to go to jail either. When they accused your father, I felt bad, but I figured it would go away after a while… and it did."

"It's okay, Skeet. It was a long time ago—and he had it comin'."

Skeet nodded. "I know. But I don't forget stuff."

"Why did you have to tell Mary about the crush I had on her?"

He hung his head and shook it slowly. "Two reasons," he said. "One, I had to say something. I got myself crossed up—thought I wanted to tell somebody about Sawyer but I chickened out. Two…" He looked up and squinted. "I actually thought I'd be doin' you a favour."

Finton thought of a couple of things he could say. That it didn't work out to be a favour. That things between him and Mary had never been the same after that. That, in some ways, Skeet had set him free from a lifetime of adoring someone he could never have. Perhaps he would never have left Darwin if he'd retained some hope, however illogical, that Mary would someday love him. "Maybe you did," he said.

When Finton left him, Skeet was making one of the barn cats chase its own tail around in a circle. "You'll be all right," he told Skeet, but in a low voice as he was walking away, so that his former best friend likely couldn't hear. He had no trouble imagining Skeet growing old in Darwin, settling for what he'd started with, getting into trouble, managing a gas station, and married to a big-chested woman like Dolly with an infinite string of youngsters following her to mass every Sunday morning while Skeet sneaked off to the tavern for a beer.

Mary Connelly was sitting on the front steps of the old red schoolhouse.

It never ceased to startle him how decrepit and sad the small building appeared, with its boarded windows and flaking paint, dried and neglected in the brutal Newfoundland weather. It was as if the front of the school was the face of a person who, day after day and year after year, had faced the tireless gale and finally regressed into a slouching, scarred version of its younger self. But the abandoned building didn't radiate resignation; with its flecks of red paint flapping like skin tags on its grey, wood siding, it appeared ready to rise up from its slumber and fulfill some long-delayed destiny.

He'd seen Mary from a distance and, for a while, denied it was even her. And yet, as he came closer, there she was—in a close-fitting pink t-shirt and cut-off jean shorts. He hardly saw her anymore—not since prom night—and it startled him to realize how much she'd grown up. When had Mary sprouted breasts? He hadn't said so at the prom, but he liked her short hair. But when had her legs gotten so long and beautiful? They were thin, however, like Mary herself.

"Nice day," he said, squinting against the sun.

"Sure is." She smiled. It was a beautiful, freckled smile with slightly crooked teeth. "What are you doin' today?" She was playing haphazardly with a blade of grass, like emerald-jade velvet snaking around her fingers. Only once did her glance go towards the rectangular package in his hands.

"I'm leaving Darwin."

She cocked her head as if trying to assess his truthfulness. "Going on a trip?"

"Going for good."

For a moment, she fell blank and seemed lost in thought, but then her grin returned. "No, you're not. You knows you're never leaving Darwin, Finton Moon. You're a part of this place."

"Well, I am."

"I said you're not. I knows yer not."

It was his turn to look at her—*really* notice the apprehension in her eyes, the insecurity in her playing with a blade of grass. In acknowledging the tremble in her voice, he realized he didn't know where her fear was coming from. She'd never loved him, so why should she care that he was going away?

"Well, I guess I'll just have to show you," he said.

She stiffened her spine and sat upright, fingers still toying with the sliver of grass. The warm July breeze swept between them and kicked dust into their faces. When she swept an errant strand of hair from her eyes, pushing it behind her smallish ears, he thought she was the cutest thing he'd ever seen.

"See you around, Mary."

"Yeah," she said. "See you—I mean—Finton?"

"Yeah?"

She stood up and approached him quickly, almost as if afraid of losing her nerve. With a firm hug and a sincere kiss on the cheek, she said, "Thank you."

He didn't need to ask what for. Sure, he could have explained it to her—why he'd sat, unacknowledged, at her side for so long. But he could never say everything, and so he said nothing, just nodded and turned away.

Alicia was working in her parents' kitchen and saw him coming. She met him on the front step, propping the door ajar with her hip and wearing tattered, brown oven mitts. She squinted against the sun, compelled to raise a gloved hand to shield her eyes; most of her injuries, he noticed, had healed quite well, with only some scars to remind them both of that awful night. When he announced he was leaving, she simply said, "I know."

"I brought you a present." He handed her the package he'd been carrying, and she slowly removed the oven mitts, clamped them together and tucked them under her arm. When she'd ripped away the brown paper, she laughed. "*Great Expectations?*"

"You can finish reading those last fifty pages," he said. "Or just read it again and keep the ending a mystery."

She opened the front cover and, with a slight tremour in her voice, read what he'd inscribed: "To my friend, Alicia."

"You should come with me," he said.

"You're nuts, b'y. What would I do somewhere else—especially with someone who doesn't want a girlfriend?"

"The important thing is to get away, isn't it?"

"Shouldn't there be something to go to?" She didn't allow him time to respond. "I'm not like you, Finton. I have responsibilities. I have to take care of everyone."

"No, you don't."

"Someone has to."

"Your mother could do it."

"She needs me." Alicia shook her head and glanced behind. There was movement in the kitchen, but, to Finton, it all appeared as indistinguishable shadows.

"Your father—"

"Oh, please, Finton—get real. I can't go anywhere." She tried to swipe away the tears that suddenly appeared at the corners of her eyes.

"You can. You just won't."

"Either way—"

"Think about it. Someday, you're gonna look back and wish you'd done different. You only get one chance like that in life—ya know?"

"Aren't you afraid?"

"Of what?"

"Of getting away and wishing you could come back. But you can't. Once you're gone, you can't come back."

"Jeez, Alicia, it's not like dyin'."

"It is, sort of."

"Look," he said. "I wouldn't tell this to no one else, but I'm actually scared to death. I could end up homeless, nothin' to eat and no place to live." She nodded as he continued, as if he'd articulated her deepest fears. "But you know what? I don't care. You can't go around being scared all the time. You just don't get anywhere that way."

"But what if the worst happens and you can't come back?"

"To me," he said, "that wouldn't be the worst thing could happen." He looked at her—really looked at her, just as he had done earlier with Mary—and saw a girl who, all her life, had been told she would amount to nothing. She was born a Dredge, lived in poverty and would never escape. Her fate was to be a Dredge until the day she died. In the eyes of Mary Connelly he'd seen the fear of loss that comes with privilege but, in Alicia's eyes he saw the resignation of the dispossessed. "You could start over."

She peered behind her, glanced towards the sink as if it were calling to her, and she sighed. "I think you should go."

"No," he said. "You saved me once, and now it's my turn. Come with me and change your life. You are so much better… than this."

"Just leave me alone—just go wherever you were always going to!" Tears streamed down her cheeks as she dropped both the mitts and *Great Expectations*, and leaped off the porch. She charged past Finton and left the door banging against the frame.

He bolted after her, but she was faster than he'd expected. They dashed, one after the other, into her backyard, which was littered with old tires and car parts as far as the eye could see. One of the scrawny fir trees had a Styrofoam tray wedged in its topmost branches. He'd never been back here—in the Dredges's backyard garbage pit—and he'd never before seen such a mess.

When she swung around to punch him, the sun beamed on her face. He turned his head slightly and saw at the farthest end of the garden, against a backdrop of scrawny spruce, a gigantic apple tree. He was so flabbergasted he forgot to duck; Alicia's fist struck his cheek and sent him reeling backwards. But he couldn't take his gaze from the sprawling, grey tree with the sunlight bursting through its branches like a holy vision.

It looked like the apple tree on the Planet of Solitude. Tall and stout, its branches overhung the ground at its roots, like someone had propped open a gigantic umbrella and stuck it into the earth—the same tree under which he had lain so many times.

"How long has this been here?" he asked, rubbing his hurt cheek.

She turned around to see what he was staring at. "That old tree? Since before I was born. But it was a lot smaller than that when I was a girl. I remember that. I used to climb it every day. But I don't anymore."

"Why not?" he asked, even as he found himself drifting towards it.

"I don't know. I just don't—I mean, do you still climb trees?"

"I guess we're too old for that now."

Standing at the edge of the tree's massive shadow, he wanted nothing more than to sit and bask in its cool majesty. But he feared doing it. He was waiting for something to happen.

"Maybe *you're* too old." Alicia shucked her shoes and rolled up her sleeves. "But I'm not."

"Hey!"

"Hey yerself!" She lodged one foot at the junction between a low branch and the gnarled trunk. "Give me a boost, if yer just gonna stand there."

As Finton rushed forward and ducked beneath a branch, he received a small, stinging gash beneath his left eye. He put his fingers to the cut, but there was no blood. Undeterred, he spread his hands on her backside and shoved her upward. Her left foot scrambled for, and found, secure placement just a bit higher than where her right foot was planted. By wrapping one arm around a branch above her head, she hoisted herself up.

"Be careful, Alicia!"

"You sound like my mother." She glanced back at him and grinned. "You're such an arse, Finton Moon." She was shaking her head as she resumed her attention to the climb ahead. "Such an arse."

Suddenly, the branch beneath her right foot snapped. Planting himself beneath her plummeting body, he spread his arms, and she fell into them. But his triumph was short-lived as his arms wavered, his knees buckled, and they fell together to the ground. His tailbone struck the root, and his head snapped back and struck the trunk. Alicia's head hit the earth with a sickening crack.

"Alicia?"

Again, he called her name as the summer wind whistled through the branches overhead. As he brushed the hair from her face, he rocked her softly. He wasn't sure when the birds had ceased singing or the various Dredges had stopped yelling, slamming doors and running machinery. And yet at some point, all activity had ceased, and Finton heard the world take a massive suck of breath as the earth fell black, teetered on its axis, and threatened to roll away into the infinite, dark sky.

She didn't open her eyes, so he shut himself down: his eyes blocked out the world, and he slowed his heart's rhythm, making it beat stronger, with singular purpose. His body stilled like a reed in a pond, motionless within, at the very source, yet bending with the breeze. Finally, his mind was freed from its moorings and he lifted them both to the sky. She was light in his arms—floating, spiraling upwards until, all around, the darkness bled light in every colour. Far below, at last, was his Neverland and, suddenly, he was there, on the grassy surface of his Planet of Solitude, beneath the white tree with the unconscious girl in his lap, while he stroked her face and spoke her name.

Her eyes came open and she smiled. *Where are we?*

You struck your head. I brought you here.

What is this place?

My home.

It's beautiful here. I'd like to stay for a while.

So he allowed her to remain, safe in his arms while he held her close. Shooting stars flew by in the distant, dark sky. A translucent rainbow bordered the planet, reaching towards infinity. The sudden memory of a *Romper Room* song made him laugh aloud: *Bend and stretch—reach for the sky!* He lifted his head to acknowledge the neighbouring planets—small and large, ringed and plain. A ripple of cool wind rushed through his hair.

He heard her small, clear voice singing the words he'd sung in his mind. Her eyes filled with tears. He swept a hand through her hair and closed his eyes, took a deep breath and finally exhaled. Involuntarily and unexpectedly, he opened his eyes to the bright, material world.

There were people standing around, peering at the two injured teenagers huddled beneath the apple tree. Gradually, his mind adjusted to his surroundings, and he realized the girl's fall had summoned the Dredges from wherever they'd been playing, working, or hiding. But the girl in his arms wasn't smiling. Her skin was pale, her features stiff.

Exodus

It rained.

All through the night, the lightning-lit clouds had their way with the ground and flooded Darwin with a torrent of biblical timbre. Finton lay in bed and watched the sky illuminate as if they were in World War II London, under siege from enemy bombs. Just before dawn, the lightning ceased, though the occasional Aslanic growl unfurled itself upon the earth, and Finton stood at the kitchen window, awaiting his moment when the rain would cease and the sky would clear. Despite his exhaustion, he was anxious to begin his journey.

He wouldn't have minded a send-off. They knew he was leaving and the acknowledgment would have meant something—although what exactly, he wasn't sure. But the fact that such kindness was withheld indicated the gesture's significance.

His mother's reaction to the news had been calm, but her eyes were nervous. He told her he might go to school or he might just wander the world and educate himself. Elsie's response was, "What do ya want to do that for?"—a question for which he had answers, but not nearly enough time, energy, or incentive to entertain. When he insisted that leaving was something he needed to do, she said cheerlessly, "You're only sixteen."

"Old enough."

"I know. But… we'll worry."

He promised he'd write now and then. She still didn't smile, but she at least relented. "I know we can't hold you here, Finton. But I hope this isn't because of what Miss Bridie told you. We always loved you, you know. Don't forget that."

He said nothing for fear of either appearing weak or opening a discussion he'd rather avoid.

Nanny Moon's disappointment was not as obvious. "Be a good lad and stay out of trouble," she said. "If you runs into anything ya can't handle, you knows where we are." She started towards her bedroom, but turned at the last second. "And go to mass." She went to the bedroom and, within moments, returned with a white envelope. "Open it in the morning," she whispered. He knew she saved money in the Jesus tin on her dresser —the one with Christ surrounded by youngsters and the caption at the bottom: "Suffer the little children to come unto me." The envelope contained three hundred and eighty-five dollars, nearly every cent she'd saved.

When he told his father he was leaving, Tom blew a smoke ring and said, "The time has come, I s'pose." Then the commercials were over, and the news was back on.

Each one had asked where he was going, and his reply was always the same: "I'll let you know when I get there." No one was satisfied with the response, but that was all the information he'd give. Clancy said, "I wish I had yer guts, b'y. Good luck to ya." Homer didn't even look up from the sawhorse, where he was cutting a large log. He looked straight ahead, paused in his sawing, and said, "You'll be back." He resumed sawing until the piece of wood fell to the ground; then he repositioned the log for his next cut.

When the rain subsided to drizzle, Finton took up his knapsack, which contained a change of clothes wrapped in a plastic bag, as well as some food, his wallet and, also wrapped in plastic, his copy of *To Kill a Mockingbird*.

One hand on the doorknob, he turned for one last look around. Over the stove, the clock kept ticking. A corner of the brown-stained wallpaper curled down from behind the fridge. The house seemed to hum a barely discernable dirge. But in his heart, there was no song, and his feet were too heavy for skipping.

He turned to leave and, even with the door more than halfway ajar, he couldn't help but turn around one more time—perhaps out of hope, or some errant sense of faith—with the expectation that his mother would bustle out, in her bathrobe, to make sure he'd eaten and had sufficient money to see him through. And maybe, just maybe, to ask him if he'd reconsider. He would reject her request. But that didn't mean he didn't hope for some last-minute attempt at familial connection.

He noted the clock that read 7:15. As he stepped into the porch and began closing the door, a glimpse of white hair and a grey nightgown made him halt.

"I just wanted to wish ya luck," she said. She gave him an awkward hug and said, "It's rainin' out, sure. Why don't ya wait till tomorrow?"

"It'll stop."

"Well, if you wants to be foolish about it, I can't stop ya. Don't forget to call when ya gets there."

"Thanks for getting up," he said.

She closed her eyes and nodded. "Your mother's feelin' pretty low. And your father's not the type, ya know?"

"That's all right," he said. "I get it."

He thanked her again and was about to leave, when she said, "I didn't like your mother once upon a time." She peered into his eyes as if to assess whether he was listening and understood the importance of her confession. "But I've come to see that she's a good woman who's done her best."

"It's too late for this, Nanny Moon."

"It's never too late. Sure, go on ahead now. That's the way of things, and it's what you have to do—although I still thinks you're a bit too young."

"No one in this house can lecture me about anything," he said. "Way I see it, there's too much water under the bridge."

"Yes. You might be right about that." She nodded sadly. "But people only do what they think is best at the time. No one meant any harm to ya. Just remember that."

Then he heard footsteps, bare feet on canvas, and a voice that gave him chills: "Finton?" Elsie emerged from the hallway in her billowy, blue nightgown, arms folded across her chest. He hadn't really wanted this. He realized that now. The mere sound of her voice made him sad. But he didn't mind leaving; he mourned the relationship they never had. "Were you leavin' without saying goodbye?" she asked.

"I didn't think you were getting up," he said. "You knew I was going."

Elsie seemed as if she was about to scold him again, but she was interrupted by the sight of Tom entering the kitchen, yawning and swiping his hand through his tangle of hair. "Jesus, b'y—you're goin' awful early, aren't ya?"

"I got a ride waitin'," he said. It was only a small, convenient lie.

"Are ya sure? I don't mind drivin' ya."

"No, that's all right."

"Well," said Elsie. "You write to us when you get there."

"Where are you goin' again?" asked Tom.

"I'll write," Finton said. "I promise."

The kitchen filled with an awkward silence that lasted only a couple of seconds, just enough to remind Finton of why he was leaving.

"See ya." He nodded, turned and then, with merciful quickness, he was gone.

His last image of Nanny Moon was her standing in her grey night dress, a sad look on her face, his mother looking perplexed in her baby blue gown, and Tom, patting his chest and glancing towards the table where his cigarettes lay beside the ashtray.

Finton closed his eyes and took a deep breath. Finally, he shuffled outside into the dark, wet landscape and shut the door behind him. Not once did he look back.

By the time he'd reached the bottom of Moon's Lane, the drizzle had misted his face, drenched his hair and soaked through his backpack's exterior. Every step he took for those first thirty minutes, he considered aborting the mission. But he soldiered on, bolstered by his out-loud singing of Beatles' songs. By the time he'd reached the bridge that opened Darwin to the rest of the island, he had launched into "The Long and Winding Road." The clouds split their seams and poured their vendetta down on his head—a baptismal soak that was to be his judgment. The weather was an obstacle, but a mere piffle to his innate obstinacy and pure determination to escape from it all.

Nearly two hours after leaving the house, he stood, soaked to his skin, at the access road. He stopped and read the sign:

You are now leaving Darwin. Come again soon!

Of course, if, by some miracle, he made his destination, that place of his dreams would be filled with everything good and there would be no need ever to return to Darwin. Another hour or so later, he arrived at the highway and stood beneath the gigantic green government signs with their bright, white lettering telling him how many miles to get from that precarious spot to everywhere. He found himself wondering—a flickering thought that briefly transfixed him—what would happen if he veered left instead of right, towards the interior—deeper into the heart of provincial darkness—rather than away from all he had ever known? Wearily, he resumed his predetermined path, trekking southward along the highway, hoping somebody would come along to offer a lift. The rain might keep people from traveling unnecessarily, but surely to God, even on such an ungodly morning, there'd be someone else escaping Darwin.

As he approached a particularly solid wall of mist and fog that seemed anchored to the road, he found himself immersed in a world of whiteness, full of silver shadows and muffled noises. Events of yesterday tumbled around in his mind.

Alicia's eyelids trembled partway open, and she gazed with concern into her father's face. When she saw her mother peering down at her, she closed her eyes again. When she opened them once more, she saw Finton, but shut her eyes.

A few minutes later, she was lying on a gurney being wheeled through the Emergency Room on her way to X-ray. A handful of Dredges remained in the waiting room because only the parents were allowed to escort her through those demoralizing double doors. Surveying the landscape—Dredge to the left of him, Dredge to the right, in front of and behind him, sitting in chairs, on the floor and under the coffee table—Finton closed his eyes and prepared himself for the long night ahead.

He endured the chatter and noise, the hum of fluorescent lights, the crying of a baby, the dull metallic groan of the Pepsi machine. But he couldn't ignore the internal chatter, reminding him that tomorrow would be even harder—and life, after that, might well be more difficult. He would get up early, creep outside and hit the road, come what may. He was finished with school and Darwin, its people and its church. The further he walked away from it all, the better he would feel, and the more possibilities he would see for himself. He didn't know what he was going to do, but getting out of bed tomorrow morning and forcing himself out the front door would be a beginning. It would be easy to just forget his plans, just stay home, and live out the rest of his days. But it would also be the hardest thing he'd ever done, and he'd never be done doing it until the day he died.

The doctor emerged and told Finton Alicia had asked to see him. The Dredge family appeared unimpressed.

She was lying in a bed, covered in a white sheet, face exposed and a white bandage wrapped around her head, her right arm in a sling. Her smile lacked enthusiasm. "Now I know why we don't climb trees anymore."

"It wasn't anybody's fault."

"Just mine," she said. "I shouldn't have gone up there. But—"

"But you were trying to get away from me—"

"I was trying to show you that we can still climb trees, silly. That we shouldn't give up on being childlike just because we're not children. Does that make sense?"

"It would make more sense if you didn't have a concussion and a broken arm because of me."

"But you saved me—" She tried sitting up, but had to slide back down again, letting her head rest gently on the pillow. "I think I might have died without you."

He stuffed his hands into his pockets because the urge to hug her was strong. "I think you got lucky."

"No—really, Finton. Did you—" Her voice trailed as she closed her eyes. Just when he thought she'd fallen asleep, she opened them again and finished: "I thought I went somewhere—with you."

"You were in my arms the whole time."

She smiled at the reminder. "Yes," she said. "We were floating. We went really, really high… and the planets were bright—red and yellow and green suns all around."

Finton tried to suppress his smile. He'd never heard anyone else describe the journey to his planet. It was as if she'd actually been there—meaning he hadn't gone there alone or just in his imagination. "I call it the Planet of Solitude."

A shadow of concern crossed her face. "You mean we were actually there?" When he nodded, she asked, "How is that even possible?"

"Don't tell anyone."

She promised not to, but her confusion was evident, and he was pretty sure his own bewilderment was obvious too.

A gargantuan black pickup truck came roaring through the fog like a colossal dragon, its bright yellow fog lamps like eyes, and chunky, black wipers swiping side-to-side like flapping wings. He stuck out his thumb and stared into the fog lamps, but his heart leadened in his chest as the driver accelerated. The tail lights winked at him just before they disappeared into the mist, and he was left alone with his thoughts.

He wished Alicia had come with him. He wished he'd never left Darwin.

He knew she wouldn't tell anyone about the Planet of Solitude. No one would believe her—or they'd think he was insane, and Alicia had sense enough not to bring that down on his head. She seemed to believe him, that the planet was real and that he had the ability to bring people there, heal their injuries and illnesses, then bring them back.

But, in this case, that wasn't what had happened. They had shared a thought, and that was that.

"It wasn't you," she'd said. "It was me."

"How do you know?"

"Because you didn't make me better. Look at me—I'm still not very good. But I'm better than I was."

"So… I cured you."

"Tell me this—whenever you healed somebody before, did they get better right away, or did they take awhile?"

"Right away."

"Exactly. Otherwise, genius, there's no miracle. You can't have a miracle after you go home and take two aspirins and call the doctor in the morning. A miracle is spontaneous. It happens right away, right before your eyes and that's how everyone knows it's a miracle. But look at me—still in bed, still in bandages—arm in a sling."

"We could take the bandages off."

"You try and you'll have to wear bandages yourself."

Finton understood. He didn't need to tell her that. He just sat by her side, listening to her talk. She was obviously already beginning to heal, and he couldn't help but wonder if he'd played a role in that. Watching her, though, he also wondered what had actually happened. She was far too chatty for someone who'd suffered a concussion.

"Are you listening to me?"

"I'm sorry—what?"

"I said, maybe that's all it ever was—maybe you never cured anyone. Maybe they healed themselves, and all you did was give them a placebo—you made them think they could be better, and so they were."

"I think you got hit a little too hard on your head."

"Is it that hard to believe? Are you that egotistical?"

"Why are you saying all this?" He stood up then, hands plunged into his pockets. "I thought you were on my side."

"I am. But I can't let you go on deluding yourself. A friend would tell you to get a grip."

"But you saw—you saw what happened with Bernard."

"It was dark. I didn't see anything."

"People came to me. And I healed them."

"No one really gets healed, Finton. They all die, eventually. You can't escape that."

"What about Miss Bridie? What about Mary?"

"Easily explained, and you know it," she said. "I think they weren't ready to go, and you gave them something—where are you going?"

"I'm gettin' outta here."

"Don't be such a—Finton!"

He didn't even say goodbye.

The blaring of a horn jolted him from his daydream. But not at first. It was more the glare of headlights, shining onto the pavement before him. Even though he leaped into a ditch and twisted his ankle, the driver didn't stop, merely leaned on his horn as he zoomed past, the wet pavement whistling through the treads of tires.

For the first time in a long while, Finton felt like crying—he just wanted to sit there in the soggy ditch, knapsack twisted around and clutched to his stomach, and bawl as if he'd just been born and slapped on his behind. But he couldn't will the tears to come. The rain pelted his face. The fog banks drifted past like mountains of mist, and right before him, in a whisper-thin clearing, stood a large, scrawny, grey dog, with its head lowered and appearing startled. As Finton stared back, the creature bared its yellow teeth and emitted a low, rumbling growl as it started to lope forward. Finton was mesmerized by its jaundiced eyes that appeared more frightened than he was himself. Still, he wondered if, after so much had happened and with freedom so near, this was how he was fated to die.

The dog—which reminded him of the "wolf" in the cage at the circus last summer—maintained steady eye contact, but it never came closer than a couple of feet as it passed beside him, slipped into the thicket, and vanished. The apparition had occurred so quickly that Finton could barely compose a thought. But, considering how far they were from the nearest town, he might well have just witnessed a kind of quiet miracle. Still trembling and yet strangely revitalized, he climbed out of the ditch and back onto the shoulder of the road, keeping a watch on the spot where he'd seen the wolf melt into the woods.

Limping slightly, he got himself moving southward again.

His heart and his clothing grew heavier with each step forward, and the deluge kept coming. Even his skin felt waterlogged beneath his clothes, inspiring the thought that he could not get much wetter unless he were water itself.

He had no idea where he was or how far he'd travelled, for the fog was so dense he could not read the signs and, without a horizon dividing one from the other, the pavement was indistinguishable from the downpour—all wet and all black. A handful of vehicles zipped by like blinkered phantasms—a school bus, a garbage truck, and a few vehicles that looked as if they were stuffed for vacation. The thought should have made him smile, but there were days when the weather on this island incited anger that could only rightly result in defeat. The very notion of travelers on the same miserable road as him, seeking heaven and freedom amid such perpetually horrific conditions, was so irresponsibly optimistic he could only shake his head.

He plodded along, sneakers squishing and backpack scraping, fifteen minutes removed from the last car sighting, so he occasionally walked on the asphalt, knowing he could easily scoot aside if a car happened to come along. The silence on the highway was startling and lonely, inspiring him to wonder how it could be that, at the moment of his greatest freedom, he felt such insignificance in the pattern of all things, such removal from the joys, comforts and concerns of humans. With the roadside trees standing silently tall, like grim witnesses to a brutal test that could only end in tragedy, it was obvious that this journey was leading in one direction, towards his own physical and mental devastation. Immersed in such unsolvable greyness, how could his fate be otherwise? Without even a fleeting light to interrupt the immortal darkness, what reason could there be for hope or faith?

It had always been like this, really. There never had been any reason for hope. Being born to a woman who could barely take care of herself, let alone an infant, what chance did he have in life? He understood why he'd been taken. No one ever spoke about the past, a policy he never understood because the bygone days were no more threatening nor darker than the present. Nanny Moon had once said to him, "Give up all hope of a better past." At the time, her words made sense. But, despite her intentions to the contrary, there was something defeatist about them—the notion that there was a part of your life—essentially, the entire mass of moments and conditions that comprised your existence—that was beyond healing. In his deepest moments, he rejected the idea, clinging to the belief that somehow he would find a way to rectify the past, to at least reconcile it within his own mind and be at peace with his own history, with the history of his people and, thus, prepare himself for a better future.

Without peace with the past, there could be no hope for future contentment—which made the present a battleground for Finton Moon. That was the last thought he had before his foot slipped into a water-filled pothole and he wrenched his already-injured ankle. Screeching in anguish, he dropped to the pavement, clasping his foot.

"Ow! Ow! Ow! Fucking ow! Ow! Ow!" he cried out as he rubbed the injured spot. His words fell dead on the asphalt and gravel, for no sound could carry far in such indomitable fog. All noises were close as if emanating from just beyond his body. He cursed the road, the Department of Highways—*what kind of godforsaken place has potholes in the middle of a highway?*—and he cursed an apocalypse on God himself. He cursed his mother and father and Bridie Battenhatch. Most of all, he cursed the rain.

A few tears rolled down his face, but that was all. He tried standing up, but the pain was too sharp and, more out of frustration than physical necessity, he again fell on his arse, plop down in the pothole full of dark water.

This time he didn't curse, only hung his head to his knees, which he wrapped his arms around and pulled tight to his chest. He was just about to launch into a round of Hail Marys when, from somewhere nearby, he heard the unmistakable whir of rubber on wet pavement as a slowing vehicle rolled towards him. He didn't bother lifting his head, for he couldn't handle the vicious cycle of hope and despair.

But he could swear this car was slowing down as it came closer. The pothole in which he sat was suddenly awash with light. The tires ceased rolling, the engine rumbling like some massive beast in suspension. Finton wondered what greater misery was about to descend. He wasn't exactly prepared to fight, but he supposed he would, if forced.

"Hello again."

A familiar voice.

Moments later, he sat in the front seat of a police cruiser across from Kieran Dredge, staring into the fog and drizzle.

"Not a fit day for a walk," the constable said.

"So I found out."

Kieran laughed. It was a warm, genuine laugh—a sound not necessarily intended to make the youth feel at ease, but it had exactly that effect.

"Your family's probably worried sick about you."

Here it comes, he thought.

"Where are you headed?" Kieran asked. The wipers scraped rhythmically, every few seconds, until their sound became a wordless song that cut right to Finton's heart.

"I'd rather not say."

"You should tell someone where you're going." Kieran paused thoughtfully. "You could tell me."

Finton maintained a steady gaze on the hidden horizon. Shapes in the mist drifted before his eyes like white watercolour paintings. In the all-consuming blankness, he saw nothing and everything. He saw his past and his future—the people he knew and those upon whom he had yet to lay eyes. But mostly he saw himself—a past barely gone, a future unwritten. "No, thanks." He sniffled as water rivered down his face and plopped onto the seat.

"Mind if I ask why?"

"Because I'm not sure who to trust anymore."

"Fair enough." Kieran sighed. "You remind me of myself when I was your age."

Again, he thought, *Here it comes—the old "you remind me of me" speech*.

"Didn't get along with my family. Thought nobody understood me. Man, I hated this place. Hated intensely. I couldn't wait to get away and go someplace better."

"Did you find it?" Finton was skeptical about where this "talk" was leading, but he played along, hoping his sociability would score him a ride for a few miles.

"What I found was, there is no place better. There are only other places."

"I don't believe that—some places have gotta be better than this shithole."

"So you would think. But when you get away, you actually miss it— the ocean, the land, the fog… and the people." He laughed bitterly. "I didn't miss them for the longest time. I missed my little sister. My mother. But that's about it."

"Did you get along with your family?"

That made him smile. "Let's just say we have different ideas on things."

"I know what ya mean," Finton said. "My family doesn't get me either."

"Anyway, I'm not saying I didn't love the city life, the girls, all the things to do. It was pretty great. But no matter how bad things were back here, this was home—a place you're always connected to, always affects you, for better or worse."

"I'm thinking mostly for worse."

"Maybe," said Kieran. "Just don't go writing people off."

"There's some pretty bad people here—you should know that better than anyone."

"Oh, yes, indeed. But it's not just here. They're everywhere. And the good ones are here too, just the same as anywhere else."

"So you're saying I shouldn't go anywhere."

"No. I'm saying, don't go havin' any great expectations."

Finton found his choice of words funny. "Do you read?"

"Yeah, I read. I read that one in school—Dickens, right? But I mostly read non-fiction. Biographies and articles. Sports stuff."

"Like Clancy."

"Yeah, I know Clancy. I was a few grades ahead of him in school. Good guy."

Finton found himself tingling with pride to hear his brother's name mentioned in such a positive manner. "He's good at cars and stuff."

"I know—he replaced a belt in my old Gremlin a while ago—before I sold it to that Stuckey friend o' yours."

"Listen," said Finton as he drew a deep breath. "Tell Alicia she needs to get out." As he steeled his nerve, a car went by, honking like a migratory goose before it disappeared into the white wall.

Kieran smiled. "She's a big girl. She'll make up her own mind."

"I just thought maybe you could convince her."

"She's still a bit young for that." Kieran nodded, his lips knotted thoughtfully. "So are you for that matter."

"I'm old enough," he said, unwilling to explain himself any more than that.

"I'll drive you down the road a ways, if you like."

"That would be great."

"But I'll ask you one more time—would you rather go back home?"

Finton considered it. He wished the weather was better. Hell, he wished a lot of things were better. He wished there was an easier way and a better way. But this was the best thing for now. "Onward," he said; within half an hour, they were rolling across the Avalon.

The ferry to Nova Scotia was bigger, brighter, and bluer than he'd imagined. He didn't tell Kieran his destination, but since he said it wasn't St. John's, the constable turned right at the Argentia access road. Somehow, he'd known. When he dropped Finton off at the ferry terminal, he wished him luck and advised him to contact his family once he got where he was going. He told Kieran, "Have a good life." Then he changed into dry clothes and tossed his old ones into the washroom trashcan. Only his sneakers were still soaked through, and they squished and squeaked with every step he took.

The boat ride went quickly—they'd left port in the evening and arrived in North Sydney a mere fourteen hours later. For sixteen years, hardly anything had changed. But in just under half a day, Finton had practically entered a new country.

Nova Scotia was vast and yet similar to the place he'd left, the only apparent difference being the sunshine. While the land behind seemed perpetually bathed in fog and snow, Nova Scotia was bright and fairly warm. The ferry ramp, the dock, the goldenrod-striped pavement, and the perky conifers that bordered the government property were all tinted golden, lending the expedition a touch of grandeur. He felt as if he were in a movie—all the people just actors, saying tired lines.

The sight, as he left the station, of a red and white flag with the maple leaf rippling against the powder blue sky made him stop and stare, wondering if this was what it felt like to belong to something bigger. The moment was fleeting, however, and he started walking alongside a narrow road that would eventually lead to the highway. Cars and trucks whizzed by him, same as before, all going some place. They might even be going to the same place as him. But he didn't stick out his thumb. He simply trusted.

It was a long time before one of them pulled over, and when he ran to the waiting car and opened the door, there was a young woman with long, dark hair and soft, brown eyes, asking where he was going.

"The Annapolis Valley."

"Well, that's where I'm going," she said. "Do you need a lift?"

In her front seat, he felt as if everything was going to be okay. In that moment, who he used to be and the place he'd grown up no longer existed. Maybe in years to come, it would all come back. He might even miss it. But from now on, he was a young man named Finton Moon and that was all. Like a snowball heading downhill, he would accumulate himself as he rolled along.

The pretty woman asked his name, and he told her.

"Where are you from?"

"A whole different place," he said.

She didn't prod, but when he asked her name, she said, "Clarity." She wasn't born with that name and yet somehow she actually had been. She had chosen it, but she'd always known it; she just hadn't known what it was till she said it aloud.

"What's in the Valley you're so worked up to see?"

He'd know it when he saw it, he said.

It was a long drive, but they conversed the whole way, and time passed quickly. He was amazed by how much she knew about everything and how little he knew about anything. But he had opinions, and that counted for something. She'd been home for the weekend, visiting family in Stephenville, but now she was back in university to finish the semester.

"I'm Wiccan," she said, "which is why I chose my own name." Then she explained that she was a witch-in-training, a member of a small coven that met at low tide for bonfires on the mud flats of Wolfville every full moon of summer and fall.

When Finton explained he was "born Catholic," she said, "No one's born Catholic. You were baptized—and you can be baptized again as something else." He liked the sound of that, the chance at starting over, not as someone else, but as the person he'd always felt that he was. Perhaps, in a way, he already had been baptized—for he still felt a chill from his hours in the rain.

By the time they reached Wolfville and were parting ways, he was already in love with Clarity. She gave him her number and a hug. She kissed his cheek and said, "If you ever need anything, you get in touch. I'm not far away."

She left him on the steps of the residence hall at Acadia University. After he watched her drive away, he went to the main office to ask for help, which another young woman joyfully provided. He showed her the letter from the registrar's assistant—a girl named Debra—but she said she didn't need it. She just gave him the directions and the key to his room. It was the most precious thing he'd ever held, in a hand that had held many precious things. No one had ever trusted him with a key before.

Because it was still summer, the residence was mostly empty, although there were several students milling around, conversing on their way to someplace else, possibly to class or out for a mid-afternoon coffee or whatever it was students did in their free time. Until now, Finton hadn't even realized there was something called free time— the adult distinction between work and leisure. Up until now, all times had been the same: a seemingly endless stretch of constant anxiety.

It took a few minutes, exploring the hallways, making a couple of wrong turns, but he finally found his room. He knocked on the door, but he knew there'd be no one inside. The girl at the desk had told him he had it all to himself. The charge would be eight dollars each night, and he could stay as many nights as he wanted until September.

Dear Finton:
In response to your letter dated May 14, 1976, I am pleased to inform you that we have dorm rooms available throughout the summer for anyone who wants them. The cost per night is eight dollars. Please let me know the dates you'll be requiring a room. I look forward to hearing from you.
Regards, Debra Huntington

The bed had a pillow and two blankets. The bookshelf was empty. A brown metallic heater was built into the wall, but there were no knobs. With his shoes on, he lay on the bed and clasped his hands on his stomach, feeling the up-and-down motion of his steady breathing. So this was freedom. He had just closed his eyes when he just as quickly opened them and sprang to his feet. He sensed it was time.

The door locked behind him, and he felt in his pocket to make certain he still had the key. Reassured, he retraced his steps and sauntered out the front door, into the warmth of the day. The sunshine on his face was a balm to his soul. He closed his eyes and inhaled, then slowly emitted a life-affirming breath.

Eyes reopened, he chose a direction and followed it. He strolled across the expansive, forested lawn to Main Street, which ran through Wolfville and connected it to townships beyond its borders at both ends. As he navigated the sidewalk past a small cemetery and a large, white theatre, he imagined one could walk for days and never encounter a bank of fog or a moose. You could go on forever without running into an obstacle, and no one would tell you that you were doing anything wrong.

He was amazed that there was a sidewalk, and the trees were so tall. He'd seen pictures of oak trees on TV and in books, and this is definitely what they were—strong oaks that had stood at least for decades in the very same spot. And they would remain there long after he'd gone; no one would cut them down for sport or out of necessity. They, and the sidewalk, were the epitome of beauty. They already made him feel that this was the place for him. But they were not what he had come for.

Onward he ambled, taking his time, knowing he'd get there eventually, for the map showed the next town was New Minas, not too far away. Somewhere outside Wolfville was what he had journeyed so far to see, to be among and to worship—to stare at in wonder: to see for himself that what he'd dreamed of was real.

Almost half an hour after leaving his dorm room, he halted in his footsteps on the side of the road. The sidewalk converted into a pebbled path that was nonetheless smooth and navigable.

When he finally saw them, he almost cried.

Their beauty was beyond anything he could ever describe, although he knew, eventually, he would have to try. *Mysterious. Hopeful. Universal. Life.* These were words that came to his mind.

As far as he could see, there were hundreds of apple trees, in infinite rows—he'd never imagined that they were planted that way. He'd always envisioned a haphazard arrangement, as if apple trees could grow wherever they wanted. But these, it seemed, were arranged that way, and there was something so utterly divine in the way they were cloistered, limbs thrusting outward, downward and yet, at their very tips, pointing towards the sky, that, just for a moment, he was certain that God existed and had a plan for him. Otherwise, there would be no such orchard, no such trees, and he would not be standing here at this moment to see their emerald leaves and life-giving fruit glistening angelically under a perfect sun.

It was the way Mary Connelly had appeared to him on that first day of school in her blinding pink jacket. The way he'd felt when he swam in the cold ocean or lay on his back in a meadow, gazing up at the stars. The certainty and wonder he felt about life before he'd ever laid hands on Miss Bridie's wound. All that time, he thought Mary's pink jacket had opened his eyes, but now he could see it had only closed them, and he had been living a sightless dream. But the spectacle of these trees had returned his vision.

He slipped under a white, wooden fence and strolled across the grass, towards the trees. There was no one else around. Behind him, a few cars slipped by. No one paid him any attention. Out here, it seemed, no one minded anyone else's business.

Dear Mr. Moon:
I am pleased to inform you we can, indeed, hire you to pick apples on Inglis's Farm from the period of August 30 until October 30. Please inform us as to the date and time of your arrival.
 Sincerely,
Martha Inglis

He chose a tree—one that seemed friendly, protective, and open—and he sat beneath it, his back up against it, his noggin against the trunk as he gazed upward, amazed. Seeing one particular apple dangling from a limb, surrounded by soft, green leaves as if presented just for him, he reached up to touch its solid, scarlet splendour. At his touch, the fruit fell into his palm with a weight that reminded him of Morgan's breast.

He brought it closer for scrutiny.

Then he realized, with brutal clarity, that, having plucked the apple, he had invoked the necessity for an unwinnable choice. For, though he dared not mar its beauty by stealing a bite, the apple could not be replaced from where it had fallen. At the foot of the tree with the sun beating down, fended off by the shade of the umbrella-like branches, he laid the lone piece of fruit aside, on the ground by his knee.

And then, at last, Finton wept.

By the middle of September, he was already having difficulty remembering who he used to be. He never called home and rarely wrote letters. Once in a while, he sent a postcard with a picture of an orchard, or the Memorial Church at Grand Pré, the sort of things he thought Nanny Moon would enjoy. He wrote a letter once explaining how he'd come to see things, how relations between them had gotten so estranged—it was because he was different, because he needed something they couldn't offer him, and it wasn't their fault, but he felt claustrophobic even thinking about that little kitchen and that tiny bungalow at the top of the windblown hill. The Valley had changed him, given him a new identity and a sense of belonging he'd never known before. But he knew in his heart they wouldn't understand, that he would only make his mother cry. So he tore up the letter.

Occasionally, when the sun was setting burnt orange in a deep, black sky, or the silver fog encroached and crept over the Gaspereau mountains to settle on the red mud plains of Wolfville, he was reminded of the people back in Darwin in images that were only shades of grey. He would occasionally have flashes of memory, of the night he put his hands on an old woman's wound and retrieved her from the dead. But, in time, he rarely even thought of that woman or considered that moment. He couldn't remember the circumstances that led to it or the years of growing up that had followed. His past became like a country he'd only traveled by train, distanced and detached from all those around—disconnected from no one so much as himself.

It began to seem as if Alicia, Morgan, Mary, Skeet and his brothers weren't real, but existed only inside his mind and sometimes not even there. Whole days went by when he thought about none of them. Months would pass when he concerned himself only with the new people he'd met—the magic of novelty and constant renewal, here where people didn't care what you used to be, only what you were now and were about to become.

At times, he would stare at his small, freckled hands in the glare of an afternoon sun while he sat beneath the shade of a parental oak. They looked as if they once could have healed, but now they were useful for writing an essay, writing a fresh story, plucking an apple from its stem, stirring sugar into a mug of coffee—or holding a girl's hand.

The scar beneath his left eye faded more with time and, although it remained visible to him on an average day, it blazed deeper on days when the memories raged.

One day as he passed by a thrift store, he saw in the window a red bicycle and a manual typewriter—an Underwood, like the one Stephen King had used to write *Carrie*. For five dollars, he bought the typewriter and took it back to his dorm room where he spent many long and glorious nights composing new stories by hunting and pecking. Eventually, he went back and bought the bicycle.

On the last day of August, he'd reported for work at Inglis's farm, and they gave him a place to stay in the bunkhouse. "You're awful small," Martha Inglis had said, sizing him up. "Are you sure you're seventeen? Apple-picking's not for the faint of heart." Only when he assured her he was old enough and would work really hard did she give him a key, show him his bunk, and introduce him to the rest of the men. He soon found out that there were some hard tickets among them, one of whom reminded him of Bernard Crowley, the way he always ribbed Finton about writing his "fairy stories" whenever he sat at the typewriter. Others of the men liked to get drunk on their time off, often sitting around and playing cards till all hours in the morning, sometimes even going to work pretty smashed. It wasn't long before he realized he didn't fit in with these crude men, some of whom couldn't read.

Maybe, he thought, *it wasn't Darwin, but me.*

On days off, he'd go exploring on his bike and, after weeks of hearing about the world-famous Tidal Bore, he went to the store and gave Clarity a call, asking her if she'd take him to see it. She greeted him that day like a long-lost friend, and they drove up to Cape Split, picnicked on a ridge and watched the tide come in. Gradually, Finton noticed that the forest above the beach was filled with a loud, hollow sound like nothing he'd ever heard before, and yet it touched his soul so deeply that he almost cried. But then, all his emotions lately were near to the surface, and he had decided to just let them be.

"What's that sound?" he asked.

"You should know it," she said. "It's 'The Voice of the Moon.'" It was a unique aural phenomenon caused by the inrush of the world's highest tides, right there in the Minas Basin, outside of Wolfville. When she told him that, he was certain that he'd made the right choice in leaving Darwin. When his fingers tingled and his palms buzzed, Finton shivered briefly and smiled.

At night, the trains would rumble beside Front Street, out near the mudflats, and make the bunkhouse rattle, the floorboards shake, and the ceiling sway. Finton's bed would quake so hard that it woke him up. He would lie breathlessly still, listening to the desolate call of a slow-moving train—one of the most beautiful sounds he'd ever heard—and wonder if soon he might be moving on. There were places to see besides Nova Scotia, places that might open his mind equally and expand his soul even more.

Those moments would stir his imagination and, when he was feeling reflective, he'd write stories about a boy who was able to heal. That same boy, in the same story or in others like it, could also levitate and sometimes fly. In those tales, there were girls who wanted to be with the strangest boy in town. He had a family who loved him in some stories and neglected him in others. But it was always the same family in every tale.

Dear Finton,

This will be short. Everything here is good. Your father and Clancy just opened a garage. I don't know where it's going, but they called it "Clancy and Tom's Garage." Your father says he'd like to hear from you if you get a chance. I told him me and him both. Homer's going to trades school in the fall. He should do all right if he can put his mind to studying. Nanny Moon gets around pretty good for her age. She said for you to be good and go to church. Anyway, Morgan's here now. I asked her over for a cup of tea. She seems lonely since her mother died. She said to say hello. Hope you're doing good. If you need anything, just let us know.

Love, your mother

Darwin was encroaching on his newly made life and, as he read the letter, he knew he'd be leaving when the blossoms returned to the orchards of Wolfville. Sure, they were beautiful. But there was no need to wait around for that which he'd already seen. He had a world to seek and a soul to heal, or maybe the other way around.

This novel has taken many different forms in the decade or so it took to fashion it into the story I needed to tell. Thus, many people have played a role in its development, as well as in my own evolution as an author.

In 2001, a very rough first draft of *Finton Moon* won the Percy Janes First Novel Award, and I am forever grateful to Regina Best, the Newfoundland Arts and Letters Awards, and especially the adjudicator, Kenneth J. Harvey, for offering me the encouragement to see this story to publication. Without that initial success, I'm not sure I would have possessed the faith and fortitude to see this journey through.

Laurel Boone, Sally Harding, Carolyn Swayze, and Samantha North were all very kind and encouraging when they read the earliest version of *Finton Moon*. Each offered advice that I've heeded, evidence of which can be seen in the published novel.

Dr. Stacy Gillis read parts of the original manuscript and offered invaluable suggestions. But it was your time and enthusiasm that meant the most to me.

Donna Francis, I can never thank you enough for your unwavering belief in my writing and patience with my process. I wish every writer could have a publisher like mine.

Pamela Dooley, thank you for the long conversations and endless good cheer in bookstores, Costcos, airplanes, and book fairs. You make promotion fun, and that, for an author, is an uncommon experience.

Thanks to my editor, Ed Kavanagh, for your patience and diligence. Your constant questioning, your eagle eye, and your uncommon instinct for logic have made me a better writer and *Finton Moon* a much better novel.

Thanks, Tammy Macneil, Rob Warner, and JoAnne Soper-Cook for weighing in on my name change dilemma at the eleventh hour.

Thanks, Todd Manning for the wonderful cover art. Also, thanks Darren Whalen for your amazing talent and hard work, and to my anonymous, skilful copy editor.

Most of all, thanks to my wife, Norma, who has read every version of *Finton Moon* since I first conceived of the idea nearly twelve years ago. You never lost faith, and you never stopped caring for and loving either the characters, the story, or me. There is no way on earth this novel would have been written and published without you being you.

I need to thank the book bloggers, the reviewers, the librarians, the bookstore owners and staff, the people who come out to readings and signings, as well as the dedicated folks at Creative Publishers, WANL, NLAC, the Atlantic Book Awards, Tamara Reynish, and the Literary Arts Foundation. We're all in this together, for the love of books and the arts, and our lives are enriched by your efforts.

Thank you to the Newfoundland and Labrador Arts Council and the City of St. John's for their financial benevolence.

Gerard Collins is a writer and teacher whose fiction has appeared in various journals and won a handful of literary prizes, including the 2012 Ches Crosbie Barristers/Newfoundland and Labrador Book Award for Fiction and the Percy Janes First Novel Award.

He was born in Bond's Path, Placentia, Newfoundland and has lived most of his adult life in St. John's. He has also resided in Nova Scotia, Ontario, and British Columbia, as well as various small towns in his home province. For many of those years, he was, alternately, a guy with a shovel, an agricultural inspector, a printer, newspaper reporter, high school English teacher, substitute teacher, tutor, vagabond, musician, songwriter, grad student, and TV background actor.

Gerard has a Ph.D. in American literature (MUN), with a specialization in ghost fictions, and an M.A. from Acadia University, with a thesis on the Gothic works of Edgar Allan Poe. For over a decade, he has been teaching English Language and Literature at Memorial University of Newfoundland while writing short stories and novels.

Finton Moon is his first novel.